Marcia Williams

Flex

The X Press

Published by
The X Press, 6 Hoxton Square, London N1 6NU
Tel: 0171 729 1199   Fax: 0171 729 1771

This edition published in 1999

© Marcia Williams 1997

Printed by Caledonian International Book Manufacturing Ltd, Glasgow, UK.

Distributed in US by INBOOK, 1436 West Randolph Street, Chicago, Illinois
60607, USA Orders 1-800 626 4330 Fax orders 1-800 334 3892

Distributed in UK by Turnaround Distribution, Unit 3, Olympia Trading Estate,
Coburg Road, London N22 6TZ
Tel: 0181 829 3000
Fax: 0181 881 5088

ISBN   1-874509-45-X

To my loving and lovely Grandma (1918-96) and Grandad (1912-96). We miss you.

To Patricia and Charles for your constant encouragement. *Flex* wouldn't have been finished without it.

Last but not least to Martin, the man of my dreams. Who says there are no good men left?

Marcia Williams lives and works in London.
Flex is her second novel.

Also by Marcia Williams and published by The X Press
Baby Mother (writing as Andrea Taylor)
Waiting For Mr Wright.

1. WHAT'S LOVE GOT TO DO WITH IT?

"Easy nuh, man. Wha' you ah hegs up over?"

Hegs up? *Hegs up?!* Bwoy, he was lucky she couldn't run down that phone line and ram her fist down his throat. Man had the damn cheek to call her number and tell her how he's thinking about her and her ripe body. Only last week she had had to throw his outta-order backside out of her house because he'd taken the damned liberty to raise his hand and slap her. Slapped like she was a child bad mouthing its mother! Had he honestly expected her to stand for that? Did he have no idea who he was dealing with? This was Joan Ross — a strong black woman. Not some dibi-dibi schoolgirl with stars in her eyes.

First, she had kicked him in the shin. And while he was bent over nursing his leg, she'd balled her fists and brought them down hard on the back of his skull. He'd looked so comical sprawled out on the carpet that, despite her anger, she had laughed hysterically. Embarrassed, his eyes full of shock, he'd scrambled to his feet issuing a stream of obscenities.

"Sticks and stones, Stevie bwoy. Sticks and stones," Joan had taunted.

He'd not touched her again, but had left, slamming the door behind him. And Joan hadn't seen him since.

All that aggro over a gallon of blasted petrol. She was glad it had happened sooner rather than later on in the relationship, when she might have fallen too deep to care. If he had filled up the car as promised, there would have been no argument. If he hadn't been such a prick she would have given him lovin' like he'd never had before. Stephen was tall, dark and athletic — exactly how she liked her men. She would have rocked his world. Oh well, it was his loss. As far as Joan was concerned, he was history. She disconnected him and placed the telephone receiver back in its cradle.

Still angry, she walked across the room to where her cigarettes lay on the armchair. She shook one from the packet and lit up. Men had to be aliens, she concluded, puffing out a cloud of white smoke. Brothers from another planet, an experiment gone wrong. Only an alien could expect a sane woman to take him back after what Stephen had done. Only aliens have brains between their legs. Only an alien would consider a hard-on to be a matter of life or death — damn the consequences as long as they can find somewhere to put it.

Since Joan had split up with her baby father (she hated that term, but she couldn't think of a more appropriate description), Martin Baker, two years previously, she'd had countless men in and out of her life. She wasn't proud of the number, but that was one of the hazards of searching for Mr Right. How else was she supposed to know if this one or that one was the right one unless she tried them out in every aspect?

Joan sighed to herself. She felt like she was the only woman in the world without a man. Her best mates were both living with their men — well, Pamela was, and Marion had her part-time lover. Even Joan's mother changed her male 'friends' with the seasons. But were any of them happy? *Really* happy? Donna, her younger sister, was already married. She seemed to have fallen off the face of the earth since her wedding day, and was now rarely seen. Donna had given up her job as a receptionist for Lewisham Housing Services because John didn't want her to work. She had lied, saying that the job wasn't that important anyway. For Joan, that had signalled the complete loss of her independence, and she had let her know what she thought about it. This is what had caused the rift between them. Joan regretted that. Donna had once also been a strong black woman, but nowadays if John didn't like something, neither did she. She even had to ask her husband for pocket money. Joan couldn't see how her sister could possibly be happy.

She lit another cigarette. She felt like a good bitching session. Stephen had wound her up and she needed to let it out. Pamela would love this one. "Kick him, yes," she'd say.

Joan had known Pamela for four years. Just like Joan, she had wasted some of her best years on one no-good, confused black man after another. And she was only seeing James because he was more like a housemaid than anything else. He was always ironing, cooking and — check this — attending to Pamela's every needs, and those of her girlfriends when they came round! Marion and Joan called him Jeeves behind his back. He even paid half of Pamela's bills! So far James had lasted ten months, but knowing Pamela she would soon get bored. She was, after all, a hot-blooded Scorpio in constant need of passion, which she wasn't exactly getting from her live-in butler.

Joan's other best mate was Marion, the youngest of them all. Joan had known her since she was eight years old and knew how gullible she was. Marion's man, Gerard, was an extremely good-looking bloke, but he was a bastard. A dominating womaniser who couldn't give a damn about Marion and what she wanted. He only visited her when he was at a loose end or when he needed a boost. Yet Marion was ever ready to forgive and forget, and would do virtually anything for him. Joan couldn't stand him. Neither could Pamela. The gossip between them was that Gerard had to have "somet'ing sweet" between his legs. There was no other explanation.

Joan uncurled her shapely legs from the sofa. Her oversized red T-shirt dropped to below her knees. Grabbing her phone index from the coffee table, she left the living room and climbed the stairs, smoke drifting like a fine mist in her wake. At the top of the stairs she stood at the doorway to her daughter's bedroom. Shereen, or Sherry, was now four years old and already talking like a big woman. Joan flicked the light switch and looked over at her daughter's bed. The girl was spread out on her back, her angelic face a picture of peaceful sleep. Her mouth hung open and she breathed lightly. This was Joan's pride and joy. She fought the urge to wake her daughter just for her own comfort.

Joan sighed. She wished she could spend more time with her daughter, but she was an ambitious woman and if she didn't work twelve hours a day she wasn't going to get far in her career. It hadn't been an easy climb to get to be features editor at Icon Press. Especially with her relationship with Shereen's father disintegrating about her.

Martin was a believer in hire purchase, credit cards, cheque books and overdrafts. It had put them in debt, which Martin had left her to pay along with the mortgage. Now she had to work all the hours she could manage, just to keep her head above water.

Stephen, the latest man in her life, had lasted two months. One thing about Stephen, he was "wicked in bed"! She was going to miss that, if nothing else. Before Stephen she had been seeing Colin, Martin's brother. Joan and Colin had been in and out of each other's lives for a year and a half. Shereen's uncle was another one of those black men who just won't/can't commit. Which isn't the same as a womaniser. Colin could stay faithful as long as he could come and go as he pleased, as long as he wasn't "living" with the woman and marriage wasn't on the cards.

It had been good at first, and Joan had felt such a fool when she'd let her feelings rule her head. She'd fallen in love, he hadn't. She had kept giving him pressure, and he'd kept making excuses. So in the end she had told him to get the hell out of her life. She was twenty-seven, and she had no time to waste on immature men. She'd wanted commitment — she still did. And all she was left with now was her phone book full of ex's.

It was eleven thirty on a weeknight, and she suddenly found herself becoming horny. She, of course, had a new, improved, bigger, better, feel-real, three-speed, pump-action, clitoris-stimulating vibrator at her disposal. But that wasn't what she wanted tonight. No, her bedside buddy wasn't enough. She wanted a man. A hard, hot body.

So there she was, flicking through her phone book with one hand, cigarette in the other, Aaron Hall telling her how much he's missing her, and getting hornier by the second. Page after page she turned, scanning the names one by one. There were so many losers among them — Joan hadn't got that desperate yet.

She had to laugh at some of the memories that surfaced from those names. There was Kinky. He would turn up with handcuffs, blindfolds and wicked leather gear. He liked to have whipped cream licked off his body.

Then there was Ego. He was so selfish that he would bring a bottle round to her house and then proceed to drink it on his own, unless she asked for some! They'd been out four times and not once had he said, "I'll pay." They'd halved the bill every time. But he always expected dinner when he turned up at her house empty-handed. He got turned on by getting Joan to remind him of how big his manhood was, how he made her feel, how jealous her girlfriends were when she told them what she was getting. And all this while they were actually doing it!

Then there was Inexperienced. She had tried to teach the boy that she had a whole body and not just a hole between her legs. She'd taught him the gentle art of head to toe massage. She'd shown him all her tender spots and asked him, God knows how many times, to slow down. But he was too eager to hit the jackpot and not interested enough to try to please her.

Oh yeah, then there was Mr Love. She could laugh about him now, but at the time it had been kind of scary. This man had told her that he loved her on the first date. Joan had laughed. "Yeah, right, you don't know me from Eve." He'd called her every day after that, told her how much he missed being with her and was forever asking if he could come over. Then he'd started to turn up at her house nearly every night, always with a little gift for Shereen. One morning Joan had picked up her mail to find there was a letter addressed to Mr Love. Curiosity got the better of her and she'd opened it — it had come to her house after all. The letter was from someone interested in Mr Love's offer to sell her house.

Mr Loverman, on the other hand, was different. Nice, easygoing, clean-cut, fair-skinned, and packing a lethal weapon. Sexual perfection!

For a moment, Joan considered calling Mr Loverman up. Just to say hi, see what he was doing and how he was doing, maybe arrange

8

to meet up — like tonight. Her thoughts were interrupted by the buzz of the doorbell. Startled, she looked at her watch. It was nearly midnight. She wasn't expecting anyone, but a sudden premonition told her who it was. She slid off the bed and crossed to the window that overlooked her front garden. A car came round the corner and lit her uninvited guest with its headlights. It was Colin.

Like an angel he had come to answer her prayers. She ran her fingers hurriedly through her short Toni Braxton style hair, to give it that casual windswept look. The cut emphasised her high cheekbones, slanting, exotic eyes and full lips. Joan was not the world's prettiest woman, but she was interesting looking, with mysterious, dark eyes that men found irresistible.

The doorbell rang again.

Joan opened the front door to a confident, boyish grin on Colin's ruggedly handsome face. He stood six foot three before her (firm from head to foot), appraising her with deep brown eyes beneath long lashes.

She looked him up and down. She caught his eyes resting on her chest, where her nipples had risen to bullets in the cold breeze. She pulled her dressing gown closed and crossed her arms over her chest.

"Yes?" she asked nonchalantly.

"All right?"

"Yes, thank you." She stared at him, one eyebrow raised in question. She knew why he was there — for exactly the same reason she wanted him there — but she was going to make him work for it. She didn't want him thinking her house was a pussy takeaway.

"So you're not gonna let me in?"

"For what?" She pushed up her chest.

He rolled his eyes. "I didn't come all this way to stand on your doorstep."

Greenwich to Plumstead. All this way?

"Then what did you drag your arse up here for?"

He ignored her rudeness. "How 'bout I tell you inside?"

Joan wasn't going to stand there and freeze her nipples off just to spite her ex-lover. She let him in and he stood in the hallway waiting for her to lead the way.

"I s'pose you want something to drink now that you've got me out of bed," she said.

"Wouldn't say no."

No you wouldn't, would you, Colin? Wouldn't say no if I dropped my drawers out here in the middle of the street. But if I asked you to stay longer than one night you'd sure run fast enough in the opposite

9

direction.

He dragged out a chair and sat at her dining table like he was at home. Damned cheek! If she weren't so hot for some action, his backside would be walking its way back to Greenwich.

"So how's Shereen?" he asked. "Bet she missed her Uncle Colin."

"Shereen's fine," Joan answered without a hint of warmth in her voice. *No thanks to you and your family*, she wanted to add. His brother had walked out on her, and when push came to shove so had he. Even their mother had taken Martin's side in the break-up. They were one confused bunch of people. But now that he was here, sitting in her kitchen, she knew that she still wanted him. She also knew that he was here because he still couldn't get her out of his system.

She smiled to herself as she made the coffee. Maybe she would just use and abuse him, she considered. Mek 'im beg. Yeah — that sounded better.

"I missed you, y'know," Colin mumbled. "You and Shereen," he quickly added.

"So?"

He huffed. "You still mad at me?"

She wasn't mad at him. What was there to be angry about? He wanted his freedom; Joan wanted to settle down. She couldn't force the man to want what she wanted. They had to go their separate ways or end up hating the sight of each other.

She handed him his coffee and, pulling out a chair, she sat down beside him and continued playing hard to get.

"Colin, I'm over that." She waved the very idea away. "Don't take it personal. You see, my mates were all settling down and I just wanted to give it another try myself." She crossed her legs and leant one elbow on the table. "You just happened to be around at the time."

His eyes dropped to the pine table, and he studied his fingernails as though he'd never seen them before. Poor Colin — he'd never been very good at verbal expression. Joan sipped her coffee and watched him over the rim of the mug. He was one hunk of a man. She was remembering his body under those loose clothes. All she had to do was reach across the table and she could have him if she wanted. She licked her lips. Colin was hung like a horse, and Joan often thought he made love like one too. Just climb aboard, do your thing, then dismount. Foreplay didn't occur to him! But that didn't bother Joan, because he knew just how to rock her world without it. She was getting goosebumps just thinking about him naked. Just then he reached across the table for her hand.

"I . . ."

"Yeah?" She fixed him with a smouldering, dark gaze.

"I . . ." He paused, frustration clear in his furrowed brow. "Cho, you won't understand."

"Understand what?"

"I'm trying to tell you . . ." He breathed a sigh. "I love you."

Joan bit her tongue to stop herself laughing but her shoulders shook anyway. Hurt, Colin snatched back his hand.

"Sorry," she giggled.

"Joan, I'm trying to be serious here." He threw his arms open, then slapped his palms on the table in frustration.

"I'm sorry, Col. But even you've got to admit, you saying 'I love you' sounds ridiculous."

"Yeah, well, I've been thinking — and I think you should give me another chance."

"To do what, Colin?"

"To check out this relationship stuff."

Was he for real? She started giggling again. "Well, if you put it like that, how could I possibly refuse?"

Colin reached up and twisted his baseball cap backwards. "Come on, man. This ain't easy, y'know."

Joan got up and walked round to his side of the table, her T-shirt clinging in all the right places. "You're serious, aren't you?"

"Ya know dat."

"Come here," she commanded in her huskiest voice.

Her juices had been flowing all night; now was her chance to satisfy her lust. Grinning like a monkey, he stood up and faced her. She looked up into his eyes. Her arms curled round his neck and she drew him down to meet her waiting lips.

That was all it took to seduce Colin Baker. He pushed himself up against her, nearly lifting her off her feet. Oh God, she loved it when men did that. He wrapped his tongue around hers, and his long, strong fingers did the same to her ample backside. She felt like singing "Hallelujah", but her mouth was too busy.

His hands travelled down to her naked thighs, then back again to her bottom. His mouth seemed to be everywhere at once. Joan's dressing gown dropped to the floor and her T-shirt rose over her head. She was standing in her kitchen stark naked while he was still fully clothed. It was her turn to do the undressing. She yanked his jacket down his back and his track suit bottoms down to his knees. Then she knocked his baseball cap off his head. All he had on now was a baggy string vest. His lips and tongue were working on one nipple and then the other. Feeling his crotch press against hers gave her a rush, his penis hanging like a baseball bat between his legs.

That was when she went weak at the knees and her legs gave way. Colin supported her. Lifting her with ease, he laid her on the dining table, panting, gasping and moaning, all ten and a half stone of her.

He mounted her like a stallion and she screamed out for Jesus. All that pent-up frustration was being exorcised like the devil from a woman possessed. He thrust back and forth as she pumped up to meet him. She could have sworn he was getting bigger inside her. Thank goodness I bought solid pine, she thought to herself. She pulled at his shoulders, begging him to make her come, and he obliged as only he could.

Joan shuddered with the after-effects of an orgasm that must have woken the neighbours. It was over in about ten minutes, but it was the best ten minutes she'd had in months.

He was standing above her, his finger tracing a line down her body from her neck to her breasts and down to her belly button.

She raised herself up on her elbows and looked him dead in the eye. "This doesn't mean we're an item again," she breathed, still catching her breath. She was telling him straight, leaving no room for doubt.

"What have I done now?" He bent over to pull up his pants and she uttered a low sigh as she caught a last view of his tight, hairy buttocks before they were tucked out of sight.

She began to feel exposed sitting there on her dining table as naked as a fertility goddess, so she covered her chest with one arm and slid off the table.

"Don't get me wrong, Col. The sex was wicked — but that's not enough any more. I don't need a man to come and go. Literally."

He had the cheek to kiss his teeth, then made her shiver by tickling her hip with a light, playful stroke.

"Who says it's gonna be like that? Ain't we having a good time?"

She couldn't be bothered to answer him or give him the chance to confuse her. She knew what she wanted. She wanted a man who was going to be there for her and Shereen. She wanted a man to be a provider, a lover, a friend, her life support emotionally and physically.

Grabbing her dressing gown from the floor, she slipped it over her shoulders, tying the belt around her waist. Boy, she needed a cigarette.

Joan left the kitchen and headed up the hall to the front room. Colin followed her and stood just inside the doorway, leaning against the frame like he was waiting for something. Joan inhaled deeply, regretting the boredom and frustration that had driven her to start smoking again.

"I know what I want,"Colin blurted suddenly. "I want you. I can't even look at you without wanting to touch you."

"Here we go again." Joan tutted. "It always comes down to sex with you, doesn't it?"

He shook his head. "Are you paranoid about sex or what? I didn't mean it that way." He came closer.

"Me? Paranoid?" A false chuckle gushed from her lips. "What do you have on your mind one hundred per cent of the time?"

"I'm a man, aren't I?" he grinned, lifting his shoulders in a shrug as if to say, "It's not my fault."

She kissed her teeth, flipping her eyes to the ceiling.

He took the opportunity to slip his arm around her waist. "I just don't want the whole marriage thing yet," he breathed in her ear.

She turned her head away from him. "Yeah? Well I do. Shereen needs a father. I need a companion. If you don't wanna be tied down, then there's the door." She pointed with the lighted cigarette. God, she wished it was a spliff.

"I can't just leave," he insisted. "I love you."

"Yeah, right. Well you might find it easy to say, but can you show me? An' I'm not talking about sex."

Colin let go of her, stood up and began pacing up and down, arms crossed over his chest. In his string vest, with his bulging muscles, he looked like he had just stepped out of an action movie. She could sense him stirring in his boxer shorts. Sex on legs.

"I think we should go back to just being friends. Like the old days."

"Is that what you want?" He looked deep into her eyes, defying her to say yes.

She caught her breath. What she really wanted to tell him, of course, was that it wasn't what she wanted. He was so much like his brother that she couldn't help but have feelings for him.

"I think it's for the best." Her cigarette had burnt down to the butt and, she decided, so had this conversation, despite its unsatisfactory outcome. She took his hand off her bottom and stubbed out the cigarette in the ashtray. Still holding his hand, she led him to the door.

"You throwing me out?"

"I've got work tomorrow. It's late." She fetched his jacket and cap from the kitchen and handed them to him.

"You'll never realise how much I care about you, y'know." He kissed her forehead. He kissed her again, on her lips this time. Give a man an inch . . .

13

"I'll call you," he promised.

"I know." Joan opened the front door to the cold once again, and pulled her dressing gown tighter over her chest.

"Colin, if you weren't such a coward, you could have had me twenty-four seven," she called after him on impulse.

He turned. "I know," he said smugly, and walked away into the night.

COLIN

Women can't resist me. I'm not boasting, honestly! They call it charm. All I know is I can weaken any woman's resistance with a touch. Forget love. I'm only interested in sex. Pure sex. Slow and sweet, or wicked and wild — it's a good way to forget your troubles. Good exercise, too.

I told Joan a man and woman can't be "just friends", it don't work. So I kinda replaced Martin, my brother, in her life. It was fun, with regular sex. I wanted her for her body and she wanted me for mine, though I liked to kid myself that it was for my mind. Then one night she turned round and asked me if I loved her. I thought it was a joke, so I laughed. Unfortunately she was being serious, and when I said no, she got vexed and locked me 'arf. Since then, it's been the cold shoulder.

I though it would be cool, y'know, plenty more fish in the sea an' all that, but I couldn't get her outta my mind. All that thinking was ruining my sex life! I didn't even feel like checking any other women. To my surprise, I found that I was in love — and I wish I wasn't. Because Joan can be one miserable woman. I blame my brother for that. He took the best five years of her life and threw them back in her face. Left her with the baby and a mortgage. Well, that's Martin for you. I am not my brother's keeper. All I can say is that his loss is my gain.

2. I NEED YOUR LOVIN'

Marion's eyes shot open. Was that the front door? She slowly eased herself into a sitting position, one ear cocked towards the bedroom door. Only one other person had the keys to her flat. She heard a shuffling of feet in the hallway. Gerard was home. She glanced over at the clock. It was nearly midnight. Some eight o'clock this was!

"Yeah baby," he'd said this morning, "dinner'll be fine. Eight o'clock? I'll shut the shop on time and come straight over."

Marion pursed her lips. It wasn't the first time he'd stood her up. Maybe if she asked him to stop making promises, then there wouldn't be any to break.

She ran her hands over her naturally wavy hair, tidying her ponytail, then swung her thin legs off the bed and smoothed down her satin and lace camisole and French knickers set. She checked herself in the dresser mirror. She'd wanted to look sexy for him tonight and had doused herself in Champagne, the perfume he'd bought her.

She hadn't meant to fall asleep. She'd wanted to be ready and alert, with dimmed lights, chilled wine, silk lingerie, seductive music — the works.

She heard him go into the bathroom opposite. Was he freshening up for her? She tiptoed to the bedroom door, opened it and peered outside. A trail of clothes ran from the front door to the bathroom — a pair of men's shoes kicked off carelessly, an overcoat thrown over the back of a chair, a tie and suit jacket thrown over the back of the sofa. She wanted to head straight for the bathroom but couldn't fight the urge to put the articles away. As if by instinct, she collected the clothes and folded them neatly. Then she knocked hesitantly on the bathroom door.

"Gerard?"

"Hi, babes," his muffled voice came through from within.

"Can I come in?"

"If you want."

She opened the door and entered the pink bathroom. Gerard stood naked, about to climb into the steaming, cologne-scented water. His shirt and boxer shorts lay in a heap on top of the wash basket, his trousers on the towel rail. The sight of his firm body still made Marion's heart race, even after a year together. She picked up the discarded clothes. The faint musky smell of aftershave wafted off the fabric before she dropped them inside the basket and replaced the lid.

"I thought you were asleep," Gerard said, easing himself into the bath with a satisfied sigh.

"I was . . . I cooked . . ." she added a subtle reminder.

Gerard Thompson was six foot two and a healthy twelve stone. His features looked as though they had been carved from marble, with a rigid, handsome jaw, high cheekbones and almond-shaped light brown eyes. He was stunning to look at. His fair, cool complexion came from a mixture of Bajan and Indian parentage. "I'm sorry, babes. Mum called. She needed some help shifting furniture. I've been promising to do it for ages. You know what Mum's like." He raised a thick eyebrow at Marion. "When she wants something done, she wants it done now. Anyway, she fed me. We'll have your dinner tomorrow, yeah?"

Marion lowered her eyes and nodded in barely noticeable agreement. No, it wasn't okay, but there was nothing she could say. Yes, she did know what Gerard's mum was like, and her son treated her like a queen. Mrs Thompson — Claudia to everyone who knew her personally — would always come before anyone else in Gerard's life.

Marion wanted to ask him why he hadn't called. What was the point of having a mobile phone if he never used it? Instead she said, "I missed you."

He grinned patronisingly. A grin that said, "Of course you did". "You too. Come here."

She stepped over to the bathtub and knelt on the mat. Gerard placed a wet hand on the back of her neck and pulled her to him. He kissed her open-mouthed, exploring her mouth with his tongue. She responded passionately.

Gerard released her suddenly and yawned. "Boy, I'm knackered. Any more of that wine left, babes?"

Wine? What did wine have to do with how he was making her feel? Was he truly as insensitive as he acted? She could feel a trickle of water running down her back as she sat back on her heels like a puppy waiting for its master's attention. Her large, naive eyes gazed at the man she loved. Gerard pretended to be oblivious to the effect he had on her. He liked to say he gave her as much as he could give — which left her wondering if that meant he had nothing else to give, or perhaps she had only a share of what was on offer.

"A little." She wiped bath water from the back of her neck.

"Get us a glass, will you?" It wasn't a request, it was an order. Gerard knew all about giving orders.

"Sure." She stood to leave the bathroom, turning at the door to look back at him. Gerard blew her a loud, theatrical kiss and she forced a smile. How did he do it? How was it that he could so easily twist her around his little finger? Why was it that she couldn't go right up to him and cuss him out for standing her up? So much for a romantic night in.

And what could she have said? "How dare you help your mum out? I wanted you here, wrapping your arms around me, covering my body with kisses and whispering sweet nothings in my ear"? No.

The one time she had tried that, Gerard had dialled his mother's number and handed Marion the phone, saying, "Tell her how you think you're more important than she is." She never did, of course.

Marion returned to the steamy bathroom with a glass of chilled wine. Gerard lay back in the bath, his eyes closed. Aching for him, Marion thought about climbing in. With a clink, she set the glass down on the side of the bath.

Gerard opened his eyes. "So," he said sleepily, "what did you do today?"

Slightly flustered, Marion answered, "I went window shopping."

"Yeah? Anything interesting?" He reached for the bath gel.

"I had a look at some rings."

Gerard sat up and sipped some of the wine, tasting it, then gulped the rest down in one. "You don't have enough rings already?" he asked offhandedly.

Marion took the gel from his hands and fished his flannel out of the bath. "Not them kinda rings. Engagement rings," she said, soaping his back.

"Why? You leaving me?" His head turned round to catch her eye, his expression serious.

Marion swallowed hard. They'd had this conversation before in various forms. There was no subtle way to broach the subject any longer. Gerard had become fed up with indulging her dream of settling down, buying a home together, getting married and having kids.

"Very funny, Gerard," she chuckled nervously. "You know we were talking about getting engaged the other day."

Gerard shrugged her hands off his shoulders. "Excuse me! You mean *you* were talking about it. I'm not getting married."

"No, not straight away," she compromised. Why was it that getting a man to talk about love and marriage was the hardest thing in the world? She had hoped that after a year of being together Gerard would feel the same way, but it didn't seem like it now.

Gerard stepped out of the bathtub, dripping water on to the cork-tiled floor. He wrapped a towel round his waist while he dried his muscled upper body with another. Marion sat on the edge of the bath watching him, her eyes travelling from his buttocks down to his tapering thighs and bulging calf muscles. God, but he was beautiful.

"I'm going out," he said finally.

Her head snapped back towards him, her eyes widening in surprise. *No, I must have heard wrong.*

"But you only just got in," she reminded him.

"So? This ain't my home. I've got some business to take care of."

He splashed Giorgio Red, his favourite *fraicheur,* under his arms and across his chest.

"This time of night?"

"Yeah, this time of night," he answered, mimicking her. He swiped mist from the mirrored bathroom cabinet and felt his chin with the back of his fingers. Deciding he didn't need a shave after all, he turned and exited the bathroom without a glance at Marion.

Tears welled up in her eyes as she remained seated on the edge of the bathtub. He wasn't wearing his favourite aftershave to go and visit his mum. She'd suspected for some time now that she wasn't the only one receiving the pleasures of his flesh. Every time they argued he would pick himself up, freshen up and disappear. At times like that it didn't seem to matter to Gerard whether they stayed together or not. She breathed deeply, trying hard to stop the overwhelming emotion that rose from her stomach and gripped her heart. What had she done wrong? She did her best to regain her composure and wiped her eyes with the heel of each hand. Seeing her cry would only make Gerard angry.

Stifling a sob, Marion left the bathroom and headed for the living room to avoid a confrontation. The stereo was already cued up, and all she had to do was press a button on the remote and the room filled with the sound of the Whitehead Brothers singing "187". How appropriate. Gerard's love was about as regular as a damned bus, and just like public transport you spent more on it than it was worth.

She flicked off the light and flung herself on to the soft grey sofa, her slim frame hardly making a dent in the cushions. She sat there in the dark, a thousand thoughts racing around in her mind. Lately, it seemed that all they ever did was have sex (it wasn't making love any more) or argue. She was tempted simply to end it, tell him it was over.

The light suddenly came on.

"Marion, you seen my pager?" Gerard walked over to the sideboard, searching frantically, lifting neatly placed ornaments, books and recently opened mail and dumping them back into disorder.

She breathed deeply, willing her voice not to break when she spoke. "I think so . . . I can't remember where."

He kissed his teeth. "Don't gimme that. Or are you trying to stop me going out by hiding my t'ings?"

"Of course not," she protested.

He came around the sofa and hunched down, facing her.

"What's wrong wid you, eh?" He brushed a tear from her cheek with his thumb. "You want to own me? I don't treat you like property and I don't expect to be treated that way either, you know what I mean?"

Marion just looked at him. Another tear trickled down. She sniffed.

Gerard opened his arms wide to show that he had nothing to hide. "There ain't no more, babes. You listening to me?"

"Yes, Gerard." Even as she spoke, Marion knew that it didn't matter whose bed Gerard ended up in tonight, she would still take him back. She knew she would let him keep the front door key and allow him to come back whenever he liked. She knew, because this was the man she adored.

"Now, if you feel bad about me missing dinner, then I'm sorry." He took her fingers in one of his smooth hands. "I'll make it up to you, okay?"

"Yes, Gerard." She felt numb.

"That's my girl. Now, where's my pager?"

She wanted him to go. *Go now*, she thought. *Leave me alone.*

"Try the bedroom, bedside drawer."

He patted her hand, then let it go. Smiling smugly, he rose from his haunches, leaving her feeling empty and cold.

A few moments later the front door slammed and Marion was alone again. She bawled openly. Her body racked with sobs. He hadn't even said goodbye. Her tears soaked into the fabric of the sofa. This was worse than not having anyone at all. She knew now that she wouldn't see Gerard for a week or more. That would be her punishment for bringing up the subject of marriage again. Hadn't he warned her about trying to corner him? Yes he had, that same time when he'd said that, as soon as he was ready, she would be the first to know.

Marion had become Gerard's property a year before, when they were both attending Lewisham College. She was twenty-one and Gerard six years older. They weren't in the same classes, but their breaks had coincided and they would meet up in the canteen. All the girls had fancied Gerard, especially those who denied it. Some of the guys probably fancied him too.

Gerard had oozed confidence, while Marion, a psychology student, had lacked it. But he'd noticed her nevertheless, one day in the lunch queue. Marion had been with her classmate Simone, who was chatting about Valentine's Day a week away. Gerard had stood two places behind with three of his friends, noisily discussing a boxing match and taking bets on who would mash up who for the heavyweight title. Simone had informed Marion loftily that her steady boyfriend, Conrad, who she had been with since she was sixteen, was taking her to Paris for Valentine's. "Four days in gay Par*ee*," she'd swooned, "all expenses paid." She was so excited, she wanted the whole canteen to share her joy, and wouldn't stop talking about it loudly.

Marion had followed her friend to a table and they'd sat down with their lunches. Half-way through the meal Marion had looked up and caught Gerard looking straight at her, smiling. She'd averted her eyes instinctively, but every time she looked back in that direction he'd been looking at her.

For several days after that Gerard would nod or smile whenever their paths crossed. Her friends would nudge her and giggle, but Marion would simply smile back shyly, too afraid to imagine that it would ever come to anything. Gerard was, after all, the resident Adonis. What could he possibly see in her?

Marion had started looking forward to every new college day, looking forward to a smile or a nod of acknowledgement. And she had started dressing better too, and making sure that her hair was knockout before she left home in the mornings.

Then one day it had happened — again in the lunch queue. This time he had been standing right behind her. She'd reached over the counter for a plate, but Gerard's hand had reached for it first and handed it to her. Her heart was thumping hard and fast as she croaked, "Thanks."

"S'all right," he'd said. "I'm Gerard, by the way."

She'd smiled weakly and turned to go.

"Hold on."

She'd turned back to face him.

He'd grinned down at her. "And you are . . . ?"

"Marion," she'd replied.

"Nice."

He'd squeezed her free hand, smiling favourably and nodding his head in approval as his eyes undressed her.

Marion had felt embarrassed as her whole body tingled and her nipples hardened. Did the "nice" refer to her name or her body, she'd wondered as she hurried off to her table.

He didn't let her off that easily, though. He had sat at her table that day and every day from then on, making her laugh and showering compliments on her. This guy wasn't just good looking, he had charm and a brain, and (to Marion's surprise) they had a lot in common. Gerard seemed to know so much and was very ambitious, just the way she liked her men. Still, she had let him ask her out four times before she accepted. On that first date at the Roof Gardens nightclub, he had been the perfect gentleman. He had done nothing more than kiss her when he dropped her home, and she'd floated through her front door deeply in love.

GERARD

No, I don't think I'm God's gift to women, I know I am. I am every woman's dream. I'm more than good looking. I've got my own business, I've got brains, I treat women well. Buy a lady presents and take her out — sometimes. Not too often, or else they start to take it for granted and then give you hassle when you don't.

I treat 'em all different, because no two women are the same. Take Marion and Debbie for instance. Marion wants me to be her exclusive property, like I'm wearing a sign saying "For Sale". I'm sure she done picked out her wedding dress and the church already. I'm not going to tell her straight out why she isn't my ideal wife because I don't want to hurt her feelings. She's too . . . fickle. She too easy fe cry. Catch her when it's her time of the month and she'll bawl for any lickle t'ing. And she spends too much time taking care of me. What's wrong with that? I don't need another mother.

Now, Debbie — she's totally different. She loves the fast life. She likes fast music, men, cars, money, food. You name it, it's got to be fast for Debs. There's no talk of babies and marriage with her. She knows what she wants and goes out and gets it.

I like being with Debs. Marion is just someone to relax and chill with. Because I can't relax with Debs, she's always on the go.

3. TWO-TIMING LOVER

Pamela King shut and locked the bathroom door. She ran the shower until it was pleasantly warm, then stepped in and let the water cascade over her body. She soaped herself vigorously, washing away his scent. Already she began to feel better.

When she'd finished, she climbed out and stood naked in front of the mirror-tiled wall. She untied her shoulder-length hair and let it fall freely. Her body was perfect. Fifty sit-ups a day made sure that her stomach stayed flat. She occasionally went to the gym, more for the social aspect than the keep fit. Otherwise, she contented herself at home with the aerobic step and video tape, the exercise bike and the stairclimber she had bought herself for Christmas.

She didn't have a mark on her smooth skin. She turned sideways. Her pert backside and firm breasts curved out sensually from her body. She leaned forward to study her face closely. Stunning brown eyes framed by long upturned lashes stared back at her. Her straight nose was almost European, her skin the colour of coffee cream. She was beautiful.

So why did she feel so damned depressed?

She knew why — and as she dried off her body with a large lilac towel she thought of the man lying in her bed. Before he had come into her life, living with someone had never entered her mind; it would severely cramp her style, she'd thought. She thought back to the days when she had three or more men virtually queuing up to be with her. She could have had a different man for every night of the week if she'd wanted it. She'd had her boops, her ruffneck, her sweetboy, her buppie — even her toy boy.

She missed those days, when she never knew who was around the corner. The unpredictability of a new lover and all the flirting, the teasing, the chat-ups, the chase and the capture. The life she was living now was just not for her.

Living with James had been an experiment. Her first married man. They met at a party. He'd been very open and had told her all about his wife and two kids. A couple of weeks into the affair, he'd suggested that he should come clean and tell his wife about it, then he and Pamela could stop all the ducking and diving and be together properly. Pamela had thought she'd dissuaded him. "After all," she had purred, "why spoil a good thing?" Two months later James had moved in, claiming that his wife had found out and thrown him out of their home. Pamela had her doubts, but he said that he had nowhere else to go, and she felt that she had little choice but to let him move in temporarily.

Now she knew what living together meant, she wanted to move on. She had had enough of sharing her possessions, fitting her life around somebody else's, putting up with habits, not being able to make arrangements without informing your partner. James would be perfect if she ever needed a housemaid. He cooked, cleaned, ironed, massaged her feet, and even did the shopping. But his idea of excitement was having sex on a Sunday morning.

Shaun, who was Pamela's ex that never was a boyfriend, had called two days earlier and asked if he could see her again. Irresistible Shaun. They'd had a thing going, on and off, for four years — before James had come on the scene. Hearing his voice again down the telephone line had made her tingle with the memories. She felt she couldn't refuse him, didn't want to refuse. Shaun was the ideal tonic to get her back in the swing of things. Boy, they had learnt some positions together. Shaun — Mr Stan' 'Pon It Long! James was no comparison.

Pamela heard the alarm go off in the bedroom. Seconds later James came into the bathroom and stood behind her, rubbing sleep from his eyes. "Morning," he grinned. He was obviously pleased with his performance half an hour earlier.

"Morning," she replied brusquely, beginning her face-cleansing routine. She removed a cotton wool ball from the tube on the low window sill and caught his eyes in the mirror. He smiled, a smile that she had once thought cute but now irritated her. Five foot eight, he matched her in height, if slightly underfed. Very fair skinned, he was often mistaken for mixed race. His hair was cut in a fashionable short back and sides. He was so thin that, when he had first moved in, Pamela had cooked everything fattening she could think of to put a bit of meat on him. She'd even suggested he visit the gym. Eight months later he was still *maaga*.

He reached out and stroked her hair. She tensed.

"Coffee?" he asked.

"Please."

She breathed a sigh of relief at his departure. *Please don't let him get horny again this morning,* she prayed silently. Once a day was quite enough. Shit, once a week was too much. He did nothing for her any more — if ever.

She was smoothing cocoa butter over her full breasts when he came back with the coffees. He placed hers on the window ledge and sipped his.

"Has something changed between us?"

Pamela held his gaze, then bent over to moisturise her legs. His eyes were on her, lustfully following the curves of her lithe body.

"Pam?"

She stood up, shook her dark brown shoulder-length hair, then pushed it off her face and took a sip of her coffee. It was perfect. She reached for her bra from the towel rail. "Everything changes, J, nothing stays the same." She clipped the front clasp of her bra and pushed her arms through the straps.

"But it's not changing for the better, is it?"

No answer, just a deep sigh.

"I mean, do you still love me?" James asked.

Pamela put her hands on her hips and turned her eyes to the

ceiling. Why in hell had he chosen this morning to have this conversation?

"Look, James, love is an emotion. It's like being happy or sad. There are different degrees of love, you know what I'm saying?"

He frowned. "You didn't answer my question." He looked like a little boy with stubble, who'd just been told he'd never see his parents again.

"I love you, James," she said softly. "I'm just not sure how much. Maybe it's not enough for you," she added lamely, trying unsuccessfully to convince herself. She pulled black lacy panties on and hoped her answer had satisfied him.

"Is there someone else?" He was looking at her with lie-detector eyes.

Where the hell did he get that from? He had been watching a lot of soaps lately. And did he suspect, or was he just groping in the dark as usual?

She hoped she was looking at him earnestly. "No. No, there's no one else." At the moment she wasn't lying.

James looked at her helplessly, then his shoulders slumped and he hung his head.

"I'm going to get dressed," she said, easing past him and out of the bathroom.

James came into the room and stood in the doorway, a midnight blue towel around his waist. He didn't look too happy.

Personally Pamela liked a good argument, but James wasn't the type. He gave in too easily and always let her win. This inevitably infuriated her, but he refused point-blank to argue back.

"I need some answers before we leave this flat today."

Pamela turned to him, her mouth dropping open. For a minute there he'd sounded angry. She placed one hand on her hip impatiently.

"Pammy, are we breaking up?" He was dead serious.

She reached for her hairbrush on the dresser and turned back to her reflection. "What makes you think that?"

"You want a list?"

"Do you want us to finish?" Pamela brushed her hair vigorously.

"No. But I don't want us to go on like this," he huffed. "You don't respond to me when we make love, you avoid staying in with me. When I suggest we go somewhere you've always got something better to do. You sleep in nightclothes every night with your back to me. I can take a hint."

She sighed and twisted her mouth to one side. "It's true. My feelings have changed." She looked at him for a reaction. His lips were tight and his eyes searched hers. "Maybe if you moved out . . . we could take it from there."

He gasped as if he'd been punched in the stomach. "Move out? But I've got nowhere to go."

"It wouldn't have to be immediately. Just start looking, eh?" She turned her back, dismissing him with a toss of her head. And when she turned back a moment later, James was gone. She heard the bathroom door shut, the lock turn and the shower begin to run.

Remorse began to rise in her chest, but Pamela beat it back down. There was little point in apologising. It was what she wanted. It was for the best, even if it meant that she would have to find his share of the rent somehow.

She pulled her hair back and braided it, tying the end with a red velvet scrunchy. A smile turned up the corners of her mouth. Today could be the start of a new chapter in her life. She punched the air triumphantly. "Yes!"

On Monday she had taken him to the annual Afro Hair & Beauty show. She had picked out what he would wear. He had to look good — after all, she did.

Pamela had tonged her hair into ringlets and expertly applied a touch of bronze colour to the ends. She'd worn a red crêpe de Chine trouser suit and silver jewellery, and to add the finishing touch she'd put on her most expensive Ray-Bans. For James she had picked out black trousers, a white polo-neck, and a black and white striped blazer. They looked like a couple out of *Ebony* magazine.

As they had driven to the Alexandra Palace, they'd passed countless groups of women of colour, all making their way to the venue: ladies with ponytails or elaborate beehives, waves, wigs, hairpieces and the most amazing outfits. The Afro Hair & Beauty show was, after all, the unofficial Miss Black UK.

It was still early, two o'clock, when they'd arrived. The air was charged with a buzz that was unmistakably a 'black *thang*'. Pamela had felt her ego rise in her chest as they'd walked towards the main hall, James two steps behind her. She knew she looked good and she knew that everyone else knew it too.

"Where to first?" James had asked, consulting his programme.

Pamela had kept cool. "Let's just walk," she'd said, taking the lead.

Having walked around the whole hall once, Pamela had regretted bringing James along. This wasn't the place to take your boyfriend to. The atmosphere was right for singles who were looking.

They'd both become bored pretty quickly. James was interested only in the "Battle of the Barbers" on the Soft Sheen stand, with four hairdressers snipping their way through the best style they could come up with in twenty minutes.

Meanwhile, Pamela had scanned the hall from behind her shades, checking out the talent. A tall, fair-skinned model had strolled by, and Pamela's eyes had followed him. The man noticed her and grinned handsomely back.

She'd turned to James. "Back in a minute . . . going to the Ladies'," she'd told him as she fell into step behind the model.

Having got Tevin's phone number, she'd circulated on her own. By the Hawaiian Silky stall she was surprised to bump into Marion's boyfriend, Gerard. His face had spread in an uncomfortable and guilty smile when he noticed Pamela. The two young girls at his side had something to do with his unease.

"Gerard! Fancy seeing you here," Pamela had smiled wryly.

"A'right, Pam." His eyes had darted shiftily around the room. He was dressed in a red blazer with a black T-shirt and trousers. His hair, recently barbered, had shone with S-curl gel, as had his immaculate goatee beard and moustache.

Pamela had shaken her dark curls, enjoying his discomfort. "Enjoying yourself?" she'd asked, turning her attention briefly to the two gum-chewing girls, barely teenagers. They'd been dressed in the typical uniform of their age group: coloured denim, baggy, with extra-extra gel on their heads just in case they ran into a tornado.

"Not really my scene, y'know. I jus' brought these two out for the day," he'd said.

"Yeah, *right*," Pamela had grinned. "So aren't you going to introduce me, then?"

"Max, get a picture of that guy on stage, that's a wicked suit, man!" the girl closest to Gerard had yelled. Max, her companion, had backed up, pulling a camera out of her pocket and taking a snap.

Pamela had waited for the introductions, and Gerard had had no choice but to oblige. "This is Debbie and Maxine, friends of mine," he'd said, emphasising the "friends". "Satisfied?"

Pamela had lifted an eyebrow. "The question is, aren't you?" she'd said pointedly. Then she had cut her eyes at him and left him fuming inside.

She wouldn't mention it to Marion, she'd decided, unless she found it necessary. It was none of her business. If Marion was naive about men she would have to learn the hard way.

By the time Pamela had got back to the Soft Sheen stand an hour later, she had collected two more phone numbers, one of which had been forced on her by a photographer who wanted her to pose for him. James had been so engrossed with the different heats of the "Battle of the Barbers" that he had barely noticed Pamela had been away.

She'd let that slide. She had managed to enjoy herself without James tagging along. The day hadn't been a total waste of time after all. And she had the phone numbers of men with potential to add to her list.

JAMES

I can't see why some men refuse to learn how to cook. I love to cook and clean. And I can look after kids just as well as any woman can. I've got three kids of my own to prove it. But I need a woman to care about in my life. I love being part of a couple.

We met at Pamela's twenty-fifth. She came over and chatted me up! Even when I told her I was married and had kids from two different women, she didn't so much as bat an eyelid. True, she was a little bit tipsy, but this woman was for real. We got on so well that I went up to see her at her flat the next day and I knew then that I was in love. Maybe I fall in love too easily. I just feel good when I'm with her. Even when we're just relaxing with a bottle of wine and playing Monopoly.

We are so different. But as the saying goes, opposites attract. Pamela likes to rave. I understand. She needs her time to herself. Why should she stay cooped up with me all weekend when she has a lot of friends to see? I don't mind. Any problems we're going through I'm determined to sort out. I can't just let it end I love her. When something's worth saving you work at it. We won't let a few ups and downs split us up.

4. TELL ME WHAT YOU LIKE

Pamela sat at home in her satin pyjama suit with a glass of brandy and Coke in her hand and sweet soul music oozing out of her stereo system. James was out visiting his children. She wasn't expecting him back until late, and she intended to get completely sozzled before then.

The phone rang, interrupting a fantasy of sex on the beach with

Shaun. She answered on the fifth ring.

"Pam, it's me."

"Maz. A'right love?" She settled down in the cream armchair, throwing her legs over the arm.

"Not really." Marion's voice sounded low, depressed.

"Man trouble?" Pamela guessed.

"Yep."

Whenever Marion needed to tell someone her troubles she called Pamela. Joan, being the eldest, would only lecture her.

"So what did the bastard do this time?"

Marion explained. Gerard had come and gone the night before without a word of when he'd be back.

Pamela listened, ice tinkling in her glass as she twirled the brown liquid around before raising it to her lips and sipping. The brandy warmed her throat and continued its heated trail to her stomach.

Pamela had heard this story before, several times in the last few months, in fact. Gerard needed someone to cut him down to size, she concluded, and Marion definitely wasn't that someone. He took advantage of her too easily.

"I've told you before, Maz, you're too good for him. He doesn't appreciate you."

"That doesn't help, Pam. I still love him."

"Don't mek love turn you fool, y'know."

Marion sighed. "Maybe it's my fault."

"You should never blame yourself with someone like Gerard." Pamela wanted to say more. She wanted to tell Marion about the Afro Hair & Beauty show, or the times she'd had to fight off Gerard's advances. About six months previously, he had found her phone number in Marion's phone index and started calling her. At first she had mildly flirted with him. He may have been her friend's man, but he was a wicked-looking specimen and she couldn't resist playing with him. She saw no harm in a little fun, but she had absolutely no intention of letting it get any further. After a few calls, though, he had started to come on strong, dissing Marion to her, and saying how he thought he and Pamela would make the perfect couple. Pamela had told him in clear, expressive terms what he could do to himself. He hadn't called again. Since that day, there had always been a frosty atmosphere between them that Marion noticed but couldn't quite place. Gerard treated Marion badly enough; Pamela wasn't about to hurt her friend further by telling her the truth.

So she changed the subject. "I haven't told you, I've got good news: I got a promotion."

"Congratulations, Pam."

"It's only temporary, but, you know, extra money for three months isn't bad."

That morning, Pamela had gone into the Loampit Vale nursery where she had worked since leaving college, and had been called into the office by the senior nursery nurse. Margaret, her first-line manager, had been ill for some time. The doctors had suspected cancer but Margaret, being the kind of person she was, had laughed it off. It had unfortunately turned out to be worse than first diagnosed.

The job would now go to Pamela while Margaret was on sick leave. It wasn't the way she would have liked to gain a promotion, but a hundred pounds extra a month was not something to be sniffed at.

"More good news," Pamela whispered conspiratorially. "Shaun's back."

Marion's voice was full of surprise. "Are you sure you want him back? That was over a year ago."

"You know it could never be over, not with Shaun," Pamela giggled.

"But what about James?" Marion asked.

Pamela tutted. "James bores me silly. I've asked him to move out, but he reckons he can't find anywhere else to go."

"How can you do that to him? He'd die for you."

"That's an idea," Pamela laughed.

"Pam!"

"I was only joking. I've been drinking — it's gone to my head. I need some excitement."

"If that's the way you feel, then go for it," Marion said unconvincingly.

"I will. We've got a problem, though."

"Yeah?"

"Well, we're supposed to go out tomorrow night. We can't use his place, his parents are staying for the week, and I can't exactly bring him here . . ." Pamela frowned. She couldn't even do as she pleased in her own flat. James was becoming a liability.

"Sorry, Pam, can't help you," Marion interjected. "I'm babysitting for Joan; she's staying over at Colin's tomorrow night, apparently."

Pamela smirked. "You're kidding! She told me they were done."

"Yeah, well, he doesn't think so."

"That means her house is free tomorrow night?"

"I suppose so."

"What d'you think?"

Marion wasn't committing herself to a promise that had nothing to do with her. "Ask her yourself. So long as you don't use her beds, there shouldn't be a problem."

"I wasn't thinking about the bed, Maz."

"The bathroom?" Marion laughed, catching the hint of what Pamela had in mind. Joan had a large en suite bathroom. Tiled floor, circular bathtub and a shower stall. The girls had often shared jokes and fantasies about using her bathroom for adventurous sex.

"Yes, girl. I'm getting goosebumps just thinking about it."

"You'd better call her, then. Let me know what she says — and, Pam, I want details afterwards."

"You know that. I'll call you later, yeah? Bye."

Pamela rang off. She sat there, easy and relaxed, with a mischievous grin on her face. She savoured the thought of Shaun and herself in Joan's bathroom. Shaun knew how to please a woman, any time, any place. She could hardly contain her excitement as she picked up the phone to call Joan.

"All right, Mum. We'll come down this Sunday for dinner."

Joan's mother kissed her teeth. "Fe dinner! I tell you I want to see more ah yuh, an' so yuh want me to feed yuh."

Joan rolled her eyes. "Look, I'll tell you what. How about if we come down on Saturday and stay till Sunday evening? I'll cook the whole weekend."

"Dat soun' bettah. I'll see you Sat'day, then."

"Yeah. Bye, Mum."

Joan hung up and reached into her handbag for a cigarette. Talking to her mum always gave her a smoker's appetite. She complained about not seeing enough of her and Shereen, but refused to come and visit, claiming she couldn't leave the house empty "fe teef to come tek weh me t'ings dem".

Joan lit a cigarette, sucked in deeply and exhaled. The phone rang again.

"Yeah, hello?" she answered abruptly.

"Hi, J."

"Pam! How you doing, girl?"

"Safe. How're you?"

"Alive."

"Oh, don't. You sound like Marion. I just spoke to her and she's depressed over Gerard."

"Yeah, I know."

Pamela kissed her teeth. "She better sort him out soon. He was

30

at the Afro Hair Show the other day, with a couple of schoolgirls."

"Yeah! Does Marion know?"

"I couldn't tell her that. Besides, I've got no proof he was *with* them."

"You can bet he wasn't there just to hold their hands, though."

"Speaking of holding hands, I heard a rumour you're seeing Colin tomorrow night."

There was the tiniest pause. "Marion, right?"

"She mentioned she was babysitting for you, that's all."

"He came round last night and we talked," Joan said wistfully.

"Yeah, and the rest. You and Colin never just talk." Pamela chuckled. "You can't hide that stuff from me. I know you too well."

"All right, nosey. I had him on the kitchen table." Joan smiled. She got warm just thinking about it.

"You lie!" Pamela screamed.

"Why would I lie? It was gooood. He's still got it."

"Well, I've got news for you too. Shaun is back in my life."

"No! What did I tell you about you two? You kept telling me it's really over this time."

"Yeah I know, but the boy is just too tempting . . . J, I need a favour."

SHAUN

You see me, I'm a sucker for pretty women with long, tight legs, clear skin, a fit body and kissable lips. But did you ever hear of someone being instantly turned on to someone else without any contact? No? Then let me tell you, it can happen. It happened to me when I was just seventeen years old, and it hasn't worn off yet.

When I first met Pamela she was the same age as me and had her own place. For a seventeen-year-old to have her own flat was wicked. A group of us would hang out there regularly.

At seventeen, girls are only for one thing. I'd had my share of them and more. But Pamela always stood out in a crowd. She had this kind of aura about her. Anyway we got close, just hanging out together. She was studying for her BTEC in nursery teaching. I had no time for school, but used to meet her outside college every afternoon. When I finally got round to asking her out, I kinda like acted like I was playing, y'know. I said, "You ever thought about us going out, y'know, as boyfriend and girlfriend?"

She looked at me with those sexy eyes and said, "Ain't we going out already?"

I tell you, my heart must have risen up outta my chest into my

31

throat and did a little soca dance. I was so choked, I couldn't speak. That night we went back to her place and made it official. I thought I was good, but she was a lot more experienced than me, and taught me about a woman's body and what she wanted. I loved every moment of it.

Even at that age I knew I didn't have anything to offer a girl like Pamela except my looks and body and what I had learned about satisfying her in bed. I had her hooked on sex with me, you know what I'm saying? We always seemed to be at it. We couldn't go to a party together without having to slip out into some back alley to get some.

The relationship was intense and we broke up and got back together whenever it got outta control. Then she moved that guy in. I had gone to visit my parents in St Lucia, and when I got back I found Pamela shacked up with some man. At the time I just said fine, it's your life, even though it hurt me. But now I've got one more chance and I'm going to make sure I get her back.

5. EMOTIONS

Music pumped out of the fifth-floor flat where Pamela lived. Marion rubbed her cold hands together and knocked again, louder this time. She hated waiting around in this neighbourhood. There was never anyone around — at least no one she would want to meet. Deptford wasn't exactly Hampstead, and the Pepys estate, with its reputation of old, was one of the least desirable addresses in the area.

Pamela finally answered the door, her face covered in a green face-pack. "Hello, love." She wore a cut-off top and a pair of shorts, emphasising her hard, flat stomach and long legs.

"Are you deaf? I've been knocking for five minutes. It's cold out here, y'know." Marion dropped her bag containing her toiletries and outfit in the hallway and shrugged off her coat.

"Sorry, Maz. Joan's got the music up loud."

Marion followed Pamela into the flat. The three girlfriends had decided to meet at Pamela's flat to get ready to go out. In stark contrast to the block Marion lived in, Pamela's flat was very stylishly decorated in cream and red. Cream-coloured leather settee and armchair, red carpet and red aluminium shelves. A glass-topped marble coffee table centred the room, and a large black-framed mirror dominated one wall.

Joan, her lips slightly puckered in concentration, sat on the settee building a spliff as Marion entered. She glanced up briefly. "Hi, Maz."

"Getting in the mood I see," Marion said disapprovingly. Joan ignored her and carried on rolling her joint.

"I'll get us some drinks," Pamela said, and motioned with her head for Marion to follow her. They stepped into the adjoining kitchen and the door swung shut behind them.

"What's happening there, then?" Marion asked. "I thought Joan had given that stuff up."

"Who knows? Colin. Her mum. She just needs to chill out every once in a while."

"Okay, it's her life." Marion let it go. "So how did it go with Shaun?"

Pamela remained cool, not giving anything away. "I'll get the drinks and then I'll fill you both in. Joan's begging me for the details too." She opened a cupboard stocked with alcoholic beverages. Bacardi, whisky, brandy, Southern Comfort and Malibu were definitely in effect.

"You planning to open an off licence?" Marion joked.

"You know I like my tipple, Maz. Besides, I often need a stiff drink when James is around." She crossed to the fridge and swung the door open. Still more alcohol. Several four-packs of lager and half a dozen bottles of sparkling wine. She pulled out a bottle of Asti Spumante and poured a glass for herself.

"Where is he, anyway?" Marion asked.

"I chucked him out," Pamela said seriously.

"You didn't!"

"He's only gone to his cousin's." Pamela threw her head back, laughing. She loved winding Marion up; it was so easy. "Look, make yourself useful." She handed her friend the ice bucket. "Take this through. I'll bring the drinks in shortly."

Joan stood by the window, gazing out over the estate. The living room was full of the pungent aroma of ganja.

Marion deposited the ice bucket on the coffee table and sat down on the settee, her short, slim legs crossed.

"Joan!" Marion raised her voice over the music.

Joan turned with a faraway look on her face. "Sorry, Maz — miles away."

"You all right?"

Joan rocked her hand back and forth. "So-so." She went over to the stereo and turned down the volume.

33

Pamela came in with the tray of drinks and placed it carefully on the table. "Get stuck in. We're gonna get well plastered tonight."

"You mean you've still got the energy, after Shaun?" Joan winked.

Pamela flung herself on to the sofa with a graceful air. "Shaun's good, but not that good. Anyway, you can talk. You've had Colin two nights in a row."

Joan and Marion exchanged looks. They both knew the truth: Joan and Colin hadn't spent the night together. They had argued, and Joan had walked out on him. She hadn't gone back to her own home because Pamela and Shaun had been there, so she'd ended up crashing on the sofa at Marion's. She hadn't been in the mood to talk about it then, and she still wasn't now.

Marion and Joan had grown up together on the Meridian housing estate in Greenwich, by the *Cutty Sark*. They had lost touch when Marion's family had moved to Abbeywood. After five years they'd met again at the funeral of Marion's younger sister, Jacqueline. For two years now the friends had been very close again, just as if they had never parted. A mutual acquaintance had introduced them both to Pamela shortly afterwards, and the two friends had become three.

"So?" Joan persisted.

"You eager, eenh?" Pamela teased.

"Don't keep us in suspense, Pam," Marion pleaded. She knew Pamela was dying to tell them about her night of lust anyway, so why the delay?

"Awright, awright." Pamela paused. "It was wicked! Five hours of non-stop bed work."

The girls let out whoops of excited laughter.

"I'm telling you, he made my toes curl," Pamela continued, gesturing with her hands. "I stopped counting the orgasms after number eight. You know when you feel like you're gonna explode . . ." Pamela went into graphic detail — of how Shaun had given her the good stuff and she had lapped it up, all of it. "I swear he's got bigger. I was like, okay, so I haven't had a decent man in months, but when I held it in my hands it was t'ick an' heavy." Pamela held one hand out as if she was weighing something in her palm. "I was feeling it all up in my chest . . . And you know what really turns him on?" A wicked grin spread across her face. "When I bite his bottom. I swear, my teeth just have to go near his backside and he goes wild."

Joan screamed with laughter and Marion wiped away tears from the corners of her eyes.

"No, I'm serious. You should try it, then tell me if I'm lying. They love it. Bite his bottom, man."

By the time Pamela had finished, Joan was on the floor holding her sides and Marion was swaying, laughing hysterically.

Pamela took a swig of her brandy and Coke. "I've got to wash this stuff off my face, I probably look like the Wicked Witch of the West. Back in a minute." With that, she disappeared out of the door.

The girls slowly recovered from Pamela's tale. Joan slid back on to her seat and reached for her cigarettes. "Pamela kills me, man." She shook her head.

Marion got up and went over to the stereo to select another CD, still chuckling to herself. She flipped through the stack, occasionally pulling one out and reading the list of tracks. She turned to look at Joan as she heard the flick of the lighter. She had been smoking a lot more than usual, and Marion knew from experience that this was a sign she was feeling low. "You sure you're all right, Jo?" she asked.

"Safe. Why?" Joan dragged hard on the cigarette and leaned back in the chair.

"You're chain-smoking again," Marion noted.

"Am I? Didn't notice, y'know." She shrugged. "I only light up when I feel the need."

"So how's Colin?"

Joan shot her friend a look of frustration. "We've gone back to being mates — yet again. He's just a big kid, Maz. I need a man." She played with her lighter, nervously flicking it on and off.

Colin had wanted them to go back to sex on casual terms. She was adamant that it wasn't what she wanted. After hours of arguing back and forth on the subject, she had given up trying to make him see her point of view.

"So you dropped him again?"

"Yeah, no big deal. We ain't got nuttin' anyway." Joan half-smiled unconvincingly.

Marion decided to let it drop. She slotted an R. Kelly CD into the machine and grabbed a handful of peanuts as she sat down again.

"How's Shereen?"

"Fine." Joan smiled. "Better than her mummy."

"I think we all need a break, a holiday."

Joan took a puff of her cigarette, rested her head on the back of the sofa and let her thoughts drift away.

Marion continued. "Like that weekend in Paris. We just packed up and went. Forgot about men, work, London . . ."

"Yeah, Maz, but who can afford it now?"

"Mmm . . ."

The conversation fell dead again.

Pamela walked back in, fresh-faced, her hair held back with a red hair-band.

"So, does James suspect anything?" Marion asked her.

"He might. He's been asking a lot of questions recently. I told him I was at Chantelle's house Thursday night. I don't care if he does think something's going on, I'm enjoying myself." She snuggled back into the leather armchair, curling her legs underneath her bottom.

"You're too wicked, Pam," Joan jokingly scolded.

"Innit, though? The man left his wife for you and, eight months later, you're cheating on him," Marion chided. She had a soft spot for James, and thought Pamela fortunate in having him.

"What's good for the goose is good for the gander," Pamela said smugly.

"Damn right," Joan agreed. She was starting to feel light-headed. "Men think they're the only ones who can play around."

Pamela grinned. "Shaun told me he loves me."

"And you believed him?" Joan sniffed.

"He was telling the truth. I know him."

"Yeah, whatever." Joan kissed her teeth and downed the last of her Malibu and pineapple.

Marion frowned. "Never mind her. What you gonna do? James loves you too."

"But he's so boring. I used to miss him like crazy, before he moved in. Now all we seem to do is watch telly then go to bed — to sleep! A woman cannot live by TV alone." Pamela raised her glass of wine to her lips and gulped down a mouthful.

"Which one of them gives it to you how you want it?" Joan asked.

"Shaun does — but woman cannot live by cock alone either."

Joan stubbed out her cigarette in the ashtray. "You two need to swap men. Gerard could put Pamela under manners, then James and Marion could live happily ever after," she giggled. "After all, you do fancy James, don't you, Marion?"

"I just think he's a nice guy, that's all," Marion murmured.

"You want him, you can have him," Pamela offered.

Marion pulled on the tops of her knee-high boots, loosening them a little. She gave an exasperated sigh. "A good man is hard to find."

Joan reached for another cigarette. "You don't really know what a man's like until you live with him," she said.

R.Kelly's "Bump n' Grind" pumped out of the speakers. Pamela threw her arms in the air. "This is my tune, man." Then she sang: "I don't see nothing wrong, with a little bump an' grind."

The girls joined in. Joan dragged Marion to her feet and started gyrating to the beat. Pamela, giggling, joined in, bumping and grinding around the marble coffee table.

"Oh God, you do it long enough, you can actually feel it," Pamela laughed.

"Feel what?" Marion asked, bumping hips with Joan.

"The man's t'ing, you dope."

The track ended and the girls collapsed on the settee. Joan picked up a magazine and fanned herself with it, beads of perspiration trickling down her nose. Pamela refilled her glass with brandy and Coke and slid back into her seat.

It was nearly time to go.

The red Maestro cruised slowly past the crowd queuing outside the South London club. Granaries was going to be packed as usual. Girls shivered in short, expensive dresses, sacrificing warmth for style on this cold spring evening, while the guys posed, looking cool in their finest clothes.

Heads turned at the sound of the heavy drum n' bass track booming from Joan's car speakers.

"You sure we're getting in there tonight? Look at the queue!" Marion shouted above the music.

"Never mind 'bout the queue, did you see the men?" Pamela craned her neck to check out two guys who were eyeing the girls as the car passed. She smiled back teasingly.

Joan turned the volume down on the car stereo. "Don't you think you've got enough men already? Girl, save some for the rest of us."

"Nothing wrong with looking." Pamela pouted into her Fashion Fair powder compact mirror and dusted her nose lightly.

Joan steered the car into a parking space round the corner. They climbed out and began to make their way back. Joan was dressed in an all-in-one flared trouser suit. Pamela wore a silver baby-doll dress that just about covered her butt by five inches — her usual style. Marion was wearing sexy black batty rider shorts with lacy footless tights and a studded bra top. It suited her petite figure like it was made for her.

It was only a quarter to one when they entered the hot and sticky club, but it was already packed. Pamela's eyes scanned the dancefloor for men with potential. A mellow soul tune pumped from the speakers as a crowd of bodies rocked gently in time.

The girlfriends made their way down the mirrored corridor and past the mini waterfall which ran down the centre of the stairwell, to the Ladies', just to make sure nothing had slipped and that they looked as good as they had before leaving home. Even the rest rooms were crowded, with women queuing for the lavatories. In front of the mirrors, a line of women touched up, made up, adjusted bra straps, straightened hemlines, pulled tummies in, pushed breasts up, and patted hair into place, before asking their homegirls for a last opinion:

"Do my boobs look all right?"

"There's nothing wrong with your boobs. You wait till you've had kids — going without a bra will be a thing of the past."

"I should have worn my strapless, push 'em up a bit."

"Leave those tits alone. Bwoy, anyone would think you loved groping yourself."

"I do!"

Pamela pouted into the mirror and giggled. She shook her breasts and concluded that they looked fine. Then the girls strode confidently back into the club.

"Ready for a drink?" Pamela offered as the girls squeezed their way to the bar. Traditionally, she always bought the first round.

Drinks in hand, they made their way back through the crowd to their favourite spot at the back of the dancefloor, by a row of small tables. From this vantage point they could observe all the talent available.

The swing beat changed to hip hop.

"Drum an' bass crew, hol' tight, your time soon come," the MC (Master of Ceremonies) announced. The roar went up from the ravers.

Half an hour later the music slowed way down to lovers. Men mopped their heads with limp handkerchiefs or flannels, and women fanned themselves with invitation fliers. On the dancefloor one of the ravers twisted seductively, her knee firmly in her dancing partner's crotch. His hands groped her backside.

Joan recognised the girl. "Look, it's Christine!"

Pam laughed loudly. "We know who's getting some tonight then," she howled.

Christine was a well-known man-eater. She was a mini-mampy with an insatiable sexual appetite and, judging by the way she was dancing, she had found another victim. Her sequined bottom rose slowly, then dipped again as she whined away blissfully.

Marion was hot. She had been dancing throughout the drum n' bass set and, as a result, her clothes were now sticking uncomfortably to her body. As she watched the couples dancing close, she wondered what Gerard was doing. She couldn't remember the last time she had danced with him. They didn't rave together any more — they didn't do *anything* together. She looked over at her friends. Pam was giving the eye to an extremely good-looking fair-skinned man who was grinning back, hand on his chin contemplatively. Marion watched as he said something to his friend, who then turned to get a good look at Pamela. He nodded and smiled as if giving his friend the go ahead. The man began to make his way over. Suddenly, from behind, a pair of arms encircled Marion's waist and a firm male body thrust up against her. She spun round, ready to slap somebody. Instead she came face to face with a pair of familiar eyes on a dark, attractive male face. A look of pleased surprise filled her face.

"Paul, baby!" She embraced him, kissing him on both cheeks.

"See how you stay," Paul joked, holding her at arm's length. "Me nuh like the way you just dash me weh. I ain't heard from you in months."

"I didn't forget you. Busy, y'know," Marion said.

"Yeah?" Paul raised an eyebrow wryly.

Paul was a memory Marion thought she had forgotten. The last time she had seen him he had a full head of hair. Now he was fashionably clean-shaven and wore an earring.

Paul looked to her left. "Is that Pam?"

"Yeah. As usual she's rubbing up man," Marion laughed. She tugged Joan's arm to get her attention. "You remember Joan."

Always the charmer, Paul took Joan's hand and kissed the back of it with a bow of his head. Then he turned back to Marion, and taking her hand in his, he flashed his sweetest smile and put an arm around her waist, drawing her to him.

"I want to talk to you," he whispered in her ear.

"Talk, then."

"Just a chat, man. Come on, I don't want to shout. Come to the bar with me. Your friends aren't going anywhere. Come nuh." His eyes smiled at her warmly.

Marion tapped Joan on her shoulder and mouthed, "Back in a minute."

Joan nodded as Paul took Marion by the hand and led her to a quiet table.

"Want a drink?" he asked.

"Yeah, a Canei, please."

Paul nodded and left her at the table. Marion watched him weave his way through the crowd to the bar. He looked so fine. He was not a tall man, five foot eight, but his ebony black physique never failed to be noticed by women. Marion remembered how he used to be able to turn her on simply by looking at her in that certain way of his. Just the thought of his dark, hard body set her skin tingling, especially his tight buttocks. Her mind drifted back to one particularly passionate night in her living room. Paul taught karate to kids, and he was good, but that wasn't all he was good at, she recalled.

Paul returned with the drinks a few minutes later and sat down beside her, the scent of Aramis oozing from his body. Marion smiled to herself as memories came flooding back.

Paul caught the faintest smile in her eyes and, full of confidence, he held the stare. Then his smiling eyes travelled down her body, from her face, to her breasts, to her legs — all the way down — and back up again. "I could eat food off your body, you know that."

Marion smiled modestly. Paul loved complimenting women. It seemed to give him a buzz.

"You're looking fine yourself. Still training?" she asked.

"Yeah, man, it's my life. So where's your man?"

Marion knew he was going to ask that sooner or later. It was pretty standard as chat-up lines go and, being a man, Paul was looking for that green light to give him the 'go ahead'. She was glad she wouldn't have to lie.

"I hope he's in bed, dreaming about me," she replied coyly.

"I dream about you." Paul ran his forefinger gently down her bare arm, looking enticingly into her eyes.

"Yeah?"

"Yeah, man, all the time." His eyes dropped to her smooth, slim legs. "Those shorts . . . I looked over and said to myself, no one else looks that good in shorts, it has to be Marion."

"Don't bullshit, Paul," she chuckled.

"Who's bullshitting?" he said with mock astonishment. "You make my nature rise, girl."

Marion fought the urge to lower her eyes to his crotch. "Stop it, Paul. I told you, I've got a man."

He leaned on the table with one elbow and rested his chin on his knuckles. "You happy?"

"Yes." She lowered her eyes.

"Like we were?" He knew she was still attracted to him.

Marion hesitated. "It's different. I don't want to talk about us, we're in the past. It's over."

The music changed to a down-tempo groove. Paul got up and offered Marion his hand. He wanted a dance — up close and personal. Marion didn't know if she could trust herself hip to hip with him, but she stood up anyway and let him pull her close. She could feel that he was already slightly aroused. He placed a hand on her lower back.

Their bodies moved together, hips rolling to the up and down beats of the track, and Marion let herself go with the flow. It didn't take long for the combined effect of alcohol, music and breathlessly good whinin' to wash away Marion's memory of her man at home, in bed and dreaming about her.

Paul's hands caressed her gently, following her spine as they danced. His warm breath, close to her ear, made her tremble. Then he nibbled her neck.

A dance with Gerard had never been this good. Not even close.

The record came to an end, but Paul wasn't finished. The next track was equally as arousing and he guided her arms back around his neck.

This guy knew how to move, and he was moving her.

She clung to him, and any thought of Gerard disappeared like a bubble bursting. It was Paul she was dancing with and that was all that mattered. Hadn't she loved him once? It was therefore not so surprising that feelings began to resurface. Not just sexual feelings either, but how Paul had loved her, *really* loved her. Yes he had, and now she wanted — no, *needed* some of that sweetness back.

Gerard forced his way back into her mind. Marion suddenly pulled herself away from her dancing partner and made to leave.

"Where you going?"

"I've got to find my friends," she insisted.

"When we gonna meet up again?" he asked, dabbing his brow with a handkerchief from his back pocket.

She shrugged. "I'll call you."

He laughed. "I've heard that before."

"No, really. I will call."

"A'right then. An' tell that man of yours, he better treat you right, or he'll have me to deal with. Seen?"

Marion smiled, she leaned towards him and kissed his cheek, stepping back quickly before he got the wrong idea.

Flustered and hot, she returned to where she'd left her friends. Both of them had their arms wrapped around good-looking men. She fanned herself with a beer mat, thinking about Paul and Gerard. It had only been a dance, but the rush of emotions it had evoked worried her. Paul was irresistible.

But what of Gerard? She was sure she loved him. Who wouldn't? A six-foot-two tower of ambition. Paul, though, had stirred up emotions Gerard knew nothing about.

Oh, cruel world that would make Paul her past and Gerard her future. Was that all there was to it? If only she could be like Pamela and share her love, with no feelings of guilt.

What was she thinking? Marion suddenly realised that she had had too much to drink.

The girls swapped notes on the car journey home. Joan had got the number of a guy named Charles. He was thirty-five years old and the manager of a busy cinema in Islington. "Dollar signs all over him. He didn't look bad either," she said.

"The guy I was dancing with last — now he was nice," Pamela interrupted.

"Another pretty bwoy." Joan tutted. "Don't you ever learn?"

"They have their uses," Pam smirked.

"I'm so glad I'm off the market," Marion piped up.

"I'm not exactly 'on the market', but it don't stop me browsing," Pamela laughed. "And anyway, didn't I see you disappear with Paul?"

"Paul's a friend," Marion said defensively.

"A 'friend' you had a passionate affair with." Joan looked over her shoulder at Marion as they pulled up at traffic lights.

"Yeah, well, I've got morals."

"Listen to her, Miss Goody Two Shoes," Pamela teased.

A black Saab pulled up beside them. The driver rolled his window down and grinned at Pamela. Pamela nudged Joan and the three of them burst out laughing.

The man was no Denzel Washington. In fact, Shabba Ranks would have been stiff competition.

As the lights changed Pamela wound down her window and shouted out, "If I had your face I wouldn't need a backside, mate."

Marion's mouth fell open with embarrassment as their car sped through the lights, leaving the other car behind.

"Nice car, shame about the face," Joan giggled.

Marion curled up in the back seat and pretended to sleep, her mind too tormented to join in the fun.

PAUL

When I was fourteen my parents split up. Dad went back to Nigeria, leaving us in England with our Jamaican mother. She struggled to bring the three of us up. No way would I let my woman or my kids struggle like that. No way.

At the moment I'm single — by choice. I haven't met anyone I want to be with. It's like everyone out there is on the lookout for a partner. I've been there, been hurt, and now I just wanna chill.

Women are like assault courses. They have their ups and downs. Some of them are easy, some difficult. The ones that look easy have their little surprises. They'll pump you up, then bring you down hard. But, hey, if the right woman came along . . . who knows? As the saying goes, can't live wiv 'em, can't live wivout 'em.

There's one woman I'm interested in. She's my ex but, hey, if t'ings never work out the firs' time . . .

She was going t'rough some emotional stuff back then. I couldn't handle it. That was two years ago. I've matured since then. And, hey, if she came along today . . . I'd gladly take the stress.

Marion attracts me like a magnet. She's so innocent . . . I jus' wanna take care of her. When I saw her at Granaries it was like sump'n jus' open up again. I'm not one of these brothers who can't express how they feel, so when we started dancing I let her know exactly how I felt with every move and every caress. Now the ball's in her court.

6. SECRET LOVERS

Pamela stirred before opening one sleepy eye. The space beside her was empty — James had already left for work. He worked one Sunday a month, and would be gone until four in the afternoon. So it was her turn to cook. As James had cooked all week, she couldn't complain.

She opened the other eye. The bedroom was a mess, clothes and underwear scattered everywhere. Even last night's raving clothes lay in a pile on the floor — surprisingly, James hadn't cleared up after her. Squinting, she looked at the clock. It was two in the afternoon. Luckily, she never got hangovers.

With a prolonged yawn, Pamela lifted herself up into the lotus position. She sat like that for several minutes, breathing in deeply and out slowly. Then she got up and, pulling an oversized T-shirt over her naked bottom, skipped across the peach bedroom carpet into the bathroom. She ran a hot bath, and added plenty of scented bath oil.

Pamela sank into the perfumed water and closed her eyes. This was like a slice of heaven. She stroked warm bubbles over her thighs and thought of Shaun. As the image became clearer, her hands became his. Her fingers moved over her body, tracing a moist path up her stomach and over her breasts. Her fingers stroked and teased her nipples into hardness. The water lapped around her as she sank lower into the bubbles. Her right hand ran down her body to her flat stomach and below to her pubic hair. She placed her painted toes on the rim of the bath and parted the fur with her fingertips, lingering on her clitoris before entering herself.

She moaned with the increasing ecstasy of her own foreplay. She dragged her fingertips slowly back up the path to her clitoris, while her left hand continued to massage her nipples. All she could feel was Shaun kissing her, caressing her, pumping away deep inside her.

She massaged her clitoris to a tempo that was getting faster with each beat. Heat was rising from deep inside, spreading over her neck, chest and face. Eventually she gasped aloud as her most sensitive nerve throbbed.

Pamela had brought herself to a delicious climax, and beads of perspiration now stood out on her forehead and upper lip.

It was James who had turned her into an expert in the art of fantasising and masturbation. He hadn't been performing to satisfaction. For weeks, the only sex they'd had was made up of quickies, amounting to little more than a kiss and a quick fumble, then off with the clothes, followed by hurried strokes as though he were running for a train — and that was it; he'd roll over and leave her to conjure up a dream lover.

Pamela had known from the start that sex wasn't as important to James as it was to her. And at first she'd thought she could cope with that. However she now knew that, far from being ready to slow down, she was hungrier than ever. Shaun, she knew, was ready and willing to satisfy her — and the more she thought of him, the more it seemed like James was history. She just didn't know how to tell him.

Perhaps her mates were right. Maybe she was a bitch. Her parents had certainly thought so. It was as though they'd blamed their only child for the three miscarriages her mother had previously suffered — all boys.

She remembered being dolled up, bows in her hair, wearing a pretty dress and her best coat, to go to church every Sunday with her parents. She recalled the boring sermons, the smoke drifting from melting candles, and all the old people. Often she would drift off, only to be rudely awoken by a nudge in the ribs from her mother's Bible or umbrella: "Wake up, child. You don't sleep in the Lord's house. Pray for your brothers."

But she hadn't known any brothers. She was the last born and the sole survivor, yet her mother would remind her daily of how she'd nearly died bringing Pamela into the world. So much pain and suffering over a girl child. Pamela was made to feel that the only way she could make it up to her mother was to do all the chores in the house.

At around the age of twelve, Pamela had begun to rebel. She knew there was more to life than the strict Catholic school she attended. Reggae music became her high, and she saved her meagre pocket money to buy herself a cheap Walkman from the market. As she got older and realised her parents would no longer lift a hand to her, she got braver. Every way she could think of, Pamela turned their rules around. They were old — what could they possibly do to stop an unruly teenager? Her parents had turned on each other instead. When she left home there was no love lost between any of them.

The telephone began to ring in the living room.

The caller was persistent, and the phone continued to ring as Pamela tried to ignore this intrusion into her private thoughts. Eventually, tutting her frustration at being interrupted, she grabbed a large towel from the bathroom rail and stepped dripping from the bath. She padded her way out of the bathroom leaving a trail of water behind her, and picked up the phone in the hallway.

"Hello?"

"Hi, babes," Shaun's crisp tone came down the line.

"Hi." Her voice mellowed instantly.

"Is the coast clear?"

Pamela leant against the red and grey striped wall, holding up the towel with one hand. "Yeah, he's out at work."

"What took you so long to answer the phone, then?"

"I was in the bath."

"So you're standing there naked?" His voice was trickling down the phone line like warm syrup.

She could almost see the look on his face. "Yeah. Nothing but a towel to hide my modesty." She was playing into his hands.

"What modesty?" Shaun laughed, sending shivers down her body.

She raised one foot and rested it high on the wall, stretching her lean muscles. Her wet hair was clinging to the back of her neck and shoulders.

She ran her tongue over her lips. "I can be modest, y'know," she beamed.

"Yeah, sure," he chuckled. "Are you doing anything this evening?"

Pamela sighed. "If you can call having dinner with James doing something, yes. Why?"

"My parents left this morning," he declared. "I want to see you."

"I want to do more than see you. I want you butt naked and

45

sprawled out on a bed," she smiled, her eyes lighting up.

He chuckled again, and lowered his voice to a sexy growl. "And then what would you do with me?"

"Wouldn't you rather I showed you?" Pamela purred.

"Boy! You've got to come round now, cause something just came up."

Pamela laughed. Men were so predictable. "What time?"

"Eight?"

"Make it seven. James might wonder if I go out that late." There it was again — having to consider James before making her own plans.

"Okay. Want me to pick you up?" His voice was eager now.

"No, I'll make my own way. Just give me a lift back."

"I'll be waiting."

"Ready and waiting?" she teased. This was so easy; he was putty in her hands.

"Damn right."

She giggled, licking her lips. "See you later."

She hung up, smiling confidently to herself. She was ready for him now.

It was just after three. James would be home in about an hour. Pamela sauntered back to the bathroom and immersed herself back in the warm water.

Tonight wouldn't be quite as boring as she had thought.

"You decide to leave that wimp yet?" Shaun nudged Pamela's naked bottom with his bare foot.

She was lying on the threadbare carpet, flipping through *Hype Hair* magazine.

It was the first time either of them had spoken in ten minutes. They had made love within half an hour of her arriving, and were now chilling out in the living room. Getting out of dinner with James had not been a problem. He hadn't stood in her way. All he wanted to know was when she was coming home. She had no idea — and that was exactly what she had told him.

Shaun, wearing nothing but baggy shorts, sat on his black foldaway sofa bed, remote control in hand, busily flicking through the cable channels. A half-eaten pizza lay in its box on the second-hand wooden coffee table. Pamela had decided that she wasn't that hungry after all, and had eaten only the mixed salad. She was dressed in a large T-shirt she'd found in Shaun's wardrobe.

Shaun nudged her again. The T-shirt rucked up, baring her

buttocks.

"He's not a wimp," she replied irritably. She hated talking about James when she was with Shaun; it spoiled the mood.

"Any man who can't please his woman is a wimp," he sneered.

Pamela sat up in front of him and crossed her legs. Her long, dark hair fell about her face. She had about her an after-sex glow that brought her natural beauty out to its fullest. "It's not that. It's just that you've spoilt me. After having champagne, who wants to go back to Babycham?" She flashed a cheeky grin.

Shaun ran a hand over his barely-there hair. He grinned back. "So, I'm champagne now, am I?" His dimples deepened.

"Yeah. Bubbly, sweet, strong, and very addictive." Pamela drew out the words sexily and let the T-shirt slip back just a bit, giving him a glimpse of her pubic hair.

But Shaun knew her too well. He knew she was avoiding the issue by trying to take his mind off it. "You didn't answer my question," he said paternally.

Pamela switched to the defensive. "Which one?" She twirled a finger in her hair, distractedly turning to gaze at the television.

"Don't play games with me, Pam. Are you gonna chuck him out?"

He was starting to sound like her father and she wasn't so sure she liked him telling her what to do. "I told you I asked him to go. What more do you want from me?" She bared her teeth and her eyes flashed fire.

Shaun, taken aback, moved to touch her.

"Just don't, Shaun." She shrugged his hand away.

"What did I say?" He lifted his shoulders.

She sighed. "It's like you're hassling me. I shouldn't have to take that from you."

"I know, but I want you to myself."

"And I don't want to make any mistakes. You know what it was like with us. There were so many ups and downs. James is stable, helpful, supportive . . ." She was counting the points off on her fingers.

"Boring," Shaun interrupted.

"Okay, so I can't have everything." She half-laughed.

Shaun glowered. "I can be all those things too, y'know. I've grown up since I was going out with you. Don't tell me you can't see that?"

Shaun's fair skin had one drawback: when he was upset, the tips of his ears went pinky red. Pamela saw this happening now and her spirits rose again. She was glad she was having this effect on him. It meant she still had the power. She raised a cynical eyebrow.

Shaun remained serious. His usually playful eyes were staring into her face. He leaned forward, resting his elbows on his knees. "Being away from you made me realise how much I want you. You're meant for me, man."

She cast down her eyes. She wasn't sure if she felt the same, but it wouldn't hurt to keep him sweet. "I dunno."

"You want to stay with him?"

"No, not any more."

"Then get rid of this geezer. I don't like sharing you."

"It's not that easy."

"Why not?" He raised his voice now. "It's your flat. Just pack his bags and throw them out. Or do you need some help?"

He was giving her orders again. "You see what I mean? A minute ago I told you not to talk to me like that. You don't listen to me." Pamela uncrossed her legs and stood up, the T-shirt dropping down to hide her nakedness. She wandered over to the glass-fronted drinks bar. This was a relic from when Shaun's parents still lived in England. Its front was the shape of a yacht and had a gold railing round the top. Pamela picked up a bottle of Southern Comfort and poured some of the orange-brown liquid slowly into a glass tumbler, her back still turned to Shaun.

As he watched her, he wondered what was going through her mind. Did she really like this guy or was she just using him? His possessiveness was compounded as he admired her small, tight buttocks moving under the T-shirt. He felt the beginnings of arousal and pushed the thought to the back of his mind. "What's wrong with you? You turning soft in your old age?"

Pamela spun round, breasts jiggling enticingly, her nipples pointing at him through the thin fabric. He licked his lips.

"Don't test me, Shaun."

"Or you'll do what?" he challenged, almost smiling. To him, her anger made her more beautiful.

"Just don't put pressure on me. I've come here to enjoy myself. Do you have to ruin it?"

Shaun couldn't resist her any longer. Fighting Pamela was like punching a brick wall — you only hurt yourself. "Come here," he said, opening his arms.

Pamela stepped lightly towards him, stopping in front of him, glass in hand.

He took the glass and placed it on the floor. "Why did I ever let you go?"

"Because you're a fool?" Her eyes were drawn to his erection.

He smiled, dimples deepening. "I *was*. I know what I want now, though."

"Yeah? What?"

"This," he said, squeezing her bottom.

"Give me time — an' you can have it all."

"Don't take too long, y'know. I got women queuing up to take your place."

Pamela thumped his arm playfully. "But you're turning them all down, aren't you?"

It was his turn to tease. "For now. So long as you keep me happy."

She grinned. "In that case . . ." She mounted his lap, wrapping her legs around his back. "I want to make you happy now." She pressed against his groin, feeling his penis jump.

"Yeah, well, I'm not in the mood," he joked, his eyes shining. He pushed her hands away.

Pamela kissed his lips, tickling them with her tongue, playfully nipping them with her teeth. She let her breasts brush against his chest. Then she slid herself down his body and nudged his semi-erection with her lips. She could see it grow instantly. She took him into her mouth and he moaned softly.

Releasing him suddenly, she grinned up at his face. "Changing your mind yet?"

"Okay, you've persuaded me." He pulled her up to him and kissed her passionately.

Shaun never let her down.

If only he didn't want to own her like all the others, she would enjoy this so much more. But right now he was pleasing her, the best way he knew how.

7. USE ME

At Woolwich, Marion stepped hurriedly from the bus clutching the bulky pushchair. She waited while the young girl with the screaming infant followed.

"Thanks a lot," the girl said, taking back the buggy and struggling to get it open. She couldn't have been more than sixteen, Marion thought, and her own mother suddenly sprang to mind. She had been younger than that when Marion was born.

She breathed in deeply and made her way across the market. Today was going to be hot. June was only a few days away, and already the temperature was seventy-five degrees.

There was only one class of people in Woolwich: working class. To Marion, they seemed to have no direction in life. Working in a library, she encountered many disillusioned faces daily.

At college, she'd had dreams of becoming a journalist. Her tutors had told her she had talent; she had the certificates to prove it. But the opportunities were few and far between. Six months down the line, she was still not in full-time employment. She had a dead-end part-time job that just about paid for her shopping every week.

But still she had a dream. Though her sights had narrowed and it was no longer top priority, it was there somewhere.

Heading towards the library, she allowed her mind to wander. It was a habit she hadn't managed to break since childhood. At school she had been one of those children who, when asked a question about the subject of the lesson, couldn't answer because she had been gazing out of the window. After Jacqueline died she had daydreamed constantly, usually in the form of "what if"s. What if Jacqueline hadn't been working so hard? What if she had gone into hospital a day earlier? What if she could have been cured? What if the consultant had been on duty when they arrived at the hospital? Could he have saved her?

What if their mother had still been around?

If anything, Marion blamed Gwendolyn, her mother — there had been no real father to speak of. Jacqueline's father was a married man, who had no intention of leaving his wife or acknowledging the baby as his own. Marion's father had been nothing more than a sixteen-year-old boy who, after being verbally abused by Marion's grandfather, was thrown out of the house and told never to come near his daughter again.

The closest they had come to a father was Derek. He had moved in when Marion was five years old, and stayed for ten years. During this time Marion's mother lost two babies by him before getting herself sterilised.

Derek was allowed by their mother to take over the girls' upbringing completely. Gwendolyn was totally under his control, so it followed that her children would be too. They were told to call him Daddy, and to follow the new rules he set out in their home: "Tidy your bedroom, you have fifteen minutes." "Do your homework by six o'clock." "Hoover up the place." "Do the washing up." "Go and get my newspaper." Fetch this, that, come, go, do, don't . . . His rules were hard and fast, and any rebellion was met with a beating from his belt. He would make them stand in front of him, holding out their small hands to receive their punishment. The girls would invariably be bawling before the strap had actually touched them, pleading with their mother, who would simply say that they should have done as they were told.

The girls hated Derek with a vengeance, and would often sit and plan how they could get rid of him. Their plans ranged from calling the police after a beating, to drugging him and throwing him into the Thames. As they were both kids at the time, there was no way they had the guts or the know-how to do it.

What their mother saw in the man, they never knew. He certainly wasn't good looking. Maybe he had charisma. He was intellectual; he'd been a law student when they'd first met. His skin was as dark as plain chocolate, and his affected Queen's English always made him sound like a foreign student. He was forever being mistaken for African. He always spoke to outsiders as though he knew what he was talking about. This superiority had fooled Marion's mother — but not the children.

The man was evil.

When the bills had got out of hand from his gambling, and strangers kept turning up on the doorstep demanding money, Gwendolyn had finally started to fight back. This, of course, made the situation worse. Derek would threaten to kill her and the children, or throw them out on the street. These turned out to be empty threats, but the beatings were real enough.

He stole from her to pay his debts, forging her signature in the social security books and drawing on her money. Many times Marion found her mother in tears, for no other reason except that he was in her life.

Eventually Derek moved on. Another woman, another life to ruin. A profound peace fell over their home after his departure. At last, they had their mother back.

Then Gwendolyn married, and practically left them to fend for themselves. Jacqueline was forced to find work instead of continuing with her studies.

Jacqueline had refused to go to their mother's wedding. From the beginning she had been adamant that she wasn't going to celebrate a marriage between her mother and this white man from Birmingham. Marion had attended simply to keep the peace, although in her heart she did wish her mother the best.

By now, Marion was a year into her BTEC in journalism at South Thames College, and was also studying psychology at Lewisham. Jacqueline had managed to get a job at Hennes in Oxford Street as a salesgirl. She never complained, but woke at six every morning to get ready, and came home in the evening shattered.

Marion promised her that as soon as she finished college they would swap over, so Jacqueline could go to college and complete her education. She wanted to be an Environmental Health Officer. Sadly, she managed only four weeks' work experience with the local council before her illness prevented her from continuing work. As the disease progressed she would sleep more during the day, and she started taking a lot more of her pills even when she wasn't in pain — or at least she said she wasn't.

When Jacqueline died, Marion felt alone until Joan and Pamela started to call her regularly after the funeral. Eventually they made going out together a regular thing. In time, her friends became closer than family. There was nothing she couldn't share with them.

Marion was the only black woman on the staff. A part-timer, she found she would often be called into work on days when promotions were happening. The week before, some bright spark had suggested they have a Afro-Caribbean make-up demonstration. They had booked a beautician to come in today to make up volunteers' faces while the onlooking public learnt what colours suited them and how to apply them correctly.

Marion was all for encouraging the black community into the libraries — but like this? Using make-up as bait was not her idea of encouragement. Why couldn't they have asked the community for ideas on what they would have liked to see? They might have had a book-signing by an X-Press author, or a speaker on black history, or a successful black businessperson to come in and say how they had achieved what they did.

Role models — that's what Marion felt were needed. Not someone telling you how to look pretty by dabbing on make-up. What about black men? Was this supposed to interest them?

About an hour before the beautician was due to arrive, Marion and Parminder, an Asian colleague, were instructed to pace the streets of Woolwich handing out flyers advertising the demonstration. They walked down Powis Street, the busiest shopping area in Woolwich, then stood outside Woolwich Arsenal station for fifteen minutes.

"You know why they picked us, don't you?" Parminder asked. She was the same height as Marion, with shoulder-length black hair, a chubby figure and a thick Asian accent.

"Course. We're their token blacks. When it suits them, we can appear to be very important to the organisation."

Parminder tutted and handed out another leaflet to a woman with a scarf round her head who was dragging three toddlers along beside her.

"You know, I've tried three times to get a promotion in this place," Marion said. "I had the experience required, and they still wouldn't give me a permanent job."

"I know. I'm a qualified librarian in my country. When I come here they tell me I must take exam again."

"So you have to start at the bottom because they think your country is too backward."

"It seems that way," Parminder said, clearly disgruntled.

Thrusting leaflets into the hands of people in a hurry was one of the most humiliating things Marion had ever had to do. Nobody was interested. After an hour or so there were flyers floating off in all directions. To top that humiliation, when the beautician finally turned up at the library she was white, had never done coloured skin before, and hadn't brought the right shades.

Five black women turned up for the session. They sat watching the chief librarian get made up in colours made for her skin colour. Every now and then they would glance at their watches. Half-way through, two of them stood and made hastily mumbled excuses before exiting. Marion didn't blame them, if she could have left she would have. She was glad she was working only until four o'clock, because her jaw ached from putting on a forced smile for each new customer during the day.

Standing once again at the bus stop, she thought about how much easier life would be if she could get a full-time job, and therefore be able to afford a car. She had passed her test at eighteen, and she hadn't been able to afford a car then either.

One good thing about working part time was that she could keep her hand in with her writing. She wrote articles for women's magazines. She knew the competition was fierce and, although she kept having articles returned, they would usually come back with a note of encouragement. Some would say that, although the article was not right for their publication, they had enjoyed it and would like her to keep trying.

As soon as she got home Marion ran a quick bath to freshen up. Lying in the water, she felt as though she'd lived in this flat forever.

It had been four long years, she thought, letting the warm water soothe her aching legs. Two without Jacqueline. When their mother married and left, they had been moved out of their three-bedroom council house in Abbeywood, into this dingy flat in Charlton.

The flat had two bedrooms: Jacqueline's room (as Marion still called it) was a narrow 6'-by-15' room with a built in wardrobe; Marion slept in the fairer-sized 12'-by-12' room. The living room was large, with doors leading out on to a self-contained balcony. The kitchen was a neat L shape, badly in need of decorating since there had been a flood upstairs.

Marion stepped from the bathroom in her bra and knickers. The scent of her Body Shop deodorant and body oil followed her into her bedroom. The room was decorated in pastel pinks and blues. She found baby colours relaxing. This was her thinking room. A small desk and bookshelf were to the left as one entered and on the other side of the bedroom stood Marion's all-in-one dressing table and double wardrobe. One side of the wardrobe had become Gerard's. It had happened gradually, starting with the odd jacket left over a weekend, then clean shirts had appeared, toiletries, a second pair of trousers, underwear . . . To Marion it felt right, even if it meant that she had to fold her clothes and use the airing cupboard shelves.

She had never understood the stories of women fighting or killing themselves over men — until she had fallen for Gerard. He knew a lot of women. On the few occasions they went out together, they would always end up bumping into someone he knew. The heat of jealousy rose up and boiled within Marion each time. It wouldn't be so bad if he didn't act as though she wasn't standing right there by his side. He would chat intimately to the females, making promises to visit them and swapping phone numbers, and not once would he introduce her.

It hurt. Once she had actually tried to introduce herself, fed up with being treated as though she didn't exist. Gerard had shot her a look that had burnt right through her, before shutting her out of the conversation again. He had a life that she had nothing to do with. It was something else she had come to accept.

She removed a simple black catsuit from the wardrobe, along with a short, crocheted cream top. Slipping them on in front of her mirror she imagined being single again. Being without Gerard. It wasn't as though she *had* to put up with him. She could get other men. It was the thought of being out there again that put her off. Meeting a man, getting to know his pros and cons, getting to know another body, judging his feelings, with him judging yours . . . Relationships were too unpredictable, yet she would rather stay in this unpredictable one than start all over again. Besides, she loved Gerard. Faults and all.

GERARD

Hot. This kind of weather makes a man restless. My mum would cuss if she saw the way I was sitting in her chair: "Tek yuh naked skin out de chair, Gerry. Yuh no have no manners?" She'd probably grab the towel from my body and whip me with it.

But she ain't here, she won't know.

I've just been for a five-mile jog. I like to keep myself trim.

I need a woman bad — right now. It would be a crying shame to let this fine body go to waste on a day like this. Debbie should be home now. She don't go nowhere on Sundays. She's at college doing sociology and psychology. She have ambition as well as beauty. We met at a dance in Dalston. She lives in Brixton. She's young, twenty one, but she have a vibrancy I cyan't resist. She's feisty too, but I like that. She can stand up for herself. There ain't no comparison between her and Marion.

Marion can cook and care for me, and she's willing to listen to my troubles and pamper me when I need it.

Debbie is wild, man. I doubt she even knows how to use a cooker. But she makes up for it in other ways. Thinking about her just mek the restlessness rise, y'know what I mean? I'm gonna call her. She'll do nicely.

8. HOT, HOT, HOT

It was a beautiful, sunny day. The sky was blue and cloudless, and a light breeze prevented it from becoming too hot. Perfect weather for a barbecue.

Joan stood in her bedroom, dreamily looking out of the window at the street below. Her Asian neighbour across the road was stripped down to his shorts, washing his dark blue Peugeot 405 by hand. Two boys raced their skateboards down opposite sides of the road, their friends cheering them on.

The little girl stepped daintily across the lavender carpet, not making a sound. A cheeky grin dimpled one cheek as she crept up behind her mother and encircled her legs in her little arms, giving them a gentle squeeze. Joan turned to look down at her daughter. "Shereen, how can you frighten Mummy like that?"

"You left me on my own." The little girl pouted. She was dressed in a pink corduroy skirt with a matching jacket and a white T-shirt, like a miniature cowgirl.

"I was only up here. You miss me?"

Shereen put on her pretending-to-be-shy look and nodded.

"All right." Joan picked up her daughter and hugged her small body to her chest, careful not to crumple the flimsy material of her own clothes. She wore a short, flowing, navy dress that moved when she did, bought specially for the occasion. "I'm coming back down now. You got your bag all ready to take to Grandma's?"

"Yes. An' I put in my Barbie and Ken."

"Did ya?"

"Yeah. 'Cause Grandma only got soft toys, not real dollies," she said with an air of authority on the subject. Joan smiled. Her mother made rag dolls and teddy bears. Over the years, they had accumulated quite a collection.

Shereen would stay at her grandmother's house on occasional weekends. For a fifty-two-year-old woman, Grace was still very lively, and Joan had no worries about her becoming reclusive. Joan's father had gone back to Jamaica ten years previously, taking her brother Patrick with him and leaving the two sisters, Joan and Donna, with their mother. At first her mother had carried on like she couldn't care less, even though she had cussed all sorts of bad words about her husband's "fancy piece dem". Then all of a sudden she hadn't mentioned him any longer. When Joan or Donna asked her whether he wrote, or if she had heard from him, their mother would pretend she didn't hear or change the subject.

Soon they stopped mentioning him altogether, as though he had never existed.

Joan drove towards Wandsworth to drop Shereen off at her grandmother's before going to the barbecue.

Charles, the man she had met at Granaries, had kept in touch. He seemed mature, interesting — and interested. But Joan had been at this stage in a relationship before, when you had met the man in question only once, in a club or at a party, but always in the dark. You'd talked a couple of times on the phone, and he'd sounded like so much fun, you couldn't wait to meet up again. And then you find when you do meet up that he's nothing like you remember and you have nothing in common.

Since she had stopped seeing Colin, and after the episode with Stephen, Joan had decided to look for someone who was more than simply a 'good man' — he would have to be a good father too. But the men she met didn't seem to know what they wanted. It was as though the older they got the more they struggled against being tied down. As soon as she mentioned children, you could see the interest drain from their eyes.

Joan pulled into her mother's driveway. The house was pre-war, three storeys high. Her mother had the first floor and basement, and she let the upper floor out to a young black couple. It was lunchtime. The smell of cooking wafted towards them. When Shereen rang the bell, they were greeted by a new face at the front door.

Joan eyed the old man suspiciously, wondering what the hell this guy was doing answering her Mum's front door. He looked very dapper in a smart suit. His hair was completely white, and he was clean shaven. He must have been at least sixty-five. She looked past him for any sign of her mother.

"Er, hello."

"You must be Joan. Come in, darling." The little man stepped aside to let them into the house and closed the door behind them.

Shereen clung to her mother's coat as they followed the stranger through the hallway and into the kitchen.

"Grace, is yuh dawta," he called.

Grace was fifty-two last birthday, and looked no older than thirty-eight. Joan's friends were always complimenting her, saying they looked more like sisters. They even wore the same sized clothes. Grace was in the hairdressers at least once a week, prettying herself up for one of her many admirers. If Joan got there early enough in the morning she could catch her mother bouncing up and down in front of the television to a keep-fit video.

Joan had to admire her mother, but she hated the fact that she still went on dates. Mothers of adult children shouldn't be doing them kind of things, she'd constantly tell her. And she refused to think about whether her mother still had sex. That was just too gross.

Grace stood at the cooker, stirring a pot of spicy chicken. Joan's stomach contracted hungrily. She hadn't eaten all day, saving herself for the barbecue food.

"Joan, you early," Grace stated, turning to them.

Joan kissed her on the cheek. "You did say two o'clock. I didn't think two hours would make that much difference. I've got some things I want to do before I go out. Besides . . ." She cast a sideways look at the man seated comfortably at the kitchen table. "I didn't think I'd be interrupting anything."

"Oh I feget, you never meet Clyde. Clyde, This me eldest, Joan. Joan, a Clyde dis. 'Im is a fren'."

"A friend?" Joan raised an eyebrow. She thought she knew all her mother's friends.

"Doan question me, Joan," her Mother warned, and turned her

57

attention to the little girl still clinging to her mother's leg. "So, Sherry, you have a kiss fe yuh Grandma?"

Shereen let go of her mum's leg and, without taking her eyes off Clyde, she ran up to her Grandma and kissed her firmly on the lips.

"Ehhh! T'ank yuh, love."

"I'm gonna go now, Mum. I'll pick Shereen up at dinner-time tomorrow."

"Yes, good. I'll see you then."

"Clyde, maybe I'll see you again. Shereen, be good for Grandma."

Shereen waved and Clyde nodded and smiled.

Boy, her mother had more boyfriends than she did. What was this world coming to?

Following the directions Charles had given her, Joan swung the car into a narrow street off the Old Kent Road. Already she could hear the music blasting from the speakers, even though she was still one block away. As she turned the car into Drovers Place, she could see people congregating outside the house, some sitting in cars, some sitting on cars. Suddenly she felt very uncomfortable about coming to the barbecue on her own. But that had been the whole idea, she reminded herself — change of scenery, different mix of people.

She parked the car around the corner from the house and checked her hair and make-up in the rear-view mirror. Charles had seemed very eager to see her again when he called. He'd made her laugh with his sarcastic humour and he'd showered her with compliments. She didn't fall for it, but it was nice getting them.

The barbecue was in aid of his thirty-sixth birthday, as if Joan needed reminding that there was a nine-year age gap between them. Charles's tastes were different to hers, and he talked about things that she'd never experienced and wasn't interested in. However, they both loved to party and Charles could really dance. He was an okay guy.

The barbecue was in full swing. The front door stood open and Joan stepped into the house. She glanced around for any familiar faces, but saw none. Most of the people seemed to be outside in the back garden. MC Hammer's "Pumps in the Bumps" was blasting out of the speakers so loudly that Joan could feel the house vibrating. Her earrings tinkled with the buzz. She edged past people she didn't know, through the living room and into the sun-filled garden.

It was an elegant affair, with 'nuff chat, food and drink. Everybody seemed to be mingling, standing in twos and threes or huddled into picnic parties on the grass. The huge speakers under the willow tree oozed music to the residents of the neighbouring streets. Joan scanned the garden, her eyes coming to rest on the plume of smoke that rose lazily into the blue sky. The barbecue. Heading in that direction, she quickly spotted Charles, surrounded by a bevy of women, laughing as usual, looking cool in black cotton shorts and a long white shirt that billowed in the gentle breeze. His hairy legs ended in sandalled feet.

Joan eased up behind him and wrapped her arms round his waist and squeezed. His body tensed, just for a second, then he craned his neck to see who his seducer was.

"Jo! Hello, sweetheart." His eyes creased as he smiled at her. Charles was tall, dark and charismatically handsome, the kind of good looks formed by personality. His forehead was lightly ridged with fine lines and tiny crows' feet adorned the corners of his eyes. Whether he liked it or not, time was catching up with him.

"Hi, Charles. I hope you've got my plate ready."

He slid a hand round her waist and answered in his natural Jamaican accent, "Everyt'ing ready. You want a drink?"

"Yes, please."

"Saaf or hard?" he teased with a glint in his eye.

Joan laughed, catching the innuendo straight away. "I'm driving. I'll just have a pineapple juice."

"Right, I'll be back. Don't go away." He squeezed her hand gently and walked back towards the house.

Alone again, Joan surveyed her surroundings. She had never been to Charles's home before. From what she had seen of the inside, he had expensive tastes. The garden was landscaped, the path from the patio doors running straight down the middle before branching off in different directions. One branch ended in a flower display, another in a rockery. The main path ended at a pond bordered by love-seats.

Charles returned with the drink. "You looking good," he said, handing Joan the glass.

"Thank you, Charles," she answered modestly.

"I did t'ink you change yuh mind."

"About what?"

"Seeing me."

"Well, I had nothing better to do." She lit her cigarette, hiding her smile.

"You t'ink yuh smart, but one of dese days, Joan, some guy gwine tame yuh."

"No one tames me until I want to be tamed."

"Awright, we'll see." He gave her a look as if to say, 'I take that as

59

a challenge'. "You hungry?"

"Starved."

"Then come nuh. Mek we fine sump'n fe yuh." He took her hand in his and led her to the front of the queue for hot food.

Time was flying, and Joan was having fun. Three hours later, although she didn't know it, Joan was pissed. Well out of it. The spiked pineapple juice had gone straight to her head.

Charles made her laugh. He'd introduced her to some of his male friends, who had taken it upon themselves to be her bodyguards for the rest of the day. Any man who came near her was politely but firmly shown the runnings.

It was now evening. She and Charles sat alone on a love-seat by the pond. Coloured bulbs strung out in the trees above their heads, cast dancing shadows over the garden.

Charles slid his arm around her waist and pulled her close. "How's my sexy lady?" he whispered softly into her ear. A light breeze had blown up, and Joan clutched his jacket around her shoulders.

"Me? I'm fine," she giggled.

"Did you drive?"

"Yeah, the car's round the corner. Why?"

" 'Cause yuh not driving home." He kissed her forehead.

"I'm fine, Chas." She didn't sound convinced. "I've only had pineapple juice — I think." Her voice didn't sound like hers anymore. It reminded her of when she was on a sensi buzz.

"You get drunk on pineapple juice?"

Joan giggled again and looked at him. She shook her head foggily and tried to focus her eyes but wasn't having much luck. "I'm drunk?" she slurred.

"Nuh worry 'bout it. Me will drive you home."

She hugged him with arms that had no strength in them. "My hero," she teased.

Charles helped her to her feet and walked her back through the house. Inside was empty, except for a few stragglers and two older women tidying up in the kitchen. Charles stopped to introduce Joan to them.

"Aunty Gen, dis is my wife," he told a tall, grey-haired woman, who turned and smiled at them.

Joan tried to smile back, but not being able to feel her lips she wasn't sure she'd managed it.

"From when you married? Chile, tek no notice of de bwoy's nonsense."

The woman had a beautiful smile.

"I don't," Joan replied.

Charles looked into her bleary eyes. "How you mean? You don't think I'm gonna mek an honest woman of you?"

"It'd be more like me making an honest man of you," Joan said. "Now take me home before you have to carry me," she said, slipping her arm through his.

"Bye, Love." Aunty Gen waved and resumed her washing up.

Joan must have fallen asleep on the way home — or passed out. Charles kept glancing over at her as he drove. She was his kind of woman. His friends had even asked him if she was available. He'd made sure they got the message: this one was his. And the only way he could be sure that he would be driving her home, was to spike her pineapple juice with Bacardi.

He wanted to spend some time with her alone, get to know her better. As far as he was concerned, she was already his. He just had to make her realise.

Charles parked the car in a space opposite Joan's house. She woke as the car's engine shut off.

"You all right?" he enquired, leaning towards her.

"Mmm," she answered, peering out of the windscreen. "You coming in?"

"If you want me to."

Joan didn't notice the seductive tone in his voice. "You might as well, unless you're gonna walk home, it's late," she yawned.

Charles wasn't going to argue.

He accompanied her inside. She kicked off her shoes in the hallway and hung his jacket, which she'd been wearing in the car, on the banister. She told him to go through to the living room while she made some coffee.

"Nice place you 'ave 'ere," Charles commented, when Joan returned with the coffees.

She walked over to the stereo and slotted a Keith Sweat cassette into the machine. "Thanks. It was hard work." She stepped back to the sofa and sat down at Charles's sandalled feet. All thoughts of sleep slowly vanished as she sipped the coffee and looked up at his handsome, mature face. A coy smile played on her lips. Soon she had something else on her mind.

"I t'ink I've met my match," he told her.

"Why do you say that?"

"Yuh mek me nervous," he said, smiling. "Look, how me hands dem ah shake." He raised a trembling arm.

Joan laughed.

"Cyan I kiss you?" he asked, leaning forward.

She regarded him quizzically. Was this guy for real? "Do you always ask first?"

"Naw, man. I tell yuh, it's you doing this to me. Yuh too *mysterious.*"

She eased closer. "Some men like mystery."

"I do. 'Nuff time pass since I met anyone like you."

"Has it?" she purred, resting her hands on his bare knees.

"Yeah." He touched her nose with a finger, and a little smile played on her lips. "You're beautiful, you know that?"

She suddenly wished he would stop talking and kiss her. A sexual tingle was rising in anticipation from her vagina. "No I'm not. An' you don't need to compliment me to get a kiss."

His smile broadened. "What me haffe do?"

"Come closer."

Charles leant forward a bit more. At first he merely tasted her lips with his own. Then, as she kissed back, he became bolder, his tongue pushing past her lips to meet hers.

He can kiss too, this is promising, Joan mused. She closed her eyes and enjoyed. The kiss lasted for what seemed like minutes, without him attempting to touch her elsewhere. Joan decided to make a move instead. She crawled up on to the sofa and climbed on top of him, still kissing, forcing him to lie back.

His hand moved up inside her top, and she gave a sigh of exhilaration. Too soon. His hand stopped. There was no fumbling for the bra strap to unclip the clasp. There were no fingers on her thighs, rising higher to search for gold. Not even an erection pressing into her stomach. She resigned herself to the fact that maybe she was just too fast. This guy obviously wanted to take it slow.

She kissed his cheeks, his neck, and slid down his body so that her head rested on his chest. His torso was soft, but she could tell that at one time it had been hard with muscle. She listened to his heartbeat.

"This feels good," he murmured, eyes closed.

Joan frowned. *What* felt good? They hadn't done anything except kiss. Could this be what older men are about? Maybe nine years was too big a gap. He only wanted a woman to be comfortable with.

His hand stroked her hair. "You know how to make a man feel good."

"I do?" She looked up at him, resting her chin on his chest.

"Yeah. I feel close to yuh, you know? Like I know yuh fe years. I jus' want to hol' yuh, not get sexual or anyt'ing. It jus' feel right, y'know?"

"Don't take this the wrong way, Charles, but I don't want to get heavy with anyone right now."

"Why not? You have someone else waiting on yuh?"

She hesitated. "I don't want to go into it. But this is our first date. I like to get to know a man a little, before planning a future together. I mean, you hardly know me."

He raised her face from his chest, his big hands gripping her arms. "I know you, Joan. I told you, dis feels right."

"For you." She could have slapped herself. What was she thinking? She might never meet another man like this, and here she was giving him the cold shoulder.

He sat up straight, forcing her off him. She sat beside him feeling awful. He held one fist in the palm of his other hand and stared at the coffee mugs, standing untouched on the table.

"I'm sorry, Charles, but I can't lie to you," she blurted. "I'm in love with someone else. He just doesn't feel the same way as I do. At the moment I feel it would be unfair to lead you on."

He cut his eye after her. "More fool you," he said tightly.

"Don't get offensive with me. I thought we were good mates. We've been getting on fine until now."

His head bobbed in comprehension. He understood what she was saying. He placed a hand on her knee. "Awright. We'll tek it slow. Is not like yuh saying yuh don't want to know . . ." He watched her face for an answer.

"No, of course not. I like you," she assured him, making her expression as sincere as possible. It was the truth, after all. It just wasn't the kind of "like" that he wanted it to be.

"Good." He stood up. "I better go, you get some sleep." Now he was back on his feet, he appeared to perk up slightly.

Joan stood up too. "Are you sure? If you wait till morning I'll drop you."

"Is awright. I'll catch a cab." He kissed her quickly on the lips. She went to kiss him again, but he gently pushed her away. "Slow, remember?"

Damn! Just now she wished it wasn't slow. She followed him to the front door, lifting his jacket from the stair banister. "You'll probably need this now," she said.

"T'anks. Later, then."

"Okay," she said.

"Bye, beautiful." He kissed her cheek and left.

For a while she just stood with her back against the door. What had happened here? Was she losing her touch, or just a little touched

63

in the head? This man would have been good for her. Single, own house, car, no live-in dependants. In the back of her mind she knew it was her love for Colin that was blocking her emotions for anyone else. She cursed him, before stamping her way up the stairs to bed.

CHARLES
There comes a time in every man's life when all him want is a good home life. I work 'ard all my life since I was fifteen. Get up early in the morning, come home late.

For eight years I had a woman in my life and I took her for granted. Now, after five years on my own, I want a woman to give me de chance to treat her right.

All it takes is someone like Joan to turn my life around, I'll show her what a real man is all about.

9. MY ONE TEMPTATION

The group of men and women filed out of the conference room, chatting, discussing work or plans to meet for lunch. Although they were smiling now, the meeting that had just concluded, between the editors and writers, had become heated. The editors had complained that there didn't seem to be any enthusiasm any more. The same old stuff was being published. They needed something for the nineties. Everyone, the boss had told them, had to pull their socks up or else outsiders would be brought in, and that would mean job losses for the existing staff.

Being commissioning editor of features, Joan had no worries about her job. She remained seated as the room emptied, scribbling mindlessly on the lined pad in front of her. Two days had passed since the barbecue, and all she could think about was Colin. The fact that she hadn't heard from him for three weeks was beginning to bother her.

Charles had called yesterday and suggested they go out somewhere. No ties. Joan had told him she would let him know. She'd made up an excuse about having a lot of work on at the moment. She had no intention of calling him again. Colin was different. With him she wanted to be more than "just friends".

"Penny for them." A voice close by brought Joan out of her

reverie.

Sarah, blonde, slim and sexy, bedroom fantasy of many of their male colleagues, perched herself on the edge of the desk. She wore a low-cut see-through blouse over a lacy slip, and a smart scarlet skirt. Her blonde hair — never tidy, she seemed to like the wild-child look — was piled high up on her head and secured with a butterfly clip. Long tendrils that had worked their way loose were falling around her face and down her shoulders like a blonde waterfall.

"My thoughts are worth more than that, Sarah." Joan swivelled her chair around to face her. "Just trying to plan my life out in my head."

Joan could always talk to Sarah. Being the only other female of her age group in editorial, they tended to find comfort in each other's company. There wasn't much they didn't know about each other's lives.

"It's not just work, is it?" Sarah asked, crossing her waxed legs.

Joan half-smiled. Was she that easy to read?

"How's the love life?"

Joan raised an eyebrow. "What love life?"

"Like that, is it?"

Sarah was in the process of buying a home with her boyfriend of three years. White girls always seemed to be getting engaged, married or moving in with their boyfriends. It seemed as though white men knew what they were doing when it came to love and women. Black men didn't have a clue — except for sex.

"I've had men throwing themselves at me, Sar, but I just keep throwing them back. I haven't found the man who's good enough for me yet. Instead I lie in bed and dream up my perfect lover."

"Colin, right?"

It must have been written all over Joan's face

"So, you heard from Colin?"

"No. Don't know if I want to, either. You know when something's just not going anywhere; I need to move on."

"Yeah, I had that problem with Graham. Plus he was cheating on me." She removed the butterfly clip and shook her hair free, letting it cascade over her shoulders before grabbing a bunch in the centre and tying it up exactly as it had been.

Joan sighed. "Anyway, I've got more important things on my mind than men."

"Like what? What do we spend most of our time talking about?"

"Men," Joan had to agree.

"We *make* them important. No wonder they feel they can treat us as they do."

"You've got nothing to worry about, anyway. You're moving in with Daniel in two weeks."

"I was lucky this time. Look, if you're having trouble sleeping at night, just call Colin. Use him. They do it to us. Why go without, 'cause you don't want the rest of him?"

Sarah could be so cocky sometimes, but she was right. Why not? It couldn't hurt, could it? "I might just do that."

"Good." She punched Joan playfully on the arm. "Fancy a coffee break?"

"Yeah, why not? Let's go round the corner to that neat little deli and order cappuccinos and a slice of that double chocolate gateau. And no more talk of sex and men, okay?"

"What does that leave us with?"

"Money and kids?"

"Oh no, how depressing. Can't we just have a little sex?"

"I didn't know you were that way inclined," Joan laughed.

They arrived back at the office just after eleven thirty. Joan went straight to her desk. Sarah took time to freshen her make-up, a routine she performed five times a day.

Joan shared an open-plan office with four others including Sarah. The editor's office was partitioned off at the end of the room.

"Anything been happening? Anyone called for me?" she asked a male colleague.

Geoffrey looked up from his PC. "Actually, yes. I wish you'd tell me when you're leaving the office," he spat indignantly. "I spent five minutes trying to find you."

"Well *excuuuse* me," Joan exaggerated. "Just give me the messages and spare me the heartache." The nerve of some people! Anyone would think she'd taken the whole afternoon off.

Geoffrey tutted, running a hand over his spiky hairdo while shuffling through the papers on his desk with the other. "Francis Dixon wants to know when her article will be published, claims we've been fobbing her off for three months."

"Damn! I'll call her later. Forgot all about that." She'd get Sarah, or her secretary, Jayne, to deal with Mrs Dixon. The woman had written an article on collecting African artefacts, and had expected it to be snapped up straight away. It was a good article, but it needed a hook. And Joan hadn't found it. She scribbled a note and handed it to Jayne.

Easing back in her swivel chair, Joan stared at the phone, fingering the cover of her phone index thoughtfully. Three weeks.

Was she really missing Colin bad? She certainly couldn't stop thinking about him. All she had to do was swallow her pride and call him. Surely he'd be glad to hear from her. After all, the last time he had come round they'd had a laugh and terrific sex too.

The thought of Colin's body made up her mind. She flicked through her address book until she found the number to the adventure playground where he worked.

"Hello?" Colin's deep voice came on the line, and Joan's heartbeat quickened just for a second.

"Col, it's me. Joan."

"J! How you doing?" His voice sounded smooth.

"Good," she answered. "And you?" She rested her elbow on the desk, a little smile dancing on her lips.

"Fine."

There was a pause. She wondered if he could hear the thundering beat of her heart.

"I miss you," she blurted out.

"Yeah?" He sounded surprised.

"What d'you mean, 'yeah'?"

"What do you want me to say?" He sounded peeved.

"You could say you missed me too."

"Joan, I've been busy."

Her heart sank. This had been a bad idea. "So what does that mean? You couldn't pick up the phone?"

"Did you want me to?"

"Of course I did! We're still friends, ain't we?"

"Friends, yeah."

"So . . . are you seeing anyone?" she asked in as casual a way as possible. She doodled on the desk blotter, squares, triangles, then hearts trapped inside them.

"Sort of." He coughed nervously.

Bloody hell, Joan thought, it was like getting blood out of a stone. "What's 'sort of'?"

"I am," he owned up.

"Oh. I see."

Silence again.

She changed the subject abruptly. "Listen, I've got to go now, but could you come round later?"

She was chasing him. It was the first time she had chased a man and it didn't feel good.

He exhaled loudly, as though it were a big decision. "Err, yeah. I could sort something out. About nine, all right?"

"Okay. I'll look forward to it."

67

"Bye."

He hung up.

Joan replaced the receiver slowly, feeling worse than she had before she made the call. She needed a cigarette break. She had already decided that she would have to seduce Colin tonight. She had no intention of giving him up to another woman without a struggle.

Joan preened in front of the bathroom mirror for the third time in half an hour. Her hair was slicked back and it gleamed in the light from the bulb overhead. She applied some more lipstick, blotted it, then dropped the tissue into the bin already full of bathroom disposables.

It was ten o'clock. Colin was an hour late. She walked over to the window and looked up and down the street. Nothing, no sign of him. She lit an incense stick, Afrodisia, to take her mind off things. Then she picked up the latest copy of *Black Beauty & Hair* magazine and sat on the edge of the sofa, not wanting to crease her white chiffon blouse. The smoke from the incense flowed like a cloud across the ceiling and was already filling the room with its pungent aroma.

The knock at the front door startled her. He was finally here. She jumped up in excited anticipation, before checking herself. *Take your time, girl. He kept you waiting.* She straightened her clothes, did a slow twirl in front of the mirror on the wall, dimmed the light, and went to let him in.

He was dressed reasonably smartly, in black jeans with a black denim shirt hanging over them. A new pair of black boots donned his feet. His height and stature gave him a menacing look that wasn't him at all.

He sat on the sofa beside her and Joan got him a drink. She wanted to jump on him and have her wicked way, but she also wanted *him* to make love to *her*. Sweet and slow. Which wasn't his style at all. Oh well, she thought, it's never too late to learn.

He was being very quiet. A wildlife programme was on the television, and instead of meeting her eyes he pretended to watch it.

"Have you gone off me?" she asked after a while.

He turned to her with a grin. "I could never go off you."

"Then why haven't you called?"

"I thought you wanted it that way."

Just like him to transfer the blame. She slid a hand on to his leg and smiled seductively. "Can you stay tonight?" Knowing that he lived alone, she knew he couldn't have an excuse not to.

"Maybe," he replied coolly.

Joan was becoming impatient. "Maybe *what*?"

"If you give me good reason to."

She studied his face, looking for any hint to what he was thinking. "I know what you're doing, you know."

"What?"

"You're playing hard to get."

He mocked her with his eyes. "Me?" He raised his glass to his lips and sipped, watching her over the rim.

"Yes, you."

"I don't know what gave you that idea. I'm just playing things the way you wanted them."

She decided to try again with the seductive tactics. Her hand travelled up his thigh. "Suppose I want to change the way things are."

Colin remained immobile. "I suppose you expect me to just go along with it."

Joan snatched her hand back. "You haven't gone off me, so what's the problem?"

"The problem is you're using me."

"How can I be using you? Or have you gone off sex?"

"Now who's got sex on the brain?" Humour shone from his eyes, but Joan was getting seriously irritated.

She pouted. "I thought we had a deal."

"Our deal, as you call it, was to be friends. Remember?" His eyes were laughing at her. He was actually enjoying this.

"Yeah, but . . ."

He interrupted. " 'But' nothing. I don't need this any more." His foot tapped the carpet soundlessly.

"You're saying you don't need me any more? So it *was* just sex. Now that you've got a replacement, you don't love me any more."

"Maybe I don't."

Joan glared at him. His face remained cool, but a little muscle in his jaw jumped, giving away his true emotion. She pulled away from him, moving up the sofa. Her lips were pushed up into an angry pout. Her eyes narrowed under a bunched brow.

Colin brushed invisible lint from his jeans. "Sorry, J."

She didn't move. "Don't even talk to me," she hissed.

"I didn't mean it." He moved closer and put his hands on her shoulders.

She felt herself melting and tried her best not to think about it. "Then why say it?"

"I've got other things on my mind. Forgive me?"

She turned to face him, tucking one leg up under the other, as she always did. It gave Colin a sense of *déjà vu*.

"You don't have to stay if you don't want to," she said, knowing full well she wouldn't want him to leave.

"I do. I still care about you," he added, "even though we are just friends." He stressed the overused phrase with a grin.

Her mouth curved ironically. She looked into his deep brown eyes and asked, "Do you still love me?"

He grabbed her, and before she realised what was happening they were on the floor, covering each other with kisses. Their hands explored each other, seeking the flesh beneath the clothes. The questions remained unanswered, but Joan didn't care. For the moment, she had what she wanted.

She threw her arms around his neck and kissed him hard. Colin sent his tongue deep into her mouth. She let one hand slide down into the front of his shirt and ran restless, searching fingers across his hairy chest.

"Do you want me, Colin?" she whispered into his ear.

His hand on her breast, he groaned, "Yesss."

She slid down his body and used both hands to unbuckle and unzip his trousers, while he worked on the buttons of her blouse. Their eyes remained fixed on each other's. Joan squeezed the strong swell of his muscled thighs as she drew his trousers down his legs. His cock was like a raging bull ready to charge, its head straining against the flimsy material of his boxer shorts.

She stood up, and with her blouse hanging open from her shoulders she turned her back to him. She let her blouse drop to the floor. Then she half-turned and glanced at him for a reaction. He had his hand on his huge erection and was working it slowly up and down. She grinned wickedly and drew down the bottom half of her clothing, bending to give him a full view of her buttocks.

Colin stood and came up behind her. He grabbed the offered flesh with his big hands and squeezed. She gasped as he rubbed his cock against the crevice offered up to him.

He was big, hard and hot. His hands travelled upwards to cup her breasts and he gave her nipples a tweak, groaning hungrily. It sounded like a grizzly bear — mean, but exciting and vigorous.

"Come on, baby, fuck me," she whispered huskily.

"I'll fuck you," he promised, "until you see stars."

She raised her entrance to him, moist in anticipation of his cock filling her. Her hands crawled around to his hips and she gripped him as he plunged deep into her vagina.

Perfect rhythm. She felt as though she could come straight away.

He seemed to get deeper with each thrust, as though she was sucking him inside her, like a kid with a lollipop.

A little harder, a little faster. They began breathing more heavily as they neared climax. She could feel his balls slapping against her, exciting her further. He felt so close, so hot, she was melting and breaking up into a million pieces all at the same time. Every nerve in her body was jumping, alive. She felt his orgasmic swell inside her, the first pulsing of his penis coinciding with her own explosion, moving ever closer, and it seemed as though her whole body shook with the final tumult of their release.

Afterwards, she lay on the floor in his arms.

He had gone quiet again. She leaned up on one elbow. "Something wrong?"

"No. Just thinking."

" 'Bout what?" Finally, she thought, he's going to talk to me. She knew there had been something bugging him all night.

"Us . . . life, y'know."

"No, I don't know. Explain." Joan sat up fully now. Her small breasts, nipples erect, hung above him.

Colin knew Joan well enough to know that she wasn't going to let this go. He also knew with a knot in his stomach that he would have to tell her.

His face was illuminated by the mute television. "I told you I was seeing someone . . ."

"Yeah, but that's nothing serious." She paused. "Is it?" A trace of worry had entered her voice.

He breathed deeply. Joan's heart lurched into her throat. She thought she knew what he was going to say. She set herself up to hear that Colin was falling in love with someone else. There was no way of preparing for what she was about to hear.

He looked serious. "I've been living with her for about three months." He hesitated, swallowing hard before he continued. "The thing is, she's pregnant."

Joan's voice was low with disbelief. "What? Is this some kind of joke?"

"I haven't finished."

"What? You mean there's more?" she gasped.

"I told her I'd marry her for the baby's sake," he blurted out.

Joan shot up off the floor. Realising she was naked she grabbed her blouse from the sofa and held it clasped against her chest. She felt as though she was in the middle of a very bad soap opera. "I can't believe you're doing this to me." Rage and humiliation swept through her, making her every nerve taut. "What we just did . . .

what was that?" She motioned at the floor with her hand as though the actions were still going on.

He sat up now, feeling vulnerable (angry women can be dangerous creatures). He knew he'd hurt her. Trying to find a way of telling her had been on his mind all night. She had to know. And yet he hadn't wanted her to.

"Answer me," she screamed.

He stood up and stepped past her. "Look, I didn't mean for that to happen. I can't resist you. I love you, remember."

"Oh, you love me so damned much that you're gonna marry someone *else*." She began to shake hysterically, torn between tears and terrible laughter.

"It's not like that. I'm doing it for my kid."

"You're telling me the only way you'd have married me is if I got pregnant?" she spluttered.

He pulled his shirt on and retrieved his trousers from the floor, dragging them on as quickly as he could. He zipped and buttoned them, leaving the belt dangling.

He bent to retrieve his boots and Joan dived for them first, and dashed them at him. "You bloody user! You're a bastard, Colin! Just like your brother! Why couldn't I see that before?"

He silently took the boots, pulled them on and tied the laces. His cheek smarted from where the heel of one of them had hit him.

She watched him with narrowed eyes, her breathing heavy. At that moment she hated him. She hated him with a vengeance that she had no idea how to act out. She'd thought she hated Martin when he had walked out, but that feeling had nothing to do with the fire inside her now.

Finally, Colin looked up. Anger like the venom of a horde of scorpions stung him from her eyes. He didn't want to face her. He stood, fully dressed now, and picked up his jacket from the chair by the door.

He turned and looked at her again. She stood there, completely naked, the chiffon shirt lying discarded at her feet, her whole body shaking with the pent-up fury inside her. All of a sudden her clenched fists flew open and she dived for him. Her hands reached for his face, open palms flailing as though she wanted to beat him to death.

Colin stood there and let her hit him, feeling her blows rain down on his chest and across his head. There were tears coming from her eyes, but Joan wasn't crying. She was screaming, yelling, venting her outrage. He grabbed her wrists as he felt her sudden strength ebbing away. "I'm sorry, J. Believe me." He let her go and she stepped

72

away from him.

Heaving, she swiped away the betraying tears with the back of her hand. "Get the fuck out of my life, Baker." Her voice sounded both harsh and winded.

"So much for friendship," he said, then ducked as Joan bent and picked up a glass from the coffee table and hurled it at him. It missed by inches. He exited hurriedly, closing the door behind him. He paused momentarily outside the door to listen to her continuing tirade.

She would get over it. They always did.

COLIN

Got in from work and Lois had cooked dinner. While I was eating she ran me a bath. This is the kind of life I dream about having when I'm sixty, not twenty-nine!

Lois was all right before all this baby stuff. There are some girls you shouldn't make a habit of, and Lois is one of them. I made a big mistake with this one. I thought we were both out for the same thing, y'know — exciting sex, a laugh, few drinks . . . Boy, I must have been tripping when I got mixed up with this one. I know she got herself pregnant deliberately. She's that type. I give it too good, that's my problem.

Why do we black men always trust you women when you say, "It's all right, I'm on the pill"? The pill ain't gonna stop me from catching sup'm deadly.

I've only known her a few months. She goes for kinky sex. Likes being tied up and covered in food, and then to have the food licked off her. That's what kept me going back, jus' to see what she would come up with next.

Her getting pregnant wasn't part of the deal. When she told me, it was like someone dropped a heavy metal safe from a great height on to my head. She took away my power and freedom to finish with her.

I have always said that the woman who has my first child will be special to me. So I had my hands tied. Lois had to become special.

There's something weird about her, though. Apart from the kinky stuff. She gets into all my business and flies into a rage for no reason. Not my ideal woman. I think she just needs a strong man to calm her down.

Me?

I don't know, but I'll give it a try.

I feel real bad about Joan. All that stuff I said to get her back. I do love her. She should have been my baby mother.

73

Lois knew all about Joan, and I know she was as jealous as hell. Boy, I should have dropped that when she started acting them ways. But as usual I was following my dick.

I don't wanna blame Joan, but in a way it's her fault too. She's the one who wanted us to be just friends. She expect me to go without, so that she can have her independence? Things don't go like that.

They say things always happen for a reason. What the reason for this is, I don't know.

10. WHO'S ZOOMING WHO?

The Indian restaurant was only half full, but the atmosphere was bordering on rowdy. A group of young white guys were celebrating something, and the beers were being consumed as fast as the waiters could serve them.

James looked up from his meal.

"The food all right?" he asked.

"Yeah, fine," Pamela mumbled unconvincingly. The rose-scented candle in the centre of the table was giving her a headache — or maybe it was making a headache that was already there worse.

James pushed his plate aside. "What's wrong? You've been quiet all evening."

Pamela looked up at him. She had invited him out because she had hoped that on neutral territory she would be able to talk to him about them going their separate ways. Now she didn't know how to start.

"Pam?" he pushed, breaking her thoughts.

"I'm tired, that's all. Don't waste your food on my account." She'd meant it to sound courteous, but instead it came out somewhat agitated.

To think that two months ago, she and James had been planning to buy a house and have children together. She shuddered involuntarily at the thought.

She regarded him with a perplexed stare. He wasn't a bad-looking guy, a bit paler than she liked her men, but he couldn't help that. He *was* in love with her. She saw it in his eyes, felt it in his touch. He never raised his voice to her in anger. He was living in her home, and he respected that. He did his share around the house: cooking, cleaning, paying his share of the bills. She knew she was the envy of many women, including Marion. What on earth was she doing? James had given up so much for her, even his wife and baby.

Pamela reached over and touched his hand, feeling his knuckles beneath her soft palm.

She smiled. "I'm sorry. I spoilt the evening. I promise I'll make it up to you later." There was a gleam of mischief in her voice.

James's expression changed swiftly from a frown to a smile of excited expectation. "I've got some making up to do myself. Why don't we get out of here?"

All the way home, James was caressing her. Although to her it felt more like harassing.

Pamela tried to get more enthusiastic about this, but the more she tried the more she thought about Shaun.

This would definitely be the last time, she affirmed. She couldn't possibly go on like this.

As soon as they got into the flat, his hands were everywhere. James was practically floating on heat.

Pamela went into the bedroom and undressed slowly. She slipped on a full-length satin négligé before going to the bathroom. She was so tense, she felt like a body builder after a workout. She shook her shoulders and arms to try to relax.

James stood in the bathroom doorway. He was bare chested, his belt hanging loose around his small waist. He watched her pull the brush through her long black hair, and then tie it back with an elastic band. He loved her hair. Indeed, he couldn't think of anything he *didn't* love about this woman. He watched her slim body move sensuously underneath the satin nightgown, feeling his manhood begin to stir. He took a stride towards her, encircling her waist and pulling her body close. Then he buried his face into her neck and took her flesh between his teeth. He was as horny as hell.

Pamela tensed as he sucked at her flesh, but she let him lift her nightie and caress her smooth buttocks. She felt him fumbling to undo his trousers, to release himself, and heard his belt buckle hit the floor.

He was nothing compared to Shaun. Shaun would at least make sure she was enjoying it as much as he was before even attempting to enter her. James simply spread her legs with his hand and pressed himself into her. There wasn't much of him; he slid in easily.

Pamela grimaced. She wasn't ready, not in the least bit turned on. She shut her eyes and thought of Shaun as James, oblivious, continued to pump in and out of her with uninspired strokes. Each motion of his hips was accompanied by a low grunt.

Pamela clenched the muscles of her vagina and moaned loudly.

"That feels so good," she cooed expertly. "Do it faster." This, of course, would bring him to a quicker climax.

He thrust into her with one final, shuddering lunge, and she felt his hot seed filling her. It was over before it had begun. James wilted, gripping her hunched shoulders, and his thrusts slowed and stopped. He withdrew. Kissing her on her shoulder and pulling up his trousers, he whispered, "I'll see you in the bedroom," before leaving the room.

Pamela froze. Was he expecting more? Hands still braced against the sink, she stood up straight and caught her reflection in the mirror. She didn't even want to face herself. Her cheeks hadn't flushed, her pulse-rate hadn't risen a beat. She was as cool as if she'd just taken a shower. In fact the shower stood more chance of stimulating her.

She turned on the taps to fill the bath. She had to wash him off her. His fluid was already oozing out, tracing a sticky path down her leg.

"Not for much longer," she hissed quietly.

JAMES

Something's going on. Maybe it's just me, but Pamela always seems distracted these days. I try to please her, and all it does is upset her. It's like she's got non-stop PMT.

I agreed to go out with her the other night. I thought she was going to come out of this mood she was in. Have a nice meal, go home, have a few drinks, and then a bit of you-know-what. It sounded perfect.

I get the feeling she's hiding something from me, but I don't know what yet. She asked me to move out of her flat about a month back. When I asked why, she said something about needing her space back. But I never get in her way or stop her from doing what she wants to do. Couldn't, even if I tried.

She keeps going on at me to get out more. What's the problem? I'm happy staying in, being with her. The way I treat her she should be ecstatic. Maybe it's just a phase she's going through.

We need a holiday, some time away together, away from distractions like her girlfriends, her work, the mystery telephone caller she keeps telling she'll call back later. I'm not a suspicious person. Everyone has their secrets, I don't think she's cheating on me . . .

No, the problem is definitely that we need to spend more time together. I'm going round to the travel agents first thing Saturday

76

morning to find a holiday to surprise her with.
If there's one thing I know how to do, it's treat a lady well.

11. BIG FUN!

Walking home, Marion struggled with her umbrella to shelter from the downpour that had seemed to come from nowhere. Gerard had called her at work to tell her he was taking her out tonight, and to be ready for seven. Marion had tried protesting — she didn't get home until seven most days when she worked late — but Gerard had insisted. So she'd taken the last hour off work and stepped out into the pouring rain.

Arriving home at quarter past six, lower half soaked despite the umbrella, she was miserable and not in the mood for going out. She had been feeling nauseous, depressed and lethargic the last few days, and today was no exception. All she wanted to do was get into bed with a cup of hot chocolate for company.

She ran a bath. As she lay in the water she wondered what the occasion was. Gerard hadn't said why he'd suddenly decided to take her out. They never went anywhere together any more, unless it was shopping. He'd told her to wear something dressy, sophisticated. She had grinned, despite her suspicion at his enthusiasm to show her off.

The bath had revived her sufficiently for Marion to start looking forward to the evening. She poured herself a glass of wine before searching her wardrobe for something suitable to wear and deciding on a lilac velvet dress she had worn only once. Gerard liked it; when she'd worn it he'd said he couldn't keep his hands off her.

Seated in front of the mirror, dressed only in her underwear, she applied her make-up while the curling tongs heated up. She sang along with Usher's "Can You Get With It?" The wine was already giving her a buzz.

She didn't like to wear very much make-up; eyeliner, lipstick and a fine layer of powder was all she felt she needed. She wrapped her hair into a french twist and a small beehive, then with the aid of the curling tongs she created tiny ringlets to fall around her face.

She slipped into the dress, feeling the smoothness of the silk lining against her skin. She stood in front of the full-length mirror on the wardrobe door and admired the way the shaped cups pushed up her breasts, giving her extra cleavage.

Gerard arrived at quarter to seven, looking stush in a bottle-green suit with a white polo-neck sweater. He wore two gold chains, one a belcher that Marion had bought him for his last birthday. He gave her a look of proud admiration as he entered the bedroom, coming up behind her and kissing her cheek.

"Nice, very nice. New dress?" he asked.

"No. I wore this the last time you took me out, remember? You liked it then too."

"Oh yeah," he said vaguely. He stood behind her, checking his hair in the mirror while she put dangling gold earrings in her lobes.

"So, what's the occasion then?" she asked.

"Sorry?"

"Why are we going out tonight?"

"Oh, a business contact invited us to dinner. They're married, so I thought I'd better bring my other half." He ran a hand over his S-curled hair, smoothing down a single stray hair, then smoothed his moustache on either side of his top lip before wiping his hands on a towel which hung on the back of the chair.

"Are we supposed to be married, then?" She applied powder to her nose and chin, spreading it gently with dabs from a cotton wool ball.

"Well, I didn't tell them we weren't," he answered.

"I suppose he'll guess anyway, when he sees there's no ring on my finger."

"Just say we're engaged then," he said, then quickly added, "but only if he asks. Wear one of your other rings on that finger. Just for tonight." He reached over her shoulder for his aftershave and sprayed it lightly under the collar of his polo neck.

Marion beamed. She turned around and kissed him on the cheek.

"Watch it, I don't wear lipstick," he smiled, swiping at his face and checking his handsome reflection in the mirror.

She watched him, feeling an admiration that was fuelled by hunger, as he dusted his spotless lapels. She didn't care that this man loved himself more than anything else in the world. He was *her* man, and she loved him.

The drive to West London took them nearly an hour. Gerard was full of talk about their host, and Marion paid attention as he briefed her on his background. "His name's Brian Mack. He owns a chain of electrical retail shops, and he's looking to get into mobile phones — which is where I come in." He tapped a finger to his chest. "He wants a partner to run that side of the business, right? So tonight, we'll . .

." he searched for the right word, "negotiate — see whether he buys me out and hires me or whether he buys into my company as a silent partner. You follow me?"

"Yeah. If you want my opinion, Ger, I don't think you should sell out. If he decides he doesn't like you, you could be out of a job, left with nothing."

"I didn't ask for your opinion," he answered bluntly. "I've thought of that already. I've got a contract to cover it — I'm no fool, y'know." A muscle bunched in his jaw and he gripped the steering wheel more tightly.

Marion knew she had struck a nerve. She wasn't sure what her purpose was to be tonight, but she hoped he wouldn't bring her into the business side of the conversation. He never listened to her ideas anyway; on the rare occasions when he did, he'd pretend he had come up with them.

A cyclist swung out in front of the car. Gerard braked sharply and slammed on the horn. He stuck his head out of the window and shouted, "Blasted idiot, shoulda killed your raas."

Marion didn't realise she'd been holding her breath until she started feeling light-headed. She let it out slowly. She reached forward and turned the car stereo on to avoid any further conversation. Gerard was obviously uptight, and this wasn't good considering they were going to a business meeting.

The car turned into a quiet residential street. Beautifully landscaped gardens lined the road. Some houses had elaborate gates surrounding them, like film stars' homes in the movies. Perfectly trimmed hedges, mowed lawns, patios . . . these houses had to be worth at least two hundred grand, Marion thought, in awe of what she was seeing.

Gerard pulled into a wide driveway outside a pretty mock-Tudor house. He parked the car outside the garage door and turned to Marion. "What d'you think?" He was smiling again, his eyes lighting up as though they had never known anger.

"This is where they live?" she asked dazedly.

Gerard just kept smiling knowingly. Marion was overwhelmed, and had every right to be — this was a world so very different from her own. Brian Mack was raking the money in, and Gerard wanted to be part of it. Electrical goods, whether they be mobile phones or start-of-the-art studio equipment, would always be in demand.

"These are white people, right?" Marion asked, opening her door.

"Nope." Gerard checked his face in the mirror before exiting the car. "One day I'll have a house just like this." He looked into her eyes for a second over the car roof.

Marion, who never missed intonations in speech, had caught the fact that he had said "I will" and not "we will". But she let it go as usual.

She slipped her arm through his as they walked up the red-brick path to the house. Gerard rang the bell and the porch light came on instantly. Marion half-expected alarms to start ringing too.

The door was answered promptly by a tall, slender, dark-skinned woman. She was dressed in a short, deep red, crushed velvet dress with a plunging neckline. Around her neck she wore a diamante choker that caught the light and completely mesmerised Marion with its brilliance. The woman's smile spread as she grabbed Gerard by the shoulders and loudly kissed the air by each of his cheeks. Marion noticed her green contact lenses and instantly disliked the woman.

"Gerry! On time, I like that." She must have been at least six feet tall in her high heels. Marion came level with her chest as she stepped inside.

"And you must be Marilyn," she giggled, brushing her hand through her long brown woven hair. Was there anything about this woman that was real?

Marion momentarily held her gaze, just as the woman's bosom held Gerard's eyes. "Marion," she corrected pointedly. Gerard dragged his eyes away from the woman's cleavage, but not before Marion caught him running his tongue over his upper lip.

They followed the woman into the hallway. It was as Marion had expected: expensive, everything dressed up as much as their hostess. The hallway and the doors were all of the same dark wood. Lamps lit the hallway, three on either side.

"Marion, this is Patrice Mack," Gerard introduced.

Patrice offered her hand. Those had to be false nails! Marion shook the outstretched claw lightly, ignoring the way Patrice had held it as though she was expecting Marion to kiss it.

"Something smells good," Gerard said, nose in the air.

Patrice took his jacket. "I do hope you like lamb. The cook didn't receive very much notice, but she has excelled herself tonight."

After relieving her guests of their outdoor clothes Patrice, to Marion's horror, took Gerard's arm and swanned off down the hall to their right, leaving Marion to follow, fuming. Gerard hadn't taken the least bit of notice of her.

They entered a semi-lit study. Brian Mack appeared from behind a large wooden desk. Marion was surprised at just how small he was compared to his tall, voluptuous wife.

"Brian, I told you to stop work for now. We have guests," Patrice scolded.

Brian Mack was a man in his early forties. His round face was bearded and the beard was speckled with grey, while his hair was dyed jet black and gently waved giving him a distinguished look. He was dressed casually in a short-sleeved, blue and white striped shirt and navy trousers.

"Gerard and Marion!" His deep voice filled the room, reminding Marion of her deputy head teacher at school, whose voice had boomed across the assembly hall. Brian stepped from behind his huge desk with his arm extended, shaking their hands in turn. "Nice to meet you at last, Gerard. Patrice hasn't stopped talking about you."

Marion's eyes whipped from Gerard to Patrice, and she caught the look that passed briefly between them. Patrice's expression was one of self-satisfaction, and Gerard's lips turned up just slightly, his eyes sparkling as if a happy memory had just come to mind.

"Nice to meet you too, Brian. Let's hope we can do business," he said in his best posh voice.

"And Marion, the good woman behind the successful man! You are the very angel I'd imagined." He held her hand a little longer than necessary and looked too deeply into her eyes.

"Thank you," she answered, pulling her hand free.

Brian turned to his wife, who was busy patting her perfect hairstyle into place. "Patrice, will you do the honours? I've just got to finish up here." He waved a hand over his desk.

"Not too long, Brian," Patrice said, once again taking Gerard's arm as though he were a blind man needing guidance.

As they left the room, Patrice continued to talk as though Gerard was the only one there. "It's such a pain, Brian working as much as he does. He really does need a partner, y'know. Then I wouldn't get so lonely." She pouted, flashing her green eyes to Marion. "Marion really is a lucky girl." They entered another room down the hall. "Sometimes," she giggled, "I fantasise about burning his study down, but that would only mean he'd be out of the house more often, in one of his shops — so I just can't win."

The room they had walked into was huge, as big as a small school hall. Marion gazed about in awe as Gerard strolled in and made himself comfortable on the sofa. At one end on a raised floor stood the dining area, six chairs surrounding a long black wooden table. Light danced off the crystal glasses placed at each setting. The entire area was seductively lit by candles. The other end of the room had probably been decorated by Patrice. There were four large framed photographs of her around the walls, each in a different pose, all very artistically composed. The largest dominated one wall. In the picture, Patrice lay back on a chaise long, wrapped only in a length of African cotton, her nipples pointing at the ceiling, her hair hanging to the floor. Those cat's eyes seemed to stare at Marion wherever she stood.

Patrice caught her looking at it. "Brian is into photography when he has the time. He likes shooting me, especially naked," she giggled.

Maybe he should use a gun next time, Marion thought wickedly. "Nice," was what she said aloud.

"Please, sit down. What can I get you to drink?"

Before Marion could open her mouth Gerard had answered for her. "You know what I drink — and Marion will have a Bacardi and Coke."

Marion shot him a look, which he ignored. What was going on here? Whatever it was she didn't like it. If she had any way of getting home on her own she would have left there and then.

It wasn't just the fact that he had ordered her drink. She wanted to know how on earth he was so familiar with this woman, and why he hadn't mentioned her before. For the time being, she knew her curiosity must remain stifled, the questions unasked. Maybe she was just being paranoid — or was that look in Gerard's eyes lust?

Gerard watched Patrice approvingly. Now here, he considered, was a black woman with class. No wonder her husband couldn't handle her, he was twice her age. Gerard had had a hard time controlling her four nights ago. Patrice was insatiable, but he'd soon tame her. He had absolutely no objections to helping her out in that department.

The merger had been Patrice's idea. She knew everything about her husband's business, and often put other firms in touch with him. She found Gerard irresistible. He not only had a face and body she wanted to eat, but a good business brain too. She was sure this was a unity made in heaven. She mixed their drinks and brought them over on a sparkling glass tray.

She took a seat in the unusually shaped cream leather swivel chair opposite, and crossed her legs suggestively. "Brian and I have big plans for your business," she purred, looking directly into Gerard's eyes.

"So do I," he answered proudly, with the same suggestive look in his eyes.

"I know. Which is why I want to get the two of you together." Her voice oozed in a sickly way that turned Marion's stomach.

Marion couldn't help but feel invisible. The only way she was going to get in on this conversation was by barging in. "So, Patrice. How long have you known Gerard?" she asked shrewdly.

Patrice answered promptly without missing a beat. "It must be two months now . . ." She looked to Gerard for confirmation.

"Yeah, 'bout that," he said, giving Marion a look of uncertainty.

Marion continued regardless. "It's just that he's never mentioned you. I'd assumed it was your husband he was dealing with." She took another sip of Bacardi.

Patrice, visibly flustered by Marion's intonation, uncrossed her long legs. "That reminds me — I'll just go and chase Brian," she said, rising from her designer chair and making her way to the door.

As soon as the door was closed, Gerard turned on Marion. "What the hell do you think you're playing at?" he exploded.

"I only said what I thought, Gerard. Maybe she's got a guilty conscience."

"About what?" he challenged her, trying to keep his voice from getting too loud.

"I don't know — you tell me." Marion knew she was pushing it. Now wasn't the right time to have this out.

Gerard pointed his finger at her threateningly. "Don't delve into my business, okay? I didn't have to bring you here, y'know. Just enjoy it — an' don't mess up." The last words were delivered through clenched teeth.

Marion's wide eyes lowered and her lips quivered. She felt her heart sink into the pit of her stomach. He had just confirmed that something was going on. She raised her eyes and stared at him disbelievingly as he downed the rest of his sherry in one gulp.

Her friends were probably right — she deserved better. Marion knew that, if only she could stand up to him without being afraid of losing him, maybe then he'd show her some respect. She felt tears sting the backs of her eyelids. She had so many questions buzzing in her head that a headache was emerging from the back of her skull and forcing its way round to her temples. She suddenly had the scariest feeling that this had been planned, just so that Gerard could show his mistress off in front of her. To show her what her competition was. Well, if he wanted a wannabe-white black woman, he wasn't the man she had thought he was.

They both started as the door opened and Brian entered, followed by Patrice. Marion and Gerard sat rigidly at each end of the three-seater sofa. You could have cut the air with a knife.

"Sorry to keep you waiting," Brian apologised. "Dinner is now served." He gestured with his hands that they should take their places at the table.

Patrice directed them to their seats. Marion found herself placed opposite Brian and next to Gerard. Patrice sat opposite Gerard. "Cecile will serve dinner. We don't always have a cook, by the way," she said to Marion. "She's borrowed from neighbours of ours. I can cook just well enough to get by," and she issued that irritating giggle again. A shudder passed through Marion.

Brian took Patrice's hand. "Not that you need to cook to win your man's heart," he said.

Marion felt a twinge of pity for this man, who obviously thought his wife was faithful to him.

"Isn't he sweet?" Patrice giggled.

"Mmm," Marion smiled back weakly.

A door opened in the panelling behind Brian and Patrice and an olive-skinned woman entered, pushing a food trolley. She placed warm bowls in front of them and served them with soup. Once she had withdrawn Brian started up the conversation.

"I see you're engaged," he said to Marion. "Have you set a date?"

"We . . ." she began.

Gerard placed his hand over hers, silencing her with a squeeze. "Not yet. We're saving first. Start things right, y'know."

"Of course," Brian agreed, impressed.

"I told you he was sensible," Patrice added.

"That you did," Brian said, nodding appreciatively.

Marion sat, quietly fuming. After the soup, Brian opened a bottle of vintage wine and poured for all of them. Marion drank hers in big gulps and prayed that no one would notice just how much she was consuming, despite her promise to herself to give it up. It was the only way she was going to be able to get through the evening.

All they seemed to talk about over the main course was business. Thus Marion was kept out of it, and the drink was dulling her senses enough for her not to care. The food was perfection, right down to the Tiramisu. While they drank their coffee, Brian never stopped complimenting Marion, while his wife giggled and made eyes at Gerard.

After dinner they retired to what Brian called his studio. It was at the top of the house, and took up the entire attic conversion. Plush cream carpet covered the floor and even two of the walls. There wasn't much furniture, except for a few low easy chairs at one end, a coffee table and a well-stocked drinks cabinet. They were told to take off their shoes at the door and to make themselves comfortable. Gerard had no trouble making himself at home, acting as though he already knew the place.

84

By now Marion was unsober, what with the drink before dinner and the wine with dinner, and now Brian offering her brandy. Before long Marion had allowed the warmth of the alcohol and the comfort of her surroundings to obscure her earlier feelings of jealousy, and she relaxed in an oversized easy chair.

Gerard sat across the room from her, Patrice snuggling up next to him.

It meant nothing to Marion.

After all, they were socialising.

Brian put on a CD and the room was filled with the voice of Diana Ross. He sat beside Marion and placed an arm across the back of the chair behind her head. "You're a very attractive woman, Marion," he told her.

She shifted away from him, feeling uncomfortable under his gaze.

He turned to Gerard. "Don't you ever worry about men trying to steal her from you, Gerry?"

Gerard seemed amused by the question. "They can try, but she belongs to me." He smiled at Marion then, and she shivered involuntarily. Suddenly she felt like the doomed victim in a vampire movie.

Brian turned back to her and took her hand in his. She was still looking at Gerard, but he was already in deep conversation with Patrice. Their eyes held each others and their voices were too low for her to hear.

"Your fiancé is a very open-minded man," Brian was saying.

"He is?" Marion could barely hear herself, as if she were speaking through cotton wool.

Brian's face loomed closer. "You know, I find it very hard to relax. Patrice is always trying to find new ways of taking my mind off my work. I think this is her best idea yet." His arm fell on to her shoulder.

Marion flinched. What idea? Her brain was doing somersaults trying to figure out what was going on. Across the room Gerard and Patrice were joined together in a passionate embrace. Her leg was thrown across him, and her fingers ran through his wavy hair. Marion giggled as she imagined Gerard doing that to Patrice and the hair coming off in his hand. She was really out of it.

Brian's hot breath was on Marion's face and she tried to push him away, but her arms felt heavy and she didn't think she could stand up if she wanted to. Brian's beard brushed against her cheek and then he was on top of her, tongue probing her lips. She was unable to stop him; his weight was crushing her into the chair. She tried to call Gerard but her voice stuck in her throat.

As she struggled Brian groaned in her ear. "Enjoy, Marion, enjoy."

Again she looked for Gerard but he had disappeared, along with Patrice. She was alone with this old man. The image of him having a heart attack on top of her made her giggle again, and she became sure she was drugged. She began to feel herself passing out, and fought it, knowing what would happen if she did.

She had no idea where the strength came from, but somehow she gathered it, and with the palms of her hands on Brian's chest she shoved, twisting her body under him.

They both tumbled to the floor. Marion moved quickly despite her intoxicated state. As she struggled to her stockinged feet the room swam around her. The door up ahead was dancing in time to the beat of "Why Do Fools Fall In Love" and moving farther away. She managed to lunge for the handle, gripping it tight and dragging it open. Brian moaned from the floor behind her — she must have hurt him, but that wasn't her concern. She just wanted to find Gerard and get out of this madhouse.

There was a key on the outside of the door and she turned it, locking Brian inside. Steadying herself against the banisters, she stepped as quickly as possible down the carpeted stairs to the first floor. She could hear the sounds of a bed creaking and muffled noises coming from the hallway to her left, so she hurried towards them, needing to locate Gerard, knowing and yet still dreading what she would find.

This door wasn't locked. She shoved it and it swung open to reveal a large four-poster bed in a semi-dark room. The two bodies on top of it were unmistakably Gerard and Patrice. Gerard, naked, was on his back, being ridden by a writhing, bouncing Patrice. His hands fondled her breasts and she was groaning with ecstasy. Marion heaved and felt a rush of vomit race up from her stomach. She bent double as it came spewing out.

She passed out, but before she lost consciousness she distinctly heard a hammering, like fists on wood, and Gerard exclaiming, "Shit!"

Marion came to in the car. Her throat was dry and she had a cramp in her stomach. Gerard was driving like a madman and she bounced from side to side as he took the corners.

"Ger?" she whispered.

"Shut up, just shut up." His face was a mask of stone.

Marion squeezed herself into the corner of the seat by the door.

86

She was shaking uncontrollably. She was sure that Gerard had planned the events at Brian's house, and she had spoiled his plan.

Knowing Gerard like she did, she was afraid she'd get more than verbal abuse if she pushed him to talk to her, so she shut her eyes to fake sleep — or further unconsciousness.

Gerard took her home, made her take a bath and then took her to bed, intending to complete his unfinished business.

He made love to her body only, and she felt as though he was with someone else. Tears filled her eyes as he rode her silently in the dark. He had used her in the worst way tonight. She wanted him to talk to her about what had happened. Why Brian Mack had expected her to have sex with him. Why he had gone off with that woman, leaving her for that old man to maul.

Marion lay still as Gerard finished. As her thoughts began to rearrange themselves, she slowly began to convince herself that the whole night must have been an awful mistake, that Gerard had been drugged and seduced also. Gerard grunted and turned his back to her. She was sure that, when morning came, he would be able to explain the whole sordid affair.

She fell asleep curled into his back. He snored lightly, completely sated. She breathed in his scent and squeezed herself tighter into his back.

Somehow that night she managed to dream only sweet dreams as her subconscious struggled to replace the nightmare.

GERARD

The best laid plans . . .

Y'know, I thought about taking Debs. But she wouldn't have fit in. Marion can look good, knows when to keep her mouth shut, and usually goes with the flow. Not this time, though.

I couldn't believe it when she burst in on me and Patrice. I was having a good time, y'know what I mean? I did t'ink Marion was too, getting herself drunk and flirting with Brian.

The way Patrice was throwing herself at me in full view of her husband! Only a fool wouldn't catch the drift. I wanted Marion to try sup'm new, different, y'know? Everyone's got this kinky streak in them, I reckon — all it takes is the right person to bring it out.

Patrice attracts me 'cause we're two of a kind. The only difference is she married money and I'm making my own by hard work, y'know what I mean? She made the first move. She walked into my shop and asked to make an appointment with the manager. She had good timing — I was running the shop that day. When she came in I was,

87

y'know, kinda worried. A black woman in a suit usually means government business, trouble. Y'know, like solicitors, fraud squad, sup'm like that. She introduced herself and told me exactly what she wanted: a piece of my action. I tell ya, I couldn't wait to get a piece of hers, jus' looking at her, y'know what I mean?

What is the big deal with women and relationships anyway? Y'know, nearly all the women I know are in their twenties and they all want me to be their exclusive property. The teenagers and the older women are the ones I have the most good times with. The babies are ripe and ready to be filled with the joys of sex; the mummies are just ready to have a sweet young boy give them the business. No strings, no hang ups.

Soon as I find a replacement — y'know, a nice lickle regular, with her own place an' dat — then Marion's gone. One t'ing, though. I'm gonna miss her cooking.

12. WHEN ONLY A FRIEND WILL DO

Marion had managed to get through a week without Gerard.

It wasn't by choice — the morning after the Macks' dinner party she had woken up disorientated and alone, and Gerard had been unobtainable ever since. Every time she called his work place she was told he had "just left". His mobile number was constantly giving her the mechanical voice: "We are unable to connect your call. Please try again later." She'd left copious messages with his mother, until Claudia had had to tell her to stop calling, to let Gerard call her when he was ready. Needing to share her worries with somebody, she had told Pamela about the planned orgy.

Pamela had gone absolutely mad. "I hope you told him where to go, Marion," she'd said in a stern voice.

"Well, I . . ."

"Don't tell me you didn't finish with him."

"All right, I won't," she'd huffed childishly.

"Marion, you are sick. Are you so addicted to this man's dick that you can't give him up? Even after this?"

"I will. There's just a couple of things we have to sort out first."

"Yeah, right. You mean he'll be doing the sorting out and you'll just sit back and take it all."

Marion hadn't been able to think of anything to say. Pamela's words had sounded too much like the truth.

"Listen to me," her friend had continued, "I don't want to hear from you again until you've sent his arse to hell, d'you hear me?"

"Pam!" Marion had gasped, affronted.

"No, I mean it. I love you like a sister, but this has gone too far."

After that, Marion didn't have the guts to tell Joan. She knew her friends only wanted the best for her, but some decisions she had to make on her own. It was her life.

Now Joan had called and invited her out tonight. A night out with Joan would be just what she needed to help her escape from her own prison of misery. Joan had said she had some good news for her. It was about time Marion got some good news. Her life seemed to be one long bad news story.

Neither of her friends knew she was pregnant.

The test had confirmed it this morning, but she'd already known what the result would be. If splitting up with Gerard had been difficult before, it now felt like an impossibility.

When Joan arrived Marion could immediately smell the ganja on her. She didn't say a word — Joan already knew how she felt about her smoking that stuff. Joan didn't need it. She was a much better person without it, in fact.

To match her mood, Marion had dressed completely in black — a short flared skirt and a long blouse, worn with her knee-high black boots and black stockings laced with silver. In contrast, Joan was dressed in white, a crocheted dress that echoed the style of the twenties.

"You ready, then?" Joan asked, eyeing the garments her friend wore. Her eyes may have been faraway, but the rest of her was alive and kicking. She seemed to be bubbling over with some kind of adrenalin rush; her body was one giant fidget.

"Maybe I should change . . ." Marion turned to go back to the bedroom.

Joan grabbed her arm. "Don't bother. We're only going to King's. You look fine."

"Joan, I can't afford a wine bar." Marion thought of the five pounds in her purse that was to last her the rest of the week.

"Hey, this is my treat. I needed a night out just as much as you," Joan said, and ushered Marion through the front door.

It was still early evening when they got to the wine bar, and the after-work crowd was still loitering. It was mostly men, some of whom turned to look the girls up and down as they walked towards the bar. A few couples sat at the bar, and people were scattered around the room at various tables, chatting loudly over the music.

Joan bought the drinks and the girls sat at a corner table by the PA system, where a young male DJ selected music for the evening. Changing Faces' "Stroke You Up" was playing.

"Remember I said I had some good news for you?" Joan beamed, her eyes staring too intensely.

"Yes," Marion said tentatively.

"You'll love this." Joan touched Marion's arm. "I'm planning a six-month series on black men in one of our magazines." Joan glanced around and lowered her voice, as though anyone might be listening in to their conversation. "I've already got a writer in mind for the job. Someone who's talented, qualified, and ready to start straight away . . ."

Marion, her mind still churning with other matters, waited for the punchline.

"Well? What d'you say?" Joan asked.

"What?"

Joan threw her hands up in exasperation. "I was talking about you, silly!"

Marion's mouth fell open. *"Me?* But I couldn't . . . I mean, I could, but . . . what about experience?"

"You've got the qualifications, it's your field of work . . . Marion, this is just what you've been looking for! I mean, what you don't know about black men isn't worth knowing."

Marion shook her head. "It'll be hard work. I don't know . . . Is there a deadline?"

"You'd have to have a draft plan of each topic ready in October." Joan reached down for her miniature handbag by her feet. "Here, I've brought a plan with me." She removed a square of paper from her purse and carefully unfolded it into an A3 sheet. Marion moved the glasses aside and they spread the plan out between them. Drawn out in different colours was a large seven-legged spider. At the end of each of its legs was a heading. On the body was written: "Project Target: Black Men", and the topics highlighted on the legs were Sex, Money, Love, Ambition, Family, and Future.

"The first one will go out in the December issue," Joan explained. "We'd want this one to catch people's attention, you know, leave them hungry for part two."

"I like it." Marion's eyes lit up as she perused the page.

"These headings aren't fixed," Joan pointed out, "we can always change one or two if a better idea comes up."

Marion's brain was already working with the topics in front of her. This was perfect. She could see her name in a by-line on the front page. This was a once-in-a-lifetime opportunity. All these months she had been scouting for work, trying to sell her articles, and now this job was being handed to her.

"Do you feel you can handle it?" Joan asked.

"This is exactly what I've been looking for."

Marion reached over and hugged her friend. "Thanks, Joan."

"Hey, we're sistas, ain't we?"

"I want to do this, Joan. This is my career, my ambition. I want to do this more than anything else at the moment." She suddenly thought about Gerard — and the baby. How would they fit in? Her eyes misted over.

"You sure?" Joan regarded her quizzically. "You look a little worried."

Marion shook off the descending black veil surrounding her. "No, I'm fine. It's not the work."

"What then? Your man?"

Marion sighed theatrically. "I think Gerard's avoiding me."

"What, again? I thought it was something serious," Joan said flippantly, and sucked on her cigarette.

"He *is* my boyfriend, Joan." Marion found herself defending him despite what had happened, probably fuelled by her friend's insensitivity rather than any sense of loyalty.

"Yeah, I know" Joan said, "but how long's it been since you had anything good to say about him?"

Marion knew now she couldn't fool herself any longer. There was nothing good about what she had with Gerard. She knew he was cheating on her — he'd done it right in front of her on the last occasion. Even when he made love to her it was like he was fantasising about other women. He cared more about his clothes than he did about her. She blinked smoke from her eyes, raising a hand and wafting it past her face.

Joan swapped her cigarette to her other hand. "I'm sorry, Maz, but you know the man's no good. For all you know he's got loads of other women . . ."

"He hasn't," Marion said a little too quickly.

Joan raised that quizzical eyebrow again.

"All right." Marion swallowed. "I think he *might* be seeing someone else." She studied a spotlight on the opposite wall until her eyes ached.

"What makes you think that?" Joan asked, brushing ash from her

91

white dress.

Marion searched for the right words. "Well, he . . . he hardly comes round any more, unless it's to eat or to crash out. He never phones. When I call him he fobs me off with excuses, but still he just turns up when he feels like it . . ."

"Because you let him, Maz."

"What else can I do? I love him," Marion protested.

Joan wanted to slap some sense into her. Sometimes women could be so pathetic. What on earth could possess Marion to love this egotistical bastard? There was nothing in the relationship for her any more, and yet she still clung to him. Her own pride, dignity and self-esteem were going down the drain. It was no wonder he treated her the way he did; he did it simply because he *could*.

Joan remembered one occasion when she had gone around to Marion's flat to pick her up for a night out. Gerard had walked into the bedroom as Marion was putting on her jewellery.

"What's that you have round your neck," he'd demanded.

Joan had raised her head from the magazine she was reading at the tone of his voice.

"What, my necklace?" Marion had raised her hand to touch the silver and gold costume jewellery she wore.

"Is that what it is?" he'd snared. "Didn't I buy you gold? What you wearing that shit for?"

Joan had had to bite her tongue to stop herself interfering.

"It goes with my dress, Ger," Marion had reasoned pitifully.

He'd looked at her with disgust. "Well you're not leaving here with that thing on."

Marion had reached up to undo the chain and take it off, and Joan found she couldn't control herself any longer. "There is no way a man could come tell me what I can and can't wear on my body!" she'd blasted. "Much less tell me I can't walk out of my own house."

Gerard had glared at her, then decided to ignore her and turned back to Marion, who held the chain in her hands, looking from her friend's face to his. "This is nothing to do with your friend," he'd said, "but if you wanna go out looking cheap then that's up to you," and he'd stormed back to the living room, slamming the door behind him.

His sudden anger had frightened Joan a little, but she was also angry at Marion. If that was the way he carried on all the time, then it was clear that Marion was living her life in fear of his dominance.

"You were never a doormat before you met him," Joan said now. "I can remember when we were kids you would even stand up to your mum's boyfriend when he tried to boss you around. You stood up for yourself."

"I don't want to have to fight, Joan. Not like my mum did. He walked out on her because of her interfering children."

"That just proves that he was no good, and only out for himself — like Gerard." Joan leaned toward her. "He's playing with you. Using you for his own satisfaction and not giving a damn about your feelings. He's a sweetboy, a buppie, a cock on legs."

Marion looked into her friend's eyes. Just who were they talking about here? "How's Colin these days?" she asked with a sneer.

Joan suddenly jumped back, shocked. "We're talking about your love life here, not mine."

"Hit a nerve, did I?" Marion was getting into this. She watched as Joan lit another cigarette with shaking hands.

"I don't want to talk about Colin." She shook her head. "I've made some mistakes in my life, and the Baker brothers were two of the biggest."

"Tell me about it."

Joan suddenly stood up, smoothing her dress down. "I'll get us a refill. Same again?" She didn't wait for an answer but sloped off towards the bar, leaving Marion wondering.

The wine bar had filled up since they'd entered. Most of the crowd hadn't bothered to dress up. There were all walks of life in here tonight, Marion considered, becoming conscious of eyes watching her. She turned around to the table to her left and saw a young black man smiling at her. She looked past him, then turned to look for Joan.

The fellow was not to be deterred. He nudged his mate, and the two of them strolled over and made themselves comfortable in the vacant chairs at Marion's table.

The last thing Marion needed was to be chatted up. She turned her back on them, having to swivel around in her chair to do so.

"Hi," the first man said.

Marion glanced at the speaker, then cut her eyes at him and turned to look for Joan. She caught her friend's eye briefly and saw the flicker of a frown as Joan clocked the men at their table. *Get back here, Joan. I can't handle this.*

"So wha'? You cyaan seh hello," the friend said. He was tall, dark and skinny.

"Do I know you?" she replied without looking at them.

The first guy dragged his chair closer and looked into her face. "No. But you will." He wasn't too bad looking. The first thing she noticed about him was his smooth skin.

"I don't want to know you, okay?" She managed to muster some sternness into her voice.

"Aah, come on. You two looked a little lonely, sitting here all alone. We just want to keep you company."

Marion thought quickly. She wasn't good at this sort of thing. "We're not alone. We're waiting for our boyfriends."

"Yeah? So where are they?" Tall and Skinny asked, smirking.

Joan reappeared by Marion's side like an angel. "Can we help you with something?"

"I can think of something," Smooth Face said.

"Yeah, so can I. But I take it you know how to walk."

"Come on, girls," Tall and Skinny chimed in, "we only want to chat."

"Can't you take a hint? When a woman tells you she doesn't want to know, she means she doesn't want to know," Joan enunciated.

"So you t'ink you're too stush to talk to us?" Smooth Face asked.

"In a word — yes." Joan touched Marion's shoulder. "Come on," she said. "Let's sit somewhere else," and she turned and made off across the room. Marion got up and tagged after her.

"Yaow, sexy! You don't know what you're missing," Tall and Skinny called after them.

The girls totally ignored him, taking a seat at the other end of the bar. It was the noisier side of the room, but at least the men hadn't followed them.

"What is wrong with some men?" Joan blasted. "D'you think if a man turned me down flat I would keep pestering him? Where is their pride?" She gulped at her brandy and Coke.

"Some of them can't tell the difference between a woman turning them down and one who's playing hard to get," Marion said.

"Whatever." Joan kissed her teeth and shook another cigarette free from the packet. "They should stick to women who at least look interested." She lit the cigarette and tapped the lighter on the wooden table in time to the music.

"Obviously you're not on the lookout for another man then," Marion said, swinging the conversation back to their previous topic.

Joan gave her an incredulous look. "You must be joking. I've had too much trouble with them recently."

"So, tell me about it."

Joan blew smoke upwards through pursed lips. "I'm still not talking about it, Marion." She seemed adamant. Her eyes flicked restlessly around the wine bar.

"Are you sure you don't need to get this out of your system, whatever it is?"

Joan's eyes became too active, darting here and there, anywhere except Marion. She tapped the lighter a little harder at double the

94

tempo of the track. "Bastards," she finally spat. "The lot of them." She crossed one leg over the other. "Y'know, if he'd have asked me to, I would have had his baby. Not without a ring on my finger first, mind you, but I would have done it. But no, what does he do? He goes and gets some whore pregnant instead!"

Marion's big eyes opened wider at the mention of a pregnancy, then she remembered Joan knew nothing about hers. She narrowed her eyes. "Are we still talking about Colin?"

"Who else?" Her voice was rising to an unnatural pitch. She rested her elbows on the table in front of her. "I feel so damned stupid. Why couldn't I see it?" She looked to Marion as though she held the answers.

Around them people chatted, laughed and carried on as if they didn't exist. Marion wondered fleetingly what their lives were like. Was there even one couple here who could say they were in a solid relationship? Finally she said anxiously, "I can't believe it, Joan. Why didn't you say something?"

"I don't want pity, Marion. And don't you dare tell Pam! I can do without the whole world knowing how I let myself be used. I mean, here I am giving you advice and I can't even see what's wrong with my own life."

Marion stifled a smile. She wasn't the only one who'd fallen for the wrong man. She'd caught her friend in a rare moment of weakness, most unlike her, and Joan had told her more perhaps than she'd intended. Would she still be handing out advice now that Marion knew she had her weaknesses too?

"It was probably a one-off with this girl." Marion allowed the smile to grow. "These things happen. He loves you, doesn't he?"

Joan cut her down. "Love? Get real, Maz! He was probably seeing her all along. He fancied a change and came running back to me, and like a sucker I let him." A vein throbbed at her temple.

Marion wished she could turn back the clock to when they had first entered. This was supposed to be an evening of good news, an attempt to take her mind off her man and her worries. The bad news had all of a sudden eradicated the good. They now sat in silence, Joan puffing away at her cigarette. If only society didn't make having a man so important to the fulfilment of a woman's life, Marion mused, she and her friends would be a lot happier.

Claudette Thompson opened the door and greeted Marion with a hug. Gerard's mother was surprisingly bubbly for a woman in her early fifties. Her jet black hair, which fell below her shoulders when she wore it down, was tied back in a loose bun. She was a few inches taller than Marion and just a little overweight, but the full figure suited her. It was a natural mother figure. She had the same mouth as Gerard, with sensual, cupid's-bow lips. She was altogether a very attractive woman, and Marion sometimes felt jealous of her vibrant personality.

Marion had called Gerard's house two hours earlier, for what seemed like the hundredth time. Claudette had answered and told her that Gerard had gone training. When she realised it was Marion, Claudette had promptly invited her round to the house for dinner. It was just the excuse Marion needed to corner Gerard.

Marion loved being in Claudette's company. She found that they could talk freely about anything, and often forgot that this woman was more than twice her age. Claudette served up a generous helping of steak, stew peas, rice, boiled cabbage and carrots, then sat opposite Marion, smiling, occasionally asking if the food was all right, telling her that she was still a growing girl. Marion laughed, assuring her that the food was fine — she just wasn't used to eating so much at one sitting. Afterwards, Claudette offered her home-made strawberry and kiwi cheesecake. Even though Marion was full, she could not refuse.

By ten o'clock in the evening Gerard had still not arrived home, and Marion was beginning to feel drowsy. She explained to Claudette that it was her time of the month and she had to go up to the bathroom. Claudette smiled — those days were now gone for her, she told Marion, and good riddance to them. Anyway, she went on, she was feeling pretty tired and would be heading for bed any minute. Used to Marion waiting for Gerard in his room, she wished her good-night and left her to her own devices.

Gerard's room was just like him. Immaculate. Yet another ego trip. It was decorated completely in black and white, with a mirrored wardrobe covering an entire wall. As if that wasn't enough, there was a mirror above the black ash dresser and another smaller one on his bedside table. His expensive aftershaves and hair-care products adorned the dresser.

Unable to help herself, Marion began to snoop, not really knowing what she was looking for. She opened the top drawer of the dresser, his sock drawer. She knew because she had organised it that way three months previously. Her fingers ran over the paired bunches. She knew several of them were silk, his favourite fabric. Tucked underneath was a small box of condoms, which she picked up, opened, counted and then replaced.

The next drawer, his underwear drawer, held no surprises. The bottom drawer however was heaped with junk. She gently pulled it on to the carpet and sat cross-legged in front of it. She didn't feel guilty about going through his things. If they were to reveal any secrets to her, she had a right to know.

Neither did she know what she expected to find. Left-over underwear perhaps, love letters, photographs . . .

Marion removed postcards, which she quickly read before putting them aside. Nothing. There were some old copies of a body-building magazine called *Work It*, pencils, batteries, receipts, guarantees, birthday cards, an address book (which she placed on her lap to browse through later), stubs of concert tickets — these interested her. They were for Aaron Hall's and R. Kelly's concerts, to both of which she had wanted to go. Gerard had known this — she had pleaded with him to take her — and yet he had never mentioned going. Marion screwed up her lips to stop herself from making a noise and attracting the attention of Claudette, and dropped the tickets by her side. Disgruntled, she continued her rummage with greater determination. There were passport-size photographs of Gerard on his own. He was smiling in only one of them, and one of the four was missing. Marion was tempted to take one of them, but she forced herself to put them back.

Her eyes scanned the remains of the drawer. Screws, envelopes, bits of broken jewellery, cassettes that looked as though they would never play again, half-melted candles — and a Colorama photograph envelope. Her hand reached for it. Dismissing any doubts about invading his privacy she opened it up and slid the prints into the palm of her hand.

Girls, girls, girls. Here was one in her underwear sprawled out on his bed. And another in a bikini sitting by the side of a jacuzzi. Here was Gerard with his arm around another.

Marion flicked through the photos one after the other, her mouth opening wider with each one. Who *were* all these women? Okay, so the pictures didn't look all that recent, and they had been at the bottom of his drawer covered in all his other rubbish, but if this sort of behaviour was Gerard's thing there was bound to be someone else keeping his bed warm nowadays.

She threw everything back into the drawer and slid it back into its slot. She stood up, the address book still in her hand, and glanced back at his dresser. There was another photo envelope, propped up against a bottle of aftershave.

A more recent Gerard, with two young girls at some kind of

event. There were several of these, all innocent enough, until Marion came across one of a smiling Pamela, at the same event, and the back view of Gerard's head.

Her heart sank. She walked back to the bed and slumped down, the offending photo still in her hand. She felt like running, screaming, yelling, ranting, throwing something, breaking something. She wanted to confront someone. Gerard would be home soon. Then she would have someone to confront. Then she would get an explanation.

Marion's full belly and the heat of the night were making her drowsy. She switched on Gerard's stereo and put a tape in, then kicked off her shoes and stretched out on his black and white duvet. Her mind was turning somersaults, but the mellow soul tune soon had her drifting into a light sleep.

The girl clung to his arm. Dizzy with alcohol, she leaned her weight on his strong shoulders. "You sure this is all right?"

"Debs, I told you, mum sleeps like a log." Gerard eased the front door open and stepped aside to let her into the house.

"It is after midnight, y'know," she informed him.

"Since when you start worrying about how late it is?" Holding the latch, Gerard closed the door silently. The hallway was dark and he made no attempt to put the light on. He took Debbie's hand and strode stealthily towards the stairs. With a finger to his lips, he nodded in the direction of his mother's room. Debbie squeezed his hand to show that she understood. They crept up the stairs towards his bedroom at the end of the landing. He flicked the light, bathing the area outside the room in a warm glow, stepped in, and froze as he noticed the figure asleep on his bed. "What the . . . ?" His arm flew up to hold Debbie back.

"What's wrong with you?" she hissed. "You almost had my eye out!" She tried to crane her neck to see what had stopped their progress. She was in no mood for games, she was feeling good — and when she felt this good there was only one thing she wanted to do.

"Hold on a minute." Gerard tried to pull the door back, but Marion had already started to wake up and Debbie had seen her.

Marion heard the voices and slowly came out of her sleep. At first she couldn't remember where she was. Then, seeing Gerard standing in his doorway, it all came back. She saw the girl over his shoulder and recognised her from the pictures. Her brain began to function again.

"Marion, what you doing here?" Gerard asked, trying in vain to keep Debbie out of sight, but she struggled past him.

"Who's she?" she squealed.

"Just keep quiet!" He grabbed hold of her arm to keep her from going further into the room.

Marion blinked the sleep out of her eyes and swung herself off the bed. "I could ask you the same thing," she said to Gerard. "Who's *she*?"

Gerard looked at the ceiling. "A friend."

"Who you calling a friend?" Debbie exploded. "You screw all your friends, do ya?"

"*What?*" Marion's eyes flared. She wasn't sure she had heard right. Was this *child* telling her she was screwing her fiancé? Who the hell did she think she was?

Debbie wasn't waiting for Gerard to make any excuses. "I wanna know who she is, Gerard. Is she another one of your girlfriends?" She faced him with her hands on hips, her large earrings jangling.

Marion stood her ground. "His fiancé," she answered for him.

Despite the increasing noise level Gerard seemed not to know how to deal with this situation. He had been standing stock still, like he was trying to blend into the wall. Now his eyebrows shot up and his mouth dropped open, but still he seemed to have been struck dumb.

"Gerard ain't marrying no one." Debbie laughed in Marion's face. She had an earring in her nose which Marion desperately wanted to rip out.

"Well, he would tell you that, wouldn't he? He's got good taste."

"What did you have to do, get pregnant?" Debbie smirked.

Marion flinched, catching her breath. "I don't have to stoop that low to get a man," she spat back, glancing uneasily at Gerard, who still seemed too shocked to intervene.

"Only to keep him, eh?" Debbie cut her eye after Marion.

"Bitch!"

"Don't call me no bitch, right? 'Cause if anyone's a dog in here it's you." She pointed a gold fingernail at Marion.

Marion dived towards her, her hands stretching like claws ready to scratch her eyes out. Gerard suddenly came back to life and stepped between them, so surprised that Marion was actually initiating a fight that he snapped out of his stupor.

"Do something, Gerard," Debbie whined, fending off Marion's grasping hands. "Tell this mad woman where to go."

"Stop the noise, you'll wake my mum," he hissed under his

breath.

Marion stopped her attempts to get at the girl. "Is that all you care about?" She crossed her arms in front of her heaving chest. "Just get rid of her. I want to talk to you alone."

"If anyone's leaving, it's you," Debbie said confidently, still ready to fight.

Gerard had heard enough. "Debs! Jus' stop, all right? I'll give you cab fare home," he said.

"You're throwing me out?" She turned to face him, a look of disbelief in her eyes.

"I'll call you in the morning." His voice mellowed as he tried to appease her.

Debbie's shock was replaced by anger. "Don't bother. I don't want to hear from your sorry arse again. I'm not that desperate." She threw Marion a look full of scorn, but underneath it Marion thought she saw a hint of pity in her eyes.

Debbie ran down the stairs. The front door slammed as she exited, no longer caring whom she disturbed. Gerard closed the bedroom door. He looked at Marion, who sat back on the edge of the bed. Her eyes were downcast, and she was close to tears.

She looked up at him. "How could you, Gerard? And with someone like that," she sniffed.

"I needed a break." Gerard shrugged. He was thinking about how to get this over with once and for all. He didn't need this kind of business going down in his mother's house.

"Couldn't you have talked to me about it?"

He looked at her as if she'd asked a ridiculous question. "Of course not. I knew how you'd react." He crossed to the bed and sat on the crumpled sheets beside her, his elbows rested on his knees, fingers clasped.

"How long have you been seeing her?" Marion asked, looking across at his solemn face.

"Not long. A few weeks, on and off."

Marion sniffed, fighting back the tears. "Do you want us to finish?" It was the last thing she wanted to say, but it was the question she had come to ask.

"Honestly. I think it's for the best. I don't want to hurt you." He forced an earnest tone into his voice. "We're just not right for each other, you know what I mean?"

"It feels right to me." As the words left her mouth she realised she was lying too. It had never felt as wrong as it did right now. Her head felt heavy again, and her eyes began to swim a little, she couldn't focus.

"But not to me. This is just too one-sided. I tried, but you're choking me. You hang around me all the time. I want to be my own man again."

His words stung. The threatening tears finally arrived and she sobbed, her body shaking with emotion. "I . . . I'll change," she promised, her dignity taking a leave of absence.

"You see what I mean? You just caught me sneaking another woman into my bedroom at night, an' you still want me. Is that normal? Aren't you angry?"

Marion felt a mix of emotions, but wasn't sure whether anger was among them. "I can't be angry with you. I love you." She touched his arm, an unconscious attempt to seek comfort.

Gerard backed away from her fingers, as though she was conducting electricity. Suddenly he couldn't believe this was the confident woman he had met just over a year ago. "It's over. I'm sorry, but that's life. Come on, put your shoes on and get your things. I'll give you a lift home."

Marion burst into fresh sobs.

Gerard looked at her in disgust. "You're only making this worse for yourself. Stop it, Marion." He grabbed hold of her arm, and she was dragged reluctantly to her feet.

She couldn't control her actions. She threw her arms around his neck, clinging to him in desperation. A voice inside her screamed out that she was losing all her dignity, making herself look a complete fool, but she couldn't help herself. She could feel herself doing these things, but it was as if it wasn't her. It was as though she were fighting for her life, trying to hold on to the only person that meant something to her. She was begging him to love her, and though she wanted to stop, she couldn't.

He'd finished with her, and she hadn't yet told him she was pregnant.

"Don't do this, Gerard. I want us to get married and have our baby."

He pushed her away roughly. "What baby? I don't want those things yet, and when I do it won't be with you. You're bloody obsessed."

GERARD

Women! I can't even come home to my own bedroom without finding one waiting for me now.

I was looking forward to a piece ah Debbie that night, man. The girl couldn't wait to get my clothes off. Instead I find that stupid bitch

Marion — on my bed!

What did she expect? That I would welcome her with open arms? Can't she take a hint, man? I ain't called the girl in weeks an' she still run me down.

She don't own me. An' I don't like women telling people they're my fiancé when they know damn well they ain't. I don't want my reputation soiled. The girl's got a screw loose. She had to go, man. This is what happens when you stay too long with one woman. They start getting ideas.

13. OH NO, IT'S YOU AGAIN

It was seven o'clock by the time Joan pulled up outside her house. She lifted Shereen out of the car and carried her towards the house. She didn't want to wake her just yet; she knew she would only be miserable until she was settled again.

She was fumbling in her handbag for her door keys, Shereen asleep and balanced on one arm, when she heard heavy footsteps coming up the path behind her. She spun around. The figure she saw caused her to freeze on the spot.

Martin Baker, Shereen's father, stopped less than three feet away from her. He was as tall as his brother, and they had the same boyishly handsome face, but Martin's was two shades lighter. He had sleepy eyes; Joan had always called them "come to bed eyes". Now she thought they looked as though he'd had too much to drink. His hands were shoved deep into the pockets of the grey trousers he wore. The navy blue blazer and white shirt did nothing to hide the fact that he had lost a lot of weight.

He stood there, a tentative smile on his face, like he was waiting for her to greet him.

Shereen was getting weighty. Joan came out of her shock and found her keys. She turned to the front door without saying a word, opened it and stepped in. Martin took this as an invitation and followed. Joan turned around as he reached the door and glared at him.

"What do you want?" she asked acidly, dark eyes flashing from oval slits.

Martin looked at her earnestly. "I . . ." He paused. "Can I come in?"

"What for?"

"I came to see you . . . and Shereen." His eyes flicked over the child still sleeping on Joan's shoulder.

"I don't think we need to see you, Martin."

She started to close the door, but he put a hand up and stopped it with his palm. "I'm here for my child, I'm not here to interfere. I just want to see my daughter."

"Couldn't you have called first?"

"I did try," he said. "You changed your number, innit? I called your mum an' all I got was verbal abuse."

"You called my mum?"

"Yeah, an' I wish I hadn't. She's still got a whiplash tongue on her."

Joan smiled inwardly as she imagined her mum cussing Martin. But she didn't want to stand on the doorstep discussing her business for everyone to hear. "I suppose you'd better come in," she said with a sigh. She walked in and Martin followed, closing the door behind him. "Go through to the living room," she instructed. "I'll be down in a minute."

She dropped her handbag at the bottom of the stairs and ascended. She placed Shereen on her bed in her pretty pink bedroom. As she removed the child's sandals, she wondered why Martin had suddenly appeared. He knew that she and Colin had been getting it on. It had never bothered him, according to Colin. Perhaps he now also knew that Colin was getting married to the pregnant cow.

She went back downstairs. She picked up her handbag and removed her cigarettes, shaking one free as she entered the living room. For some reason she was feeling nervous. She couldn't believe it. She had known this man for seven years — minus the two that she hadn't seen him — what on earth was there to be nervous about? Her palms were slick with perspiration as she bent down for the table-lighter. It was shaped like a baseball cap and looked tacky and out of place compared to her other ornaments, but Colin had bought it for her in Blackpool and it reminded her of the good times.

"You look like you're doing all right," Martin said, looking around the room.

"Not as well as I could be. We just about get by."

She leant back in the armchair and crossed her legs. She was sure Martin hadn't turned up just for a chat. After not communicating for two years, he had a lot of bottle to turn up on her doorstep at all.

"So?" she said impatiently.

"How's Sherry?"

"Our daughter is fine. She started school a few months ago."

"Yeah!" He grinned proudly. "Does she like it?"

Joan blew a stream of smoke into the air. "Yeah, she does. They told me she's one of the brightest kids there."

"That's my girl."

Joan gave him a look of contempt. "So — you've come to see her?"

Martin nodded. "And to make arrangements to start giving you both some money."

Joan pulled the ashtray towards her and tipped ash into it. "And what do you want in return?"

"Just to see my daughter when I can. I've never set out to hurt either of you," he said frankly. "I'm trying to make amends."

"Why now, all of a sudden?"

He shrugged. "I have to face up to my responsibility some time," he said, toying with a large gold and onyx ring on his finger. "I've been out of work for a year and I didn't want to make promises I couldn't keep." He chuckled nervously. "I kept expecting a letter from the CSA any day." He smiled at Joan, but she didn't return it and the smile dropped like a stone. "I started a new job with British Telecom last month. I can afford to be a father to Shereen now." He said it as though he expected Joan to be proud of him.

"You don't buy love, Martin," she told him, unimpressed by his feeble show of responsibility. "I'm sure your daughter would have been happy to see you even if you'd turned up in rags. You're still her father, with or without money."

He met her eyes briefly before guilt gripped his insides and he dropped his gaze to the carpet. "I've got my pride, Joan. I couldn't come back empty-handed." He stood up suddenly and pulled his wallet from his jacket pocket. Removing three notes he walked over to her and handed her the money.

Joan took the notes from his outstretched hand. Sixty pounds. She felt like throwing it back in his face. But why should she? Money is money after all.

"I'm sorry it's not more, but I owe more than I earn. I'll give you what I can. Tell Shereen I called, yeah? I'll be in touch."

He dragged his feet into the hallway. Joan stood up and followed him out, fighting an uncontrollable urge to slap him for the last two years absence. She wondered if this small donation was the real reason he had come.

"Aren't you going to ask for my new number? I wouldn't want you just turning up again, I might be . . . *engaged*." She made sure he got the meaning by the tone of her voice.

"I s'pose I better." He turned back towards her.

Joan went back into the living room and scribbled her number on a Post-It note. She took it back out to Martin. He glanced at it before folding it and slipping it into his inside pocket.

"I'll be in touch, then," he said again. He didn't seem inclined to say any more. He leant down and kissed her awkwardly on the cheek. Joan visibly tensed and he hurriedly retreated. She closed the door behind him and strolled back towards the kitchen.

Many times she had imagined what it would be like if he reappeared, but she hadn't expected anything like this. It was curiously disappointing. He hadn't asked her about her love life. He hadn't tried to seduce her, so that she could reject him. He hadn't applied for custody of his daughter. All he seemed to want to do was see Shereen occasionally.

After getting herself that cold drink, she decided to call Marion. She had to tell someone. She lit another cigarette as she dialled. The phone rang and rang. Marion wasn't in. So she called Pamela instead. Pamela would cheer her up. For some reason she suddenly felt like the most undesirable woman alive.

Pamela's answerphone clicked on and Joan listened to her friend's husky voice telling her she wasn't in. Joan knew how much Pamela hated people not leaving a message, so she waited for the bleep. "Hi Pam, it's Joan . . ."

There was a whirring click and the line opened up. "J! How you doing, girl?"

"Who you trying to avoid now?" Joan asked.

"I was just being lazy," honestly. "So, what's going on?"

"If I told you that Martin was just here, would that give you a clue?"

"You lie!" Pamela said.

"No. He reckons he came to see Shereen."

"And?"

"He gave me money."

"How much?"

"Sixty pounds."

"Is that all, after . . . how long is it?"

"Two years," Joan informed her. "It's not what we deserve, but it's a start. He says he's going to give us money regular."

"So, what did Shereen do?"

"She was sleeping, didn't even see him."

"What a shame. You gonna tell her?"

"I don't know. I don't wanna get her hopes up in case he doesn't come again."

"You know your daughter better than anyone else, so it's up to you. How do you feel about seeing him?"

"I'm still in shock, Pam. I didn't know what to say or do. He told me he'd called my mum to try and get my new number. She cussed him out — you know what my mum's like, innit?" Joan laughed.

Pamela joined her. "Good, the bastard. Some of 'em need a good cussing. Like Shaun the other day, getting on my case about when am I gonna throw James out."

"Are you?"

"Eventually, in my own time. I can't go on like this for much longer, though. I can't take the hassle. I'm losing sleep. I'm sure I saw a grey hair this morning."

"Men!"

"Who needs 'em?" Pamela kissed her teeth.

"We do," Joan joked.

"You got that right." They both cracked up. "Listen, girl, I was thinking. Why don't we have a drink up? We haven't had one since last year. We could invite Paul and his mates. Christina and Melanie. It would be a laugh."

"You know, that's just what we need. When?" Joan asked keenly.

"About three weeks, nearer pay day."

"Okay. Let's do it. I'll start making a few phone calls this week. We all pitching in with the food?"

"Yeah. I'll do the curry goat and white rice. Let Maz do the chicken and rice and peas, that leaves you to do simple salads."

"Thank you, Pam. You know I hate cooking, innit?"

"Yes, girl."

"So — you inviting Shaun?"

"D'you think I should?"

"Why not?"

"No, I couldn't. Not if we're having it here. James and Shaun in the same house . . . can you imagine?"

"We'll have it at my house, then. That way you won't have to tell James. Just say you're going out."

"How'd you get to be so devious?" Pamela gave a little laugh.

"You're my teacher." Joan grinned into the phone.

"Hey, I'm not that bad," Pam said with mock innocence.

"Look who you're talking to. This is me. I know about both the men, remember?" Joan laughed. "I also know about you using my house to carry on your sordid affair. So don't come tell me you're 'not that bad'." She mimicked Pamela's voice.

Pamela laughed. "Hold on a minute, J."

Joan could hear a male voice in the background. Then Pamela

106

came back on. "Listen, J. I've gotta go. James just got in and I wanna talk to him before he goes out again. I'll call you during the week, yeah?"

"Yeah, okay. Bye."

Joan decided she still had time to go ahead with her plans for the rest of the night. Martin hadn't totally ruined her evening.

Now, where had she put that bag of weed?

MARTIN

I know what you're thinking — just another absent father. But I have my reasons. A lot of black men couldn't tell you why they left their wife and kids. I know why.

She drove me away. While she was just a clerical assistant everything was fine, then within three years she got two promotions with Icon Press. We never saw each other.

She was always working. She'd leave before I got out of bed, leaving me to take care of Shereen, make her lunch, get her bathed and dressed and then drop her at the minder's before I went to work.

Then she would bring work home with her, as if it wasn't bad enough that she was at work nearly twelve hours a day. There was no room in her life for me any more. I wasn't important. She became this New Woman. Strong, ambitious. Cold. And always too tired for sex.

I know this is gonna seem like a cliché, but I had to find someone to fill the empty space she had left in my life. There was this girl at work. I didn't mean to have an affair. I took her out to lunch to start with. Then we would meet after work for a drink. Then she would invite me round for dinner. We understood each other. It felt good to enjoy myself with a woman again. A woman who was interested in me. She wanted me, made me feel good about myself. After six months of seeing her we decided it was time I made a decision. Things were getting pretty serious, and I'm sure Joan knew all about us, but either she was waiting for me to tell her or she didn't care.

The way I left her was cowardly, I admit it. I couldn't tell her face-to-face, so I just waited until she'd gone to work as usual, took Shereen to the minder's, then went back home, packed and left her a note. I had taken voluntary redundancy from work without telling her, so she couldn't reach me there. I just disappeared from their lives.

It's hard to go back. But I want my daughter to know her father cares.

I know angry women can use their children against their absent fathers, and I never want that to happen to us.

14. I'M GOING FOR MINE

A heavy rain tapped ceaselessly against the windowpane like hundreds of tiny fingers, bringing Marion back to the land of the living.

She had slept only fitfully, the kind of sleep brought on by an exhausted mind. Gerard had driven her home from his house the night before. They'd sat in silence for the entire journey. The only sounds were the traffic and her sniffing and sobbing. He'd opened the front door with his key, then pressed it into her hand, saying he wouldn't be needing it any more. He'd helped her undress, as though he were undressing a child. He'd tucked her in, kissed her forehead, then switched off the lights and left. She'd felt physically and emotionally paralysed. She'd eventually cried herself to sleep.

Now her head felt heavy and her eyes ached. It hurt to open them. The last time she had felt this way was after Jacqueline died. Her sister was only nineteen when sickle cell had claimed her life. Marion had cried for three days before drying up into a state of numbness. Then it had started all over again at the funeral. Marion now felt the same empty, worthless feeling. What was the point of life? What did she have left to live for?

She ran her hand across her flat tummy. She did have something to live for. Gerard's baby was growing inside her. Only five weeks old now, and its father didn't even know. He wouldn't want it even if he did. This thought brought fresh tears, but it hurt to cry and she forced herself to stop. She turned over on to her stomach and pulled the cover over her head. What had she done? She would now have to face the world as another single black mother, just like her own mother had done. Once, she had promised herself she wouldn't let her children go through that — struggle, stress, stepfathers . . .

The phone rang and startled her. She snatched up the receiver. "Hello?" she answered breathily, expectantly, the vague notion that it might be Gerard filling her with anticipation.

It was Joan.

"Maz? Did I wake you? Sorry, I just had to talk to someone. I tried to call you last night . . . Maz? What's wrong, babe?"

Joan could hear nothing but anguished cries on the other end of the line. Her voice became concerned as she immediately forgot her own problems. "It's Gerard, ain't it?"

"J, I don't know what to do." Marion hitched and coughed.

"I'm coming over, all right? Right now."

"But Shereen . . . ?"

"She's at a neighbour's. School holidays she's round there most of the time. See you shortly."

The connection went dead as Joan hung up. Marion felt like such a fool.

Forty-five minutes later the doorbell rang and Marion dragged her feet to the front door.

Joan dropped her handbag and shook raindrops from her jacket. She hugged Marion's tiny frame to her as they stood in the hallway. "You don't even have to tell me what happened," she said. "That bastard wasn't good enough for you anyway."

Marion made a dry clicking sound in her throat, as though she were trying to swallow something that didn't want to go down.

"I bet you haven't even had a hot drink yet," Joan said, walking her back to the living room. "Come and sit down and I'll get us both a cup." She made sure Marion was comfortable on the sofa before she went into the kitchen.

She took off her damp jacket and put the kettle on. "What was it, then? Another woman? He just couldn't keep himself still. What did I tell you about them sweetboys?" she yelled back to Marion.

Marion slumped back into the sofa, not seeing, hardly hearing. Her head throbbed and she wanted to curl up into a ball.

Joan's voice continued in the background: "I knew you'd get hurt, but you can't say anything to a woman in love. I know. My mum warned me when I told her I was moving in with Martin, but I was in love. He promised me marriage, and I went ahead and had his baby. Now where is he?" She came back into the living room with two steaming cups of coffee and put Marion's mug on the coffee table. "That'll wake you up a bit." Then she sat next to her friend on the sofa. "So — talk to me."

Marion, dressed only in an oversized T-shirt and panties, looked at Joan with red, swollen eyes. Joan shook her head in pity. She thought that her friend looked like a mirror image of herself after Martin had walked out on her. She put her arm around Marion's shoulders.

"It's over. He told me," Marion said. "I went round to see him. To find out where I stood. I was going to tell him about the baby, I nearly did too . . ."

"What baby?" Joan interrupted.

"That's exactly what *he* said. Then he said he wouldn't want me to have his kids anyway. Joan, he had a girl with him . . ." Tears threatened again with the memory. "She laughed at me when I said I was his fiancée. She didn't even *know* about me."

Joan's face registered incredulity. "Hold on a minute." She raised a hand. "Rewind. You're pregnant?"

Marion moistened her lips and reached for the chain she wore around her neck. Her sister's. She toyed with the small gold key on the end of it. "Yeah. Five weeks. And he still doesn't know."

"Boy, Marion, when you keep a secret you keep it good. I don't believe that guy! The bastard was dipping elsewhere and you were pinning your hopes on marriage." Joan shook her head again and handed Marion her coffee.

"There's something else," Marion said quietly.

Joan studied her face curiously.

"I think he might be seeing Pamela too."

Joan smiled. "Get outta here! Our Pamela?"

"I saw photographs of them together." Marion looked up at Joan with a dead pain in her eyes.

"What do you mean 'together'? Kissing? Naked? Holding hands? What?"

"They looked as though they were just talking. It was at that hair and beauty thing. Pamela told me she went with James. She never mentioned seeing Gerard there . . ."

Joan shook her head, stifling a laugh. "Pam *did* go with James. She told me all about it," she explained. "She bumped into Gerard with two girls there. Come on, Marion. You know how Pamela hates Gerard. What, did you think she was making it up? She wouldn't do that to you."

"But she was always trying to get me to leave him. And why didn't she tell me she saw him there?"

"Marion . . . Maz," Joan comforted, "she didn't tell you because she didn't want to upset you. She wanted you to break up with him for your own good, not so that she could have him."

Marion realised that what Joan was saying was true. "I'm sorry," she said, "I haven't been thinking straight. Tell me how stupid I am."

"No, it wasn't your fault." Joan squeezed her shoulders. "Pam will probably die laughing when I tell her." Her tone became more serious. "But why did you let yourself get pregnant?"

Marion's eyes told her what she had already guessed, and she answered her own question. "You hoped it would save your relationship."

"Now tell me how stupid I am." Marion gulped the warm coffee; it felt good going down.

"So you're gonna have an abortion?"

"No!" Marion's answer was sharp, direct. She was hurt that Joan would automatically expect her to get rid of her baby.

Joan's mouthed dropped open and she stared at her friend in

disbelief. "What?"

"I'm keeping it. It's my baby too. I got pregnant deliberately, how could I just kill it?"

"You know I'll be here for you." Joan squeezed Marion's hand. She didn't agree with most things Marion did, but when you can't change a friend's mind you support them the best you can. "Does your mum know?"

"No. She'll probably kill me. I'll tell her over the phone, it'll be safer. Besides, I'm in no mood to go trekking up to Birmingham."

"Maybe you should go an' visit for a while. You could get away from things. You wouldn't accidentally bump into Gerard." Joan raised her eyebrows meaningfully on the word "accidentally".

"I wouldn't do that, Joan. But you're right — I should go away for a while. I couldn't face work now anyway."

"You're too naive for your own good, you know that? Right now I feel like hugging you and slapping you at the same time."

Marion laughed, surprising herself.

"That's better." Joan smiled. "I suppose you'd better call your mum."

"No, not yet. I've got some things I want to clear up first, bills to pay, y'know. Thanks, Joan. I don't know what I'd have done if you hadn't come round. I haven't cried so much since Jackie . . . y'know."

"Yeah." Joan gave her hand another squeeze. "But believe me, men aren't worth it. D'you think he's losing sleep over this? I doubt it. Especially as he's got this other woman."

"Girl," Marion corrected. "And she blew him out anyway. I swear she was about nineteen. I could've killed her."

"Remember, she didn't know about you either. It's him you should have killed."

Marion had called the library on Monday morning and taken the rest of the week off. She'd told them she had a family crisis, too personal to go into. It was true, in a sense, so she hadn't really lied.

It was now Wednesday evening. She lay in bed, the sheets twisted around her body, staring at the Artex ceiling, but not seeing. Jodeci played on the cassette player on her bedside table. An empty packet of headache pills lay next to the machine, along with three mugs with varying amounts of coffee in them. Discarded clothes, newspapers and magazines lay scattered on the floor or half hanging off the bed.

She'd tried to begin working on the assignment from Joan, but writing about men wasn't easy when you were trying to recover from a break-up. She'd tried to write to Gerard. She knew the message she wanted to send him should have been angry, remonstrative, but all she had managed to produce was a series of pleading letters. Then it was poetry, reminding him of how it had been in the beginning. None of her attempts had got further than the waste bin.

She took a couple more pills and vomited them back up a few minutes later. She knew it was morning sickness, but nobody had prepared her for feeling so wretched.

The phone rang. She let it ring several times before reaching over and picking it up.

"I'm still waiting for that call," a distinctive male voice told her.

"Paul?" Her voice was hoarse, sleepy.

"Yeah — Paul. You were supposed to call me, remember?"

She remembered. She had meant to call Paul ever since their last meeting, but other things had crowded her brain. "Yes, but . . ."

"No buts, Marion. What's happening? This man got you under manners?" he joked.

What man? she thought glumly. "No, Paul. In fact, we . . ." she coughed, "err . . . broke up." She had to force out the words.

"Sorry, babes."

She heard the smile in his voice, and imagined him gloating. "I haven't called anyone in a while."

"You sound terrible. Want some company?"

"I don't know, Paul. I wouldn't be very good company." She didn't know if she could face another man right now. There was too much to think about. but then again she needed a break from thinking, especially about Gerard . . .

"But *I* would. I could be there in half an hour."

Marion sunk back into her pillow and made up her mind. "Okay. But make it an hour."

"Yeah? I can come up?" he asked, somewhat surprised.

"Yes," she gave in.

"Want me to bring anything?"

"A bottle of wine would be nice."

"You got it. I'll see you later then." Paul spoke jubilantly.

"Bye."

She hung up and looked around the room. The whole flat was a mess. She couldn't let Paul see the place like this.

As she set to work tidying hurriedly, she caught sight of herself in the dresser mirror and couldn't believe what a wreck she looked. Puffy bags under her shrunken eyes, dry skin and chapped lips. She went into the bathroom and turned on the cold tap, splashing her face with icy water. Then she ran a bath, took off her bra and panties and stepped into the water. She scrubbed her body, feeling it tingle with life as she rubbed the soap over her still flat tummy. When she'd got out she covered her body in Body Shop musk oil.

Going back into the bedroom she found a purple satin french knicker set, that Gerard had bought her on one of their shopping trips, and put it on. She massaged Luster's Pink Oil into her hair and tied it back into a ponytail. She sat on the white stool in front of her white dressing table, and selected her favourite lipstick. Gerard hated the scarlet red. He said it made her look like a whore. Marion, though, thought it was sexy, and put it on. She smiled at her new defiant spirit, and applied eyeliner.

She put on her dressing gown and went to the living room, where she brought the large mirror out from behind the sofa where it had been hiding for a week and hung it back on the wall. She was practising seducing pouts in front of the glass when the intercom rang.

Here he was. Paul. She took the offered bottle from him and placed it gently on the floor. He took her into his arms as she closed the door behind him, and she buried her head in his neck and squeezed him back. He kissed her tentatively on the lips. She returned his kiss, surprising herself. So he kissed her just a little harder, plunging his tongue between her lips.

His hands held her in the centre of her back, drawing her into his embrace. Marion felt her body responding, her panties getting wet, as his sense of urgency rubbed off on her. Backing up against the passage wall, she let him open her dressing gown and grind his hips against hers. Then he began to travel down her body, kissing her breasts, sucking her nipples, taking her flesh between his teeth, exciting her further. He gripped her bottom, pulling her so close that there was no air between them.

Marion felt only the slightest pang of guilt as she led him into her bedroom, teasing him with her body, her lips, her eyes. She ran her fingers over his shaved head. He didn't need any encouragement; he was already hers. Neither of them said a word as he removed the skimpy lingerie she wore and showered her body with kisses and love bites. She totally succumbed to Paul's lovemaking. His jacket had fallen on the floor by the front door. His T-shirt was at the bedroom door, his shoes at the bottom of the bed, and now his trousers were being worked slowly down his hips.

His breathing was coming hard and fast as he moved her hand to his strong erection. He was as hard as the head of a hammer, hot and thrusting. She guided him, wanting him inside her body, needing him to come inside her, then gasped as she took the full length of him. Her brown legs wrapped themselves around his buttocks. He kissed her cheeks and neck more excitedly and drove his hips faster against her as they approached their climax.

They came together, his muscular body tensing as it shook with the sexual explosion. She clung to his broad shoulders, her nails leaving indentations in his back.

"Girl, what did you do to me?" He rolled off her, breathlessly, on to his back.

Marion turned over and leant on one elbow, her other hand resting on his chest. She studied his features. His jaw reminded her of Gerard's, strong and chiselled, but there the similarity ended. His skin was dark, like chocolate, and shiny with perspiration. She ran her fingers through the curly hairs on his chest. Gerard's chest was smooth, hardly a hair on it. They were so different. Light and dark, tall and short, headstrong and easygoing. They would make very different babies . . . Marion pushed that thought to the back of her mind. She had loved Paul once, and she could again — for her baby's sake.

PAUL

You know, I've known Marion a good two years now — and if anybody did tell me dat one day she would seduce me, I would have put money on it never happening. Marion's not that type. But sometimes it's good for a man to be in the right place at the right time. When a woman jus' break up with her man, the next man moves in and dries up all the tears.

From her performance tonight I feel sure Marion wants me back.

Like that night at the club. I'm no mind-reader, but I know she was feeling the feeling.

If we're gonna try this thing again, I would have liked to go slower. Give her time to get over her man. Give me time to get to know her all over again.

But I guess it's all out of my hands now.

15. WINE, WINE, WINE

Carnival bank holiday was here again, and this year it promised to be one of the best. Thirty years old, the carnival was now the biggest street event in Europe, and literally millions of people were flocking to the few streets in West London for the biggest alldayer of the year.

As usual the forecast had been for rain, but so far the clouds were staying scattered and, despite the cold breeze, the sun looked like it was here to stay.

Joan, Pamela, and her old schoolfriend Rebecca (Marion had decided that, in her condition, carnival wasn't for her this year) sat in the Ford Fiesta in a typical carnival traffic jam. Carloads of ravers were on their way to the festivities. On the pavements, posses of people were following each other in an expectant procession. The sound of revellers could already be heard from the Harrow Road. Soca music, whistles and foghorns blasted their welcome.

Half a million men in one place! Pure manhunt ah gwaning.

Rebecca drove. With her Brownstone cropped hair, dyed cinnamon for effect, and her tight, slim body enclosed in a simple grey track suit bottom and a clinging white bodysuit, she cast a striking figure. Pamela wore a baggy white T-shirt over track suit bottoms, and Joan had opted for a tight-fitting lycra shorts catsuit.

"Hey, Ladies! Any room in your car for me?" The young man spoke with an American accent, and his flashing white teeth immediately drew the girls' attention. They looked with amazement at the vision by their car. He was beautiful from head to toe, dressed in navy and white Fila shorts and jacket. His hair was waved high at the front and gelled back into waves at the back and sides. His fair skin was smooth and spotless. A wicked looking specimen.

"Oh yes, baby," Rebecca replied, winding her window all the way down. "Just park yourself right here on my lap."

The man grinned. "See you there, ladies. I love you all," and he blew them an exaggerated film-star kiss before jogging back to his friends on the pavement.

The girls erupted into screams as they caught a glimpse of the other guys, craning their necks to get a look. "Oh God, they're gorgeous," Joan gasped, leaning over Rebecca to ogle them.

"Follow them, Bec." Pamela shoved the back of the driver's seat as if it would make the traffic disappear. "Did you see his eyes? Oooh." She bounced up and down in the back seat.

Rebecca laughed. "How can I follow them when I can't even move forward?"

Joan watched the men cruise out of their lives. "We are definitely going to enjoy this carnival."

Pamela caught the eye of a tall, dark-skinned brother who nearly walked into a lamppost with distraction. "Men — men everywhere," she sang to the tune of "Trailer Load Ah Girls". "From London, Canada and the USA. Men, men everywhere. I wanna give you one, so bring your body right here."

"Bwoy! I jus' caught a glimpse of that guy's chest," Joan said, half-hanging out of the window, a bottle of Cisco in one hand. "Yaow, big chest!" she yelled across the street.

Several heads turned, including his, and he flung his jacket open, revealing that he had nothing but his jeans on under it.

The girls burst into catcalls as the traffic started moving again. "I woulda loved to rub my hands all over that body," Joan cooed.

"Yeah, well, you'd have had to race me for it," Pamela teased.

It took them ten minutes driving around the back streets of Kensal Rise to find a parking space. They finally slotted the car into a gap just vacated, and walked the three quarters of a mile back to the centre of activity. Whistles at the ready, bottles of Cisco grasped in their hands, mini rucksacks strapped to their chests, the three girls merged into the throbbing crowd that was milling around Ladbroke Grove.

With eyes like a radar, Pamela was homing in on every good-looking male they came across, which began to be so many that eventually she gave up looking in four directions at once and concentrated on looking ahead.

As soon as they hit Ladbroke Grove station the movement came to a congested stop. A float carrying gaily dressed dancers was trying to drive down the road while crowds of people were trying to get around, backwards and forwards. The impatience of the younger, fitter party-goers forcing their way through by whatever means necessary was causing children and the elderly to be squashed in between. Tempers were fraying. Dragging their belongings with them, the girls emerged on the other side of the commotion and forged ahead, regaining their composure.

They followed the rhythm of a drum n' bass track and headed east. This is what they had come for — to rave. They blended into the crowd, jumping to the beat. Whereas there had been a slight chill in the air before, the girls were now feeling the heat of all the bodies around them: twisting bodies, dipping bodies, pumping bodies, gyrating bodies, jumping, dancing, pushing, groping. There was so much going on that if you stopped to think about it, it would make you dizzy. The heady smells of Caribbean chicken, patties, sugar cane, coconut, and the smoke from charcoal barbecues filled the spirited air.

Having finished the drinks they had brought with them, Pamela queued up to purchase some more. Handing over the bottles of Thunderbird wine from behind his wooden blockade, the Asian storekeeper grinned. "All for you?"

"Naw, man. It's for me and my sisters," Pamela replied with an air of street tough.

"You very pretty. Come back later. You teach me dance, yes?" he leered, baring yellow teeth.

Pamela shook her head, laughing. "Naw, mate. You stay there." She giggled to her mates, making fun of the man who hadn't quite got the joke.

Joan placed a hand on her shoulder. "Pulling crusty Indian geezers now, Pam?" she jibed.

"That ain't funny. Don't go spoiling my rep," Pamela mock-scolded.

Father MC's "Hit You With a Sixty-Nine" came blasting from the speakers some way up the road. The three girls linked arms in a bid not to lose each other as they rushed towards the heavy bass, whistles to their pouting lips.

By nine o'clock, all the sound systems had packed up and the remaining revellers followed the carnival floats or chilled out by the mobile food stalls. Food and drink was not cheap, but as they say, "when you belly bawling for hungry, if you have the money you pay". The girls bought chicken, a drumstick each, which didn't even touch their hunger. It seemed that people just did not want to go home. The floats were now travelling down the main road on their way out of the route, and yet people were still dancing in the streets, caught in the hypnotism of carnival.

After having countless male members shoved up against their backs all day, the aches and pains began at eleven thirty, and the girls decided to make their way back to the car with the phone numbers they had collected. Pamela had the most numbers, never failing to catch the males' attention and hold it. Rebecca had bumped into old friends, and Joan had bumped into old boyfriends. Taking their numbers had been nothing but a courtesy.

"Bwoy, my legs are gonna be killing me tomorrow," Joan moaned, slowing down her pace now they had left the crowds behind. She was glad Rebecca was driving.

"Naw, it's my back, that's where I can feel it." Pamela placed a hand on her lower back and rubbed with her fingers.

Rebecca groaned. "Can't you feel any pain in your pelvis, all that 'wuk up yuh waist'? Mine feels like it's gonna drop off."

Joan laughed, leaning on Rebecca's shoulder. "God, we mus' be getting old."

"Oh, don't!" Pamela gasped. Only twenty-five, old was the last thing she wanted to feel.

They turned on to a long residential street — and realised they were lost.

"We didn't come this far up." Pamela looked up and down the street. She was positive they had walked too far.

Joan on the other hand felt they were still on the right track. "Yes we did. Don't you remember? I was complaining we'd walked miles," she corrected.

Rebecca cut in. "No, I think she's right, Joan. We've come too far up. Let's walk back a bit."

They turned on their heels and went back the way they had come. Three guys stood on the corner they'd turned. Rebecca recognised them as guys they'd met during the festivities. She made a comment about how they hadn't got their numbers.

As soon as the words were out of her mouth, one of them turned and addressed Pamela, who was lagging behind.

"So, you can't even stop and say hello?"

Pamela stopped, squinted her eyes at him blankly. "Do I know you?"

He raised his eyebrows in surprise. "You don't remember me?"

Pamela looked him up and down. He was quite presentable. Intelligently good-looking, and had a friendly smile. No, she didn't remember him, and she told him so.

Rebecca jogged her friend's memory. "You remember, Pam, when we were dancing at that soul sound system — the one that got shut down 'cause of the fight."

"Yeah." The guy nodded, pleased one of them recognised him. He turned back to Pamela — obviously that was where his interest lay.

Realisation dawned on her heart-shaped face. "Oh yeah. I remember now," she smiled.

He put on an offended look. "Huh! Diss me like that after I told you how good you can dance . . ."

"Sorry." Pamela touched his arm, already going into a natural flirt.

"My name's Gary, by the way," he said.

"Pam." They shook hands.

"So, where you going?" Gary asked, his friends still hanging back.

The shorter of the two was wrapping his arms around himself in a bid to keep warm; the other, a tall fellow in red corduroy, was eyeing Rebecca.

"We're trying to find our car," Joan said, wrapping her cardigan tighter around herself.

"Yeah? So are we. It's around here somewhere."

Rebecca, ever so quick, suggested they look for the vehicles together, then whoever found theirs first could give the others a lift to look for theirs.

"Come on, then. It's cold out here, y'know," said the short guy.

"So, what's your names, then?" the guy in the red corduroy asked.

The girls introduced themselves, and the other two men gave their names as Desmond and Marcellis. Joan fell in love with the name Marcellis. It was so different. She decided to take him under her wing, and as they walked down the road automatically pairing off into couples, she wrapped her arm around his shoulder.

The girls found their car first. The six of them piled into the Fiesta and followed the guys' vague directions. When finally they came to the car nobody moved. They had got into the flow of easy conversation, and nobody seemed to want to end it just yet. And so they chatted for hours in the confines of the Fiesta.

The men appeared to have their heads screwed on. They were all employed in good, professional jobs, and seemed interested in what the women had to say. Joan told them about Marion's writing, and the fact that they were looking for men to interview. The guys jumped at the chance of having their views published. So Joan steered the conversation to sex and relationships. Desmond came over as being very bitter about women, claiming that he had to ask a woman what she wanted all the time. Women, according to him, didn't communicate. Gary, on the other hand, said that women didn't know what they wanted. They said they wanted one thing, and when they got it they still weren't satisfied. Marcellis, the youngest and quietest of the group, said that he enjoyed being single. There were times when being part of a couple was something that he wanted, but he wasn't ready for long-term commitment.

The conversation continued long into the night, the six of them so relaxed — perhaps as a reaction to the day's frantic activity — that they were soon talking as though they were friends of old. It was five o'clock in the morning before everyone decided they would have to go home and get some sleep — they all had work the next day.

They swapped phone numbers, and Pamela suggested that the boys should come to their party.

By the time Rebecca had pulled out into the empty West London streets, Joan's mind was buzzing with ideas for the articles. She had taken Marcellis's number only because he seemed like promising material — plus he had promised to pose nude for her — a picture for her bedroom wall.

If that wasn't worth a phone call, what was?

16. WHEN YOU LOVE SOMEBODY

"Mummy, I'm thirsty." Shereen looked up at her mother with her father's sleepy eyes.

Joan was in no mood to be hassled. "In a minute, Shereen," she said. It was hot, she was tired, and this was the third time the child had asked for a drink in five minutes. They had been shopping for Shereen's school clothes for the new term in September.

"Mummy! Look, Mummy! It's Uncle Colin."

"Where?" Joan asked distractedly.

It was him. Wearing a black track suit and baseball cap. His muscular arms bulged beneath the vest he wore. The girl beside him, with her arm around him, kissed him. Colin smiled sweetly at her.

"Why don't we go and say hello, Mummy?" Shereen whined.

Joan had to think fast for an answer. "We haven't got time love," she said. "Come on." It sounded weak, but Shereen was tuned in enough to her mother's moods not to press the point.

It was very crowded in Lewisham today, as it was most days. They walked down the alleyway commonly known as the Black Market. Here there were shops and market stalls that sold clothes, Jamaican patties and West Indian bread, a black greeting card shop, and a hairdressers.

Joan was seething. She had finally seen Colin's pregnant girlfriend. They were shopping together. Probably choosing paint for the baby's room. Her heart jolted at the thought. That girl was going to have Colin's baby. Joan suddenly felt a deep sense of loss.

She had thought she was over Colin Baker, that nothing he did mattered any more. But that wasn't true.

Joan unlocked the car door, still in a daze. Shereen clambered into the back while Joan unlocked the boot and slung the bags of shopping in. She couldn't get Colin out of her mind. She swung the car around and headed towards Wandsworth. Shereen would be spending the rest of the weekend with her grandmother.

"Hi, Mum." Joan kissed her mother on one of her soft cheeks.

"You awright? You look a bit peaked."

"Yeah, I'm fine." Joan lied.

They entered the house. Joan took Shereen's bags into the back bedroom. As she came out she bumped into her daughter running back up the passageway, a handful of jelly beans in each of her little fists.

Grace sat in her favourite armchair, a green velvet recliner with its own built-in cushions. Its position gave her a view of the street and anybody approaching her house, which was why she had reached the front door before they were out of the car. She had picked up her knitting. A beautiful soft beige speckled mohair wool hung from the needles.

"What you making this time, Mum?"

"Somet'ing nice and warm fe de winter. You like it?" Grace held up the side she had nearly completed.

Joan picked up the pattern from the table beside her. "Oh yes, that's nice. Can I borrow it when it's done?"

Grace laughed. "Me len' you anyt'ing, me naw get it back."

Joan regarded her mother with a hurt look. "That's not true, Mum. What about that long black dress?"

"De ongle reason yuh did bring dat back is 'cause yuh hav' nuttin' to fill it wid." Grace laughed heartily, pushing her glasses back up on her nose.

Joan lifted the shopping bag she was holding. "All right, so I didn't inherit your chest."

"You going out tonight?"

"Yeah. Night club."

"I hope seh you meet a nice young man."

Joan thought of Colin. "I'm not looking, Mum."

"Dat is when yuh fine dem."

"Don't start, Mum. I've had it with men."

Her mother gave her a knowing look. "So you seh."

Joan quickly changed the subject. "You heard from Donna lately?"

Her mother huffed. "De laas me hear from your sister, is a pos'cyard she sen' from . . ." She frowned, trying to remember where her younger daughter had gone on holiday.

"Canary Islands," Joan filled in.

"Yes. She nuh call me. She doan even visit her own madda. You hear from her?"

Joan shook her head. "Same as you, Mum — a postcard."

"She t'ink seh she big now she get married, she doan need family no more."

Joan wasn't worried about her sister. As far as she knew, her husband John took care of her as he should. But she was upset that Donna wasn't keeping in touch. Last Christmas she had gone to John's family instead of visiting Grace, and on New Year's Eve she'd turned up on her own.

"Mum, I'm gonna go. Got lots to do."

"Okay, bye then," Grace said without looking up from her work.

"Bye, Shereen. Be good."

"All right, Mum. Bye." Shereen's eyes were fixed on the television.

Joan left thinking how lucky she was to have her family.

So why did she still feel so unfulfilled?

COLIN

I want respect from my woman. You know, I want her to look up at me and feel proud. I want respect for what I do, what I achieve, what I am. Money is only one way of gaining respect. You have to prove that you deserve it. A man who doesn't respect himself can't expect it from others.

Bwoy, did that come from me? I must be getting deep.

You know who should hear me talk like this? Joan.

17. ON THE ROCKS

The cooing of the pigeons strutting outside his bedroom window brought Shaun out of his sleep. He stirred. With his eyes still shut, he became aware of the warm body by his side. He turned over, leaning on one elbow, and gazed down at her.

Pamela looked as innocent as a baby. He had never known another woman to look this good after what they had done the night before. Her black shoulder-length hair half covered her face, and he swept it clear with a single stroke. A quick glance at the alarm clock told him it was time to wake her up. He leaned over and ran his tongue over his lips, wetting them before placing a tender kiss on her neck. Then he ran his tongue down her neck to her shoulder.

Pamela moaned and turned on to her back.

Shaun's eyes travelled down to her full breasts. "Pam," he said softly. She didn't move. He called her name again, this time shaking her gently.

Pamela groaned and threw her arm over her eyes. "No more, Shaun. I'm tired."

Shaun threw his head back and laughed heartily. "I'm not offering you anything. Get up." He gently shoved her again.

"What?" she cried irritably.

"Didn't you tell James you'd be home this afternoon?" he asked with a smirk on his face.

"Shit! What time is it?" She sprang up, her hair falling about her head like a badly fitting wig.

"Three thirty," Shaun informed her, slightly amused.

Pamela flung the covers off. "God, Shaun! Why didn't you wake me?" She jumped naked from the bed.

Shaun leaned back on the headboard, arms folded behind his head. He watched her with a grin as she stalked about the room, grabbing her clothes from the floor.

"I'm sure I've told you this before, Pam — your body is a gift."

"Shaun, don't go getting horny on me now. James is probably already suspicious." She turned to him, not completely unaware of the effect she had on him, and yawned. "Make us a cup of coffee, will you?"

"Is that an order?"

"Damn right." She reached for the door handle and Shaun made as if to get up and go after her. She dashed out of the room, laughing.

Slowly Shaun got out of bed. He could hear the bath water running. She was going back to her man. Or was that her *other* man? The irony of it hit him: Pamela belonged to no one; she did exactly as she pleased, when she pleased. The thought of sharing her angered him, but he had no choice. She had already told him it was share or get nothing, for the time being anyway.

She was too good for James. The wimp. She'd told Shaun she had stopped having sex with James since she had started seeing him again. And he believed her. After all, James couldn't be much of a temptation compared to him.

He ran his hand over his short, neatly cut hair, and wondered if Pamela wanted his company in the bath. He smiled to himself, showing perfect teeth.

Pamela's call from the bathroom brought him back to the

present. "Shaun, where's my coffee?"

"Coming," he called back. Forget the coffee — he would give her something to think about on her way back to James. Soon she would be back with the wimp, but one day she would be Shaun's for ever.

Pamela bounced into the flat. She was in a good mood. The only damper was coming back home to James. She could hear the sound of the television coming from the bedroom, and assumed that was where he was. She dropped her bags gently in the hallway. It wasn't until she reached the living room door that she heard music coming from inside. Puzzled, she opened the door and stopped in her tracks.

James sat on the floor, his legs underneath the coffee table, his back resting against the leather two-seater. He had a drink in his hand, and she could smell the pungent aroma of ganja. It hung in the air like a cloud; he could only just have finished smoking.

His slightly red eyes rose to meet hers. "So, you decide to come home?" he slurred.

"I told you I was coming back this afternoon." She crossed the room to the window and pushed it open.

His half-shut eyes followed her. "I thought you meant lunchtime. I cooked for us." His voice was unusually rough.

"Oh, good. I'm starving." She tried to remain cheery, but James's behaviour worried her.

She made her way quickly to the kitchen, avoiding his eyes.

"You mean Rebecca didn't feed you?"

"Sorry?" she called back.

"You were at Rebecca's, weren't you?" he asked accusingly. He had got up and followed her to the kitchen, moving with a sluggish, apathetic tread. Now he stood in the doorway, barely filling the frame.

She turned to face him. He looked paler than usual. A faint shadow covered his chin and cheeks, as though he hadn't shaved in a couple of days. She'd only been gone for the weekend. "Yes. Look, what's all the aggro about? I'm hungry and tired." she said, forcing toughness into her voice.

"Up all night, were you?" He raised his eyebrows questioningly.

"We were, as a matter of fact." she turned to the pots on the hob, switching the gas on low, "watching videos."

"Why are you lying to me?" he yelled suddenly, startling her.

"About what?" she said, her pretty brown eyes taking him in.

His hand turned into a fist. "Rebecca called last night, asking for you."

Pamela's heart stopped and then started again, beating twice as fast. She pushed past him and stepped into the living room.

He grabbed her arm. "How do you explain that?"

Her heart was in her throat, but she said calmly, "What time did she call?"

"What difference does that make?" he sneered.

"Because I stopped at Marion's first, then got to Rebecca's a bit late. I probably hadn't got there yet."

"You're still lying to me!" His grip on her arm tightened. She was more surprised than frightened. Was this really James?

"What do you want to hear?" Her voice rose again, letting loose her anger. "That I spent the weekend with another man?"

She dragged her arm away forcefully and marched into the hallway. She lifted her bags and carried them into the bedroom, where the TV still blared.

He was right on her heels. "Well? Did you?"

"Just stop this, okay?" She crossed to the television and switched off Patricia Routledge in mid-sentence.

"No! I want the truth. Are you seeing someone else?" he asked directly.

Pamela no longer saw any reason to deny it. She figured she had nothing to lose. She pulled herself up to her full height. "All right. Okay. You want the truth? I *am* seeing someone else." She said it almost with pride. "I've been seeing Shaun again."

His eyes widened, and then narrowed to tiny slits. "I *knew* it! He hasn't been back two minutes and you're jumping back into his bed. Fine. If that's what you want, I won't stand in your way." He sidestepped past her, went over to the wardrobe and, bending over, removed his suitcase from the bottom shelf.

Pamela was suddenly cautious. "James, you don't have to leave."

He continued opening drawers and loading his stuff into the case. "Do you honestly think I want to spend another night with you, when you've been with him? I can't believe I wrecked my marriage for you."

Pamela sat on the edge of the bed. "I didn't tell you to leave your wife. I was happy the way we were."

"So why didn't you say so?" He stopped packing to glare at her.

"You were the one who kept saying you wanted to tell her about us. I thought I was ready to settle down again. At first it was nice having you around."

He rounded on her. "*Nice!* You mean like having a dog, a friendly companion?"

"No. A companion, yes — but not a dog, James."

James sat on the end of the bed, his back to her. "How could you do this to us? I thought we had something good." He glanced at her briefly before facing the dressing table again.

She could see his reflection in the mirror. His face started to crumble and for one awful moment she thought he was going to cry.

"We did once," she said.

"Then *why*? And with Shaun — when you know how I feel about you and him."

"I wouldn't have done it with just anyone. You know I still have feelings for Shaun. I can't help that. I had to find out if there was still a chance for us," she said calmly.

"What you really mean is you couldn't control yourself, right? Is that how it was with me? You just lost control and I got sucked in?" His anger was rising again, his moment of weakness gone.

"Listen to me, for God's sake," Pamela said earnestly, almost fiercely. "This isn't all my fault. I gave you a chance to save this relationship."

James stood up. "What — by throwing me out?"

"I asked you to move out," she corrected, "to give us some space. I wanted to see if I could miss you again. I used to enjoy waiting for you to come round; it was something to look forward to."

He waved her explanation away. "That's your excuse. You just wanted me out of the way so you could move *him* in."

"You think I'd move you out to move another man in?" she asked seriously.

"Why not, if you can jump from one man's bed to another?" he shouted at her, a look of disgust in his eyes.

There was a tense silence for a few seconds. James started to pack again. Pamela felt her blood begin to boil. He had no right to make her feel this way. This was her life, and she intended to live it the way she wanted to.

"If that's what you think," she said, "then you might as well go."

"Well, what do you expect? I feel used. All I can think of is you and him . . . together."

"I felt exactly the same way about your wife."

"Don't change the subject," he snapped. "We're talking about you and Shaun here. I've never even met the guy and I hate him. Does he know about me?"

"Of course."

"Then maybe you two deserve each other." He jabbed the air with a thin finger. "You both couldn't care less about the people involved when you take someone's partner."

Pamela raised her hands in the air to halt his tirade of verbal

126

abuse. "Hold on a minute. *Take* someone's partner?" she said, incredulous. "You *gave* yourself to me. I saw you more than she did because you were using the brain between your legs and not the one in your head."

James's hand swung up and he took a stride towards her. Pamela flinched, expecting some kind of violence, but his arm dropped by his side.

"You don't know how close I came to hitting you."

"So why didn't you?" she dared, knowing she would have grabbed the nearest lethal object and killed him with it if he had.

"Don't tempt me," he muttered, walking past her into the hall. He removed his training shoes from the hall cupboard and proceeded to put them on.

Pamela looked at his pitiful figure and mellowed a little. He didn't have anywhere to go. He'd probably end up on a mate's settee. "I know you're feeling hurt, but I never wanted us to finish like this." Her voice was calmer now, though still a little shaky. "I wanted you to realise it wasn't working out."

"Maybe you should have thought of that before . . ." He paused, sucking air between his teeth, his face a picture of restraint.

"Before what, James? You might as well say it — you can't hurt me any more than you already have done."

"Before freeing up yourself for another man."

He ignored the look of horror on her face and grabbed his jacket from the cupboard, slinging it over his arm. Without looking back, he opened the front door. "I'll be back tomorrow to pick up the rest of my stuff. Then you can have your key back."

He left, slamming the door as hard as he could.

Pamela jumped. She was so angry she felt like breaking something. After all she had done for this guy, he had turned round and insulted her. As far as she was concerned, it was good riddance to a dull ride. She had already made up her mind that she was never going to put herself in that position again. From now on it would be me, myself and I.

JAMES

I can't believe she did that to me — to us. I know I'm not the most passionate of lovers, but I make up for it in other ways.

I feel used and betrayed. Pamela took my heart and ground it into the dirt with stiletto heels. I don't think she even realises how much it hurts. As far as she is concerned she can do as she likes, by whatever means necessary. And yet, even after the way she treated me, I still can't bring myself to hate her.

Maybe I was too hasty in leaving.

When I left Pamela's I jumped on a bus and headed straight for Brixton, to my brother Phil's place. I told him I had had enough of living with someone. I needed to play the field for a while. I told him I had given Pamela the push. Phil slapped me on the back and said he was glad I had come to my senses, he was beginning to think I was a Boops. If only he knew the truth.

I wonder if Darlene will take me back? After all, it was only my first affair. There was bound to be a few hiccups in the first years of marriage. Besides, I still own the house. I'll make a trip up to Stockwell to see her.

I miss Pamela so badly. I've already phoned her three times today, but she hung up on me.

18. THE PRESSURE

The conference room had been arranged for Marion's presentation to the members of the features team and six magazine editors. Marion had been working for a month on the outline for the articles. Joan hadn't seen the finished draft yet, and she was just as nervous as her friend, who was being extremely secretive. Apparently there was a new man in her life, but as yet she was keeping him under wraps.

There was a tentative knock on the conference door, and Joan's secretary Jayne entered, followed by Marion.

Joan crossed the room to greet Marion as Jayne left them alone. "How d'you feel?" she asked.

Marion forced a nervous smile. "How do I look?"

Joan looked her up and down. "Skinny, but you'll do," she laughed. "No, seriously, you'll be fine. Just think confidence. You certainly look the part."

Marion did indeed look businesslike. She wore a dark red and white vertically striped blouse under a red skirt suit. The brooch on her lapel was eyecatching without being dazzling, and her hair was tied back neatly with a maroon scrunchy.

Jayne appeared again with two steaming cups of coffee. The two friends sat opposite each other at the conference table. Marion had brought an A3 portfolio with her, which she opened between them.

"Did you get the photos of the guys developed?" she asked. For the past two weeks they had been scouting for volunteers. It seemed that men were only too glad to have their views heard. It had been easy to get them to pose for pictures too.

"Of course," she replied. "The slides are all set up and ready to go."

They continued to look over Marion's plan until the executives started to arrive. They all looked so formal and efficient that Marion's earlier nervousness rose again. But there was no going back now. Adrenalin was pumping fast around her body as Joan got up to introduce her. The room hushed.

"Ladies and Gentlemen, Marion Stewart on black men."

Joan met Marion's eyes and gave her a smile of confidence as she rose on shaky legs. They shook hands before changing places.

Marion cleared her throat. "Thank you, and good morning." She nervously smoothed her skirt down over her narrow hips. Removing the film of moisture from her palms, she took a deep breath and stood up straight. "As you know, I have been commissioned to write a series of articles on black men."

She turned to the flipchart behind her. On the board were the topics' titles in the order they were to be published. "The mysterious black man," she said in eerie voice. "What makes them tick? I see we have a few sisters in the room and only one black brother." She looked directly at the man sitting at the back of the room. He was a well-dressed fortysomething, and he shuffled irritably in his seat. "Don't worry, I won't embarrass you." She gave him a friendly smile before turning back to the rest of her audience.

"Wouldn't we all like to know what was going on inside the heads of our partners? When they say one thing, do they really mean another? How many of us read between the lines, or even insert lines ourselves to fill in for the unspoken words? And how many of us get it wrong?"

She smiled again. There were enthusiastic nods and a few coughs from the men in the room. "Well, hopefully, after reading my articles you'll never have to ask these questions again. You'll know."

Her audience were now all leaning forward with interest. Including Joan, who seemed entranced by Marion's transformation. Joan glanced around and took in the same look on the faces around her.

Marion continued: "We have selected twelve men from our community to tell it like it is. Jayne, the slide, please . . ."

Jayne, who was sitting at the back of the room, turned off the lights before switching the projector on. One by one images of the twelve black men were flashed on the screen, accompanied by a short verbal commentary on each one.

"Every one of these men has volunteered to give us his honest, unbiased views on sex, money, love, ambition, his family, and the future." Marion noticed everyone was busy scribbling on their notepads. She swallowed. "The age groups range from eighteen to thirty-five years. The majority are in the twenty-one- to thirty-five-year bracket. This was intentional: most of the black magazines target this group also, for advertising purposes."

The last slide was now showing, containing all twelve men. "These are the representatives of the black male community in London. You have in front of you an outline of all the topics. Now I'll take you through each one, detailing exactly what we are looking for from the men."

Marion was very thorough in her breakdown of each article. Basically, each man was to be given a set of questions and a tape each month on which to record their thoughts and opinions. The tapes would be sent back to the office and Marion would use the best selection in her articles.

When Marion finally finished, Joan led the applause. "Brilliant, Maz! You were great," she congratulated.

Marion beamed. She felt good.

"Ready for some questions?"

"Yeah," Marion said confidently.

The questions focused mainly on the method of collecting data, how honest it would be, and how much would actually be expected to go into print. Marion answered them all without hesitation. She had thought it all through thoroughly.

The assembled executives were each given a draft of the first article so they could see the points of interest for themselves. As they filed out of the conference room they all shook Marion's hands. Then Marion and Joan left to celebrate over a cappuccino and chocolate gateau at the local deli.

The phone was ringing as Joan hurriedly turned the key in the front door. Leaving it open, she dashed to pick it up. Shereen came in behind her and shoved the door closed.

"Hello?" Joan answered breathlessly.

"Jo? It's me." Her sister's voice was almost unrecognisable. She sounded like she had a mouthful of marbles.

"Donna? You sound terrible?" She hadn't heard from her sister in three months?

"Jo, I'm in the hospital . . ." came the reply.

Joan's head suddenly became light and she sat down hard on the edge of the sofa. "What? What's wrong? What happened?" she asked in quick succession.

Donna's breathing was laboured. "I want you to come, Jo. I'll tell you when you get here. They're taking me up to X-ray soon, but I'll leave a message at reception for you. Please come soon." She sniffed, and then breathed deeply into the phone.

X-ray! That meant she had broken bones! *Oh my God.* "Where are you, Don?"

"King's College."

"Okay. I'll be about half an hour, Sis. Hold tight." She hung up.

The pictures that raced through Joan's mind were not pleasant — all she could think of was that Donna must have been in some kind of accident. She hesitated by the phone, wondering if she should call their mother, then decided that Grace couldn't do anything from where she was. She didn't want to take Shereen to the hospital. She grabbed her handbag and called Shereen back from upstairs. "Shereen? You're going to stay with Natalie for a while, okay?"

Joan dropped her daughter off at their neighbours' house and drove to the hospital.

The man behind the reception desk stood up slowly as Joan approached. Jowly and red-faced, he held her with dull, yellow, glassy eyes, peering out from a field of flesh. "Can I help you, miss?"

"I'm looking for Donna Marcus, my sister. She told me she was in here."

The man tapped out a few keys on his keyboard and squinted at the screen. "Down the corridor, to your right, and through the double doors, love. Cubicle six." He pointed with a fat finger.

Joan absolutely hated being called "love", but she ignored it and followed the man's directions. She stepped through the plastic swing doors and looked along the curtained cubicles. Number six was on her left. She wandered over and gingerly pushed the curtain aside. Donna lay on her back on a cot. Her eyes were closed. She held a bandaged arm across her chest and her breathing was deep and rasping. Her cheeks were bruised black and purple, and there was a nasty gash on her forehead.

Joan brushed her cheek lightly with her fingertips. Her eyes flickered open. They were still vague as she focused on her sister.

"Jo?"

"Hi, babes. What happened to you?" she enquired softly.

"John . . ." Donna's throat clicked as she tried to swallow. She

131

lifted her eyes to the glass of water on the bedside trolley.

Joan brought the glass to Donna's lips and let her sip until she raised her good arm to stop her.

"He's not here?" Joan asked.

Donna tried to shake her head and winced. "He came in drunk this evening," she said through swollen lips. "He jus' started hitting me . . ." She sucked back saliva that was trickling from the corner of her mouth.

Joan's eyes opened wide in horror. "John beat you up?" she uttered hesitantly, hoping she had heard wrong. A flare of anger ignited in her head.

"I swear, Jo. I didn't do anything to upset him," Donna sobbed.

Joan leant over and put an arm around her shoulder, mindful of her bandaged arm. "Men don't think they need an excuse," she said between clenched teeth. "Where is he now?"

"I dunno. He ran out when I blacked out. I tried to fight back but it only made him worse."

Joan felt tears come to her eyes. She tried to hold them back. "Have you told the police, Don?" Her face became authoritative.

Donna closed her eyes and took a sharp intake of breath. "No," she whispered.

"Why the hell not? Don't tell me you're letting him get away with this." Joan's voice had risen to a yell before she remembered where she was and brought herself under control.

Donna sniffed pitifully. "I can't, he's my husband. For better or worse, remember?"

Joan glared at her sister as if she'd gone completely mad. "You've got to be joking! Well if you won't, then I will." She made as if to get up and leave.

Donna's good arm shot up and grabbed her jacket. "Please, Jo. I can't leave him. He's not always like this," she cried.

She was pitiful. Joan kissed her teeth and gave her sister a look of contempt. She had read about women who stayed with abusive husbands, but she'd never thought her sister would be one of them. She had never thought of the women in her family as weak, now here was her sister telling her she can't leave a man who would beat his wife up. How could she still think of that bastard as her husband?

She sat back on the edge of the bed. "You're going back to him, then?"

Donna continued to sob.

"Why on earth did you call me? You knew how I'd react. You'd have been better off calling Mum."

"Mum would have made me . . ." she sniffed, "come home."

"Wouldn't you be better off?"

"I married *him*, Jo."

"That doesn't mean you have to live a life of misery. I mean, look at you." Joan's eyes scanned Donna's injuries. They had cleaned her up pretty good, no doubt; she must have looked as though she'd been in a car accident. "How did you get the gash on the head?"

"I fell over the coffee table."

"God, Donna!" Joan sprang up as if pricked by a needle. "I can't take this. You're not going back there. You're going to come home with me, and then we're going to the police and we're getting him slung out."

"Don't, please, Jo."

"I don't want your waterworks. I'm doing what's best for you," Joan told her. Her patience was wearing thin. "Mum and I'll take care of you. You can work, y'know. Just 'cause he didn't want you to, it doesn't mean you can't."

"Jo?"

"Yes, babes?" Her voice softened.

"I'm scared."

Joan climbed on to the bed and stretched out alongside her sister. She took her in her arms. No words were needed. Donna knew her sister would take care of her.

On Monday afternoon Joan left work early and went round to Donna's flat. She knew John wouldn't be around. He'd probably be running scared. The flat was dead quiet. It didn't look as though anyone had been there since the incident. In the kitchen, a pot he had thrown across the room lay on its side on the floor. Congealed gravy spotted the walls.

Joan left it all and went into the bedroom. She found a holdall and packed Donna's belongings. She threw things from the bathroom into a carrier bag, along with some of Donna's cosmetics from the dressing table.

Joan left the flat in a hurry. She didn't want to hang around to face that madman if he returned.

She had already planned to move the sofa-bed into Shereen's bedroom. Donna could stay with her in there. Their mother would have to be told, of course. She would suspect something anyway, as soon as she knew Donna was staying with Joan. Grace was the least of their problems, however.

John would come looking for her eventually. Hopefully, before that happened, Joan could persuade Donna to have him arrested.

Joan arrived later that afternoon at the hospital to find Donna a lot more cheerful. She was sitting up in bed chatting to a young black nurse.

"Hi, Sis," Donna smiled through her bruised lips.

Joan looked at her. "You've cheered up. What's happened?"

The nurse turned to Joan. She was pretty, with soft, wavy hair and the kind of eyebrows Joan had always envied, naturally arched. "Your sister is a very brave woman. You should be proud of her." She turned to smile at Donna, and patted her on the hand before leaving the two of them together.

"Well? You gonna tell me what happened?"

Donna grinned shyly. "He turned up here, Jo."

Joan was ready to explode. "He *what*?"

"It's all right," Donna calmed her. "I told the staff what happened and that I wanted to report it to the police. They called the police for me."

"You mean he's been arrested?"

"Yes. I gave the police a statement."

"Oh, Don. I'm so proud of you." Joan got up and hugged her sister. Relief flooded through her and she squeezed Donna a little too hard.

"Joan! Mind, nuh? I'm still bruised all over."

Joan eased off. "Sorry, hon. So when can you come home?"

"I can go as soon as I want. No broken bones. I'd dislocated my shoulder, and it's still killing me, but I'll be all right."

"Good. You're coming home now. Shereen will love having you there."

The two women grinned at each other, and love flowed between them.

19. IN AND OUT OF MY LIFE

"Someone turn that music up," Chantelle yelled from the kitchen, her curly extensions bobbing with her head to the beat of Tag Team's "Whoomp There It Is". Chantelle was a friend of Pamela's. Her favourite place at a party was always the kitchen, she was proud of telling people, because that's where the food and drink are. As no one else wanted the job of serving people tonight, Joan was only too glad to let her do it.

Chantelle was sixteen stone and five foot seven — a woman not to be trifled with. Dressed in a red lace and satin ragamuffin outfit, she gave a massive first impression that always got a second look. Her bubbly personality and perpetually smiling face kept everyone in good spirits.

Behind her, Joan had just finished blending the vegetables for the coleslaw. She tipped them into a bowl and poured on an entire jar of mayonnaise. As she stirred the ingredients together, she rocked and bumped to the music, laughing at Chantelle's antics as she bounced around the kitchen.

Their "drink-up" had turned into a full-blown party. Pamela had gone mad with the invitations. It was only ten o'clock, and so far they had about thirty guests here, only six of them women. They were expecting about a hundred, and Joan hoped more women would turn up. They only seemed to know men, but they knew from experience that men wouldn't hang around for long if women didn't turn up.

Marion hadn't arrived yet. She had spent the whole day with her new mystery man, so only God knew when they would drag themselves out of the flat. Pamela and Donna were upstairs getting changed. Joan hadn't changed yet, as she had been busy preparing the food.

She finished the coleslaw, covered the container, and put it on the only shelf in the fridge that wasn't fully occupied with drinks. Then she checked on the curry goat Pamela had prepared, which was bubbling away on the hob.

"Chantelle," she shouted over the music, "turn that off in half an hour, all right?"

"Yes, sista." Chantelle raised her hand.

Joan laughed and, moving the table that blocked the doorway, she passed through into the hallway. She nodded or raised a hand to people she knew as she made her way upstairs, taking the stairs two at a time.

She knocked on her bedroom door. "You decent, Pam?" she called.

"Yeah, come in."

Pam stood in front of the full-length mirror on the wardrobe door. The dress she wore was red leather, the sides held together by laces. It just about covered her bottom. Her hair, which had taken an hour and a half to do, was a mass of small tonged ringlets with gold spray on their ends.

Joan raised an eyebrow at her. "Who you planning to give a heart

135

attack tonight?"

"Do you like it?" Pamela grinned, doing a spin.

"It doesn't matter what I think, I'm not a man. But if I was, I'd have no choice. Ain't you cold?"

Pamela laughed, turning to get a back view of her dress in the mirror.

"Where's Donna?"

"In the bathroom."

Joan looked at her own short black dress hanging on the wardrobe door as she undressed. The dress had a bra-shaped top, and was covered in beads and sequins. She had thought it quite revealing before she saw Pamela's dress, now she would feel overdressed.

"What's Marion wearing tonight?" Pamela asked. She bent over to get her shoes out of the carrier bag she'd wrapped them in.

"Sequined shorts and a bra top. She reckons it'll be the last time she'll be able to fit into them. She's still as skinny as a stick, but she says she feels bigger already." Joan, now undressed to her bra and knickers, walked over to the dressing table. "Has she told you who this man is yet?"

"No. But we'll find out tonight. I wonder if he knows she's pregnant." Pamela buckled her shoes and stood up straight, testing the feel of them. "I don't want children. I haven't got time for a kid." She crossed to the dressing table and, removing a Kleenex from its cube box, blotted her lipstick. "And what's she gonna do about her writing when the kid drops?"

"She'll manage. She's come a long way since dropping Gerard." Joan placed her hands on her hips and watched Pamela pouting in the mirror. "Will you stop admiring yourself and go down to greet our guests, dear? Chantelle can't run this thing on her own — and besides, they're mostly your friends."

"All right." Pam ran her tongue over her teeth to remove a smear of lipstick before striking a pose in front of Joan. "How do I look?"

"Like shit, but you'll do," Joan said in a matter-of-fact voice.

"Shut up. Jealousy is a sin, you know that."

Joan grabbed a hairbrush off the bed. "Go, or I'll mash up your hair with this."

"I'm gone, I'm gone," Pamela screamed, ducking out of the door.

The music got louder as the door opened, then muted again as it swung shut. Joan stood back from the mirror and studied her body. Not bad, she thought. Never be a size twelve again, though. Having a baby had made her a permanent fourteen. Chantelle had styled her hair for her. It was tonged then brushed into a page-boy style.

All she had to do now was shower and make up, then slip her dress on.

Donna emerged from the bathroom, freshly scented with a towel wrapped around her slim body.

"About time, too. How long have you been in there?" Joan joked.

"I was relaxing," Donna said defensively. "Boy, can't have a moment's peace in this house." She stomped over to the dressing table.

Joan frowned. She had noticed a distinct change in Donna's attitude. All day she had been distracted, and her mood was getting progressively lower.

She moved to her sister's side. "What's up, Don?"

"Nothing," Donna replied, a trifle sharply.

"Don't give me that." Joan caught her eyes in the mirror. "Has John been in touch?"

Donna looked back, surprised. "How did you know?"

"It's the only thing that gets you down."

Donna turned and shuffled over to the bed. She sat down on its edge. "He finally got bail," she said fretfully. "He called here. He knows where I am."

"Mek him come," Joan retorted. "He can't take on both of us, and if he tries, he's gonna be banged up for so long he'll have plenty of time to regret it." She sat next to Donna on the bed, sensing there was still something else her sister wanted to say. "Why didn't you say something before?"

"I didn't wanna spoil your party." Donna sighed. The bass beat of the music coming from downstairs could be felt through the floor. "He wants me home."

"No!" Joan shook her head vehemently. "It's not your home any more."

Donna said nothing, but averted her sister's gaze

"What the hell are you thinking, girl?"

Donna looked Joan in the eye defiantly. "I married him. I should give it a try, shouldn't I?" She spoke with a faltering passion, doubting her own words.

Joan stood up and pulled Donna up to face her. "Don't talk no stupidness in front of me! You don't need him, all right? When I think of how you looked a week ago, in that hospital . . . It makes me sick that I didn't kill him myself."

Tears of frustration began to well up in Donna's eyes.

"Look, don't cry." Joan's voice softened. What was she going to do with this kid? She realised her sister needed support, but she also needed some good solid professional advice. Joan didn't feel equipped to give her that.

"We are going to party tonight, right? Forget John. I'll go and see a solicitor with you next week, and we'll get a restraining order or something. I won't let him touch you."

Donna wiped away her tears. "Sorry, Jo."

"Come on, wipe your face. I'm gonna shower and then we'll go downstairs and rave."

Donna forced a smile on her face and let her sister lead her to the bathroom.

Joan sometimes wished she could lock Donna away for her own good. But it wouldn't solve anything. She would always be the way she was. No, Joan's job was to bring her daughter up right, to instil a pride in her that would allow her to live her life to the full, not to be dependent on her mother or a man to give her what she deserved.

There were a few good-looking men downstairs. If Joan had been in the swing of things she would be making her move right now, but she wasn't in the mood — for men or a party.

Marion would have her new man. Pamela would have Shaun, or whoever else was handy . . . This was a bad idea, Joan suddenly thought. It was going to be one long night. She decided she'd get totally out of it, on alcohol and the good weed.

Marion's hand rested on Paul's leg as he drove towards Plumstead and Joan's house. She was feeling so good. Happiness flowed in her veins like wine. Before they had left her flat Paul had made love to her in a way that Gerard never had. His sweet kisses had landed all over her body. He'd even kissed her fingernails, which had made her laugh. His excuse was that he wanted to taste every part of her. He had kissed her feet, sucked her toes, and eaten his way up her body. He hadn't entered her once, and yet she felt as though she had gone to heaven and back. He made her feel confident, beautiful and loved. God, was she loved! It didn't stop.

She couldn't help comparing him to Gerard. She compared everything, from the way they dressed to the way they made love. Gerard could do with tips from Paul on how a real man treats his woman.

Marion looked across at him now, and feeling her gaze on him he turned and smiled at her. His hand touched hers and he squeezed her fingers gently. She felt her heart rise in her chest.

The only thing that bothered her was that, when they were apart, she didn't miss him. She still missed Gerard. Though she wanted to forget him, he was always in the back of her mind. The fact that she was carrying his child meant that he would forever be a part of her life, whether she liked it or not.

She breathed in deeply, inhaling the smell of Paul's aftershave. Calvin Klein. The sweetness of the cologne mixed with his fresh-from-the-shower scent made her want to snuggle up close to him.

She thought back to last night, when he had carried her to the bedroom. She had felt so happy and cherished in his company, it was like the rest of the world didn't exist. They'd talked, and he'd listened to her. He supported her in all she wanted to do. In a couple of weeks, she thought, she would be able to tell him her secret and she would know just how much he cared.

The car pulled up four doors away from Joan's house. Paul switched off the engine and got out, taking the keys out of the ignition. Marion got out and stood by his side, watching him with admiration as he opened the boot and leant inside for the case of lagers he had bought earlier. He was dressed casually in a red sweater and jeans. His hard body was like a mould underneath the material.

"Don't go straining yourself now," she joked.

"As if!" His eyes smiled back at her.

Inside, the party was hotting up. As Marion and Paul were let in, Joan spotted them and came rushing over to hug Marion.

"Girl! I thought you weren't coming." There was a glint in her eyes as she looked over at Paul. She asked Marion with her eyes if this was *him*.

Marion nodded, grinning back.

"Paul — how you doing, man?" Joan slapped his arm playfully.

"Fine thanks. You?"

"Yeah, good." She turned back to Marion. "This man keeping you too busy. Don't let him take you away from us, y'know."

"It's her fault we're late," Paul defended himself. "The girl tried on everything she had and then went back to the same thing she had on to start with."

Joan laughed and waved Pamela over. Pam was in the arms of yet another tall, handsome man. She tiptoed to shout something in his ear, he released his grip around her waist, and she sauntered over, her tight dress not hindering her lithe movement in the least.

She grabbed Marion's small waist in both hands. "You're still so skinny!" she exclaimed loudly.

Marion stiffened. Taking hold of Pamela's hands, she pushed them away somewhat roughly. "Not as skinny as you. Where's my drink?"

Pamela hadn't got the hint. "I suppose you'll be off the booze now."

Marion nearly stopped breathing. Paul, still standing by her side, seemed none the wiser. She slipped her arm through Pamela's and headed off towards the bar. Pamela, bemused, was forced to strut alongside.

As soon as they were out of earshot, Marion hissed at Pamela: "Paul doesn't know about the baby."

Pamela looked at her as if she were crazy. "So when are you planning on telling him?"

They reached the bar and Chantelle leaned over to give Marion a hug. "How you doing, Marion?"

Pamela was staring at Marion, one hand on her hip.

"Fine, Chan. You look well," Marion replied, aware of Pamela's piercing gaze.

"Meaning I look fat." Chantelle made a face as if to say "Don't try to fool me".

"Naw, Chan. Just well fed." Marion laughed and ducked as Chantelle's huge hand came flying towards her. "I think you should sack your bar staff, Pamela. Too violent."

Chantelle laughed. "What you having?"

"Babycham, please, Chan," Marion replied.

"Yeah, me too," Pamela said, then changed her mind. "No — give me a brandy an' Coke instead." She turned back to Marion. "Well?"

"I'm not telling him until it's possible it could be his," she whispered.

Paul had come up behind them and they stepped apart to allow him to pass the crate of lagers to Chantelle.

Marion smiled at him and he touched her arm lightly before leaving them again. Pamela watched him go, waiting until he was far enough away and distracted by Joan.

"You're gonna con him?" Pamela said with horror.

"Don't start, Pam. I feel bad enough as it is," Marion said despondently.

"How could you do that to him?"

"Please, Pam, just support me on this. I can't lose Paul too," she pleaded, her eyes searching her friend's.

Pamela held up her hands in a submissive gesture. "Leave me out of this one. If he finds out — which he will when the baby is born looking like Gerard — he's going to hate you."

By two o'clock the party was in full swing. There was a queue at the bar and a queue for the toilet. The three guys who were running the sounds had put a tape in and were busy checking girls around the room. No one seemed to mind: the drinks were flowing and everybody was dancing to whatever music came on.

Pamela was drunk. Out in the middle of the living room she and her mate Christine were whining around each other to a soca track, their audience cheering them on. A couple of equally drunk men joined in, whining in time to their movements and the music.

Joan was amazed at how Pamela managed to dance in that dress. She sat on the living room windowsill, smoking her fourth spliff. She had got fed up of seeing Marion and Paul smooching. They seemed to be joined together at the hip.

"Hiya, Joan!" A woman's voice brought her out of her thoughts. She looked up and squinted through the haze of smoke at the familiar face.

"It's me — Sharna," the girl obliged.

"Oh God, Sharna!" Joan exclaimed with an air of pleasant surprise. She stood up and embraced her friend.

She had met Sharna at a pre-carnival party the year before, they had met again at the carnival, and had stayed in touch with the occasional phone call ever since. She had posted her an invitation to the party, but hadn't expected her to come.

"Good to see you," Sharna said, hugging her back. "I thought you'd forgotten me." Sharna had a husky voice which made her sound a lot older than her twenty-three years.

"You looking good." Joan eyed the red catsuit Sharna was sheathed in. It fit her slim figure like a second skin.

Sharna took in Joan's sequined outfit with a glance. "Thank you. Love the dress."

"Just a little something I chucked on," Joan laughed. In truth the dress had cost her ninety pounds — it was a treat she felt she deserved. "Who did you come with?"

"Those girls over by the door." Sharna pointed. "So — you all right, though?"

"Getting by, y'know how it is." Joan shrugged and screwed up her face in a fed-up way.

Sharna nodded distractedly. "Some nice looking guys here." She surveyed the room. "Looks like the girls can have their pick tonight."

"Most of them are Pamela's ex's." Joan pointed out Pamela, who was laughing hysterically with a group in the opposite corner.

Sharna twisted round to look. "She looks like fun. Where's the rest of her dress?" she asked sarcastically.

"Leave her. She always dresses like that. Likes to flaunt what she's got."

"Yeah? Well I better find myself a man before they start queuing up for some a' dat." She pushed a loose strand of hair out of her eyes.

"You go, girl. See you later." Joan smiled encouragingly.

Sharna danced back into the partying crowd and rejoined her friends.

Joan remembered at the carnival Sharna had gone wild, whining up with nearly every good-looking man available. Every time Joan had turned around she'd been with someone else. She knew how to have a good time. If Joan was in the mood now she would have joined her. Even Donna was out there enjoying herself.

She walked back through the house, pushing and squeezing past hot bodies to the makeshift bar at the entrance to the kitchen. On the way she was stopped several times by friends and acquaintances who wanted to say hello.

Chantelle stood with her back to the door, resting her ample bottom against the table cum bar. She had company. Rebecca, wearing a long, black, tight-fitting dress, waved to her as she got closer.

Chantelle rose heftily to her feet and turned with a plate piled high with curry goat, rice and coleslaw. "Hi, Joan. What's up, babe?" She swiped at her lips with the back of her hand and placed her meal on the table.

"I'm bored, Chan," Joan sighed, and took a puff of her roach before dropping it to the floor.

"How can you be bored when there's a party going on? 'Nuff man out deh, y'know." Chantelle planted her fists on her large hips.

Joan leaned wearily against the door frame. "Yeah, well, I'm not interested."

Rebecca stepped forward. "I love your house, Joan. Nice and big," she smiled. She had a wide, friendly smile, the kind that made her look as though she was getting ready to laugh.

"Thanks. Chan, d'you want a break? I'll take over."

"Yes, please. Just put my food in the oven for me." Chantelle was already moving the table from the kitchen doorway and giving Joan access. "Come, Bec, let's go shake a leg."

"See you later," Joan called to Chantelle's retreating back. Rebecca turned and smiled at her.

Chantelle had been a perfect barmaid. The kitchen was reasonably tidy, the sink was piled with plastic cups in case they ran out and had to wash some.

Joan lit a cigarette and poured herself a half-cup of brandy. She was feeling very light-headed, but it hadn't succeeded in stopping her from thinking. People spend most of their lives looking for someone to love, she pondered. She thought she had found it with Colin, but was now feeling worse than before. Why did love have to hurt so much? All she wanted to do was to get on with her life, but to do that she had to forget Colin Baker.

Sharna, who had been doing a pretty good job of circulating, took an opportunity to get some background information on a guy she had just danced with. She weaved her way through the ravers, searching for Joan, eventually tracking her down in the kitchen. "Joan. You have got to tell me some more about this guy — he says he knows you," she said, leaning her palms on the table.

"What guy?" Joan asked moodily, not in the least interested.

"Come out here and I'll show ya. He says his name is Marcellis."

Joan remembered the name. He was one of the guys from the carnival. She also remembered that he had been a good looker with a brain. "No, Shar. I don't feel like it," she protested, holding her cigarettes to her chest like a comforter.

Sharna shoved the table out of the way and reached round for Joan's arm. "What is this — a party or what? You are going to enjoy yourself if it kills me."

"I can't just leave the bar."

"Like hell you can't," Sharna said, and pulled Joan from the kitchen, forcing her to rejoin the party.

Joan could hardly see anything, it was so dark. The drink and ganja didn't help. She scanned the hallway through squinted eyes and noticed a tall, big-built, light-skinned guy entering the living room. Her attention perked up — he looked all right. The tall man stepped aside and she saw who he had come with. Colin.

Joan's heart stopped and then quickened. She caught her breath and looked around for Pamela. Sharna still had a hold of her hand and was pulling her forward. Towards Colin.

Joan stopped abruptly and managed to drag her hand away from Sharna's.

Sharna turned round and questioned her with her eyes.

"Catch you up. Jus' saw someone I know," Joan yelled over the music and whirled back the way she had come.

Marion was coming down the stairs with Paul close behind, and Joan managed to hail her. "I've got to talk to you," she shouted when Marion reached her. Paul hung back, waiting patiently.

"What's up?" Marion asked.

"Colin's here." Joan laced and unlaced nervous fingers.

Marion looked around. "Where?"

"I've just seen him go into the living room. Pam must have invited him."

"Didn't you tell her about . . . ?"

"I couldn't."

"How could he turn up here? I'll tell him to leave." Marion started to walk towards the living room.

Joan grabbed her arm. "You can't do that."

"Joan, this is your house."

"I know. Look, I'll just keep out of his way."

"You sure? I could get Paul to do it," Marion offered.

"Just leave it. You go back to Paul before he starts to miss you."

Marion questioned Joan with her eyes before squeezing her arm reassuringly and returning to Paul.

She lit another cigarette and decided to go upstairs for awhile. She passed Marion and Paul and made her way to the staircase, looking towards the living room door in case Colin came out and saw her. She was so busy looking the wrong way that she walked right into him.

She looked up, straight into his eyes, immediately became flustered and tried to push past him to get to the stairs, but he gently grabbed her arm, not budging from her path.

"Joan . . ." Colin began.

"Leave me alone, Colin," she hissed.

He kept hold of her arm. "I've got something to say to you." His jaw was determined and his eyes sincere.

"What? That you need a bit on the side?" she replied viciously.

"Come outside with me?" he asked.

"Hell, no!" She stared down at his hand. "Let go of my fucking arm." Her voice was rasping with barely controlled emotion.

Colin let go of her, and she immediately turned to walk back the way she had come. He stepped in front of her.

"Get out of my way before I dig this cigarette in your eye," she threatened, raising the cigarette to head height.

"Joan, come on, man." He spread his arms amiably. "Five minutes. I won't touch you. After that you can just walk away."

He dared to look at her with those damned gorgeous eyes.

Joan turned and stomped towards the front door. It was open and she stepped out into the cold early-morning air. The chill hit her to the bone but she marched on anyway. She could hear Colin's footsteps right behind her and she speeded up, trying to put as much distance between them as possible.

She risked looking back at him. He beamed at her confidently, with more bottle than Wray & Nephew.

Colin took his jacket off and draped it over her shoulders. Joan shot him a look of scorn, but pulled the jacket around her cold body none the less. Colin, feeling even more confident, walked by her side with his hands thrust into his trouser pockets. Joan continued to ignore him.

"Can I talk to you?" Colin asked affably.

She didn't reply.

"I take that as a yes," he said sarcastically. He breathed out deeply, trying to figure out where to begin. "Joan, I'm trying to apologise here. I was totally in the wrong. The way I told you . . ." He seemed to be trying hard to find the right words. "Lois was no good, she tried to trap me," he explained, his voice tight in his throat.

Lois! What kind of a name is *that*, Joan thought, images of Lois Lane in Superman's arms springing to mind. She wanted to laugh in his face. So his woman had kicked him out, had she?

Colin continued to speak. "She told me she wasn't pregnant when we were having an argument. She tried to fool me. I tell you, you women are the best bloody liars alive."

Joan stung him with another one of her looks.

"We're finished," he pointed out, just in case she hadn't caught his gist.

There was still no reaction.

"I'm single again, Joan. Remember what you were saying that night, about changing the way things were?"

She glanced up at his brown eyes. He smiled at her and she turned away fast enough to give herself whiplash.

Colin licked his dry lips and got out some more words. "We can do that now. I still love you, y'know."

Joan broke her silence. "What about Lois? Did you love her too?" she spat.

"I thought I could, but you were always on my mind."

Joan stopped and sat on a garden wall. They had reached the bottom of the road. She hated to admit it, but she had missed him. And now here he stood facing her, head bowed, wanting her forgiveness. Many nights she had lain awake dreaming of this moment: Colin crawling back on his hands and knees. Just as she had done two months ago. Making a fool of herself.

She took a step towards him. "What's wrong with us, Colin?"

He looked down at her, meeting her slanted eyes. "What d'you mean?"

Joan lifted her arms and his jacket fell to the ground as she placed them on his shoulders. Colin was caught unawares by the way her anger and hostility had suddenly vanished.

"I love you, Colin. We love each other, don't we?" She waited for his acknowledgement.

"Course." His lips turned up in a sexy grin.

Joan pressed closer and felt his rising erection hard against her stomach. "Then why do we keep pushing each other away? All I want is you." She seductively stroked the back of his neck.

He licked his lips and leaned down to kiss her. She felt his breath against her mouth and could almost taste the kiss. "Take me, Colin. I wanna be yours again."

He wrapped his arms around her waist. Heart racing, a strange excitement churned within her. As she gripped Colin's shoulders she swiftly brought her knee up hard into his groin, feeling it connect with his erect penis and testicles. As he hollered in pain, crumpling as though someone had just removed his spine, she jumped back out of reach.

His eyes popped wide with pain and disbelief. Both hands gripped his crotch.

"Don't take me for a half-wit, Colin Baker! Joan Ross ain't no fool. Stay the hell away from me and Shereen. I only wish I'd had something sharper to hand, then your worries about becoming an accidental father would be over." She glared down at him as his watery eyes came to rest on her. His teeth were clenched and he seemed to be having trouble breathing.

She smiled a wicked grin. "Dog!" she yelled, then she turned on her heel and marched back up the road towards her house.

Marion went into the kitchen, where Pamela was helping herself to a plateful of curry goat and rice. Pam's curls had dropped, and where her make-up had worn off she had a sheen to her skin. Chantelle was asleep on a kitchen stool, her head resting on the kitchen counter.

Marion realised she hadn't seen Shaun all night. Pamela must have invited him; in fact she remembered Pamela going on about how no one would see her all night 'cause she would be busy.

"What happened to Shaun? I thought he was coming." Marion poured herself a glass of orange juice.

"You asking me? I don't care what happened to him, I'm not his keeper."

Chantelle started to snore. Both girls looked at each other and burst out laughing.

"Boy, she's like a baby, sleep anywhere," Pamela said, glancing at her friend.

Marion smiled. She left Pamela in the kitchen and walked up the hallway. The house was now completely empty. All the remaining guests were outside, chatting on the deserted streets. The moon was dropping and the sun was beginning to lighten the sky. She could see Paul outside the open front door, deep in conversation with a guy she didn't know. She smiled as he looked her way, and he raised a hand and carried on talking. She left him to it and went into the living room to start clearing up.

Plastic cups, cans and bottles littered the floor and every surface. The air was still grey with cigarette smoke. Marion sighed and went back to the kitchen to arm herself with a dustpan and brush and a black rubbish bag.

She was on her way back when Joan walked in through the front door. She was grinning from ear to ear.

The girls sat around the kitchen table, a glass of fruit juice in front of each of them. Marion had cleared the kitchen of debris while Joan had relayed what had happened between herself and Colin. They were all physically exhausted, but found that they had so much to talk about they weren't ready for bed. Paul had taken Chantelle home and hadn't arrived back yet. The door was left on the latch for his return.

Pamela leaned back on her chair carelessly. "You know what I fancy right now?" Without waiting for an answer she told them. "A man eating my body from head to toe." She closed her eyes, conjuring up the image.

"So where *is* your man?" Joan asked.

"Shaun? He's not my man. He's my part-time lover. I've finished with relationships. Did you see that guy I was chatting to?"

"Which one?"

"The dark guy with the moustache. His body was hard. You know, if this was my house I'd have been upstairs with that one."

"You old tart," Marion joked.

"Whatever." Pamela waved her hands matter-of-factly. "I just tell it like it is. Why lie?" She looked pointedly at Marion. "At least *my* men know what I want them for."

Marion winced. She knew what Pamela was referring to. But she didn't retaliate. Although she didn't feel good about what she was doing, she also knew she didn't have to explain herself to anyone.

Joan diverted the conversation. "I've got some strawberry cheesecake in the fridge. Anyone fancy some?"

"Yes, please!" Marion answered without hesitation. She hadn't eaten throughout the entire party, and dinner the previous evening had been beans on toast.

"Well, I shouldn't really — I'm watching my figure," Pamela joked. "But go on then."

"Girl, you've got plenty of men who'll do that for you," Joan said. She took the cheesecake from the fridge and placed it on the counter.

Marion stood up and got some dishes out of the cupboard. "So, Pamela, looks as though you're the only one who's got to sort out your love life," she said.

"Does it?" Pamela looked up curiously, still tilting on her chair, her hands clinging to the edge of the table.

"Well, Paul and I are having a baby, and Joan's finally got rid of Colin. But you, you don't get rid of one before you start with another."

"And I'm staying that way. I can find more exciting things to do than changing nappies or cleaning up after a man," she returned, making a face.

Joan carefully laid a slice of cake on to a plate. "It's not as bad as you make out, Pam."

"Isn't it? I've been there. I mean, you start out all lovey-dovey, and as soon as the guy knows he's got you where he wants you he's playing the field again. I love men, but I couldn't limit myself to one for the rest of my life — and I wouldn't trust a man to do that for me."

Marion slid Pamela's plate across the table to her.

"Thanks, Maz." Pam picked up a dessert spoon.

Joan had been letting what Pamela had said sink in. "Yeah, but, I've had all that, Pam. I'm twenty-seven now, and I know I'm ready to settle down again. I want to meet a man I can love and trust, a man who makes me feel good about myself. I want to be important to somebody." She looked to Marion to support her.

"You're right, Joan. Love is hard to find. The way I see it, when you find it, hold on to it."

"I'm not saying you shouldn't. I'm just saying I don't think I could," Pamela said through a mouthful of strawberry cheesecake. "The man would have to satisfy my every need. I've not found a man who could do that yet." She took another mouthful and closed her eyes in ecstasy.

"Besides, I've got Shereen to think of," Joan said. "I can't keep parading all these different men in front of her. What kind of example is that to set for my daughter?"

For a full minute the only sounds were the scraping of cutlery on plates. Joan was digesting the fact that she had finally finished with Colin. It felt good but, still, there had been a second of panic there, when she had nearly apologised for hurting him. But she was bigger than that. One thing she knew how to do was rise above her emotions.

Marion was wondering if Paul would ever propose. Or whether, when he found out about the baby, he would run a mile. She felt she was prepared for all eventualities.

Pamela was enjoying her cheesecake and wondering if both her friends had gone off their heads, talking about settling down at their age. They were all still young. Why on earth would they want to end their freedom? But they were her friends, and if that's what they wanted she would be happy for them, when and if it ever happened. She pushed her empty plate away from her and reached for her fruit juice. "By the way, Joan, whatever happened to Charles?"

"Yeah, what *did* happen to him?" Marion asked.

"I think I frightened him off."

Marion was intrigued. "How?"

"Well, first I tried to seduce him on our first date. Then I told him I was in love with Colin."

"You never!"

"I thought it would be better to have everything out in the open," Joan said.

Marion looked puzzled. "But you and Colin weren't seeing each other then," she said.

"I know, but I still wanted him. I didn't want to hurt Charles." Joan placed her elbows on the table and laced her fingers, making a bridge.

"That's sweet, Joan, but the guy had money!" Trust Pamela to bring it down to material things.

"Money isn't everything. I didn't feel anything for him." Joan shrugged.

Pam giggled. "You mean he didn't make your toes curl?"

"My mum's got this saying: 'New broom sweep good but old broom know de corner dem'. That's me and Colin," Joan said haughtily.

Pamela chuckled. "Yeah, well, my parents had a saying too: 'When old stick bruck, you mus' push new one in deh'."

"You lie. You jus' made that up," Marion accused.

"God's truth," Pamela said with a serious face. Then, as she thought of her parents ever using a sexual innuendo, she burst into laughter, slapping the table with her palm. She shook her head, sending her dropped curls swinging round.

Marion wasn't sure she found it so funny. To her it sounded as though Charles was a romantic. The man was probably falling in love with Joan. Her friends were much too hung up on good sex.

Although she didn't see anything wrong with it, she knew all relationships can't be based on it.

They heard the front door open and close. Paul must have just returned.

"And the man had such a safe body. He used to work out three times a week," Joan continued.

"What a waste," Pamela sympathised, shaking her head. "You know what I'd have done?"

"No, what?" Joan asked expectantly.

"Just flung him down and ripped his clothes off. Or ripped my own clothes off, spread my legs and said 'Take me'." Pamela threw open her arms in a submissive pose.

Joan and Marion both screamed with laughter. Even Marion couldn't resist Pamela's humour.

"I couldn't," Joan said. "He would have run a mile. He seemed to have the idea that I was a decent, good woman. He was looking for a wife type. Maybe I should introduce him to you, Marion . . ."

"I've got a man," Marion said proudly.

"Yeah, but does your man have money?" Pamela made them all laugh again. Marion shook her head. Pamela's idea of a good catch was a rich man with a big dick.

Pamela squirted dairy cream on to her plate and stuck her finger into it. "What does this remind you of?" She held her hand in the air, letting the cream run down her finger.

"A premature ejaculator." Joan cracked up.

Pamela screamed, "James!" She held her aching sides in mirth.

"Martin!" Joan yelled.

"You two are disgusting," Marion said, turning her nose up.

"All this talk about sex is getting me horny," Pamela said shamelessly. "I'll have to go home and call my remote-control cock." Standing up, she stretched her arms in the air.

"And who is that this month?" Joan asked, beginning to clear the dishes from the table.

"Shaun, of course!"

"After he stood you up tonight?" Marion asked.

Pamela rolled her eyes. "He *didn't* stand me up. And besides, I only want him for one thing. Whatever else he does is his business," she said brazenly.

"I'd better go as well," Marion said. "I want to do more writing again later. You wanna catch a lift with us, Pam?" she offered.

"Might as well." Pamela pushed her feet back into her shoes.

Marion went to tell Paul she was ready. She came back carrying her and Pam's jackets.

"I'll call you during the week." Joan hugged her back. "It was a good party though, wasn't it?" She was beginning to feel lonely already.

"Yeah, our best," Pam answered.

"Course, we should have a Christmas one, or New Year's," Marion suggested.

"You'll be sitting down by then," Joan said, reminding her of her condition.

"Naw. Baby's gonna dance too." Marion lowered her voice as Paul came out of the living room into the hallway.

Joan walked them out to the door, where Paul waited.

He kissed Joan's cheek. "See you soon, yeah?"

"Definitely," Joan told him.

She watched them walk down the quiet street to the car before going back inside. In the living room she switched off the stereo. There was nothing left to do down here, so she climbed the stairs. She went into the bathroom and ran a shallow bath. She was washed and out in ten minutes, drying herself wearily, her arms suddenly feeling heavy.

She walked out of the bathroom completely naked, put her head around Shereen's bedroom door to check on Donna, then entered her own room. As she turned to get into bed she noticed the shape of someone under the covers, and recognised the back of Colin's head.

"Colin?"

"Mmmm." He rolled over on to his back and opened his eyes. "Thought you were never coming to bed," he said, throwing back the covers to reveal his long, hard body.

Joan almost fainted with the rush of blood to her head. Was this guy so thick-skinned that he still didn't get the message?

"W . . . wha . . ." she stuttered. Then she took a deep breath. "Where are all your clothes?"

He sat up. "Over the back of the chair." He nodded towards the window.

Joan stormed across the room. She grabbed his clothes with one hand and pushed the already open window wide with the other. She swung her arm back and the clothes went flying through the air to land in her front garden.

Colin sat there, mouth open. "What d'you do that for?"

"What will it take to get through to you, Colin? Get out of my damn bed, my house and my life!" she yelled, her arms flailing wildly with each order. She grabbed her robe from the bottom of the bed and pulled it on.

Colin swung his long limbs off the bed and crossed the room to the window. He peered out, looking for his garments.

Joan stood behind him, hands on hips. "You better go after them before some tramp claims them," she said icily.

Her coldness had absolutely no effect on him. He knew her too well. "I ain't going nowhere until I make you see sense." He stepped towards her and she stepped back.

"What do you know about sense? It's clear you haven't got any or else you wouldn't be here."

Colin continued to advance on her, his flaccid penis bouncing with every step. Her foot touched the edge of the bed and she lost her balance and fell backwards.

Before she could get back on her feet, Colin was on top of her.

"Oh, so you're gonna rape me now!" she scowled.

His eyes penetrated hers. He was serious, but not threatening. "I won't have to." He pinned her arms to the bed, knowing it was the only way to keep her still. "You know you want me, Joan. Why don't you just give in to your brain? You're always fighting what you feel."

She could feel him stiffening against her thigh. "What makes you think that?"

"I know you. I know you like you're a part of me. I know you're scared of being hurt again. But you can't keep pushing me away."

She kissed her teeth and twisted her head away from him to face the wall, her lips screwed into a tight pout. What did he know?

"You know I'm not lying. Look at me and tell me I'm lying," he said.

Joan was suddenly beginning to feel tired. Tired of running, tired of fighting. Tired because it was seven in the morning and she hadn't slept yet. Her body relaxed underneath him. "You gonna trap me like this all day?" she asked, still avoiding his eyes.

"Just promise me one thing."

"I'm not promising *you* anything."

"Then we stay like this." He grinned, pressing himself closer.

Joan could feel her body betraying her, becoming as aroused as he was. Damn him! "Okay. What?" she said. Anything to get him off her.

"Let me stay. And no more attacks on my physical being," he added.

She turned to face him. "That's two."

"Well?"

She sighed and whispered, "All right."

"Sorry?" He turned his ear to her.

"All right," she said louder.

Colin let go of her arms and rolled off her.

"The things men do to get their own way," she said, rubbing her wrists.

"Sorry, but you're dangerous let loose."

She had to smile at that. Her mother had always taught her to fight back, and she wasn't going to stop now that she had grown up. She pointed in the direction of his groin. "How d'you feel . . . you know, down there?"

"Can't you tell he's ready and rearing to go again?" He lifted it twice like a lever.

"You're sick, you know that."

"Makes two of us," Colin joked back.

"Nothing wrong with me."

"Oh no?" He raised his eyebrows. "You're the one who's in love with me."

"Yeah . . . that qualifies me all right."

They laughed together. Joan stood up and made for the door.

"Now where are you going?" Colin asked, already making himself comfortable at the head of the bed.

"To get you sheets and a pillow. You'll need those for your bed."

Colin opened his eyes wide. "What?"

"You said you wanted to stay here — you didn't say where." She laughed wickedly. "You're sleeping on the floor, Mr Baker. I want to make one thing clear: we share the same bed only when *I* want to. It's not up to you when you have my body."

He shook his head. She was sharper than he expected this time of the morning. He was just grateful he had got her to calm down. She wasn't screaming at him any more.

Colin made the most of his makeshift bed on the floor. He placed it right by her bed and held her hand as he poured out his heart to her. He would have promised her anything that night.

By the time Donna burst into her sister's room later that morning, Colin was sharing her bed.

COLIN

Oh boy! What have I done? I think I must of drunk too many last night. I woke up in Joan's bed. She turned over and smiled down at me and said, "I will be Mrs Baker after all." Yeah, I said, then it all came flooding back.

Caught up in the moment I had proposed to her. Or did I? As I remember the conversation went something like this:

She said, "So where do we go from here?"

I said, "Marriage, I s'pose." I was mucking around, didn't think she'd take me seriously. But she jumped on it like a drowning man to a life raft.

"You serious?"

I couldn't take it back. "Well, why not?"

"Okay, then," she said. "Let's do it."

That was it. I was committed. No way back. At the time it felt right. We were saying all the right things an' that. I wasn't thinking past getting in bed with her.

The thing is not to let Lois know I'm seeing Joan again, and not to let Joan find out I'm staying in Lois's flat. Nothing's going on between us. I wouldn't sleep with her again if she paid me — and believe me, she's tried. It's just that I needed somewhere to stay and Lois offered her place. Now that I've got Joan back I've got to sort out the rest of my life.

I may be allowed back in her bed, but that's as far as it goes for the time being. Sex is out until I prove myself worthy.

Shouldn't be too long now though.

20. REAL LOVE

The nursery was just opening up. Parents and children buzzed around, falling in line for the routine of hanging up coats and booking lunches with the secretary. Pamela was chatting to a parent who was concerned that her little boy kept wetting himself at school whereas he never did it at home. Was he being mistreated? she wanted to know. Pamela, who was used to parents' concerns like this, told her that this kind of thing was quite common when children were still settling in, and that if she wanted to she could make an appointment to see the child psychologists who were available for consultation. Immediately the woman's view changed. All of a sudden there was nothing wrong with her child.

Pamela finally turned her attention to the little brown-skinned boy tugging at her shirt hem. His gorgeous hazel eyes blinked adoringly up at her, his cheeks pushed up in a toothy grin. He wore his favourite baseball cap with the peak at the back.

"Hi, Mikey!" She hunched down and gave the little boy a warm hug. He was one of her favourites. So cute, and he was well behaved. "Where's mummy today?" she asked, looking towards the door. Cheryl, his mother, had become a good friend. She would often stop

154

for a cup of coffee and a chat after dropping Mikey off. Cheryl was a gossip. Little happened in her own life, according to her, but she knew everything that was going on in her friends' and neighbours' lives.

"Daddy brung me today," the four-year-old told her, and pointed towards the door. Pamela followed his tiny pointing finger and caught her breath, as in walked God.

She froze, unable to take her eyes off him.

This man was Mikey in twenty-five years' time — the same hazel eyes, the handsome, self-assured grin — except that he didn't have the baby cheeks, he had a strong jawline and cool milk-chocolate-brown skin. He must have been at least six foot four.

He strode towards them confidently, his hand raised in greeting as he approached. "You must be Miss Pamela," he said, in a voice that seemed to originate in the pit of his stomach and reached across the air to grab her attention. It was deep and mellow, and flowed like a caramel river.

Pamela stared at his mouth, his beautiful lips, full and kissable. She stood there like a fool, looking at him like a hungry man looks at a plate of his favourite food.

He was dressed in a navy business suit, with a navy tie over a white shirt. He carried it so well it could have been made for him.

"Shake his hand, then," Mikey ordered, his baby voice bringing Pamela back to reality.

Pamela's face broke out of its trance. "Sorry." She smiled, showing pretty white teeth, and offered her hand. "Yes, I'm Pamela."

He introduced himself. "Michael." His handshake was firm.

Pamela's hand stayed in his until he let it go, embarrassed. She still couldn't help but stare uncontrollably. This guy even had sexy eyebrows. They were smooth, thick and silky. Pamela had the urge to run her fingers along them; it took a great effort to control the urge. "Is Cheryl all right?" she managed.

Michael nodded. "Yeah, she's fine. She's got a job interview, so I said I'd bring Mikey in for her." He looked down at her and smiled provocatively. "I'm glad I did."

Oh yes, she thought to herself. Yes, yes, yes.

Michael looked around for his son. "Mikey? Come give me hug, I'm going now," he called. He looked round and caught Pamela staring at him again, a stupid grin on her face. He smiled back — encouraging her, she thought.

Mikey dropped the bricks he was busy carrying from one end of the room to the other and ran into his father's arms. Michael hugged his child to him with genuine affection, and kissed his cheek. Mikey

155

immediately wiped the spot with the back of his hand, and Pamela laughed with his father.

"Cheek!" Michael said, as his son ran off again to his bricks.

"He's a lovely little boy. I want my first to be just like him," Pamela said.

"First? You mean you haven't started yet?" Michael asked.

"Haven't met a man worthy enough to have my child," she said smugly.

Michael looked into her eyes as if trying to read between her words. He must have liked what he saw, because he nodded approvingly and threw her a little smile. "Maybe I'll see you again sometime," he said in that deep well of a voice.

"Sure." Pamela couldn't think of anything else to say. She felt awkward.

Michael was already walking towards the door as she came up with a brainstorm. "Michael?" she called, quick-stepping towards his waiting figure — and what a figure. "We've got a parents' evening on Thursday night. Why don't you come along? Cheryl said she won't be able to make it, and I bet you don't get much of a chance to see Mikey's work."

He hesitated, striking a pose with one hand stroking his chin thoughtfully. "You're right — I don't. What time?"

Pamela stepped back just a little as she realised she was close enough to smell the mints on his breath, and might not be able to control what her hands might do. "Between four and six thirty."

"I'll be here." The corners of his eyes crinkled engagingly. He moistened his lips with his tongue, then pulled his bottom lip in with his teeth, slowly letting it go, leaving white bloodless tracks for a fraction of a second. "Later then." He brushed her arm fleetingly.

Pamela was hypnotised. "Later," she replied, feeling her knees buckle as she tried to walk away. She felt as though she were floating a few inches above the ground.

She had been hit by the thunderbolt.

Oh my God, a voice inside her declared. I'm in love.

Pamela arrived home at nine that evening, exhausted as usual. Keeping control of twenty children under five was tiring work. After work, she had gone straight to the Wavelengths leisure centre for an hour of aerobics followed immediately by another hour of gym. As she had begun her work-out the adrenalin rush had taken over and she'd recovered enough to complete her exercise routine. Now she was completely shattered.

Since James had left, home had become very quiet. The men in her life still called, but she wasn't interested. Sex, she was beginning to realise, wasn't everything. She wanted someone to be there for her. She actually found herself missing James. Not for himself, but for the massages and cuddles, the breakfast in bed at the weekends, the morning cups of coffee. Dinner when she came home from work . . .

Her friends were right — James had been too good for her.

She stripped off her clothes as she walked around the flat, feeling filthy and grimy with perspiration. She ran the bath and went to fetch a robe from the bedroom.

The phone rang on her way, and she picked it up in the living room.

"Pam?"

She recognised Shaun's voice and sighed internally. "Yeah. Shaun." She ran a hand through her greasy hair.

"What's up? You sound down."

"I'm tired," she replied. "Shaun, my bath's running. Can I call you later?"

"Yeah, all right. Talk to you later, then."

"Bye."

She hung up. Even Shaun was getting boring.

The last time he had come round she had fallen asleep next to him. She just hadn't fancied the same old routine.

After she emerged from the bath feeling drained but clean, she still wasn't in the mood to call Shaun back. Let him cuss, she said to herself, switching on the answerphone.

She was tired of him; she was tired of them all. They swanned through her life, leaving her unfulfilled and still searching. She knew deep down she was a good person: she didn't bitch; she didn't want to tie a man down with kids; she was fit, attractive, good in bed . . . her problem was that the wrong men were always falling for her.

The men she wanted, the men who attracted her sexually, were the ones whom so many other women wanted as well. Which was why they felt they had to spread it around, not to leave anyone out. They were unreliable, couldn't make promises (let alone keep them), and only turned up when they wanted something. She understood these men. Hell, she had acted like them enough times.

On the other hand, the ones that promised love, fidelity and total devotion bored her, and they were always the ones that fell for her. They could only ever be taken in short bursts before it became too heavy and she had to escape.

She thought about Michael. Which category would he fall into?

She had a pretty good idea that he would be the spread-himself-thin type. But what the hell, she thought. She desired him too much to care and she couldn't see him putting up much resistance if the opportunity arose. Somehow she had to find out if he still shared a bed with Cheryl.

Pamela lay on her bed above the sheets, wearing nothing but a crumpled pink T-shirt and panties. Her hands were clasped behind her head, her knees drawn up making twin bridges. She allowed her thoughts to drift in and out of her mind, unable to sleep and yet not having the inclination to do anything else.

Thursday arrived. The day couldn't go fast enough. For Pamela it had been a long week so far — three days of undeniable anticipation and excitement. One person had stayed on her mind night and day. She felt like a teenager again. Even choosing something to wear to work had been an ordeal.

When Cheryl had brought Mikey in on Tuesday, Pamela had fished around for information about the boy's father. But Cheryl didn't want to talk about Michael — she'd told Pamela he was interested only in his son, and that was fine because she wanted nothing more to do with him.

Pamela had smiled to herself. Michael was as good as hers.

Tea breaks and lunchtime came and went. After the afternoon session the children went home, and preparations for the parents' evening began.

"Should be an easy evening," Annette said to Pamela. Annette was a nursery assistant and had been with them for a year. She was nineteen, and all the kids were fond of her. She had the ambition of going into primary teaching; this, she said, was just a stepping-stone for her.

Pamela looked up from her reports. "Oh?"

Annette was chewing gum vigorously, and moved it with her tongue to the inside her cheek as she spoke. "Yeah. We've only had ten definites."

Pamela put on her voice of authority. "It doesn't mean others won't turn up, Annette. I've been receiving verbal confirmations all week." She was wound up tighter than an elastic band around a pencil.

"Yeah, well, we don't wanna hang around longer than we have to, do we?"

"We'll hang around for as long as it takes," Pamela snapped. "You *are* being paid."

Annette swallowed her gum, her eyes widening in astonishment at Pamela's unprovoked outburst. She scuttled away to her chores, muttering under her breath.

Two hours into the parents' evening, Pamela was getting to breaking point. Keeping her eyes open for Michael, it was hard to concentrate properly on her job, and she was rushing the other parents through their interviews and not giving them the chance for questions. She was vaguely aware she was doing it, but couldn't help herself. She was as nervous as a cat walking past a dog pound, and her jaw was aching from forcing a smile at so many people for so long.

By six fifteen, with fifteen minutes to go, she was convinced he wasn't going to show up. She had seen her share of the parents and the rest of staff were leaving. She began to put away her notes, disappointedly. Lifting the files from the desk, she turned to walk back to the office and nearly bumped into Michael.

"Not too late, am I?" His voice was breathless, as if he had been jogging.

"Michael! No, of course not." Her eyes travelled down from his face to his smart attire. He was wearing a cream sweater and a pair of smart black trousers. He looked gorgeous. Pamela's pulse quickened. The smile that spread itself across her face now didn't have to be forced, it had a will of its own.

She fought to regain her composure, confidence and professionalism taking the place of girlish excitement. "As you can see, everyone else has left. You just caught me."

"I'm sorry. I had to get here from Finchley. You have no idea how many speed limits I broke to do it."

His voice was just as she remembered it, deep and sexy. It wasn't a fantasy after all. She wondered what he did for a living. Did he have a huge wage packet to match the rest of his assets?

"Glad you could make it." She extended her hand to shake his, and dropped the pile of files. "Shit!" she exclaimed, and then immediately covered her mouth with her hand. "Sorry."

Michael laughed, his hazel eyes filled with amusement. "Don't worry about it. I'll give you a hand."

They both bent down, and together they shoved papers back into folders and piled them back on the desk. As they reached for the last file together, their hands touched. It was like a bolt of electricity.

Pamela pulled her hand back, and Michael's eyes met hers. Right then she nearly kissed him, their heads were so close. Instead she caught herself, stood up on weak legs, and took the files from his arms.

"Thanks. I'll be with you in a minute," she said, turning her back on him as he rose slowly from the floor, eyes burning into her retreating figure.

Pamela had needed a chance to get her breath back. She had wanted to impress him and show him how classy she was, how in control she was, and boy, had she messed up. She was the one who was supposed to be in charge of developments. That was the way it had always been. But now she felt disturbingly uncertain.

She walked back into the nursery hall with long, smooth strides, aware of him watching her. Walking straight was not easy; right now she would rather be lying down — preferably with him. What was he like naked? She planned to find out. He didn't leave much to the imagination anyway. Sex-appeal oozed from his every pore.

She took him over to a desk in a corner and opened up Mikey's file. As she spoke she was aware that he was probably not listening to a word she was saying — but that was okay, because as far as she could make out she was mumbling a load of rubbish anyway.

His hands were clasped on the table in front of him. "Do you want to go somewhere afterwards?" he suddenly interrupted.

Pamela was taken by surprise. She swallowed hard and nervously shuffled a couple of pages back into the folder. "I . .. I . . ." she stammered. What on earth was wrong with her? She *never* stammered.

He covered her shaking hands with his. "I'm moving too fast, aren't I?"

"No!" she gushed. What must he be thinking of her? She wanted a chance to show him the real Pamela. "Why don't you come back to my place? We could get a takeaway, some wine . . ."

He leant closer across the table, his eyes swallowing her whole. "Sounds good to me. You finished here?" He nodded at the papers in front of them.

"I've just got to lock up." She closed the file in front of her and smiled at him. "Five minutes."

They hardly spoke as he led her towards his car. He drove a late registration Laguna. You've landed one this time, girl, she thought as she admired its sleek lines. He opened the door for her and she slid into the comfortable passenger seat.

Michael slid a CD into the player and the sounds of Jodeci issued forth. "Where to?" he asked.

The Caribbean. That was what she wanted to say. "Pepys Estate," she replied.

She gazed out at the passing scene as they drove off towards Deptford, occasionally turning to glance at his profile without being too obvious.

His lips were parted as he sang quietly along with the music.

They drove through New Cross, and within ten minutes Pamela had directed him to where she lived. He pulled up outside the tower block. On the way up, they chatted about the state of the area. Pamela told him that if she could afford to move out she would.

"You sure you can trust me to come in?" Michael asked once they had reached her front door.

She gave him a cynical look. "Why? Are you some kind of serial killer?"

"I'm hardly going to admit that now, am I?" His rich voice was heavy with sarcasm. He reached over and touched the back of her neck with soft fingers, smiling slyly.

She shivered. "Well, if you are, then I'd better warn you — I've got a black belt in Tae Kwan Do."

"Yeah, and my name's Michelle," Michael smirked.

"Hello, Michelle." She chuckled and let him into her humble abode.

"I've found my future husband."

Joan laughed sarcastically, pressing the remote control she held in her hand to lower the television's volume. "Yeah, right, Pam. How many times have I heard that? Has he got nice eyes, a firm arse, or just a big cock?"

"All ah dat. But that's not it. I haven't even had him yet. I know this sounds corny, but I think I'm in love."

Joan laughed again. In love! Pamela had to be winding her up. The word "love" wasn't in her vocabulary, much less her heart.

"So . . ." She controlled the giggle. "Tell me, then. What has this great man done to make you feel this way?"

Pamela hadn't been able to wait to tell her friends all about Michael. He had literally swept her off her feet. Last night had been the best night she'd ever spent with a man without having sex. She didn't know whether it was just the fact that he was so good looking, or the fact that he was a gentleman, or his voice, or just the way he'd treated her. One evening — and she felt as though she could spend the rest of her life with him. "I'm telling you, Joan, this is nothing like Shaun or even how it started with James. Michael took me home last night. We were supposed to get a takeaway, and I swear the thought of food went clean out of our heads. I'm gonna be honest, right? I thought the man was after sex like they all are. I know *I* was . . . We were in my living room, I got us some wine and put a soul tape on — the one you made up for me, with 'Slap n' Tickle' on it. We sat there chatting, and then he asks me to dance . . ."

"What — in your front room?"

"Yes," Pamela chirruped. "So I says, 'All right,' and he took me in his arms in the middle of the front room. I can't even explain how it felt. We just moved together like it was . . . I dunno. It just felt right, y'know? Then 'Nice and Slow' came on — you know what that record does to me . . ." She didn't wait for Joan to answer. "And he kissed me. He can kiss! I wanted him badly, and he must've felt it. I was trembling all over, but he just held me, stroked me — and boy did he move me." Pamela screamed. She was so excited she was rambling.

"So . . . what stopped you?"

"I don't know. This is what I'm saying about this guy. We danced, talked, drank a bit too much. He told me all about his job in computers and what his plans for the future are. He even stayed the night — and all he did was hold me. He told me he wanted to enjoy every minute of our time together." Pamela sighed. "I called in sick this morning and we spent the whole day together. He went out and bought us Chinese for lunch." She giggled like a schoolgirl.

Joan was amazed at what she was hearing. Prime steak laid out in Pamela's bed, and she didn't eat it! "There must be something wrong with you," she said, "or there's something wrong with him."

Pamela's voice was all dreamy. "This is different, J. I know I'm falling in love. I understand what you and Marion were going on about now — an' *that's* saying something."

"Love . . ." Joan sighed and went into big-sister mode. "You know, love comes with responsibility. You don't know this guy from Adam; how do you know he's not some sort of con artist? Sweet you up one minute and tek all your belongings the next."

"I hear you, Joan. I'm not stupid. I'll take it easy," Pamela assured her. "He's coming back tonight. I'll ask him where this is going."

"You know I only want the best for you. But I know you; you've never been committed to one man in your life. And what about Shaun? Doesn't he think he's your man?"

Pamela held the phone away from her ear and grimaced. Joan had to go and burst her bubble. But she was right. To make a go of it with any man she would have to make a lot of changes to herself and her priorities. Shaun believed he was her man. She would have to come clean with him. Anyway, the relationship had gone as far as it was going to go, she thought. There was no point in it any more. She wanted to move on.

"You listening to me?" Joan pressed.

162

"Shaun's no problem. I'll give him the elbow, an' I'll be free to do as I please," Pamela simply replied.

"Boy, you're certainly working your way through the population."

Pamela laughed. "I'm slowing down now."

Although she wanted it to be true, Joan doubted it. Lord knows, she'd been where Pamela was now. A new man who promised the world — until things started to get too heavy. But if that was what Pamela wanted, then Joan resolved to be there for her. She asked if he had any kids.

"Didn't I tell you? His little boy goes to my nursery."

"He's a single parent?" Joan seemed impressed at the thought of a black man raising his child alone.

"No. The kid lives with his mum. I must have mentioned Cheryl."

The penny dropped. "Oh, her! Mikey's mum. So Mikey is Michael junior . . ." Joan was getting a warning feeling in her stomach. Pamela had mentioned Cheryl, and Joan had the impression that the woman was the kind you didn't mess with. "It is *finished* between them?"

"Yeah. I even asked her just to make sure. She doesn't want him."

"Did you find out why not?" Joan enquired.

Pamela tutted and rolled her eyes. "It's over, that's all. Do you have to be so suspicious?"

"Let me meet him. I'll look him over for you. I've got women's intuition."

"You'll meet him. Not that you're any authority on Mr Right."

Joan laughed. Even women with women's intuition didn't get it right all the time. "Okay. I'll back off. But jus' you take care. Test the waters before you jump in, and keep me informed."

"I will. I'll see you soon anyway."

They said their goodbyes and hung up. Pamela shook her head at the way Joan was carrying on. Not *all* men were bad. You just had to know how to handle them.

Michael had left Pamela's flat at three o'clock that afternoon. At seven he'd phoned her, just minutes after she'd spoken to Joan. During the four hours in between, Pamela had become completely useless to herself. She'd tried to do housework, but had managed only to move things from one area to another before sinking again into thoughts of Michael. He crowded into every compartment of her brain, invading her mind in a way that confused her. She almost resented it. It was a new feeling for her, and she didn't know whether to fight it or go with it.

When the phone rang she'd been redoing her hair for the fourth time that day. She'd hurriedly grabbed the receiver and issued a breathless hello.

"Hi, babes. It's Michael," he'd said. There was no mistaking his voice anyway.

She'd forced a controlled calm into her voice. "Hi, Mike."

"You all right?"

"Yeah, fine. Jus' doing some housework. How're you?"

"Still at work. Should finish soon, though. You know I was supposed to start at two o'clock? I missed a meeting in Kensington. The boss wasn't too happy." She'd heard a smile rising in his voice. "But it was worth it."

Pamela had remembered the morning and her heartbeat had quickened. She had never believed Marion when she told her how Paul made love without actually "putting it in her", but that was exactly what Michael had done — and he had managed to satisfy her. She'd recalled the whiteness of his teeth and the light in his hazel eyes, his strong jaw, and the dampness between her legs that was a direct result of her contact with this man.

"What're we gonna do, eh?" She'd spoken her thoughts out loud.

"What do you want to do?" His voice had been thick with innuendo.

"I'm not sure, but whatever it is it includes you."

He'd laughed then, loud and richly musical. The sound had travelled down the phone line to grip her stomach in a nervous reflex action. She'd wondered if she'd been too presumptuous. They had only had one night together — one sexless night. Maybe to him it was no big deal.

"So, is it all right for me to come round tonight?"

"Of course."

"Good. Do you have candles at home?"

Pamela had frowned, puzzled. "A couple, I think. Why?"

"A surprise. Don't eat until I get there. By the way, what's your favourite food?"

She'd shrugged, searching her brain. "I'm not fussy. So long as it's not too fatty, I'll eat it."

"I'll be there in about half an hour."

"Okay. I'll see you later."

And now he was here on her doorstep, dressed completely in black, carrying several foil containers of Indian takeaway. Pamela was fascinated by this man's cool confidence.

They spread a tablecloth on the floor and took cushions off the sofa for seats. He lit the candles and placed them in the centre of the

164

spread. He served the food, poured the wine, and generally took over.

Michael's conversation was intelligent, and he seemed interested even in the mindless gossip that she contributed. He had a habit of watching her mouth as she spoke. She found it intriguing, if a little disquieting. Later on, she promised herself, she would stand in front of the mirror to see what was so interesting about her lips.

"So, tell me something." He swallowed and placed his fork on the side of his plate. "This guy Shaun you were seeing . . . is he definitely out of the picture?"

Pamela nodded enthusiastically. "Yes. It was nothing." She waved a hand in the air.

"When you say nothing, you telling me you were just friends?" Michael quizzed.

Pamela thought about her answer. If there was one thing she'd discovered about Michael in the short time she'd known him, it was that he never asked a question unless he wanted an honest answer. It was his way of getting to know someone, being very direct. "No. More than just friends. We go way back, to when we were teenagers. But over the past few months it's been just a sexual thing, y'know."

Michael raised his glass to his lips, his hazel eyes watching her over the rim. "I can't believe a man would use you just for sex."

Pamela nearly choked on her biryani. "Use me! Naw, luv — it was the other way round."

Michael scrutinised her across the makeshift table, taking in her body language. "Did he know?"

"What?"

"That you were just using him for sex?"

"Well, I didn't tell him any different."

"That doesn't mean he saw it the same way as you. He could've been under the impression that you were his woman."

"Get real!" Though it had a ring of truth about it, she snubbed his suggestion.

"I just don't want to step on anyone's toes. If you're seeing me, I don't want to imagine you with someone else. Unless I'm not good enough for you — then I'd rather you told me and I could back out."

Pamela was completely taken aback. Was he trying to tell her she was going to become his possession? She beat down the urge to tell him where to go with that attitude. But he had a point. If he liked her as much as she liked him, then he had every right to lay down a couple of ground rules. "Does that mean that you'd do the same?" she asked.

"Sure. But I'm telling you now, unless you don't want me, you've got me to yourself."

"Fair enough," she said, and swallowed a mouthful of white wine.

Michael spread out on to his side on the carpet, draping one long leg over the other. He rested on one forearm. "You know, there's something about the way you treat men that makes me think you're a little bitter," he said.

"Bitter?"

"Yeah, like the last two men in your life. You seem to have something against men falling for you."

What was he now? A Psychiatrist? "What're you getting at?" Pamela placed a palm on her chest dramatically.

"I want to get to know you, Pamela. I want to know every detail, but also I need to know if I'm just gonna be another plaything, someone to pass the time with until the next stud comes along. You get me?"

"Michael," she said, placing her glass gently on the floor, "I'm not into mind games. If this was just gonna be a fling I'd have flung by now." She smiled honestly. "I want to get to know you too."

He smiled his bright, white smile and his hazel eyes flashed their satisfaction. "You know, I've been asking all the questions. I probably know more about you than you do about me. Do you want to ask me anything?"

"I don't do that," Pamela replied. "I get to know a man by his actions, not by how he answers my questions. I'd be a fool to take every word you said as the truth, now wouldn't I?"

Michael laughed, the sound ranging from a deep and throaty rumble to a light chuckle. "You always have a knack of saying the right things. I'll have to watch you." He leant over and kissed her lips.

He held her hand as they continued to eat, taking her breath away with the promises in his beautiful eyes. He made her think before she spoke — which was definitely a new one on Pamela. And this was only the start of a perfect evening . . .

Later, they lay together on the soft leather sofa, illuminated by the flickering light of the muted television. The gentle soul music of Aaron Hall was playing low in the background. Michael's hand stroked her back and he placed light kisses on her forehead.

Pamela felt secure. No man had ever made her feel like this. It was alien to her, and to be honest a little frightening. She felt as though she were in a dream and had to keep kissing him to make sure he was real.

"Michael?" she whispered softly.

"Yes?"

She hesitated, choosing her words carefully. "Are you sexually attracted to me?"

"What do you think?" His eyes sparkled at her.

She could feel that he was aroused. She raised her head and giggled, her long hair falling around her face. "I know you're *ready*, but . . ."

He stroked her hair back off her face with his huge hand. "You want to know why we're not having sex yet?"

"Well," she replied hesitantly, "yes."

Michael sat her up, took her chin in his hand and made her eyes meet his. "Is that all you want?"

Pamela felt the first ripple of anticipation spreading from between her legs. "What?" she asked, for a second forgetting the thread of the conversation.

"Sex."

She looked directly into his beautiful eyes. It wasn't as though she didn't know how to seduce a man. But for some reason she didn't want to do it with Michael. She wanted *him* to take *her*. Wanted to know that he felt the same thing she was feeling. Seducing him would be too easy.

"It's just . . . what I'm used to."

Michael shook his head. "I want this to be different." He took her cheek in his hand and stroked it with his thumb. "I want you, but I want it to be special." His eyes passed over her like a slow caress, and a shiver ran along her nerves.

This was the same feeling she got when he kissed her, of every bone in her body being turned to water. "I'm gonna feel really stupid after I say this, but I have to. I . . ." She swallowed. "I've never wanted one man this badly." She continued quickly before he had a chance to laugh at her: "I know I don't know you. I just feel like this is gonna be more than just sex." She watched him, looking for a hint of understanding.

"Why do you think I want this to be different?" His voice was soft and deep, like the caress of a warm breeze, warm water, warm sleep. She looked into his eyes, and the expression there took her completely by surprise. She saw open longing there, and desire she couldn't have imagined. He kissed her and she fell into his arms, melting into his body. He covered her face and neck in kisses until she was gasping.

Suddenly he stopped and Pamela groaned.

"Let's take this to the bedroom," he said. "I'll show you what I mean."

Pamela was already aching for him, and she led the way to the bedroom without letting go of his hand. She moved lithely to the bed in the dark, and subsided on to the red satin sheets, fully dressed.

Michael stood at the doorway. "No," he said. "Come here."

He switched on the light. Pamela walked towards him, watching him with puzzled eyes. Her legs felt weak. His hazel eyes were smouldering with desire, taking her in from head to foot as they had done earlier. She stood so close her nipples brushed his chest. As she looked up at him, he smiled knowingly, teasingly. He ran one finger from her nose to her lips, where he let her kiss them before continuing the journey down her body. He gently cupped one firm breast in his hand, rolling the nipple under his thumb. She shivered. His other hand followed the curve of her waist, her hips, and then her buttocks. His eyes never left hers.

Pamela helped him remove her T-shirt and it dropped to the floor. The clasp on her bra was released and it too was discarded. Her breasts were rising and falling with her breathing. He continued to caress her nipples with his thumbs as he ran his tongue over his lips, wetting them before bending to take a nipple in his mouth. Pamela's arms rose to his broad shoulders and ran down his muscular arms, marvelling at how hard his body was. Michael's breathing became heavier as he took her in his arms. He kissed her slowly but passionately, handling her like a delicate antique doll.

She was crying out for him now, mentally and physically. She murmured, "I need you now, Michael."

"I know, baby. I know," he replied, his voice even deeper than usual. He slid her leggings down, leaving her standing in her black lacy panties. She gripped his shoulders as he took her buttocks into both hands, lifting her off her feet. She wrapped her toned brown legs around his torso, lacing her ankles behind his back, grinding herself against his taut body — still fully clothed in contrast to her own semi-nakedness — as if her life depended on it. He let her body slip down his until she was standing on her feet again, her breath coming in short pants, a film of perspiration covering her entire body. Never before had she come so close to an orgasm without penetration.

She stepped backwards and eased herself down on to the satin sheets of the bed. Michael stood in the middle of the room. She watched eagerly and somewhat impatiently as he undressed for her. His chest was as she expected: big, broad, a weightlifter's torso. His arms bulged with the strength she had felt when he'd carried her. His abdomen was hard, the muscles standing out under his skin. He unbuckled his belt and unzipped his trousers slowly. He was watching her watching him, showing discernable pride in his manhood, which stood to attention as he let his boxers drop to the floor. Pamela sighed with anticipation, sure she had died and gone to heaven. She had never seen one that big — and she had seen many . . .

She stifled a scream as he crept towards her. Starting at her feet, he kissed, nibbled, sucked and stroked his way up her body. Then he rolled her over to give her the same treatment on the back. Every nerve in her was sparking like a live wire. She was moaning his name as he explored erogenous zones she had forgotten existed. The sensation was incredible, unbearable.

His tongue probed her wet vagina. He played with her clitoris, teasing her to orgasm by sucking and licking her just right. He could certainly teach a few men the art of going downtown. It was a skill most men only thought they possessed.

As he came face to face with her and she could feel his hardness pressing for entry, she drew her legs up to allow him access, gripping his smooth buttocks in her slim hands. Still he took his time, opening her up with an expertise she admired, finding her magic button. He was treating her like a precious flower he didn't want to damage.

A wave was building up inside her, threatening to break the dams and flood them both. She felt she could drown in her own wetness, and still his finger moved faster in and out, gauging the rhythm. She finally spilt over and shuddered with a huge orgasm, her vagina clenching his knuckles.

Then he entered her, moving his penis inside with a slow, shallow pumping motion at first, then speeding up and deepening until she thought she would explode, then withdrawing again, leaving her gasping, before changing position to start all over again.

She was totally out of control. They rolled around on the bed, pleasing each other equally, until finally Michael joined her in a climax, his eyes screwed tightly shut in the agony of sex. She bit into his shoulder as they collapsed back on to the bed, moulded firmly together.

Hours later, she still lay in his arms. They were both covered in perspiration and had no need for sheets. She fell asleep feeling like the most fulfilled woman in the world.

Pamela awoke to an empty bed and the sounds and smells of cooking coming from her kitchen. For one horrifying moment she thought of

James, that last night must have been a cruel joke played on her by her mind. But as she yawned and stretched she smiled to herself, remembering Michael's body. No, it had been too good to be a dream.

She slipped out of bed and ran a hand through her tangled hair. Her mouth still tasted of last night's lovemaking. Wrapping herself in her short dressing gown, she went towards the sounds.

Michael stood at the cooker, his back to her. He was dressed only in his boxer shorts. She crept up behind him and circled his waist with her arms.

"Good morning." He turned round and smiled down at her. She stood on tiptoe to kiss him on the lips. "I hope you're not a vegetarian. I couldn't find anything except cereal, fruit and vegetables, so I went out and did some shopping. We got bacon, sausages and eggs."

Pamela grinned and her eyes sparkled. She must have been sleeping deeply — she hadn't heard him leave or return. "What you trying to do, fatten me up?"

"All the better to eat you," he said. Opening his mouth wide and baring his teeth, he brought his lips down to her neck.

Pamela laughed. "You're too much."

"You didn't complain last night," he said with a grin.

"There wasn't — and still isn't — anything to complain about." She kissed him again and he gave her a quick squeeze before turning back to his bacon.

"It'll be ready in about ten minutes," he informed her. "I was going to slip back into bed with your breakfast on a tray, but you beat me to it."

Pamela silently cursed her luck. "Well, I'll go and freshen up then." She turned to leave the kitchen.

"Don't have a bath yet," he called, his back to her.

Pamela stopped in her tracks and raised an eyebrow at him.

He turned and grinned engagingly before turning back to the frying pan. He used a spatula to flip the bacon over. "We're bathing together, after breakfast. Any objection?"

"No, sir!" She saluted.

Michael laughed. Even his laugh was sexy.

They sat cross-legged on the floor of the living room, the October sunlight giving the room an eerie glow. Michael fed her breakfast from his plate. He liked the floor for eating. He said chairs were too formal.

He noticed the book on the coffee table. "You're reading Terry

170

MacMillan?" he observed.

"Yeah," she said through a mouthful of toast. "Only just started that one."

"I haven't read it. Any good?"

"You read novels?"

"What? You thought I couldn't read?" he said with mock indignation.

"It's not that," she said, dusting crumbs from her bare legs. "I just don't know many black men our age who read. Out of about five men I know, I bet not one of them has read a book since they left school."

"I'll read to you in the bath," he promised, as if to prove the point. "Unless you don't fancy it . . ."

"Well . . ." She paused, running her tongue over her lips. "I can think of better things to do." She grinned wickedly.

"I know what's on your mind, babe." He spoke directly to her eyes. "But you can get that anytime. I told you I want this to be special. I guarantee you'll enjoy it," he said sincerely.

Michael was right. They lay in the bubble bath, her head resting on his sculpted chest, and he read to her. One hand held the book while the other caressed her body with warm water and bubbles as he spoke in a rough American accent.

Pamela never wanted this to end. Michael was hers, and she had no reason to think that this wouldn't last.

MICHAEL

I've got no intention of trying to get back with Cheryl. She's a bitch. She bitches about money, about me not spending enough time with my son, turning up when I feel like it, and sometimes she just bitches about nothing in particular to get my back up.

Now before you get the wrong idea about me, I'm gonna set you straight. I can't fall in love. No — that's not right — I can, but I refuse to. It's like this fear comes over me. And then I run. I don't like doing it. I don't want to hurt anyone — especially someone as fine as Pamela.

I thought I could make it work with Cheryl. We were together five years. I'm telling you, I tried. Now I want to try again. I want to fall in love with Pamela. If it doesn't work out, it won't be for the lack of trying.

21. I THANK YOU

The day of reckoning had arrived, and Marion felt like the world's wickedest bitch. Today was the day she planned to tell Paul about "his" baby. She had convinced herself that the child was his — it would make the lying so much easier. Having gone over the details many times — just as she had when Gerard was going to be the recipient of the news — it was hard separating the truth from the lies.

Paul was coming to pick her up from work in the afternoon, ostensibly to give her a batch of interview tapes he had collected from Joan. She knew she would be a bundle of nerves. After all, this would make or break their relationship.

She had hardly mentioned kids with Paul since they'd got back together. He liked kids, she knew that, but he'd always said he wanted to be set up financially before he had his own. The fact that he loved her gave Marion strength. After all — love conquers all, doesn't it?

Her writing had pushed her problems to the back of her mind. Joan had bought her a book called *Interviewing Techniques for Writers and Researchers*, which she had used to compile her questionnaires. One of the interviewees, Marcellis, seemed to know exactly what he wanted in relationships, and was anxious to show a woman he cared for that he was willing to please her. There would be no messing about in his relationships, Marion thought. He would make some woman a considerate husband.

There were other men who reminded Marion of Gerard with their attitudes. Some were bitter because they had been hurt before, and vowed never to let a woman get that close again.

She had read an article about black women travelling to America to find partners. Apparently, England was running short of eligible professional black men, and women were getting desperate. There was an upcoming television programme on Channel 4 called *Shopping for Mr Right*. Marion would make a point of watching it.

She was definitely enjoying writing again, especially using this enlightening method. Paul had even volunteered to be one of her subjects.

The day ticked by slowly. Five minutes before the library finally closed, Paul turned up. He smiled at her over the counter, his eyes sparkling.

"Can I get some service over here?" he said.

Marion leaned on the counter with her forearms and kissed him on the lips. He looked so handsome, dressed in a navy blue sweater that laced up from his chest to his neck, and black jeans. He had just had his hair shaved again, and was looking dashingly masculine.

"You ought to leave that till you get home," Sandra, a colleague of hers, called over from the enquiry desk. "You're making me jealous."

Paul chuckled.

Marion turned back to him. "Never mind Sandra," she said, loud enough for Sandra to hear, "she's got a list of men waiting to kiss her."

Sandra laughed and tossed her long brown hair back from her face.

Paul took one of Marion's hands and kissed it. "I'll see you outside."

She put her smile back on again. "Yeah. Won't be long."

Paul left and Marion sighed. She didn't know if she could go through with this.

Sandra brought her mind back to earth. "Cor! He's good looking, ain't he? Good bod too."

"Thanks, Sandra. And he's all mine."

"Well, you know where to send him when you've finished with him."

Marion smiled.

Paul's attempts at conversation fell on deaf ears as they drove home. Marion's mind was elsewhere. Eventually he gave up and they sat in silence.

Autumn leaves blew around their feet and fell like snowflakes from the trees as they walked hand in hand towards the flats. Paul had asked her if she was all right as they'd left the car. He was concerned. Marion had told him she was fine — just tired, that's all. He had given her a warm hug before taking her hand. She wished he wasn't being so loving. Not now, when she was doing this to him.

Paul opened the door with his own set of keys. Marion followed behind, unease churning in her stomach. Paul took her jacket while she went into the living room.

"Fancy a cuppa?" he called after her.

"Not now, P. I'll have one later." She slumped into the armchair. With her head rested on its back, she closed her eyes. She had deliberately chosen the armchair so that he couldn't sit next to her while she told him.

She heard him come into the living room and stop by the side of the chair. "What's wrong, Marion? I know when something's bothering you."

He was always so sensitive to her needs.

She couldn't put it off any longer. She wished she had thought of writing a note, going away for a couple of days and waiting for his reaction on her return. But it had to be now. They were alone. She had no excuses left. This was it.

She cleared her throat.

Paul sat on the arm of the sofa opposite. She didn't look at him. Instead, she played with her sister's chain that she wore around her neck. "I've got something to tell you," she said quietly, frowning, her head bowed as she spoke.

Paul leaned forward, hands on knees. "Is this bad news?"

"How would you feel . . ." she began, and then stopped to clear her throat again. "What would you say if I told you I was pregnant?" Her heart thudded loudly in her chest as she waited for his answer.

Paul's face, which had been wearing a worried frown, now held a look of puzzled surprise. For a second she thought he hadn't got it. There was a silence during which Marion felt as though she was going to pass out. She could hear children playing on the balcony outside — carefree, young and innocent. She wanted to be that young again, never growing up, never having to go through the stress of being an adult . . .

"Are we having a baby?" Paul came over and hunched down in front of her. He took her shaking hands in his and observed her.

She held his gaze, wishing it were possible to read his mind.

She nodded.

He searched her eyes, her face. "How?"

What did he mean, *how*? Why was he making this harder than it already was? A sudden thought occurred to her: suppose he was sterile or something. She raised an eyebrow at him, and a smile slowly spread across his lips and lit up his eyes as he laughed.

"I mean, I thought you were on the pill or sup'm. I seen you take 'em."

Marion had pretended to take the pill. She kept a packet on the bedside table and pressed one out every morning, disposing of it. She pondered for a minute before beginning her rehearsed speech. "The week I broke up with Gerard I stopped taking them. I didn't think I'd be with anyone so soon . . ." The lies started tripping off her tongue with ease. "The night you came round, I wanted you . . . I wasn't thinking straight. I'd been off the pill for a week. I missed my last period and put it down to stress. I did a test a week ago."

Paul stood up and walked slowly to the window. He rubbed his hands across his eyes, then shoved them into his trouser pockets. His back to her, his strong shoulders rose and then came down slowly. "A baby," he said.

Marion stared at her hands clasped in her lap. "I can understand if you don't want . . ." she began, but he rushed over to her.

"Don't say what I think you're going to say. Our baby!" He pulled her up to him and folded her into his arms.

A great tide of relief surged in her heart. "You don't mind?"

"We're together, aren't we? How can I mind?" He held her away from him and looked into her moist eyes. "It is mine, isn't it?"

Her voice remained low, her eyelids shading her usually jovial eyes in a modest downward look. "I can't be one hundred per cent sure, but I never missed the pill with Gerard. He made sure of that."

Paul grinned. "So when's it due?"

"May."

The baby was actually due in April. She would carry on as though it was premature when the time came.

"Another Taurean like me!" He manoeuvred her over to the sofa and they sat down.

"Can we afford it though, Paul?"

"I'm working. We've got this place. We'll manage." He kissed her forehead.

Marion's eyes flitted to the ceiling. She said a silent prayer: *Thank you, God. I'll never ask you for anything else again.*

Later, Marion woke uneasily in the dark. Disorientated, she looked over at the luminous clock on the bedside table. Three twenty-three. She tried to remember what had woken her. A nightmare? If it was, it was already fading fast.

Rolling on to her stomach, she hugged her pillows to her. They were soft and comfortable, but tonight they weren't comforting. She was aware of something in the dream, something only partially discernable, as if it lay behind a veil, there for her to see but still out of reach. It was as though her subconscious was putting something precious somewhere safe, never to be found again.

She turned over on to her back and listened. She could hear the rumble of traffic coming from down below, the distant sounds of her neighbours doing whatever people do at this time in the morning. She felt for Paul. Her hand slid along his hot back. He was always hot. She prodded him gently, wanting him to wake up.

Paul shifted slightly in his sleep, but didn't wake.

Marion lay with her eyes open for a while, listening to his shallow breathing. As sleep slowly descended upon her once more she closed her eyes — and all of a sudden the dream came rushing back.

Her eyes flew open again, warding it off. It was about the baby. Her baby was going to be deformed; something was going to be terribly wrong with it. She had lied, and for her sins her baby was going to be cursed.

Paul was a decent guy, who through no fault of his own was being misled, and this deceit would lead to his ultimate unhappiness.

Marion sat up in the dark, feeling claustrophobic. She reached for the lamp and switched it on. The whole room came to life, and the shadows which had crowded her consciousness shrank back into the corners.

She looked round at Paul, who was flinging back the sheets and struggling to wake up. "Marion, what's wrong?" he whispered hoarsely.

She took his hand in hers. "I had a bad dream."

"Come here," he said, pulling her back to him. He smoothed her hair away from her face and kissed her forehead.

As he drifted back to sleep, blissfully unaware of her inner torment, Marion lay in his arms, still feeling uneasy. Over and over in her mind she struggled to relieve herself of the terrible guilt and fear that had gripped her. She had had a bad dream, that was all. The baby would be fine, she and Paul would be fine . . . They were happy. That was all that mattered.

PAUL

Honestly, I couldn't think of anything that would make me happier than I feel now.

I love kids. I've always wanted to have my own — with the right woman. I'm twenty-four years old, and I'm ready for some responsibility. I want to be able to to take care of my own family, show people that it's not every black man who runs from the responsibility of bringing up children.

Me and Marion are good together. We jus' cool, yuh know. A kid of ours couldn't turn out wrong. This is our baby, and we both want it. Yeah, maybe I would have wanted to wait a bit longer, if we had the choice, but these things happen.

22. DOWN TO EARTH

Pamela's reflection stared back at her from the shop window on Peckham's Rye Lane. She had been admiring the snazzy red sequined dress on the emaciated mannequin, and had been staring so hard that she began to see herself in it.

In the fantasy that slowly began to form in her mind, she was on a stage with Satisfaction, the male strippers. They were wearing dinner suits, and it was her role to undress them, one item at a time, moving from one pumped-up body to the next. She would remove a garment slowly and seductively, toss it aside, and then proceed to caress and squeeze their biceps. This would go on until they were down to their pouches. The oil would come out next, and she would smother their rippling muscles from head to foot. Then it would be their turn to help her off with the sequined dress . . .

In her mind's eye she turned to them for the finale, and found they were all wearing Michael's face.

She snapped out of the daydream as suddenly as she had fallen into it. Jesus! She was becoming some kind of nymphomaniac. All she ever dreamed of was naked men, and nowadays they always seemed to end up being Michael.

She strolled up the road to the meat market. It was early morning, the best time to shop. Hardly anyone was on the streets. Any later, and getting from one end of Peckham to the other became an assault course, especially at Christmas.

Peckham had always felt like home to Pamela. Her parents had lived here until she was twelve years old. She remembered standing by her mother's side and listening to the conversations she had with her acquaintances as they travelled this very street. Her mother had always bumped into people she knew, from church, from back home, and people who had moved away but still came back to Peckham to shop.

"How you do, Miss P?"

"Bwoy! Not too good, yuh know."

"Wha'appen?"

"Me art'ritis ah kill me, Ma."

"Ah so? So wha' de doctor seh?"

"Dacta! All him a gi'me ah drugs fe mess up me head."

Or, "Ah Pamela dis? Look 'pon how she a tu'n big ooman now."

"Not too big to know her place," her mother would huff, pushing up her chest with crossed arms.

"Is true! Too much ah dem pickney nowadays ha' no respec'."

"Is de parent dem! Spoil de pickney, tu'n dem fool."

"Yuh nuh hear seh Miss Bea son lack up inna jailhouse again?"

"No! Fe wha'?"

"Ah no, me jus' tell yuh so, but de bwoy mash up some white gal face, near kill her."

"Ah true?"

"Then whey me jus' seh? Dem tell me de gal did sleep wid one nudda man."

"Well, she did get whey she ah look fa."

Gossip.

Then her mother would go home and relay it all back to her father, word for word.

Pamela felt her stomach tighten at the thought of her parents. She hadn't seen them in five years. She had no one except herself to care about.

That was good, wasn't it?

The only family she had now were her friends. Her mother and father didn't want to know. Every year she sent them a card. Not once had she received one back.

To them, they didn't have a daughter.

She sometimes regretted the way she had parted with her parents, helping herself to the cash savings they kept in a box under their bed. But at the time she'd felt she was entitled to take something on her departure.

Only once had she attempted a reconciliation. Her sour-faced mother had slammed the front door in her face. Her father had come to the living room window of their semi-detached house and peered out at her, stone-faced. When the tears had threatened she'd turned and run away from the hurt and humiliation.

Now, Pamela always spent Christmases with Joan and Shereen. This year, Joan and Colin had invited her and Michael for Christmas dinner. Joan still hadn't met Michael, and was dying to see the man that had managed to conquer Miss Pamela King.

Pamela had bought presents for both Joan and Shereen (Marion was away with Paul and wouldn't be around to share Christmas with them), but Michael's present was harder to choose. It would have to be something unique, and it would have to mean something to both of them.

Back in Deptford and her lonely flat, Pamela picked up her mail at the front door and switched on the answerphone while she unpacked the shopping.

"Pam, it's Joan. Call me back. See ya."

"Hi, babes. Michael. I'll be round eight o'clock. Later." Pamela smiled at the sound of his voice.

"It's Shaun. If you're there, pick up . . ." Pause. "I want to see you. Call me."

Pamela thought it was probably time to change her number, as Joan had done. Like a spring-clean thing.

The shopping unpacked, she picked up her mail and flipped through it as she crossed back into the living room. Phone bill, junk mail, Christmas card, and a letter from an organisation called NORCAP — probably some charity.

She started with the Christmas card — good news first. It was from an old schoolfriend, Yvette. They never saw each other, or even exchanged words on the telephone, but every year without fail Pamela would send her a Christmas card and would receive one back. This year Pamela had forgotten, but it wasn't too late. She put the card aside, a mental picture of what Yvette must look like now entering her head. She had two kids now, and had been engaged for two years. Good for her.

Next she opened the phone bill. Eighty-four quid! She slapped a hand to her forehead. Shocked, she unfolded the itemised statement and perused the list of numbers. She counted fifteen calls to Michael on his mobile number. She would have to stick to using his land line from now on.

The last envelope was the one from NORCAP. She opened it and read the letterhead: National Organisation for the Counselling of Adoptees and Parents. Her brow furrowed as she read further.

Dear Ms King

We are writing to you on behalf of Mrs Eileen Cummins. Your parents, Mr and Mrs King of Howden Street, London SE15, have given us permission to inform you of your adoptive status. Mrs Cummins, your natural mother, wishes to make contact with you. We realise that a considerable amount of stress is brought about by these circumstances, and want to help both parties through this.

Of course, the decision is yours, and no further contact will be made unless you inform our office, quoting the above reference number, to let us know that you want more information. Mrs Cummins does not have your details, and knows only that we have successfully traced you.

Please do not hesitate to contact us if we can be of any further assistance.

Yours sincerely
Karen Tomkin

The pages fell to the floor. Pamela closed her eyes, but the words still swam behind her eyelids: *Adoptive status . . . Natural mother . . . ADOPTIVE STATUS.*

Marion got up from her desk and closed the window. A football match was going on in the square outside her flats, which made concentration very difficult.

Another batch of tapes had arrived yesterday. She had spent all morning on just three of them. These were for the Valentine's Day issue: Black Men on Love.

There was a definite pattern emerging from listening to these guys talk about their feelings. The interesting thing was that they didn't really discuss their emotions. Anger and frustration, perhaps, but when it came to love and intimacy they either skipped it altogether or watered it down. Men, Marion concluded, clearly have their own language, which women have no chance of understanding.

Some men talked of how they could get out of arguments with their women with simple white lies. They would say things like "I'll call you", which simply meant goodbye. They would give potential girlfriends work or mobile numbers, so that their woman wouldn't know they were fooling around. When some said they needed their own space it meant they were seeing someone else. Instead of telling their women how they felt about them, some said they would buy gifts, take them out, or offer to decorate.

The male ego was something that manifested itself strongly in the recordings. Men with no money would come out with, "I believe in equality," when what they really wanted to say was, "You can pay your share; I'm skint."

Marion was concerned by the discovery that a man finds it hard to admit to his woman when something is wrong. If he has problems, he'd rather not share them with his partner, because he would see it as a doubling of the burden, a weakness. How could she possibly help?

One subject explained in detail why he didn't phone his partner if he was going to be late meeting her. It was because he would usually be with friends or colleagues, and a phone call to his partner would make him look henpecked, like he had to ask her permission.

Men hated to ask for anything. "Why should we have to ask when it's our right to receive?" said one. If his woman ever turned him down for sex, he would demand to know who else she was getting it from.

Communication was a big problem. Marion's questions included what men talked to their partners about. The responses ranged from work to what they were going to eat tonight. One topic they always seemed to avoid in long-term relationships was their feelings. Most subjects said they felt they knew when their partners were happy or sad, so they didn't need to ask them. They said women needed to communicate more as well; even if it meant a disagreement, at least the man would know how they felt.

There were also a few very considerate men, men who talked and listened to their partners, men who expressed their true emotions rather than what they felt their partner wanted to hear, men who put their families before their friends and careers. One such example was a twenty-five-year-old who said he was raising his two-year-old daughter on his own because when his girlfriend found out she was pregnant she didn't want it. He'd persuaded her to have the baby and had promised to take the child off her hands and raise it himself. Which he did, and never regretted it.

Joan flipped the catalogue shut. She had ploughed through pages of children's toys looking for a present for Shereen. She knew what her daughter wanted: another Barbie doll. Martin had promised to buy her the latest one, which could say twenty different phrases. But Joan was hell-bent on buying her something educational. A computer would be ideal, and it didn't have to be expensive for a four-year-old child.

It was at times like these when Joan thought of how lonely Shereen must be, lacking any brothers or sisters to play with at home. And yet she didn't seem to mind. It was the norm for her. When Joan had the time she would read or draw with her, do quizzes, watch her play. These times were very precious to them both: mother and daughter in perfect harmony.

Joan would sometimes find herself envying Barbie and Ken. The plastic couple shared their baby duties, spent evenings in on the sofa, sunbathed on their roof garden, went raving together, and slept side by side in the same bed under the roof of the Barbie dreamhouse.

At least Martin was back on the scene now — even if it was as a part-time father. Despite Joan's doubts about his intentions, it still halved the burden. She didn't have to be alone any more.

And Colin was just as much a father as an uncle to Shereen. She had asked her daughter what she thought of him coming to live with them. In reply, Shereen had asked why Daddy couldn't come and live with them again, and Joan had patiently explained once again that Mummy and Daddy didn't love each other any more, and that now Mummy loved Uncle Colin and wanted to be with him.

It was hard for a four-year-old to grasp, Joan knew, but Shereen had shrugged and said she didn't mind, so long as Daddy could still come and see her.

More than anything else right now, Joan wanted a stable family life for her daughter. She knew Colin was trying, but he had a lot to learn about commitment and about sharing someone else's life. In time, Joan hoped, and with her help, he would learn.

It was also nice having her younger sister living with her, albeit temporarily. They could do stuff together like shopping for clothes, pigging out on a Friday night with a video and a bottle of wine; they had a laugh. Plus, Donna was a permanent babysitter and someone to help with the housework and cooking.

The only problem was the lack of privacy. Upstairs was banned for sex unless Donna was out; Joan's creaky bed would give her away every time. There was a new "Do Not Disturb" sign for the living room door, designed by Shereen, for when Colin came round.

For the first time in years, despite all the recent changes in her circumstances, Joan felt as though her life was coming together.

23. FAMILY

The Victoria coach terminal was very busy. It was Christmas week, and everyone seemed to be heading somewhere to visit friends or family.

Marion pulled her coat tighter around her as Paul took her arm and they dashed across the road to where the coach was filling up with people. They were on their way to spend a week with Marion's mother in Birmingham.

Paul had finally persuaded her to tell her mother about the baby. Sooner would be better than later, he had reasoned, and at least they would be telling her together. They were also bringing the good news of Marion's first published article. She had a copy of the magazine in her luggage.

Marion had let Paul take charge of the arrangements. He'd

decided he didn't want to drive all the way to Birmingham, saying he wouldn't have much use for his car there. His real reason for taking the coach was that he wanted to be able to relax with her.

Marion was now six months pregnant — five, if you asked Paul — and the bump was just beginning to show. She was feeling a lot better these days. Ever since she had told Paul about the baby the morning sickness had virtually stopped. The dizziness and lethargy she'd suffered now came about only when she was tired. And Paul was taking good care of her. They were living together now, albeit unofficially. Paul only went home a couple of days a week. He would pick her up from work and make sure she was comfortable at home, sometimes helping out in the kitchen. She'd been teaching him how to cook. He'd said he had to learn, so that he could take over once the baby was born.

She began to nod off half an hour into the journey. They had left home at eight o'clock that morning, having been up at six to check the packing and get organised. Paul cradled her head on his shoulder and wrapped an arm around her shoulder. If there was one thing that Marion could be certain of in her life, it was that Paul loved her.

The coach jolted to a halt and Marion awoke. She straightened up in her seat, blinking the sleep out of her eyes.

"Hi." Paul gave her a squeeze.

She kissed him lightly on the lips. "Hi yourself." She gazed out of the window. "Where are we?"

"Just a coach stop. You all right?"

"Thirsty," she said, licking her dry lips.

Paul reached into their holdall and produced a bottle of orange juice. He twisted the cap, breaking the seal, and poured some juice into a plastic cup for her.

She accepted it and drank it down in one go. Handing the cup back to him, she smiled. "Thanks, hon."

"Anything for my girl." He smiled back. "You still nervous?" He stroked the soft skin of her forearm.

Marion tilted her head back against the headrest. "Aren't you? You've never met my mum and stepdad. It isn't going to be easy. I don't know how you talked me into this." She regarded him with serious, dark eyes.

"You can't tell me that you'd prefer to turn up one day on your mother's doorstep with a child. You have to tell her now."

Marion sulked. "S'pose so."

"I am right," he told her.

"I know." She put her head on his shoulder, her lips pouting a little.

He kissed her forehead. "Get some sleep — you'll need it."

"Mmm," she yawned. She closed her eyes and let him hold her, rocking her back to sleep.

The minicab deposited them outside the row of cottages at the top of a steep hill. Marion had only been here once before, eighteen months earlier. Paul held her gloved hand, carrying their suitcase in the other. Marion had deliberately chosen loose clothing to cover the evidence of her pregnancy. She wore a big baggy jumper over leggings. They stood outside her parents' front door, shivering with the cold and nervousness, daring each other to ring the doorbell.

"Please, Paul. You do it," she asked.

"What's wrong with you?" he laughed. "It's your mum."

"I'm not ready for this. Can't we go somewhere for a drink first to calm my nerves?" She tugged at his hand.

"Later. Let's get this part over with first." He dropped the suitcase to the ground at his side and rang the bell in the centre of a seasonal holly wreath.

The door was opened almost immediately, as if the woman had been standing behind it all along. They looked at each other, and Marion smiled despite herself.

Paul felt relieved. He'd had no idea what to expect at this reunion. The last time he had seen Mrs Wilkins was at the funeral of Marion's sister. She looked a lot healthier now. Gwendolyn Wilkins could have been Marion, only twenty years older. Their facial features were identical. They were about the same height, but Paul hoped Marion's figure wouldn't spread quite that much with age.

Gwendolyn held out her arms to her daughter. "Marion," she uttered.

"Hello, Mum." Marion stepped into her mother's arms and they hugged.

As they stepped apart, Marion's mother let her eyes flit over Marion's body. "You do look well. Rosy cheeks."

Paul cleared his throat, and both women turned as if surprised that he was there.

"Oh, Mum — you remember Paul, my boyfriend?"

Gwendolyn held out her hand to him and he stepped forward. Instead of his usual greeting of a peck on the cheek, he shook her hand formally. "Nice to see you again," he said, switching on his smiling eyes — and Marion watched Gwendolyn try to restrain her smile.

"Likewise, I'm sure." She stepped back to let them into the house. "Come in, bring your things. Thomas isn't home yet, but you'll see him later." She ushered them through the pastel-coloured hallway, her bottom rolling from side to side under the black pinafore dress she wore.

There was a smell of baking in the air. Marion recognised the aroma of her mother's cinnamon scones, and memories came flooding back. Her mother had always been in the kitchen when they were little, cooking, baking, washing, cleaning. The house always had to be just so, with breakfast, lunch and dinner served at the same time every day.

The low afternoon sun shone on the walls, and sunbeams danced in the air above their heads from a window at the top of the first flight of stairs. Gwendolyn showed them into the living room, where they sat on a cosy rose-coloured sofa that looked brand new. Marion was sure it only looked that way because this was the room they used only for visitors.

Her mother went off to make hot drinks for them all, leaving them alone for a few minutes.

"I can't see what all the fuss was about." Paul shrugged.

"Mum's all right on her own. Wait till *he* gets home," Marion warned, removing her gloves.

Paul couldn't believe it would be as bad as Marion was making out. Her mother seemed to like him, and there didn't seem to be any animosity between the two women.

He looked around the modest room. It looked very cosy, but rich. Not exactly the kind of place you would let a child roam free in. A large decorated fir tree stood in the corner by the fireplace. The white lights blinked on and off as if following some inaudible tune. Brightly wrapped gifts already sat beneath it.

Gwendolyn came back in with the tea and sat opposite them in the matching rose-coloured armchair. She told Paul he could call her Gwen. Mrs Wilkins was much too formal.

Gwendolyn and Paul were getting on like old friends. He complimented her and made her laugh with tasteful jokes and anecdotes of his experiences.

Marion was amazed at the way he manipulated her mother. She couldn't quite believe that this was the same woman who had left her two years ago. Paul held Marion's hand the entire time. Every now and then he would give it a little squeeze or turn to smile at her, his eyes sparkling with charm.

Her mother was gently grilling him. She had a way of gaining information that made it seem like simple curiosity. She seemed to want to know every detail of his past, and his plans for the future. Paul coped with it with admirable ease.

As she sat beside him, Marion began to realise just how much she loved this man. Over the past four months she had still feared she might be in love with Gerard. But the truth of the matter was, she had never been in love with Gerard. The realisation flooded her mind as she sat in her mother's living room. She had been in love with what other women thought she had. The actual man was nothing but a fake.

Paul looked over at her and she smiled, realising she had been staring at him. She leant her head on his shoulder and he moved his arm, wrapping it around her waist.

Gwendolyn noticed this, and with a silent smile she stood up. "I'll just clear these things away. Paul, I'll show you where the two of you will be sleeping — you can bring your things."

"Yeah, okay," he said, standing up to follow her. He turned to Marion as her mother left the room. "You all right?"

"Yeah, sure." She nodded. In fact she had never felt better. She added, "I love you, Panther."

It was the first time she had told him, and she knew it had been worth it to see the look on his face. His eyes smiled at her and he leant over and kissed her on the lips.

"Love you too."

He was grinning as he left the room to catch up with her mother.

Thomas Wilkins was a big man — six foot five — and he looked as though he had done weightlifting in the past and then let himself go. The fact was that he had spent his youth loading ships and lorries in Liverpool, and his muscles were natural. His features were naturally stern, and he didn't say much.

He arrived home just before dinner. During the meal the talk was light. Thomas said very little.

After dinner they went back into the living room to catch up on all the news from both sides. Thomas put the television on — a Des O'Connor Christmas special.

"So, how is Joany?" Gwendolyn asked, pouring a glass of sherry for them all. She had been calling Marion's friend Joany ever since she was about eight years old.

"She's fine, Mum. She's just got engaged, actually."

Gwendolyn looked up, astonished. She turned to her husband. "Joany getting married! Isn't that nice, Tom?"

Thomas nodded. "Nice," he growled, his eyes not leaving the television screen.

Marion frowned. She doubted he even remembered who 'Joany' was, having only met her once, at the funeral.

"Mum, we . . . er, have some news for you as well," she said, reaching for Paul's hand.

"Yes?" Her mother's eyes travelled from Marion to Paul expectantly.

Marion swallowed hard, trying to find the words she needed to explain her situation to her mother. The lights on the Christmas tree carried on their merry dance as if mocking her. What made it harder was her stepfather had suddenly become interested in the conversation.

Paul carried on for her. "I want you to know that I love this woman." He glanced at Marion. "She's brought purpose to my life, and I'm not planning on letting her go again."

Gwendolyn looked over at Thomas, who was now leaning forward in his chair, elbows on his knees. His grey eyes scrutinised the pair, waiting for the news. He had suspected there was more to their visit than a family get-together; now it seemed he was going to be proved right.

"We're going to have a baby," Marion blurted out, unable to take the pressure of the situation any longer.

She waited, watching her mother's face for a reaction. Her heart tried to escape by beating its way through her chest. Gwendolyn's face had frozen, except for the corners of her mouth which had dropped to form an unhappy arch.

"Oh," she issued.

"Hmm-mm," Thomas mumbled, and leant back in his chair, a smug look on his face.

Marion ignored him. "We want the baby, Mum. Although it wasn't planned, we really love each other, and we'll do our best to bring him — or her — up."

"Marion, you have *no* idea," Gwendolyn snapped, cutting her short. "How could you let this happen? After all I've been through with you and your sister, trying to bring you up properly . . ." Her lips trembled and her voice began to quaver.

Thomas broke his silence. "You have disappointed your mother, young lady. When she heard that you were coming to visit with your young man, she had hopes of hearing a wedding announcement — not *this*."

"Tom!" Gwendolyn held up her hand, halting his speech. She held her head high, her eyes hard, and turned on Marion. "Don't get me wrong, Marion. I'm happy that I will soon be a grandmother. But you don't know how much bringing a child into the world takes from you."

Paul stepped in to share the abuse. "We have thought about this, y'know, Gwen. We know what we're doing," he said positively.

Gwendolyn cut her eyes after him and continued talking to Marion. "How long have the two of you been back together? Six months?"

Thomas got up and walked over to the large bay windows, his back to them, feigning interest in something happening outside.

"I'm sure you feel as though you'll never part now — but you wait until that baby is born," Gwendolyn continued, her hands and arms emphasising her words with wide gestures. "When it's screaming in the middle of the night, when you're buried in housework, bills, too tired to make love — then we'll see if you still feel the same. An' how do you even know that this *boy* will stick around when the going gets tough, huh?"

Marion wanted to scream. It was right there at the back of her throat. She wanted to yell at her mother, tell her that she wasn't a lonely teenager — as her mother had been the first time she fell pregnant. She had Paul, and she had her friends. She stood and walked out defiantly under her mother's angry gaze. She was so upset she couldn't even retaliate, knowing it would mean the end of any kind of decent relationship between them.

Paul stood as well, wanting to go after Marion but feeling he hadn't said what he knew these people needed to hear. He heard Marion's footsteps on the stairs, and then a door slamming above them. He remained standing, and addressed the two people in the room as if from a pulpit. "How could you say somet'ing like that to your only daughter? You don't know what she's been through since you left her. You don't even find out firs' if yuh daughter and I are capable of bringing up our child! Cho', people like you need to sit down and t'ink about what is important in your lives before putting judgement on others."

Thomas bristled — Paul could almost see the hair on his head rising — and moved to his wife's side.

Paul started to walk out to find Marion and comfort her, but turned back again. "Y'know, when she told me she didn't want to tell you about the baby, I couldn't understand why she was so worried. I mean, you're her mother. How could you not be happy about a new addition to your family?" He clenched his teeth. "We shouldn't have come. I can tek care of her on my own!" He whirled out of the room, leaving the husband and wife staring at the empty space he had just vacated, their mouths hanging open.

The next morning the four of them sat down to a full breakfast of fried dumplings, ackee, fried fish, plantain and hard dough bread.

Marion and Paul had talked through most of the night. Paul had said that he didn't want her to fall out with her mother again, especially not over their child. Marion had persuaded him that they should retreat, go home — that they had been doing fine without family involvement, and could go on doing fine. Paul had given in because he could see her getting more and more upset. They would go to his mother's home instead, he'd suggested. His brother and sister were also going there for Christmas. They would be welcomed with open arms.

It seemed that Mr and Mrs Wilkins had also had a talk of their own.

Breaking the dough bread, Paul informed them that they were leaving on the next available coach. His announcement was met with silence, and furtive glances between Gwendolyn and Thomas across the table.

Thomas eventually broke the silence. His stern face showed no emotion as his grey, glassy eyes turned to Marion and Paul. "Gwendolyn has something she would like to say to you both." He nodded at Gwendolyn.

A smile found the corners of her small mouth. "Marion," she breathed, reaching across the table for her hand. Marion let her mother's hand rest on her own, but made no move to reciprocate. "You know how much I care about your welfare," Gwendolyn continued.

Marion still held some bleak anger within her, and couldn't bring herself to speak to her mother, much less look at her. She kept her eyes downcast.

Gwendolyn went on: "When you told me about the baby, all I could think about was myself at sixteen. I was pregnant with you; your father was too young to care, and my parents turned their back on me. I was alone and scared. I know that you're older than I was — and you have Paul, who has proved to be a very caring young man." Her eyes travelled fleetingly to Paul's face, a shadow of regret and apology being conveyed to him. "I want to say I'm sorry, and beg your forgiveness."

Marion looked up at her mother. Tears came to both their eyes. Marion stood, and walked around the dining table to her mother's side. She leant towards her mother and let herself be hugged.

Paul smiled and turned to Thomas. He offered the older man his hand across the table. And black and white met in a friendly handshake.

The decision was made. They were staying for Christmas.

During the week, Marion and her mother went shopping for presents and baby things. They also visited Gwendolyn's friends and neighbours, sometimes with Paul in tow. Gwendolyn's closest friends came round and shared the news which she was no longer ashamed of.

Christmas day was the first traditional celebration Marion had had since her mother had left London. She missed her friends, but a phone call took care of that.

The fact that Marion had Paul with her made everything perfect.

By the end of the week, they had so much extra luggage that Thomas offered to drive them back home. They accepted gratefully.

The goodbyes were tearful on the women's side. Both promised to keep in touch regularly. The men stood by, hands in pockets, not knowing whether to chat, hug or what.

Back in their own flat, Marion sank into the armchair and kicked her boots off. "I'm exhausted," she sighed.

Having switched the heating back on, Paul entered the living room and hunched down in front of her. "Now that we've got that out of the way, don't I get a thank you?" He took her small stockinged feet in his hands and rubbed them gently.

She smiled indulgently. "Of course you do. Thanks, honey. I couldn't have done it without you."

"You wouldn't have to." He reached up and kissed her, pressing his thumbs on her instep before moving up to her toes. "I've been thinking. Wouldn't it be a good idea if I jus' moved in? What do you think? It won't be long before the baby's born, an' I want to be there with you."

Marion relaxed and issued a moan of pleasure. She was so glad he had brought the subject up; she hadn't wanted to put any more pressure on him. This time it was his decision. "How soon could you move in?"

Paul grinned and, letting her foot go, he hugged her. "Tomorrow soon enough?"

"No. How about right now?" Her wide, childlike eyes danced.

"You got it."

Families. The house was buzzing with the noise of a family get-together. Joan, Donna and Grace were in the kitchen preparing the Christmas dinner.

Choice FM kept them entertained as they chatted and worked. It was the first time they had prepared Christmas dinner together since Donna had left home three years before.

Colin was playing Connect Four with Shereen in the living room — and losing badly, to Shereen's glee. Her babyish laughter could be heard throughout the house. A repeat of *The Snowman* was showing on the television.

Donna had started divorce proceedings against John, on her sister's advice. Joan had changed her number again to stop him harassing her. He wouldn't have a chance to see her unless he was brave enough to risk jail by breaking the injunction.

Although Colin and Joan had decided to get engaged, they had resolved not to tell their families and friends until they were sure it was going to work out. There was nothing worse, in Joan's opinion, than being premature with an announcement.

There would be seven for dinner this year, with Michael and Pamela coming too. This was going to be an occasion to be remembered. They would miss seeing Marion this year, but she was doing the right thing by going to see her mum.

Peeling potatoes for roasting, Grace sat at the kitchen table. Donna sat opposite, mixing batter for the Yorkshire puddings.

"So — Colin. You and him is more dan fren' now?" Grace asked for the second time that day.

The first time Joan had informed her that Colin was coming to have dinner with them her mother had wondered why. Joan had simply told her that he was family and had every right to.

Joan now bent down to the oven to check the turkey. "I've told you, Mum, we've started seeing each other recently."

"How yuh mean, seeing each udder? Yuh sharing a bed?"

"Mum!" Donna giggled.

Joan shook her head. Her mother always spoke her mind. She had taught them to do the same. "Yeah, we sleep together sometimes," she admitted, feeling a heat in her cheeks that wasn't from the oven. "But we're not living together yet," she added.

"Yuh don't t'ink is about time Shereen get a brudda or sista?" Grace dropped the last peeled potato into the bowl and handed it up to Joan.

Taking the bowl, she crossed to the sink to wash them. "I know,
191

Mum, but you don't rush these things. When I'm ready I'll decide with the baby's father."

Grace now turned to her younger daughter. "Dis one married, divorce, and don't even produce one gran' pickney. Nuttin' to bless de union wid."

Donna glared at her mother. There was no way she had wanted to have a child with John. What kind of father would he have been?

Joan jumped in to save her sister. "Don't start on her, Mum. She's young, plenty of time . . ." She was thanked by a look of appreciation in Donna's eyes.

Grace huffed and stood up to wrap the potato peel in newspaper and throw it in the bin. "You two always stick together. Patrick was de ongle chile I did have pan my side, and yuh faada tek him wey."

Joan tutted. "That's not true, mum. You spoiled Patrick — that's why he was closer to you than us. While Don and I did our chores — and his, sometimes — he was out with his mates. You always let him off."

"We always got the washing up and cooking and cleaning," Donna agreed. "All he ever did was carry the rubbish out every Thursday and hoover the carpets."

Grace screwed up her face. "Cho, a man don't have to learn to wash pot. Dat's what they have ooman fa."

Joan and Donna exchanged looks. Even though their mother was now independent, and had proved to herself and her daughters that she didn't need a man, she always made it clear that it was men who needed women. In Grace's eyes, men left their mothers to live with women, and thenceforth expected the same treatment — their clothes to be washed and ironed, cooked food ready when they got home — plus the added bonus of sex.

Joan deftly moved the conversation on. "So, Don, I forgot to ask you how you got on at that employment agency."

"Oh, they took my details, but I haven't done anything in administration for a while. They want me to take some computer course to get up to date with the systems."

"That's no problem. Community college has loads of courses."

Grace joined in. "Yes. Me will bring you de brochure from home."

"I think that's too far out for Donna, Mum. She's better off picking one up at the local library."

"She should be living back at home now, anyway. You have your man and yuh dawta to tek care of. I have plenty room, and I could do with de comp'ny."

"Maybe you're right, Mum." Joan dried her hands on a tea towel and took a seat at the table. "I could do with my privacy again. And

192

Donna could have much more of her own privacy with you. Sharing a room with her baby niece isn't right for a woman her age."

Donna listened to them discussing her life as though she wasn't there. It made her wonder what they said when she wasn't around.

Families!

Pamela and Michael arrived, dressed immaculately, just as the table was being laid.

Joan looked at the tall, dark, handsome man in the pure wool jacket, and wondered why she couldn't have met him first. "So, this is Michael?"

Pamela introduced him to everyone. Michael nodded at the smiling female faces, and then Joan took him through to the living room to meet Colin.

Michael immediately homed in on the computer game Colin was playing. "Is that Mortal Kombat?" he asked, settling down on the sofa.

"Mortal Kombat II. You wanna game?" Colin asked, glad for the male company.

"Set me up."

The girls rolled their eyes and left them to it.

"What d'you think of Michael, then?" Pamela asked eagerly.

"If I didn't have Colin I'd be in there making my move right now," Joan told her. "He is *gorgeous*. What possessed Cheryl to let him go?"

Pamela chuckled. "I don't think she could handle him."

"Well, you can tell him from me that when he gets bored of you, I'll handle him any time."

Pamela slapped Joan's arm playfully. "Hands off," she warned. "And none of that footsie under the table."

Michael and Colin had become instant mates. The talk over the lunch table was football and boxing — boxing being Colin's first love. The women stuck to gossip and their plans for the new year. Grace had already decided Donna was moving back in. Donna told her she had decided to put her name down with the council. It shouldn't be too long, she said, before she moved out. Pamela shot that remark down as optimistic. She told tales of friends who were stuck sleeping on mates' sofas for years because they were single with no dependants. "You'd have to get pregnant to get a flat off those people."

That started Grace on her gran pickney yearning again.

Joan told them that she was planning on changing her car. The Maestro was getting outdated. She wanted a car that matched her status. So, for the new year she wanted something sporty and flash ... and yet feminine. The guys joined in at the mention of cars, and there was a heated discussion about what a woman could and couldn't handle.

After a long and indulgent late-afternoon lunch, the women let the men clear the table while they retired to the living room. Shereen was shortly thereafter put to bed, followed closely by Grace an hour later.

The youngsters (as Grace called them) spent the evening chatting, laughing, playing music, drinking — and finally settled down to watch a video.

The two couples paired off.

Donna decided to slip away and retire upstairs to cuddle up to her niece.

24. LIES

Spring. A new year, a new season. A time for new beginnings; a time for the problems of the past to be resolved and put behind you. But whatever problems people manage to solve, others always seem to emerge ...

That evening it was Martin who put Shereen to bed. Joan had used the time to catch up on some work she had brought home a week ago, and was now clearing the kitchen.

Martin entered the neat room and leant against the counter by the sink.

Joan looked up at him and smiled. "Did she settle down all right?" she asked.

"Yeah. She was tired." He rested his palms behind him on the counter. Joan looked so relaxed and at ease with life and everything, that he felt an urge to encircle her waist and pull her close. But he knew it wasn't worth risking what he already had for the satisfaction of a basic human instinct.

He had been there for three hours. Usually, after Shereen went to bed, he would leave. Now he was arousing Joan's suspicion by hanging around.

"I saw Colin yesterday," he said.

Joan turned to look at him as she replied. "Yeah? How is he?" She tried to sound genuinely naive. They still hadn't told anyone about the engagement.

"He looked good. His woman must be taking care of him," Martin said, grinning.

Joan smiled to herself; she knew Colin was getting it good. But what was Martin getting at? "So, he's got a woman has he?"

"Didn't you know? He's been living with this girl in Deptford now for eight months. He's still there, so it mus' be good."

Joan stared at him with disbelieving eyes. The plate she was rinsing slipped from her hands and splashed back into the sink. "Y . . . you're joking," she stuttered.

"Naw, straight up! I was shocked too, believe me. Colin never stayed with no one for that long. I was telling him just the other day how he ought to settle down . . ."

Martin carried on talking, but Joan had phased out. There was a rush of blood pumping quickly to her head, her temples were pulsating; she fought to control her breathing but was fighting a losing battle. Something was using a tiny hammer and playing drums in her ears. Colin was deceiving her again. How could he do this to her? They were practically engaged, for God's sake! Tears of anger and frustration pricked her eyes and she pretended to sneeze to cover it up.

". . . So when he told me he was serious about someone I just had to meet her, you know what I mean?"

"You met her?" Joan whispered. She turned a plate over in the rack and reached into the suds for another.

"Yeah! They didn't seem real close or nothing, but maybe it's just 'cause I was there, you know?" He nudged her playfully with his elbow.

Bastard, bastard, bastard, she screamed in her head, and slammed another dripping plate into the rack. A grimace attached itself to her face.

Martin turned to her. "You want some help? You look kinda tired."

She shook her head. "I'm all right," she said, then she gazed back at him as a new thought entered her mind. Martin was still an attractive guy. She had loved him once; and now she loved his deceiving brother. What sweet revenge, to sleep with Colin's brother again . . . She was sure that she could play Martin straight into her hands.

She dried her hands on a dish towel. "Want a drink?" she offered.

Martin looked surprised. "Yeah," he said, unsure. "Why not?" She had never encouraged him to hang around when Shereen was absent. She had always made it clear that the only reason he was here was because Shereen needed her father. Now she was practically giving him a come-on. Women were the strangest creatures alive.

She crossed to the fridge and produced a bottle of Canei.

Martin watched her, trying to figure her out.

"Let's go and sit down," she said, grabbing two glasses from the cupboard. She handed him the bottle and led him through to the living room, where she sat on the three-seater settee and patted the space beside her, giving him the full works with her eyes. "I get so lonely sometimes in the evenings," she said. "Not having a man to talk to . . ."

Martin sat by her side and twisted the cap off the wine bottle. "Yeah, I know the feeling." He filled the wine glasses. Their eyes locked as they took the first sip together.

Joan pulled one leg up under her so that she was half facing him.

"You've really been taking care of yourself." His eyes flitted over her casual jogging attire. "Do you remember when we first met at that party?"

Joan nodded, smirking. "In New Cross. Yeah, I went with Marcia."

"All my friends were after you that night." He licked his lips. "But I got there first."

Joan leaned towards him. "I remember, you told me."

He put his glass on the floor by the settee, and his hand found itself on her knee and then rose to rest on her thigh. "You haven't changed a bit."

"Oh, so I've still got an eighteen-year-old body, have I?" she giggled.

His voice became husky. "Your body will always be the same to me."

His mouth was now so close she could feel his breath on her lips. "So tell me," she said matter-of-factly. "What's she look like?"

The spell was broken. Martin drew back, a puzzled frown on his face. "Who?"

"Colin's girlfriend."

He pulled his hand away and rested his head on the back of the sofa. "When were you going to tell me?"

Now it was Joan's turn to frown. "Tell you what?"

His eyes drifted to a framed portrait of Joan and Shereen on top of the TV cabinet. "Shereen reckons her Uncle Colin is coming to live with you."

Joan gasped, flustered. Kids! Never know how to keep something to themselves. "It isn't what you think . . ."

"How do you know what I think? You've been seeing my brother for months, from what Shereen's been telling me, an' you couldn't even mention it."

Joan stood up and turned her back to him. "Colin and I have been seeing each other, but it's only just got serious. We didn't want to tell anyone because we weren't sure how it would work out."

"I'm his brother, for goodness' sake! Family!"

Joan remembered that she was trying to get information out of him, not argue about her personal life. She returned to the sofa and looked him in the eye. "Martin . . . this other woman, that was just to wind me up, right?" she questioned hopefully.

Martin smirked. "No. He really is living with a girl in Deptford."

Joan felt her heart stop for at least three seconds. She dry-swallowed. "But didn't he ever mention me?"

"No. Jus' like you didn't mention him."

Her anger rose again, and she jumped up and paced the room.

Martin watched with a critical grin on his face. He found the whole situation hilarious. "So, you want to tell me about you and Colin?" he asked.

Joan didn't know where to begin. She decided that the the beginning would be best.

"When you left, we started seeing each other." She paused. Martin already knew that his brother had caught Joan on the rebound, although perhaps he didn't know the extent of their involvement. Either way, it hadn't seemed to affect him that much. His eyes were serious, expressionless, waiting. "We were just friends at first; nothing happened until I was sure I was over you . . ."

She told him everything, right up until the last time she had seen Colin. She even told him about how Lois had pretended to be pregnant to keep him, to trick him into marrying her.

"Yeah?" he chuckled. "Jus' like Colin to fall for that one. She mus' know him well."

Joan took offence at that remark. The only reason Colin had "fallen for it" was because he cared what happened to his child. She wanted to blast Martin with that one, but there was still information to get from him, and she didn't want to rock the boat.

Martin had raised his eyebrows at the fact that they'd got engaged.

"I wanted him to tell you," she said earnestly. "It was so childish not to tell the family. It was the best way, though. You know Colin — heaven only knows how long it was going to last before he got itchy feet again."

Martin nodded vaguely. He looked up at her as she paused in mid

197

stroll. "You going to dump him?"

She looked shocked at the suggestion, as if it hadn't occurred to her. "I can't. Well, not until I talk to him about it."

Martin raised his hands in a "keep me out of it" gesture. "Don't say it came from me. Colin and I are on shaky ground as it is. You know we weren't talking for a while."

Joan knew all about the year the two of them hadn't talked to each other. Colin had taken her side in the break-up, and was putting pressure on his brother. His mother had taken Martin's side, and the family had become split. Their mother had finally brought them back together the Christmas before last.

"I need his address, Marty. I'll tell him someone else saw him going in and told me about it. No names, I promise."

Martin almost laughed. "Shit, Joan. I can't." He placed his palms on his knees as though he was getting ready to stand.

"I promise, he'll never know," she begged. She got down and kneeled comically at his feet.

"He'll guess." Martin avoided her eyes.

She changed tactics. "I thought you cared about me," she said.

Martin sighed deeply. Women! They always come out with that line when a man tries to assert himself. "I do, but—"

"How else am I gonna find out the truth?" she interrupted. "He'll deny it unless I catch him in the act."

Martin leaned back and thought about it. "He's living in Dolphin Towers. Eighty-nine."

Joan memorised the address and squeezed Martin's hand. "Ta. And don't look so worried. You're doing this for me." She smiled appeasingly, her Egyptian eyes enchanting him.

She poured some more wine and the two of them sat and chatted until the early hours of the morning. Joan had wanted to go straight to Dolphin Towers that night.

She was going to get her man. Tomorrow would do just fine.

It was ten o'clock at night when Joan pulled up outside the block of flats. As she stood outside the flat, she could hear the sound of a radio and imagined them together in there. She had had to psyche herself up on the way over; now she had to again before knocking on the door. Her heart was beating way too fast. Her palms were sweaty, and a fine sheen of perspiration glazed her top lip.

She breathed deeply and knocked loudly. She heard the sound of a door opening and the radio momentarily getting louder, then slippered feet coming towards the front door. She drew her chest up, hands by her side military style, ready for the confrontation.

The door swung open and the same young woman she had seen that day in Lewisham stood before her, dressed in jeans and a jumper.

She looked Joan up and down. "Yes?" Hostility was harsh in her voice.

Joan didn't let it deter her. She cleared her throat. "Is Colin in?"

"Who're you?" the girl asked, standing her ground.

"Just get Colin. He knows who I am."

"He's sleeping," the girl lied.

"Well, wake him up." Joan was getting ready to barge in if she had to.

The girl looked her up and down again, a malignant scowl on her face, before stepping back into the flat. She wasn't much to look at: plain and flat-chested, with short, unstyled hair and a huge backside. Whatever it was that had attracted him, it wasn't her looks.

A moment later Colin came out. The look on his face was nothing short of comical. Joan would have laughed if she wasn't so angry.

He shut the inner door behind him. Dressed in black track suit bottoms and a white T-shirt, he looked as though he hadn't slept for a couple of days.

They faced each other, Colin leaning against the wall in that easygoing way of his.

Joan stood with her hands thrust into her jacket pocket. "Was that Lois?" she asked.

Colin looked down at his feet. "Yeah. How did you find out where I lived?"

"Why didn't you tell me?"

He shrugged. "This looks bad, doesn't it?" He peered at her from beneath his long eyelashes.

"Damn right it looks bad. What the hell d'you think you're playing at?"

"She's renting me a room."

Joan rolled her eyes to the ceiling. "And just what *else* is she renting?" she jested sarcastically.

He shrugged again, his muscular shoulders hunched in disgrace. He was like a little boy caught stealing. "This isn't what you think. I wouldn't two-time you." He sighed deeply. "I was evicted from my flat. It was before we got back together. I moved in here because there was nowhere else to go," he explained.

"Not good enough." Joan put one hand on her hip. "After what she did . . . Why didn't you tell me you needed somewhere to live?"

"Because I've *got* somewhere to live! I wasn't out on the streets."

Joan screwed up her face in disgust. "With *her*?"

Colin raised his hands and glanced towards the inner door. "Keep your voice down — she's a funny person."

"I don't give a fuck what kind of person she is. You're my man, or so I thought. If what you said is true, then she's got no hold over you. You could leave with me right now."

Colin kissed his teeth. "What're you talking about?"

"I'm talking about you moving in with me. Get your things. The car's downstairs."

Colin was shocked; he couldn't move. He studied her eyes. "Are you sure?"

Joan stood up straight, asserting her seriousness. "I wouldn't say it otherwise. It seems the only way I can keep an eye on you is if you're coming home to me every night. So — are you coming or not?"

He grinned out of the side of his mouth. "You giving me orders now?"

"If that's the way you want to see it, yes I am."

"You don't believe me, do you?" He searched her still angry eyes.

"I'll believe you if you go in there and come out with your things packed," she told him.

"Okay, you got me." He was still grinning as he stepped towards her. "I do love you, y'know. Even though you're a mad, impulsive fool."

She remained dead serious; she would deal with him properly at home. "Need any help packing?"

His hands dropped to his sides. "I don't think that's a good idea. Why don't you wait in the car?"

Joan huffed and ran a hand through her short, bobbed hair. "Why?"

"Well, Lois ain't gonna be too happy about losing her lodger."

"I think I'll wait right here I wouldn't wanna miss the big farewell," she said defiantly. She was well aware of what she could learn from the next two minutes. If this was an affair, it would be more than a simple goodbye and a handshake.

Colin went back into the flat, closing the front door. There was a lot of talk going on inside. Joan strained to hear what was going on, resorting eventually to pressing her ear against the front door.

"Who is she?" she heard Lois say with some spite.

"None of your business."

"Where d'you think you're going?"

"Home."

"Don't talk to me like that!"

"Where's my blue jacket?"

"You can't just leave in the middle of the night."

"Try stopping me."

"You don't care about me."

"You got that right."

Joan heard a loud thump, as if something had hit the wall, and she sprang back as the front door opened.

Lois's voice followed Colin out of the flat. "Get out! Jus' get out! Mek sure you tek everything, else it ain't gonna be here when you come back!"

Colin struggled out with two huge holdalls bulging with clothes and a rucksack on his back. "Grab these for me. I'm going back for my stereo," he said, handing her the bags. Joan dragged them over to the lift and pressed the down button.

The lift arrived as Colin was coming back out of the flat. Joan heaved the bags in and turned to him. He carried his stereo in both arms. He smiled. She smiled back. This was finally going to be it. Colin was hers.

Neither of them was prepared for what happened next. There was an unearthly scream from behind Colin, and over his shoulder Joan caught a glimpse of a raised arm that ended in a kitchen knife. The arm swiped downwards towards Colin's back. Acting on sheer instinct, Joan had grabbed his jacket and pulled him towards her, but the knife caught him in the arm.

The stereo dropped with a load crack as it hit the concrete floor, half in, half out of the lift. Colin uttered a strangled cry and tried to clutch at his injured arm; the knife had pierced the sleeve of his jacket. There was a stunned look on his face as he stumbled and fell, and the lift tried to close on his legs, automatically opening again.

He wasn't too badly hurt, and he pulled himself into a sitting position. There was already blood seeping through his thin jacket. Joan glared across at the woman holding the knife and fury welled up within her.

As Lois came at them again, Joan, free of any baggage, climbed over Colin's legs and ran head-first into the girl's stomach. The wind knocked out of her, Lois retreated and stumbled back against the wall, the knife flying out of her hand. Joan went for her again, dragging her up by her short hair and digging her nails into her scalp. She balled her hand into a fist and slammed it hard into the girl's face, feeling it connect with the bridge of her nose. Then she open-handedly slapped her across her cheek.

Lois struggled, yelping and screaming, to grab Joan. She parried a clumsy blow and struck out with her left foot. But Joan was bigger and stronger. She threw the girl hard against the wall by her hair and blood splattered from the girl's nose which, Joan suspected, she'd broken. Splashes of blood landed on Joan's cream blouse and jacket.

Lois went limp, and Joan let her fall to a heap on the concrete floor by her front door.

A door opened cautiously down the hall. Joan ignored the African man who came out to stare.

Colin was leaning against the lift door, blood dripping from his arm.

"You okay?" she asked him breathlessly, kneeling by his side.

"Me? I'm fine. Let's just get out of here." He eased himself against one wall of the lift, Joan dragged his stuff in behind them, and they descended.

Back home that night they took a bath together. Colin's stab wound wasn't as bad as it had at first appeared. Joan had bandaged it tight to stop the bleeding. Now she sat opposite him at the tap end of the bath.

He lay back with a flannel covering his boyish face.

"Colin?"

"Mmm?"

"There must be things you don't like about me."

He removed the flannel from his face and lowered it into the warm water.

Joan placed a hand on his knee. "You know I can't be perfect. What would you see as my faults?" she asked.

"Well . . ." he thought, "you always see the bad side of things . . ."

"Uh-uh," Joan interrupted, shaking her head. "I'm a realist. I don't sugar-coat things. I tell it like it really is."

"Yeah, whatever. It comes over as pessimism, though. You have bad mood swings too." He paused for thought. "Like when you're angry at me. All of a sudden you come over all passionate or sweet, and then you're angry and bitter again. I hate that. I never know where I am with you."

Joan frowned. Maybe this wasn't such a good idea after all.

Colin continued none the less: "And I don't like the way you lump all men together and judge us as one. We're *not* all the same. You say 'the Baker brothers' as if there's no difference between us. Nobody is perfect, but we're all individuals. Let a man prove himself before judging him."

"I'd have to have a man prove me wrong before I made a decision
202

to treat him any differently," Joan said, grumpily squeezing out her flannel and then soaking it again. "Anything else?"

He opened his eyes and blinked a drip of water from his long lashes. "Not for now, but you can tell me what you don't like about me."

He watched her as her eyes travelled to the ceiling in thought.

"Okay — where do I start?"

Colin twisted his mouth to one side. He looked worried.

"I got one. I don't like the fact that you take advantage of the way I feel about you."

"How?"

"Because you know how I feel, you think you can always come back no matter what — and you've been right so far."

He grinned.

"But did you ever think about how I *really* feel? It hurts to see myself weaken. I hate weakness in emotions."

Colin said nothing, letting her continue.

"Another thing is, all the years I've known you, you've never changed."

Colin sat up now, drawing his knees up to his chest. Water dripped down his hairy chest and back into the bath.

Joan regarded him across the water. "You look the same, dress the same, you're in the same job . . . People think you've got no ambition. They look at me and wonder what I see in someone like you. I know you've got ambition, but you're just not doing anything to make it happen. I want other people to be able to see what you're all about."

"I don't care what other people think. I'm me . . ."

"I know you don't. But it's not about what they want, it's about doing what you need to do to improve yourself."

Colin nodded his head in silence.

"Another thing — you're insensitive," she told him. She fished the soap out of the water and lathered her flannel. "You don't know how to make love. We have sex. Sometimes I just wish you'd kiss my body with little tender kisses from my head down to my toes. I'd love a gentle massage occasionally. Even just to have you lie down with me and hold me without it leading to sex . . . When I say no to you, you just think I'm playing hard to get. You don't listen to my needs."

"Well, you've never complained before," he remonstrated.

"You don't *notice*. As I said, you're insensitive. As soon as you get turned on you're only out to satisfy number one."

"That's not true. I go down on you — not many black men do that."

"No, and not many black men know what to do when they get there," she replied pointedly.

This was turning into a massacre. Colin glared at her. "Is that it?"

Joan laughed. "No. One more. You know how to say 'I love you' now. Just try *showing* it a little more often. And I'm not talking about sex now."

He frowned. "You talking about presents and taking you out and stuff?"

"Not necessarily. Asking me how I am, cooking for me, taking Shereen off my hands when I need a break, giving me a massage when I've had a hard day. Sharing time with me . . ." She looked into his attentive brown eyes to see if he understood.

"Bwoy!" He scratched his head. "This relationship t'ing nuh easy."

Joan laughed again. "We'll work on it together."

"Mmm, I don't know about that now." He grinned cheekily, the gap in his teeth giving him the look of an urchin.

"Yeah, well, you're in my house now — and I ain't asking you, I'm telling you."

"Yes, miss."

Joan threw the wet flannel at him and it splatted his face with suds.

COLIN

I knew that Lois was a nutter. There was something unhinged about her from the start. I can't believe that the girl would've killed me, though.

But my woman come to my rescue. That's what I call love. Yeah, I like that. My future wife is not only tough where it counts, but she's got muscle power too. Warrior! From the way I see her throwing those punches I better watch myself. I might end up on the end of one of them any time I upset her.

Looks like that's it, then. I'm living in my fiancée's house, with my brother's daughter. I've got myself a family.

Time to grow up, I suppose.

Yikes!

25. MANCHILD

Marion's eyes flew open in the darkness as a contraction jolted her out of her sleep. She turned over and faced the clock, watching the time before the next one. It was fifteen minutes before she felt the tightness again. They were mild contractions, but she knew they could still signal the birth of her baby.

But before she woke Paul she had to be sure. He wasn't expecting anything for another month. She had to make it a convincing "premature" labour.

She slipped out of bed and went to make herself a cup of tea. The contractions eased off for about an hour, then started again more intensely, the time between each one shortening. She told herself she would wait until they were coming about five minutes apart, but the pain was becoming unbearable. It felt as though her middle was trapped in a vice that was tightening with every new contraction. Beads of sweat stood out on her forehead. She sat on the sofa, her feet placed wide apart, and breathed through them as she had been told to do, until finally she could stand the agonising wait no more. She waddled back to the bedroom intending to wake Paul, but as she crawled in next to him he turned to her, already awake.

"Is everything all right?" he asked.

Marion tensed as another contraction immobilised her. "The baby's coming," she panted.

Paul shot upright as though on a spring. "It can't be — we've got weeks yet." He placed his hand on her tummy.

"Don't panic. The baby's fine. I think we should get to the hospital, though."

Paul threw the covers from his legs and reached for the phone on the bedside table. "Where's the hospital number? I'm sure you left it by the phone."

"By the phone in the front room, Paul."

"Oh, yeah." He smiled before hurrying from the room.

Marion lay back on the pillows and felt a kick from the baby. "Not long now, soldier," she whispered. "I can't wait to see you either."

Paul drove like a madman to the hospital. He accompanied her to the labour ward as planned. Marion was already ten centimetres dilated by the time she was wheeled into the delivery room.

Propped up on huge pillows, her knees drawn up to her chest, Marion panted and sweated while Paul held her hand and rubbed her back. It was too late for pethidine. Instead she gulped gas until she was seeing the staff and Paul through a fuzzy haze.

"Do you feel like you need to bear down yet?" the midwife asked. She was a chubby woman with rosy cheeks and a permanent smile, and the trace of an accent that Marion couldn't place.

Marion strained to see through the cloud. The woman's face came into focus for a couple of seconds before fading out again. "The baby's coming on its own," she gasped.

The midwife moved to the end of the bed and examined Marion. "You're right! I can see lots of thick black hair. Let's get this baby born, then."

Marion forced a smile as Paul kissed her cheek and whispered, "I love you."

"Now. On the next contraction, Marion — push."

The wave of another contraction began to build and Marion gasped, catching her breath. Oh God. The pain!

"No, no, honey. Breathe with it, you'll find it a lot easier. Breathe out slowly. Breath in . . . then out. Push, Marion."

Marion screwed up her face and bore down with all her might.

"Okay, now pant . . . good girl. Another contraction, big push this time, and we'll have baby's head out."

Marion pushed. The pain was unbearable. She felt as though she were trying to give birth to a water melon, and it was ripping her in half. "Never again, Paul. Never again," she hissed.

Paul chuckled nervously.

The midwife was busy turning the baby's head and checking the neck for any sign of the cord. "Listen to me, Marion — your baby's head has been delivered. Now I want you to give one more push and it'll be over, honey. Here we go . . ."

Marion sobbed. "I can't! Please. I can't do it. Paul, I want to go home," she whimpered.

"You can do it, babes. Just imagine, our baby will be coming home with us . . ." He gave her a squeeze as the next contraction rolled in.

Marion gave it her all. There was a rush of fluid, and their baby slid into the world. Marion collapsed back on to the pillows.

It was over . . . and she was still alive.

"You have a baby boy, Marion. A beautiful baby boy." The midwife held him up for inspection. "I'll just do his checks, and then he's all yours."

A few seconds later the baby howled, and a shiver ran up Marion's spine. Her baby's first sound. Tears sprung to her eyes.

After efficiently inspecting the infant, the midwife handed the tiny bundle over to Marion. She lifted back the blanket to see her baby's body. He had skin the colour of a Chinaman. Marion looked at the tiny features; he had her small mouth, his father's arched eyebrows, and . . . she studied his face . . . she was sure his nose would be Gerard's as well.

This child was definitely Gerard's. It would be obvious to anyone who knew him.

Tears rolled down her cheeks.

Paul and the nurses took them to be tears of joy, and Paul hugged her as she held her son. "He's perfect. Thank you," he whispered.

"I know." The baby gripped Marion's thumb in a tiny fist and made sucking motions with his mouth.

"Hungry already?" Paul asked the baby.

A nurse came in and took over from the midwife. "Baby boy? We'll have to weigh him and do his checks, and then you can have a go at feeding him. How are you going to feed him?"

"Breastfeeding. For a while, anyway."

The nurse smiled and held out her arms for the baby. Marion reluctantly handed him over and watched as the nurse walked away with her son, gibbering baby-talk to him.

Paul left her a few minutes later to call Marion's family and his own, and their friends.

After the baby had been returned to her, Marion stood by the plastic crib and looked down at him. He slept peacefully. He was so delicate and tiny. He had silky black hair which was still stuck to his head like a skull cap. Marion placed a hand on his back, reassuring herself that he was still breathing. She could feel the rapid up-and-down rhythm of his tiny lungs.

His father didn't even know he existed.

His loss.

She had decided to call him Diallo. She hoped the name would make her son as great a man as she had been told his namesake was.

Paul left them an hour later. He was bushed, and had to work later that day. Kissing Marion hard on the lips, he promised to come back that evening with a couple of members of his family.

Marion slept until she was awoken by familiar voices.

"There she is!" That was Joan.

"Let me see him." And Pamela.

Marion sat up sleepily as the girls rushed over.

"Hiya." They hugged her in turn before surrounding the crib.

"Oh, Maz, he's beautiful," Pamela cooed.

Joan pulled the blanket back off him. "Dead stamp of Gerard."

"Don't say that around Paul," Marion warned.

"He's so tiny. Can I hold him?" Pamela asked.

The girls sat around, chatting and passing the baby back and forth. Joan and Marion compared labours, Marion breastfeeding as they talked.

"I remember my breasts the day after the birth," Joan said. "Rock hard, they were. You wait till your milk comes in."

"I know. My mum told me she was leaking through a whole packet of cotton wool a day," Marion said.

"I could do with rock-hard tits," Pamela said, pushing her chest up.

Joan gave her a critical look. "I don't think you could take the pain," she said.

"Ask Michael if I can't take pain," Pam answered with a smile.

Her friends looked at her. *Everything* had to come down to sex with Pamela.

"And how is Michael?" Marion asked. "You seen him recently?"

"Nearly every day," Pamela replied haughtily.

"It happened too fast with you two, don't you think?" Joan put in. "It's like James all over again."

"This is nothing like me and James. That was a mistake." Pamela changed the subject. "How does Paul feel about his son?" she asked, emphasising the "his".

"He thinks he's perfect. He didn't even say anything about the dates."

"I think you're good to go on so long without telling him," Joan said. "Although, you know one day he is going to find out."

"I know. And when that time comes, I'll be ready," Marion declared, her warm gaze coming to rest on her sleeping infant.

East Street, one of the busiest markets in London, was packed with shoppers, the usual Saturday crowd. It was the start of the spring sales, and people were already buying clothes for the summer.

Paul had parked the car in Elephant and Castle, and they had walked up to the market through the shopping centre hand in hand, window shopping as they went. Marion carried Diallo in a pouch on her chest, her arm serving as a protective barrier for his delicate head. At six weeks old he was already starting to feel too heavy for her to carry.

"We'll have to look at christening outfits soon," she said as they passed a children's clothes shop.

"Yeah. But let's leave that till he's about six months,"Paul advised.

"Why?"

"It just seems the right time to do it," Paul said, and Marion shut up.

They stopped and looked at the pushchairs in the shop's window. They hadn't bought one yet. Their cot had come courtesy of her mother, and Joan had given them a baby chair. A pushchair hadn't seemed an essential, but from the speed by which Diallo was growing it soon would be. They decided to go and have a look inside, but as they reached the door a hand grabbed Marion's arm and, startled, she turned to face her accoster.

"I thought it was you!" Claudia Thompson's voice sing-songed. It had been a year since Marion had heard it, and her heart nearly stopped. Gerard's mother stood in front of them, grinning for all she was worth.

Paul was half-way into the shop and stopped in the doorway, standing behind Marion as she turned to face Claudia.

"Claudia! How are you?" Marion asked with exaggerated calm.

Claudia's eyes were on the tiny bundle hanging from her shoulders. She ignored Marion's greeting. "No one never tell me you have baby," she said.

"Six weeks now," Marion said, and immediately regretted it. Claudia hadn't asked how old he was, and it was a clue to his father's identity. Unconsciously, she shielded the baby with her jacket.

But that wasn't putting Claudia off. "Let me have a look, then. Girl or boy?"

Marion reluctantly lifted Diallo into view. "Boy." She watched Claudia's face, knowing the woman would see the resemblance straight away.

Claudia looked from the baby to Paul and back again. "That's a handsome baby boy you have there," she said.

"I know. Thank you," Paul answered, and placed a reassuring hand on Marion's tense shoulder.

"Yes, he is a handsome boy. Who does he take after?" she murmured, so that only Marion would hear.

Marion was so tense, every muscle of her body began to ache. "I really do have to get on, Claudia. It was nice seeing you," she said hastily.

Claudia gave her a look that said everything. She knew. "Buying baby things?" she carried on. "Expensive, 'int it?" She had a wry smile on her chubby face. "Well, I better go meself, dear. I'll be in touch. You tek care now, y'hear?" She smiled at Paul.

Marion was sure Claudia was going to say something incriminating. But her expression changed and she touched Paul's arm briefly. "You tek care as well. Bye, Marion."

"Bye, Claudia," Marion said. Her throat clicked with dryness and she tried to swallow.

Claudia walked away and Marion turned to walk into the shop.

"You okay?" Paul asked.

"Why shouldn't I be?" she snapped, and walked past him.

Paul stood behind her, bewildered. He knew Marion well enough to realise she was upset. And it had something to do with that woman.

Marion remained quiet and disinterested throughout the rest of their shopping trip. The appearance of Claudia Thompson had ruined her day. All she wanted to do was go home and shut herself in. She felt her life crumbling around her.

Gerard was Claudia's only son. Which meant — if he didn't already have children elsewhere — that Diallo was her only grandchild. There was no doubt in Marion's mind that Claudia would tell her son about the baby.

What he'd do after that was anyone's guess.

GERARD

Now I know my mum is getting on a bit, and sometimes she get mix up — but this time she's gone too far.

As soon as I came in this evening she start on me: "How can you let some other man be taking care of your child? Marion is such a lovely girl. How can you have a son and never tell me 'bout it?"

I thought the old lady had finally lost it. After I sat her down and made her some tea, she told me how she's seen Marion in the market with her boyfriend and a baby. So? I says. She told me how old the baby was and how he look jus' like me. She had already worked out the dates of when the baby would have been conceived and born.

It got me thinking . . . Marion was always going on about wanting a baby . . .

Mum was on at me to go and see her. The last thing I wanted to do was go and see my ex-girlfriend and accuse her of having my child.

I don't know if I wanna get involved in dem kinda business. If the kid is mine — an' I'm still not convinced it is — then it's mine in blood only.

Mum isn't gonna let it rest. She's got this big t'ing about having a

grandchild to spoil. I'm gonna put her off as long as possible. I don't
wanna have to meet up with Marion again. I'll give mum some story
about Marion not wanting me to see the kid.

Women!

26. FREAK 'N YOU

Sunday morning, and the air was crisp and fresh. After breakfast in
bed, Pamela and Michael showered together before getting dressed
and going for a walk to get the papers.

On Saturday they had spent the whole day in bed. Breakfast and
lunch had been served on trays by Michael, and Pamela had got up
to prepare and serve dinner. It seemed she just couldn't get enough
of him. The past few months had gone by so quickly, yet the feelings
she had for him had grown to such proportions that she was
beginning to miss him as soon as he'd walk out of the door. She
couldn't imagine life without him — and that feeling was definitely
a new one on Pamela.

Life with Michael was full of new experiences. Only last week
he'd taken her for her first taste of Thai food. They'd feasted on
squid and oysters — exotic food to enliven her tastebuds — and
afterwards they'd taken a romantic walk by the *Cutty Sark* in
Greenwich, watching the ships drift by on the Thames.

Now her arm was around his waist and his around her shoulders
as they walked up towards Evelyn Street. Elderly ladies smiled at
them approvingly as they passed. Younger people smirked
uncomfortably as the couple stole quick kisses.

Neither of them had yet used the L word.

They walked through the sixty square feet of greenery that
constituted a park on the estate. The sounds of the Sunday morning
traffic and the chirping of the birds were the only thing that invaded
the space around them.

Several times they had discussed her dilemma with her parents.
It wasn't easy deciding what to do. Michael had said that if he was
in her position he would much rather put it all behind him. Pamela
had tried that, and it didn't work. She was too curious about her
natural mother. What did she look like? What was she like as a
person? Was she anything like Pamela? What had made her give her
daughter up? And the big question: who was Pamela's father? All

these questions, and more, needed to be answered.

Joan had been with her when she'd called the agency. They had been very understanding and offered to send someone round to advise her and give counselling. But Pamela had changed her mind at the last minute; she just wasn't ready to accept her new status as an adopted child.

She felt like a nobody. She had no history — except her false one, which she was only too happy to forget.

A March wind blew up as they turned the corner onto Evelyn Street. Michael pulled her closer, closing the collar round the neck of her jacket with his arm. He had the ability to take her mind off her problems. If she ever needed to talk, he was there. They took the Sunday papers back to her flat. Michael made coffee and they lay on the living room floor, on the lambswool rug he'd bought for her, the papers spread out between them and his *Sounds of Blackness* album playing in the background.

Pamela opened a colour supplement and flicked straight to the fashion pages. "Mike, what'd you think of that on me?" she asked, pointing to a picture of a long, slinky, backless dress.

"I'd love you in that, but for my eyes only." He turned a page of the newspaper.

"What's the point of that?" She rested her chin on her palm. "Wouldn't you rather take me out and show me off? You could say to the other guys, 'This is my woman. Look, but don't touch'." She giggled.

His hazel eyes came to rest on her lips. "I do that anyway. Whatever you wear you look good in."

"Thanks, baby." She leant forward and kissed him. "You do too," she said — and meant it.

"I do what?"

"Look good in whatever you wear," she told him. "Especially your birthday suit."

Michael flashed that incredible, sparkling smile, and his eyes opened in amusement. "You're too rude, y'know that?" He touched her nose playfully.

"Mmm-mm, so I've been told. Would you like me to show you how rude I can get?" She edged closer, already feeling the heat radiating from his body.

"You did. This morning, last night . . ."

"See what you do to me?" she interrupted. "Turn me into a raging nymphomaniac."

Michael turned on to his side so that he was facing her. "I think it's the other way around. When I leave here I'm no good to anybody.

212

You drain my energy like a vampire."

"Tell me you don't like it and I'll stop."

"Would you?"

"No. I just said that to test you."

Michael shook his head in mirth and moved closer. He had this way of pulling his bottom lip in and drawing his top teeth across it when he was thinking about something sexual. It was a tell-tale sign to Pamela.

She closed her eyes before they kissed. There was no resistance in her body or mind. She gripped his firm, round arse and pulled him to her, kissing, stroking, the feel of him and the smell of his favourite aftershave filling the space around her until nothing else mattered. Newspapers crinkled and tore as he climbed on top of her and plunged his tongue between her small lips. He pushed his groin against her, knowing she could feel every inch of his growing erection. His tongue traced a path from her ear lobe to her neck.

"Michael?"

"Mmm?"

"Do you love me?" she breathed.

Michael groaned. "Mmm? What?"

"I just asked you if you love me."

He released her suddenly, rolling over on to his back. "What for?"

She frowned. "I thought it was a fair question."

He stared at the ceiling. "Depends why you want to know."

"I only asked." In reality, Pamela had no idea why she had asked. But as he protested it became more important to know the truth.

"You asked for a reason." He sat up now, the mood lost, his huge shoulders hunched over his knees.

"So — you can't answer yes or no. I'm not asking you to say you'll marry me."

"I don't know," he faltered. His hazel eyes came to rest on her lips. "I know I care about you. A lot," he added.

"Yeah. And?"

"Jesus, Pam. What is this about?" Irritated and suddenly restless, he stood up.

Pamela followed suit and moved to sit on the sofa. "It's about us, and where this relationship is going."

"Don't do this, Pam. It doesn't suit you. Has one of your friends been putting ideas into your head?"

He bent down to pick up the newspapers from the floor.

"I don't need my friends to tell me how to lead my life, Michael. Why are we arguing over this?"

"I don't know. Why did you ask?"

The conversation was going round in circles. Having placed the folded newspapers on the coffee table, Michael crossed to the window and pushed it open mechanically. Cold air entered the room, turning the already chilly atmosphere icy.

"All right! Just forget it, okay?" Pamela raised her hands in submission. "It doesn't matter."

A silence fell between them. Michael tucked his sweatshirt back into his trousers and looked at his watch. "I've gotta go. I promised to drop in on Mikey this weekend."

"You're running away," she accused.

"Oh come on, Pam. This isn't us. We were doing fine, weren't we?"

"Just go, Michael," she dismissed him.

"I'll call you later," he said, picking up his keys.

Pamela stood up and breathed deeply. She was surprised by this elusive side to Michael, but even more amazed at how upset she was.

They walked to the door together. "You all right?" he asked, stroking her back.

"Course." She looked up at him. "I'll talk to you later, then."

He kissed her on her nose, and was gone.

Disturbed and frustrated, Pamela went back into the living room. She switched on the television, not caring what was on. Tired now, and unable to get him out of her head, she turned over on the sofa, her back to the television. Everything smelt of Michael.

Her confused brain fighting with the niggling intuition that it was over, she fell into a dreamless sleep.

Pamela replaced the receiver and sat staring at it for a moment. She decided she would dial again in a few minutes.

Outside, the wind had dropped slightly but the rain had intensified. It slapped against her living room window, the constant patter sounding like a thousand birds pecking at the glass. The cheap double glazing rattled in its frame.

She reached for the phone again.

No, she thought. Leave it. Instead, she hauled herself off the sofa and padded into the kitchen, opening cupboards and the fridge. But she wasn't hungry. Not for food, anyway. She poured herself a brandy, dropped two ice cubes into it, and left the kitchen.

Michael hadn't called for four days now. On Monday she'd paged him and left a message to call her back. She'd left a message on his answerphone too, and still hadn't got a reply. The agony of waiting had made her lose her appetite, and she was having trouble sleeping. Her zest for all things fun in life had walked out of the door with him. She couldn't believe she was falling apart over a man, and so she began to convince herself that it was the stress of her recent discovery of her adoptive status that was getting her down.

Now exercise was the only thing that kept her sane. She worked her frustrations out on her stairclimber and jogged four miles a day. Then she would go to work like a zombie, come home and chat to her mates on the phone — making sure the call-waiting function was in operation — until it was time to go to bed.

She'd been sure Michael felt the same way she did. So she had opened up to him, and now he had thrown it back in her face.

She stomped into her bedroom and sat at the head of the bed. On the table was a photo of Michael she had taken outside the flats. She picked up the frame and touched the image of his face as if to feel the smoothness of his skin.

She reached for the phone again, jabbing out the digits of his mobile number.

Just let me hear your voice . . .

The phone went on ringing, no answering service this time. That meant he had picked up his messages and left the phone switched on. Still, he didn't answer her call.

Where the hell was he? Pamela took a sip of brandy, still holding the phone to her ear.

Pick up . . .

The ringing continued until she slammed the phone down and unplugged it from the socket. Fuck him! she thought. If he wants to hide, let him. Forget him. Men were like children, she decided. Never said what they meant.

It wasn't as though she was soft. Pamela knew she could take it if he called and said it was over. It was the not knowing that got to her. The fact that he knew she must be trying to get hold of him hurt even more. He was deliberately avoiding her.

She downed the rest of the brandy in one and went to the kitchen to get a refill. Deciding it would be easier simply to take the bottle back with her, she did just that.

She slammed his framed photograph face-down on the table. "Fuck you!" she told it, and threw herself backwards on the bed.

MICHAEL
So what? It's not all my fault it ended up like this.

I thought Pamela and I were on the same level. Why can't a woman just put two and two together and make four? They've always got to look for the hidden agenda.

I've been with her now for — what? — about eight months or so. We ain't had no problems — an' you know why? Because we didn't mention love and commitment. We just went with it.

I care about her. She knows I want to be with her, because I'm always there. A man don't need words when he can show how he feels. Putting how you feel in words is like giving a woman ammunition to get back at you with. The only way to keep a woman interested is to treat her right, but to keep an element of mystery there. Something of a challenge, something to keep her digging.

When Pamela came out with that "Do you love me?" line it struck me like a kick in the crotch. I guess I'm still not ready.

I need time to think.

I listen to her message on the answerphone. I want to call her, but I know what she's going to come out with and I'm not ready for that yet. I've got my career and my son to think about. Pamela is important, but that will sort itself out one way or the other.

I'm not even thinking about ending what we have.

27. COME AND TALK TO ME

Enough time had gone by since the accidental meeting with Claudia Thompson in the market place for Marion to feel she could start to relax. For the past two weeks, every time the telephone had rung she'd felt her heart-rate accelerate, every time the intercom buzzed her breathing had nearly stopped. But now the summer was finally here, and June had brought with it long, hot days. Bright, warm sunshine streamed through the curtains this morning, and Marion took this as her cue to stop hibernating.

Paul had noticed her changes in mood. He knew her too well. He had made it his duty to read her needs. In the two and a half months since Diallo's birth he had amazed her by showing a side of him she had never suspected. She would never have guessed he could be so gentle with a new-born baby.

Diallo was filling out nicely. He was a cuddly bundle of joy. The only times he seemed to be miserable was at night, when he was put in the cot on his own, and more often than not he would end up sleeping in the bed with them. He was spoiled by his surrogate father. Paul changed, fed, bathed and played with him. It made Marion feel as though nothing could destroy their bond. The three of them were meant to be together. Even if Claudia had told Gerard about the baby, there was nothing he could do to break them up — and she doubted he would even try. Gerard was only interested in himself. What would he want with a baby?

Paul's help had given Marion time to continue her writing in the evenings and at weekends. She had received several offers of work since her articles were published, and *Essence* magazine in the States had commissioned her to do a series on nineties black British women in comparison to their mothers in the fifties and sixties. All the extra cash she earned was being spent on Diallo, and the list of things he needed seemed to grow every month.

Marion pulled on a pair of shorts and a baggy T-shirt. Her figure had sprung back since giving birth. Paul had treated her to an exercise bike, and she rode ten miles a day.

She put the sun canopy on Diallo's brand new pushchair, dressed him coolly in light blue shorts and top, with boots and hat to match, and left the flat, wheeling the new buggy out into the heat of the day, feeling the sun's rays lift her spirit.

Joan and Pamela would both be at work now, and Marion decided to pop into Pamela's nursery for a visit. Pamela hadn't seen Diallo in nearly a month, and would be grateful for the company.

Marion caught a bus on the Woolwich Road and headed for Lewisham. This part of town was the usual hive of activity. The Lewisham 2000 project was causing chaos for pedestrians and confusion for drivers. Roads had been dug up and diverted, and there were temporary crossings and signs everywhere. Marion found herself manoeuvring the pushchair through the crowds with some difficulty.

She bumped into a couple of people she knew. One was a friend of her mother's, and the other was Carmen, an old schoolfriend from her days at St Theresa's. Carmen cooed over the baby, and told Marion how she hadn't changed, saying she still looked sixteen. Carmen didn't have any children yet. She was still looking for the right man. Marion told her she had already found hers and was very happy.

Making her way towards Loampit Vale Nursery, Marion thought about how good she felt. Her life was in order. She had a baby, a man who loved her, friends who supported her, and a caring family. One thing she did miss was her sister's company. Jacqueline would have loved to be an auntie.

As Marion entered the coolness of the nursery she spotted Pamela talking to a small child. "Excuse me, any chance of enrolling my son?" Marion said loudly to catch her attention.

Pamela turned to the voice and her face instantly lit up. "Marion, hi! Why didn't you tell me you were coming?" She approached her friend, dismissing the little girl at the same time.

"I thought you liked surprises."

Pamela's attention was already drawn to the baby in the pushchair. "Aaah, look at his little shoes." She worked at the straps of the pushchair and lifted him free.

Diallo was fast asleep. Pamela held him in the crook of her arm. "He is so gorgeous, if only he was twenty-five years older . . ."

"You leave my son alone, you. You'll be corrupting him before he can talk," Marion laughed.

They went over to the book corner. It was the only carpeted area of the room, with cushions and bean bags on the floor.

Once they were both comfortable, Pamela asked, "So how are you, girl? I hardly hear from you these days."

"Not too bad. What about you?"

"You know . . ." Pamela shrugged and mopped the corner of Diallo's mouth with his bib.

"Michael?"

"Nothing's wrong exactly." She paused. "It's just . . . well, I haven't seen or heard from him in a while. I thought we were getting on fine, and then he just went cold on me."

Marion nodded.

"I've called, left messages. He doesn't answer."

"Yeah?" Marion was having flashbacks to her days with Gerard. She remembered exactly how that felt.

"I know I probably rushed into it, but all he has to do is to tell me to back off, you know. He led me on, Maz. I told you about how he used to treat me, didn't I?"

"Yeah." Marion nodded and crossed her legs. Diallo gurgled in his sleep and his eyelids fluttered.

"If I wasn't so caught up in this love thing, I'd forget him. You know me — plenty more fish in the sea an' all that. The only problem is the way I feel about him. All I want to know is where I went wrong — not that I'm blaming myself," she added hastily, "it's just that I want to know one way or the other what's going on."

"Sometimes men need their own space. I've been there, remember?"

Pamela tutted. "This isn't the same. Gerard . . ." She paused and turned her eyes to the ceiling, trying to find the right words without offending. "Gerard didn't care about you. I know how that sounds, but you know what I mean."

Suddenly Marion needed the comfort of her baby in her arms.

She reached for him and Pamela handed him to her.

"Has he been in touch?" Pamela asked. Marion had told her about meeting Claudia.

"No. And I pray to God every night that he doesn't. I have nightmares about it." She shifted Diallo around so that he lay on her thighs, feet touching her stomach.

"I bet you do. And how's Paul?"

"Paul's still as loving as ever." She looked down at her baby. "To both of us."

"You should see Michael with his son. They're so much alike, except Mikey . . ." She trailed off. "Can't stop thinking about him."

"Not easy, is it?" Marion sympathised.

Pamela shook her head, her ponytail swinging. "Anyway, when're you gonna start raving again? You must miss it."

"I'm not ready to leave him yet." She nodded towards Diallo.

"Don't you trust Paul alone with him?" Pamela asked, incredulous.

"I trust him. It's just that . . . I think I'd still be worried no matter who had him. I haven't left him with anyone since he was born."

"Love, eh?" Pamela smirked, her pretty eyes sparkling.

Marion smiled back at her.

"I'll make us a cuppa." Pamela put on her cockney accent. "Then we can catch up on some news."

Marion stayed at the nursery for an hour and a half. As the afternoon drew on a breeze blew up, dropping the temperature by a few degrees, and when it was time to go Marion wrapped Diallo in his shawl so that only his head showed above the fluffy white wool.

As Marion left, she told Pamela she was glad she wasn't on the market any more. The days of having to be out there, getting mucked about by men, were over. There was no doubt in her mind.

She got home at around four o'clock. The atmosphere inside the flat was still warm, so she left a window open to circulate the air. Diallo sat in his chair in the living room, entranced by the dancing net curtains. Marion left him there while she went to put the dinner on.

While she was in the kitchen the intercom buzzed. Marion didn't even stop to wonder who it might be, but wiped her hands on a kitchen towel and went out to the passage to answer it.

"Hello," she called cheerfully.

"Marion, it's Gerard," the voice came back at her.

Marion was sure she'd stopped breathing. She leant her weight against the passage wall, stomach churning, pulse hammering, the intercom receiver clutched to her chest.

Diallo began the first hiccoughs of a cry. Marion pressed the door release button and hurried to her son. A minute later, Gerard entered the flat. Marion stood in the middle of the living room and faced the doorway waiting.

Pamela locked up the nursery door as usual, and waited while the alarm checked and switched itself on. Then she slung her handbag strap over her shoulder and strolled up towards Lewisham High Street.

Recent events had taken their toll on her state of mind. Another man had brought her down again. How many times had she said never again? Well, she thought, Michael could keep his love, and his charm, and his good looks and his hard body — she sighed at the thought of his body.

But he had been all she wanted in a man.

Pamela had got the idea that if she talked to Cheryl she could get some insight into what was happening. She couldn't think where else to turn. Cheryl had gone out with Michael, lived with him, for five years. If anyone else could shed some light on the subject, it would be her. So Pamela had called her just before leaving work. Cheryl had invited her round and sounded as though she'd been expecting the call.

Cheryl was very thin and tall. She had the Somalian look of high cheekbones and meek brown eyes. She let Pamela into her council flat. The smell of cooking wafted out of the kitchen and seemed to grab Pamela's insides, pulling her in. As she entered the flat, Mikey ran up to her and reached up for a hug. Even though they had only seen each other an hour before, he always carried on as though he had missed her.

"Leave the woman alone, Mikey. You finish yuh dinner yet?" Cheryl nagged.

Mikey skulked away, pouting at being scolded in front of his teacher.

"Sorry to barge in on you, Cheryl . . ." Pamela began.

"Don't be stupid, it's good to have some company." Cheryl waved away Pamela's apologies and motioned towards Mikey with her head. "As soon as he finishes his food he'll fall asleep in front of the TV."

Pamela followed her into the kitchen where Cheryl was preparing her own dinner. She took off her jacket and hung it over the top edge of the door.

"Wanna drink?" Cheryl asked.

"Yes, please. Something cold." Pamela perched on the bar stool by the kitchen counter.

Cheryl went to the fridge and brought back a blackcurrant cordial. "We haven't had a chance to chat for ages. How're you doing?"

"Not too bad, y'know . . ."

Cheryl poked a finger at her. "I know you — you're a raver. What you been up to?"

Pamela shook her long hair off her face. "Too busy to even rave these days," she lamented.

Cheryl cocked her head to one side. "Oh yeah? Doing what?" she asked slyly. She poured cold water into the glasses and handed one to Pamela.

"You know — work, socialising, dating . . ."

"Still up to your old tricks?" Cheryl winked at her as she began chopping onions on a wooden board.

"Naw, man. I'm thinking of settling down now."

Cheryl flashed a quick glance of amusement. "What — you?"

"That's exactly what my other mates say. D'you think I'm that bad?"

"Bad ain't the word for you," Cheryl chuckled, looking attentively downwards.

Pamela had to blurt it out before she lost her bottle. "I'm seeing your ex. Michael."

Cheryl paused for just a second, but her face showed no hint of surprise. "I thought so."

Pamela looked at her, one eyebrow raised. "What would make you think that?" Mikey came to mind as the source, but she was wrong.

"Him asking about you. You asking about him. I'm not stupid."

Now Pamela felt guilty for not telling her, for making it seem like a conspiracy. "I was gonna tell you, Chel, I just didn't know how you'd take it."

"It's nothing to do with me." Cheryl poured the onions into the steaming casserole on the hob. "Michael and me had it good once." She glanced out of the window. "Yeah, it was good — but these things happen." She wiped her hands on a tea towel and turned her back to Pamela.

"What did happen between you two?" Pamela enquired. "He never said."

Cheryl reached for a pot from the wooden shelf above her head. "He split us up. I don't think Michael can take pressure."

"What d'you mean? He was with you for five years."

Cheryl put the pot on the hob, added oil and turned the flame up. "Michael can be a good man, but he tries too hard." She paused again, reminiscing, then turned to Pamela and rested her back on the counter. "He pleases others before himself, and then when he realises what he's missing he goes looking for it. Then he can turn into the most selfish bastard alive."

Pamela shook her head, wondering if they could be talking about the same person. She'd thought Michael didn't have a selfish bone in his body. Up until a month ago he had always put her first.

Cheryl watched Pamela through knowing eyes and saw the disbelief on her face. "Believe me, Pam, I know what I'm talking about. I know him better than he knows himself."

"I think he's in love with me," Pamela told her, hoping it would change the negativity that Cheryl was giving off.

Cheryl smirked. "Has he said that?"

"No, but men don't," Pamela gushed. "The way he treats me—"

"Means nothing," Cheryl interrupted.

"Maybe it meant nothing with you, but whatever he sees in me must be something you didn't have."

Cheryl bristled. Her eyes turned to daggers, but she breathed deeply and turned back to her cooking. "I don't want us to fall out over a man, Pam. If you want us to stay friends, don't bring Michael up again."

"Fine." Pam stood and reached for her coat. "Thanks for the chat."

"Where you going? I thought you were staying for dinner."

"Sorry, I don't think I've got the time. I'll see you next week, Cheryl."

Cheryl walked Pamela to the front door. "Take care, yeah? I didn't mean anything by what I said, you know. I don't want you to take it the wrong way."

Pamela touched Cheryl's arm, briefly squeezing it, and gave her a look of pity. "Thanks," she said, and left.

The sky had become overcast, threatening rain. Pamela pulled her collar up and put her head down against the driving wind. A car turned into the road as she took the corner, a car she recognised, and its driver recognised her. The car slowed, pulled over, and Michael stepped out.

Pamela had stopped on the kerb. She waited as he approached her. He wore an uncertain smile, but his eyes sparkled with charm all the same. Pamela stood with her hands in her jacket pockets. He stopped a foot away, unsure of her mood.

They stared into each other's eyes.

They stared into each other's eyes.

Marion felt brave. She had her son to defend, and like a lioness she intended to do just that. This was her home, and Gerard had no right ever to set foot in it again. She held Diallo close to her, resting his head on her shoulder.

Gerard stood in the doorway nonchalantly, one hand resting on the frame. He looked even more handsome than she remembered him. His eyes strayed to the baby in her arms, then met hers again.

"Why didn't you tell me?" His voice was unnaturally low, as though he too felt he shouldn't be here.

"Tell you what?" Marion wrinkled her brow as if she didn't know what he was talking about.

He looked down at his shoes and shifted his position in the doorway. This seemed to be hard for him too. Marion could sense the turmoil within him. It was very rare for anyone to see Gerard unsure of himself. The only times she had seen him this humble was when he spoke of his father.

He spoke now to the floor, eyes and head cast down. "Mum told me she saw you the other day." He coughed. "Is he mine?"

Marion remained silent. She gazed at him with round-eyed perplexity. Diallo shifted his head, trying to turn to the strange voice in the room. Marion placed a protective hand on the back of his head and kissed him.

"Well?" Gerard's eyes came to rest on her once again.

"Your sperm may have created him, but he's not your child."

"What kinda rubbish is that?" He took a step towards her.

Marion backed up, feeling threatened. "What d'you want, Gerard?" She spoke firmly, asserting the fact that she didn't want anything from him.

"Jus' tell me if he's my son." He put one hand to his forehead, rubbing at his temples before letting it drop back to his side.

"I've told you . . ." she began.

"You've told me nothin'," he erupted.

The baby started to cry. Gerard saw the fear in Marion's eyes and breathed deeply. "Look, sorry. I didn't come here to upset nothin'." His voice mellowed. "Can I see him?"

Marion brought the baby down from her shoulder and held him in the crook of her arm, so that Gerard could see him. Gerard held his arms out, but Marion only gripped him more tightly. "You can look at him, but I can't let you take him."

Gerard laughed at her. "What d'you think I'm gonna do? Run off with him?"

"I don't know what you're here for." She took a step towards him and they met in the centre of the room. She watched his expression as he took his first glance at his son. She was surprised to see a genuine smile, his eyes actually lighting up. It was beautiful. Gerard looked at the baby with the same expression she had seen on Paul's face many times. His eyes met Marion's and she tried to suppress her own smile.

"He is my son," Gerard said with a hint of wonder. He stepped away from her and sat down hard in the armchair, taking a deep breath.

Marion frowned. This wasn't what she'd expected. She didn't want him to care. "Gerard, he's registered as Paul's baby. You can't claim him as yours . . ." She stopped as Gerard gave her a look that was half disbelief and half anger.

"Why?" he asked.

"What did you expect me to do? You didn't want me. You wouldn't have wanted our baby. Paul wanted both of us . . ."

"So he knows it's not his?"

Marion lifted Diallo to her shoulder and sat down on the sofa opposite Gerard. She avoided answering the question. "He loves Diallo," she said.

"You named him after my dad?" Gerard's voice broke on the last word, his pitch lowering a little.

"I'm sorry . . ."

"No." Gerard held up his hand. "Dad would've liked that."

There was a silence between them, as if they were paying a tribute to the dead man. Diallo was hungry and began sucking at his fist and turning his little head to nudge Marion's full breasts. Marion, being by now used to breastfeeding in company, didn't think twice about lifting her T-shirt to feed her baby. Diallo sucked hungrily on the offered nipple.

Gerard stood up and crossed the room to sit next to her. Marion watched his approach and let him sit close to her without budging. He took one of Diallo's hands in his. The tiny fingers gripped his thumb and a smile broke out on his face once more.

"Does he know Diallo isn't his?" Gerard asked again.

"No."

He searched her eyes. "Are you going tell him?"

"Not if I don't have to." There was a hint of pleading in her voice.

Gerard noticed it. Clearly she didn't want her new life disrupted. But didn't he have rights too? Some other man was playing happy families with his kid, and he wanted a taste of this life. "I want to see my son," he said.

Taken aback, Marion stared him in the eye. "No," she said adamantly. "You can't do that."

Gerard jumped up. "What do you mean I can't?" The tranquillity of the past few minutes was shattered in a second.

"Paul would be hurt if he found out."

Like a firecracker, Gerard was off again. "I don't give a damn about Paul. He's my kid. I wanna see him grow up."

The sound of a key turning in the front door startled them both. Marion's frightened eyes flew to the clock on the wall. It was six thirty. She had forgotten that Paul was coming back home for his kit. She shoved her breast back into her bra, disturbing the semi-sleeping baby, who began to wail.

Gerard had spun around, also surprised by the intrusion. They stood side by side, looking guiltily towards the door, as Paul appeared.

"Hi," he said.

"Hi yuhself," Pamela replied, looking up at him.

"I tried to call you," Michael said, shifting from one foot to the other.

"Oh yeah?" She remained cool. "When?"

"Just now. I've been trying for an hour."

She chuckled sarcastically. "Funny. I've been trying to call you for two weeks."

His gaze never faltered. "I've had some things to sort out. I was kinda busy."

"Too busy to pick up the phone? Or did you lose my number?" He reached out for her arm but she snatched it back.

"Don't be like that, Pam."

"Don't be like *what*? I'm not some young gal you can just mess around with for a lark, Mike. I'm a woman who deserves respect."

"Course I respect you, babes," he said in his rich, sonorous voice.

"Don't 'babes' me, Michael. You did get my messages, didn't you?"

"Yeah, but . . ."

She waved away his excuses. "Do you think I would treat you that way? You know how I feel about you, and yet you treat me like that. I don't have to wait around for you, you know."

A middle-aged woman dragging a shopping trolley slowed as she approached, the argument between these two lovebirds seeming more important than getting the tea on the table.

Pamela shot her a look. "Can we help you?" she asked rudely.

Flustered, the woman tightened her scarf around her neck and bustled on her way.

Michael rubbed his hands together and then folded them across his chest. "I apologise. I didn't mean to upset you."

"Upset me!" she yelled. "Who said I was upset?"

Michael laughed. "If you're not upset, you're doing a pretty good impression of someone who is."

"Don't laugh at me, Michael." She turned her back to him, hiding her expression. "You have no idea what's been going through my mind. I was thinking you could've been in an accident."

"You serious?" He grinned.

She turned again to face him. "D'you think I'd make that up? I don't like men using me, Michael."

"But it's all right if you use them."

"What? I never used you."

"No. But you used the last two men in your life."

"Oh, so this was to teach me a lesson, was it?"

"This has nothing to do with your past. This is me. Things were just getting too deep, y'know?"

"No, I don't know."

He shuffled his feet awkwardly. "I wanna do the right thing by you. I wasn't sure what I was feeling, you know . . ."

"Did you sort it out?" Pamela asked.

"I think so."

"That's not good enough, Mike. The way I feel about you, you've got to be sure or that's it."

"How can anyone be sure? People are getting divorced every day. I jus' know I want to be with you. Let's go somewhere on neutral ground. I need to talk."

"You're not getting out of it that easily. And weren't you going to see Mikey?"

"I was, but they weren't expecting me. I'm not trying to get out of what I have to say. I just want to do it properly."

He moved in on her then, and Pamela let herself weaken. She wanted him with an undeniable ache. He kissed her forehead, her nose, and finally her lips, with a gentleness that made her want to cry out with pleasure. She knew her heart was his again. She had needed to let off steam, and now she felt she had — some of it, anyway. Tonight, though, they were going to talk seriously. He wasn't going to get away with puny excuses. Everything he told her from now on would have to hold water, or else she was getting out, love or not.

The smile Paul had been wearing dropped from his face as he studied the stranger in his living room suspiciously. Marion felt sick to her stomach. Faint. There was a hammering in her chest as her heart speeded up. Her legs felt weak. Diallo was stirring fretfully in her arms and she wanted to put him down in his cot, but couldn't.

Gerard stood with his feet wide apart in a challenging stance. Marion was sure he was planning something. The old mocking glint had reappeared in his eyes.

Paul looked from Marion to Gerard, and back again. Marion was about to speak when she saw Gerard's hand come up. She watched helplessly, riveted to the spot, as he stepped towards Paul. The silence was deafening.

"I'm Gerard, Marion's ex," he said amiably.

Paul looked over at her again. She could only offer a weak smile that didn't touch her eyes. He shook Gerard's outstretched hand and introduced himself.

Gerard turned slightly and smiled at Marion. It was a crooked smile, that said 'I've let you off this time'. "Anyway," he breathed, "must be getting on. I'll catch you later, Marion. Paul, more time, yeah?"

He raised his fist for a touch and Paul returned the gesture. Their fists met in the air. "Yeah, safe," Paul replied with a feeling of unease.

He escorted Gerard to the front door. Marion waited until she'd heard it shut before she moved. She left the living room as Paul was coming back down the passageway, and they met at the bedroom door.

He stood behind her as she put Diallo down. "What was he doing here?" His voice held only plain curiosity.

"Just passing by, you know." She shrugged.

Paul walked around to the bottom of the cot and looked down at the baby. "How's Diallo been today?"

"Good. We went for a walk, popped in to see Pam at work." She turned to leave the room.

"Marion?"

She stopped and turned to him.

"What was he *really* doing here?"

"What d'you mean?"

"Come here." He held one hand out to her, and she approached hesitantly. "I know when you're lying to me. Is something bothering you?" He regarded her with burning intensity.

"Why?"

"Jus' answer me, Marion."

"No," she said, looking past him at the cot mobile.

"Look at me and tell me there's nothing wrong."

She couldn't. She wanted to pull away from him. She was crumbling, her whole world falling apart. She had always known the day would come when he would have to learn the truth, but she would have been happy to postpone it for ever.

Now it seemed the moment had arrived.

"Don't make me tell you, Paul," she said. "I can sort it out." She tried to make her voice sound cheerful as Paul continued to gaze at her enquiringly.

"Sort *what* out? We're in this together. Talk to me, man."

"I can't, honey." She tried the sentimental distraction; it had worked before. She put her head on his chest and pushed her arms around his waist.

His arms remained by his side. "You're shutting me out," he said.

"I'm not."

"Is it me?"

Marion shut her eyes and prayed this was all a nightmare. She could hear his heartbeat. It seemed to speed up like a drum roll.

"Marion, I can't go on like this, man."

She opened her eyes. "We're doing all right, ain't we? Does it matter what's on my mind?"

"It matters when I walk in and find your ex-boyfriend in our home, and you're acting as jumpy as a rabbit. I don't like being kept in the dark. What's going on?"

"Don't, Paul," she whimpered. She didn't want to cry, but couldn't help it.

"Is it that bad?" he asked, concerned now.

She sniffed. "You . . . you . . . don't realise h-how bad," she stuttered, tears streaming down her face.

He led her out of the bedroom and into the living room, to avoid waking Diallo. They sat side by side on the sofa.

He let her cry for a while before trying to talk to her again. "Marion, I've got a class at seven thirty. I've gotta go. When I get back later, we're going to talk, you hear me?" He spoke as if addressing a small child.

She nodded, sniffing, and wiped her face with the back of her hand.

"Good." He got up and left the room to get his martial arts kit. "I'm gone. I'll see you later," he called from the hallway.

"Bye, Paul."

The front door shut, and Marion had a sudden, mad impulse. She would take the baby and leave right now. Paul would never know;

she would never have to tell him he had been living a lie for nearly a year.

She picked up the phone and dialled Joan's number, convincing herself that this would save everyone a lot of grief.

No one could make her tell Paul — not now, or ever.

Paul arrived home two hours later to find an empty flat. A handwritten note left on the coffee table read:

Dear Paul,
    I've gone away for a while. No one will know where I am. Please don't try to find me. I'll contact you when I'm ready. Don't worry, we'll both be fine.
Marion

He ignored her request and immediately picked up the phone, pressing the automatic dial button for Joan's house. The phone rang continuously. He tried Pamela's number and got her answerphone. Slamming the receiver down, he ran out of the flat, got into the car and drove.

He would find her, the silly woman.

Just what was she running from?

It took a week before Joan broke down and told Paul everything from the beginning. He had worked on her relentlessly. When he wasn't at her home, he would call Joan hourly to ask if she had heard anything. Then he would talk about how much he was missing Marion and the baby, how quiet the flat was without them. What really got to Joan was when he burst out crying, saying he didn't think he could go on without them. She couldn't take it any more. She had to put him out of his misery. He had a right to know. So she broke her promise to Marion.

Even as she told him, Joan knew he would head straight for Birmingham.

PAUL
I had everything, and I find out I got nuttin'.
    Of course I'm going to Birmingham.
    I never figured Marion for the devious type. Perhaps deviousness is in all women.

I'm driving, an' all I can see is Marion, Diallo and that fancy ex-boyfriend of hers. I'm so tense. And I'm angry.

Damn! I need to stop thinking for a while to clear my head. I'm on my way to bring her back and I don't even know if she wants to come back. Shit, I don't even know if I want her back.

Someone else's baby. What a come-down. How can I tell anyone? I hate her for putting me through this. Yet I still love her.

Shit! I'm so fucking mixed up.

28. SUMMER MADNESS

Marion's mum's house held the summer's heat like a furnace. She couldn't stay indoors, but couldn't find the energy to go out anywhere.

She took a book from the bookshelf. It was Jilly Cooper's *Riders*. Not exactly her type of reading material but, unable to find anything better, she poured herself a glass of home-made lemonade and took it outside to the spacious, well-kept garden. This was the kind of home she wanted to bring her son up in.

She lay on the sun lounger, shaded by the umbrella that was attached to the head of the seat. This was more like it. It was the first time Marion had relaxed all week. Her mother and Thomas had taken Diallo out shopping, to show him off.

Marion still hadn't called Paul. She felt guilty about leaving him the way she had. She'd convinced herself she was doing it for his own good; it made her feel better to see it that way. She didn't want to see him hurt. But if it were possible to turn the clock back, she would have done everything differently.

The sun burnt her legs as she lay in its heat. One chapter into the book, she began to doze off. She dreamt. She was back home with Paul and Diallo, and Gerard had never existed. They were happy, until one day when the doorbell started ringing . . .

A doorbell really was ringing, somewhere outside her dream. Marion drifted back to reality. The doorbell rang again. She sat up too quickly and a wave of dizziness made her stop to regain her balance. She stood slowly, making sure the disorientation had passed before getting to her feet.

She opened the front door, a smile readily prepared on her face. And at the sight of her boyfriend — here, at her mother's front door in Birmingham — she began to back up. The banister stopped her progress. She gripped the post with one hand, the look of a cornered animal on her face. What was he doing here? Did he know?

Paul entered the thick, motionless heat of the hallway and closed the door behind him. Although he had shaved before leaving home and his hair was neatly cut, he had the hard look of a vagrant on his face. His jawline stuck out meanly. His dark eyes shone unnaturally, emotionlessly. Dressed completely in black, he looked like a possessed priest out for vengeance.

"Are we alone?" he asked, his voice hoarse. He looked around, listening, taking in the stillness of the house.

Marion nodded and backed further up the stairs as it became apparent that he *did* know. "I can explain," she blurted.

He approached her stealthily. She cursed the house's shadows — they were making him look like a psycho from a horror movie. The thought sent goosepimples shooting up all over her body.

She took another step upwards. He was only two feet away now. Suddenly frightened by his silence, she turned and darted up the remaining stairs. The bathroom door had a lock on it; she could shut herself in there and pray for someone to come in time. But Paul was fit and flexible. He bounded up the stairs and she screamed as he grabbed her arm, turning her to face him as they reached the first landing.

Tears filled her eyes as she began to blubber, "Oh God, Paul. I'm so sorry. I didn't mean to hurt you. I love you, Paul. I wish he was yours, honestly." She reached up to him and saw a flicker in his eyes — sentimentality. It was there for only a couple of seconds before clouding over again.

He took her head forcefully in his hands and pulled her to him. He kissed her hard, thrusting his tongue deep into her mouth. She responded hungrily, her mind racing.

Paul was forcing her down on to the stairs, fumbling under the flimsy dress for her panties.

"Not here, Paul," she protested, trying to stop him, but he was past listening and ignored her feeble protests. He was already freeing himself from his own clothes. She felt his hardness probing for entry and, although this wasn't Paul's style at all, she opened up for him. She kissed him, wanting to make it up to him. The stairs were hard against her back and buttocks. He thrust into her, deep and high. He grabbed her hair, pulling her head back, giving himself leverage.

For a few seconds after he'd satisfied himself they both lay still, breathing heavily. One of Marion's hands clung to the banister.

Suddenly Paul stood up and began pulling his clothes together, fastening his trousers. He looked down at her with those hard eyes she'd seen before.

She slowly sat up, waiting, thinking it was time to tell all and get it over with.

"I'm going home to pack," he said.

Marion's eyes flew wide and she felt cold.

"You see how it feels to get used?" he continued. "Yeah, I remember that day. You must have seen me coming. I walked right into that trap. Well, don't expect me to do it again," he sneered.

The tears that had only threatened before now came full force. "Don't do this, Paul. I said I was sorry," she cried.

He laughed derisively. "You're sorry? For ruining my life? You used me as a meal ticket, for you and your kid. I bet you don't even know if Gerard's the father either." He spat the words at her.

Marion cringed, bringing her knees up to her chest and hugging them.

Paul turned as he walked down the stairs. "I'm only taking what's mine from the flat." He shook his head. "You should take up acting, y'know that? You had me fooled."

With that he left, walking out of her life.

Marion sat at the top of the stairs like a tiny orphaned child. She held her knees in her arms and rocked backwards and forwards. She felt as though she could never cry again, she was all dried up.

It had happened again. She had lost a man she loved.

Whose fault was it but her own?

PAUL

I'm not proud of what I did. Shit! If I could apologise, or even face her again, I would. What's stopping me? Pride. I'm a man. Men don't go crawling back, begging forgiveness. You cut your losses and move on.

The woman made a fool out of me.

Marion and Diallo became so important to me that all I wanted in life was to make them happy. Nothing else mattered. No wonder she found it so easy to use me. I know how she must be feeling. What I did to her must have cut her up bad. But, boy, everyone must take responsibility for their actions. You can't use somebody for your own gains and not expect to pay a price.

I'm a man. I've got nothing to prove, except that I'll stand up for what I believe in. But let me tell you something . . . men get hurt too.

29. LOVE MAKES A WOMAN

July. The flat had a party atmosphere. It was a double celebration: Marion's birthday — plus yet another job offer. This time Marion was going on the box. Channel Four had been in touch. They were running a new six-week series called *Mantalk*, and they wanted Marion to be the guest 'expert' in each programme. She hadn't been able to sleep for a whole week after she had received the letter.

Windows were open in every room to let what little breeze there was flow through the flat. Marion tipped a packet of peanuts into a dish and put glasses and a bottle of sparkling wine on to a tray. She headed for the living room, where Joan and Pamela were rocking to the ragga track on the stereo. Donna was in the bedroom with Diallo — she would be babysitting tonight.

The girls were raving for the first time since Marion had had the baby. She had stayed at her mother's for a month, and had arrived back this week feeling revived and ready to face the world again. Pamela had dyed her hair brown two days previously, and she'd had it cut into an ear-length bob. The final part of her make-over was for her to go out and enjoy herself.

Paul had been truthful about only taking what was his from the flat. He had left everything that had anything to do with her. He had taken Diallo's framed baby portrait, though, despite what he now knew.

Marion had coped well, considering. She now felt at peace. She had direction in her life now — a career, and her son to concentrate her energies on. She tried not to think of Paul, it only ever resulted in sadness.

"Marion, did Joan show you the ring?" Pamela asked as she entered with the tray.

"What ring?" Marion looked to Joan.

Joan held her left hand out. "He thought it would make it official," she explained. "It's no big deal. We've been engaged for months anyway." Though a big kid in some ways, Colin was trying hard to be a responsible father and future husband. Joan loved being part of a couple again. It was good for her.

"The ring is a big deal, believe," Pamela told her. She grabbed a handful of peanuts from the bowl and dropped them daintily one by one into her mouth. "He's showing everyone that he's made a commitment."

"It's perfect," Marion said dreamily.

"It's all right, I s'pose." Joan looked at it, grinning from ear to ear.

Marion sat next to her and took a sip of wine. "So, where's Michael tonight?" she asked Pamela. Pamela and Michael had become a regular item. Every time one of her friends called her, Michael was there or he'd just left or was on his way. They'd joked about him moving in. Pamela had immediately put them straight: no way; no matter how good he was for her, she wasn't giving up her independence again.

"He's at Tony's," Pamela replied. "They're coming to Sharna's party later."

Joan raised her eyes to the ceiling before turning to Pamela. "You know what that means. You're going with us, but you'll spend the night with him," she said.

Pamela waved her away, her scarlet nails catching the light. "He's going with his mates an' I'll be with you lot. We're not joined together, you know, not like you and Colin."

"Don't tell me it hasn't crossed your mind, though," Joan pressed.

Pamela smiled, modestly brushing salt from her black jeans. "All right, I've thought about it."

The truth was that Pamela and Michael had an agreement, and that was that they wouldn't put any pressure on each other. They already knew how they felt about each other. It wasn't necessary to try to force words and action from the other to prove it.

"Shaun stopped calling?" Marion asked.

"I ain't heard from him for about four weeks. I think he finally got the message."

"Boy, that was one stubborn black man," Joan affirmed.

"You're not wrong. I thought of all the men I've been with he would understand the difference between lust and love."

Joan nearly choked on her drink. "You what!" She gave Pamela an incredulous stare. "Maz, back me up on this. Wasn't this the same girl who just a few months ago was saying how no one man could satisfy her. An' how all she wanted was sex?"

Marion nodded and Pamela laughed. "Oh come on, guys, you know what I was going on about."

"No. What?" Marion asked.

"Put it this way. I hadn't met him then — and now I have."

"Hmm-mmm," Joan teased.

"Shut up, you!" Pamela picked up a cushion and threw it across the room at Joan, who screamed and ducked. The girls cracked up with laughter.

"On a more serious note," Joan said, "aren't you going to tell Marion about your *meeting*?"

Pamela had totally forgotten. She had called the agency and

spoken to a very nice woman, who'd passed on the details of her natural mother. "I'm going to meet my real mum next week."

Marion's mouth fell open. "I don't believe it! You're actually going o go through with it?"

"I have to. They say curiosity killed the cat — well, I'm not dead yet. I have to know."

"Well, good luck to you." Marion turned to Joan. "You got a date for your wedding yet?" she asked. She had a lot of news to catch up on.

"Mmm — about this time next year." Joan sipped some wine. "I'll have to talk to Mum first. Finances, y'know."

Marion suddenly looked at the clock and then back to her friends. "Guess what?"

"What?" they said together.

"You lot have been here three hours and Joan hasn't lit up once."

Pamela now turned to Joan. "Shit, she's right."

"Didn't I tell you? I haven't smoked in a month," Joan said proudly.

"You're kidding me!" Pamela said, shocked.

Joan shook her head. "Honestly, I don't need it any more." She had also lost a stone in weight, but she wasn't bragging.

"You see what good love does for people?" Marion grinned as if she had given the love to her friend. She got up to put a new tape on.

"So, what has love done for you, Pam?" Joan asked.

"Who, me?" Pamela asked, feigning surprise. She thought about it for a while, then answered slowly, "I'm gonna get real deep here. Love has given me a sense of worth. A respect for men I never had before. Black pride." She raised her hand in a fist and the girls copied her, punching the air. Pamela continued: "I am now more self-confident, proud, and filled with absolute joy. I have a man who I love, and who loves me back." She paused, letting the momentum of her statement build.

"Get on with it," Joan said, reaching for the cushion on the floor.

"All right . . . And I'm having the best fucking sex I've had in my life!" She cracked up.

The other two laughed with her, enjoying the feeling of unity. Pamela put on her best cockney accent. "Ain't luv grand?"

Marion sat down on the floor crossed-legged, her features becoming melancholy. She drained her glass of wine and poured some more. Her friends exchanged looks, their smiles fading as they realised they were probably being insensitive.

"You know, Michael's friend Tony is single," Pamela hinted.

Marion ran her finger around the rim of the glass. "I'm not

interested. I'm tired of all that. I've got Diallo to think of now."

Joan tried to console her. "Maybe Paul will have a change of heart. You know he really loved you — the two of you."

Marion smiled weakly. Did Joan know something she didn't?

The telephone rang, and Marion was glad — she really didn't want to talk about Paul. "Hello?" she answered.

A muffled but vaguely familiar male voice came down the line: "Hello?"

"Yes?" Marion said, then the line went dead.

Her friends turned to look at her as she held the phone aloft and shrugged her shoulder. She replaced the receiver and they soon forgot about the call as they got chatting again, gossiping about life, love, sex, their future plans, and upcoming raves.

They were all a little tipsy when, half an hour later, the door opened and Donna entered the room holding Diallo on her hip. The baby, three and a half months old now, gazed around at the drunken women sprawled over the living room. He spotted his mother and grinned toothlessly.

"Marion, there's a man at the door," Donna informed her. "Says he knows you."

None of them had heard the bell.

"Oooh, a man! Is he gift-wrapped?" Pamela giggled from her place on the floor.

"Room service! Bring him in, Maz. We'll share him," Joan laughed, sliding off the chair to slap palms with Pamela.

Marion struggled to her feet and left the room, closing the door behind her. It was late for visitors, and she wasn't expecting anyone.

Joan already knew who it was, but she'd been keeping it to herself. This visitor was to be a birthday surprise. Joan had been keeping him up to date on how things were for the past month, and so he knew all about the TV offer. If there was one thing Joan was good at, she silently congratulated herself, it was being a friend and counsellor. This was one case she was not going to lose.

Donna shook her head in dismay. Sometimes, she thought, her sister and her friends acted like teenagers. She hoped she wouldn't be like that in five years' time.

Paul stood in the hallway, hands clasped in front of him. The front door stood open behind him. To Marion, he looked like a lost little boy.

A feeling of total euphoria came over her. She was feeling extremely light-headed, and wondered if she was hallucinating.

Paul looked uncomfortable, shifting from one foot to the other. "Happy birthday," he said, smiling shyly.

"Thank you," she replied, not knowing quite what else to say.

He made an attempt at humour. "You can throw me out if you want."

Marion didn't know how to react. She remembered how she had felt the last time she'd seen him. How hurt they had both been. She wasn't sure what his motives were this time, and wasn't going to let herself be trapped. "I have visitors," she slurred, her wide eyes trying to stay open.

"Yeah, I heard," he smiled.

They were silent for nearly a minute, neither of them knowing what the other's next move might be. "I need some air. Why don't we go outside?" she suggested finally and he followed her out.

They took the lift in silence, Marion watching the numbers descend above the door. All sorts of things were going through her head.

Paul pointed as they exited the flats. "My car's just up there."

Marion followed him. They reached the car and Paul opened the passenger side for her. Before she got in, she turned to him, "That was you on the phone before, wasn't it?"

Paul nodded, embarrassed.

Marion frowned and got into the car, and Paul walked around to the driver's side. On the dashboard there was a single red rose with a card attached. Marion glanced at it and then at him.

He nodded at the rose. "It's for you."

Marion hesitantly picked up the flower and removed the tiny card from its envelope. She read the handwritten words.

Darling Marion,
    Please forgive me. I want you. I need you. Without you I am worthless. I love you always, for ever, for eternity. I can't breathe without you.
Panther

The words wrapped themselves around her heart, and she read them again as her nostrils filled with the flower's scent. She gazed through the windscreen, her face holding none of the mixed emotions she was feeling inside.

"Are you sure, Paul?"

He leaned towards her and reached for her hand. "I thought about this for over a month. Why d'ya think I'm here? I really care about you . . ."

He reached to embrace her but she pulled back. "What about Diallo? Could you accept him too?" she asked, looking deep into his eyes.

He pondered the question for a moment, but he already knew how he felt. "For a year I thought he was my kid. I love him, Marion. I missed both of you." His eyes glistened with the unshed tears of remembered pain.

She looked down at his hand holding hers, and knew she felt the same as he did. "Paul, I'm so sorry . . ."

She leaned towards him, and this time he pulled back. "Hold on. There's something else." He swallowed nervously. "I have to know that you want *me,* and not just a replacement for Gerard."

"That's over, Paul. Whatever I felt for him is gone. I love *you.*"

Satisfied, Paul reached over her and opened the glove compartment. He handed her a small velvet box. "Happy birthday," he said again.

She accepted the box with tear-filled eyes — tears of joy this time. It clicked open to reveal a gold multi-stoned ring.

"It's an eternity ring," he told her.

As if she didn't know. She had certainly gazed at enough of them in jewellery shop windows. "Why don't you put it on for me?"

She handed him the box and held her left hand out. He slipped the ring on to her ring finger. Their eyes met, and as they drew closer their lips did too.

They were together again, and that was all that mattered.

Paul thought of a saying his mother loved to recite: "Learn from the past and look to the future."

He thought they had both learnt their lesson.

The future was for them to make a go of it — honestly, as a family.

COLIN

I've been tamed — under manners, as they say. It ain't that bad. Joan is still Joan. I still love her, an' I want to marry her. I have this feeling . . . our first will be a boy.

Yeah, love's so fine.

GERARD

Nothin's really changed for me, you know. The mobile phone business is going good. I've I'm shacked up with a girl named Beverley now. She's a good cook, takes care of my needs. It's nothin' serious, but she don't know that.

Marion and her man decided it was bes' if I stay out of my son's life until he's old enough to understand. Mum has visiting rights, though. Marion an' her got on.

Paul — he's all right, y'know. Respect to him still — 'cause he's raising my boy.

I'm not ready for Miss Right. Maybe one day . . . you know how it goes.

MICHAEL

When I think back on what I could have lost, I have to kick myself.

Pamela and I have an easygoing relationship. She does her thing, I do mine, but we're doing it together. There's no more playing around. We both know what we want now, but we're not pushing it down each other's throats.

I just hope I don't have a relapse.

Fingers crossed, yeah?

PAUL

I've got no complaints. My chile, my wife, my home — perfect. I have it all again.

Marion's career has taken off. Diallo's getting bigger every day.

How do I feel about him not being mine? At firs', it was hard. I kept trying to distance myself. It's still hard, I suppose. But I can't see myself without him now. Blood or not, I love him.

Marion keeps hinting at marriage. It's a good idea, but right now we can't afford to do it properly. I'm working hard though.

End

For a full colour catalogue featuring all the current X Press titles including Marcia Williams' other novels, write to:

Mailing List,
The X Press,
6 Hoxton Square,
London N1 6NU

or fax us on 0171 729 1771